NOCINO NOIR

FRANKI AMATO MYSTERIES BOOK 9

TRACI ANDRIGHETTI

Limoncello
Press

NOCINO NOIR

by

TRACI ANDRIGHETTI

***

 Formatted with Vellum

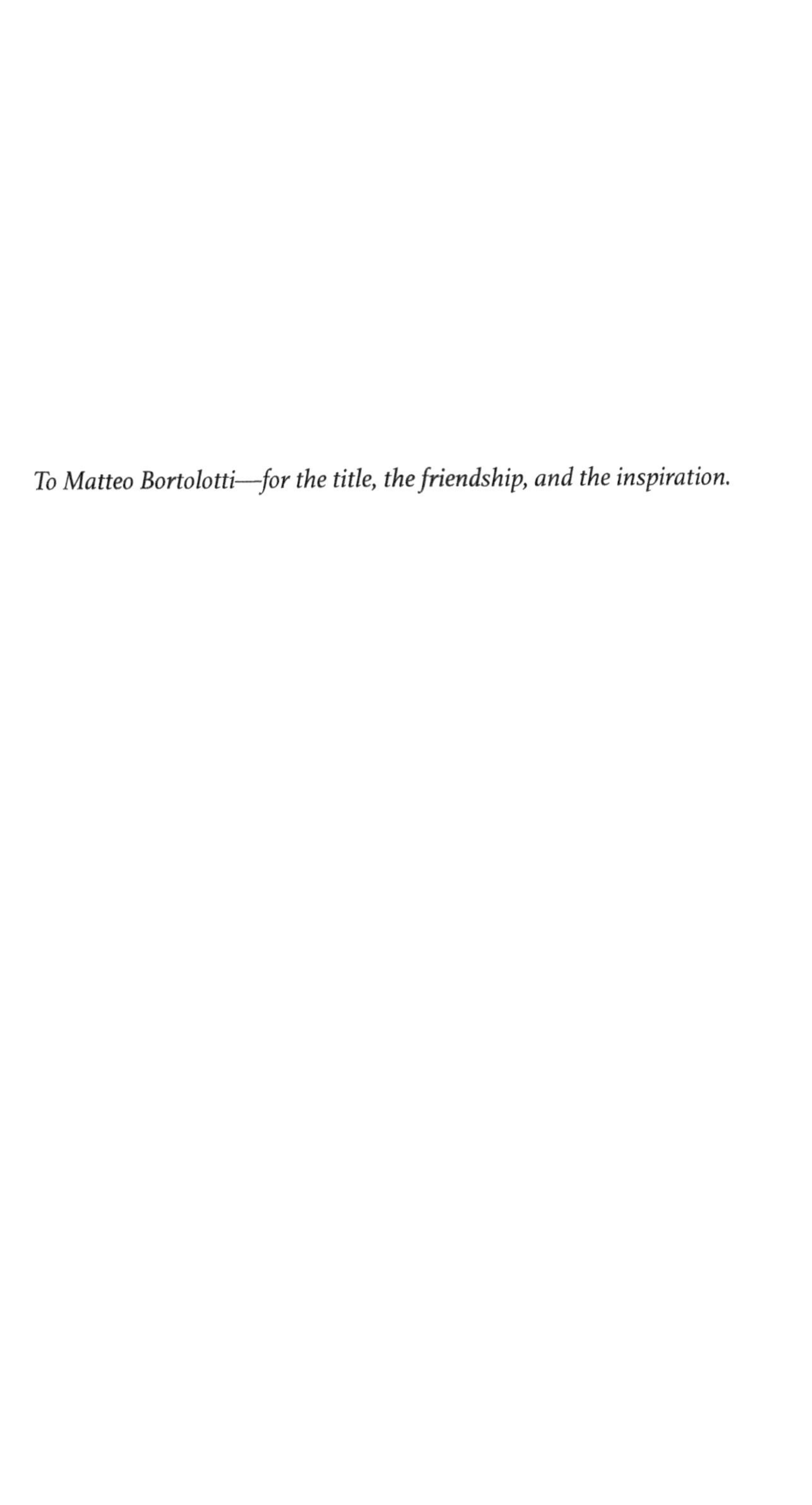

To Matteo Bortolotti—for the title, the friendship, and the inspiration.

1

———

"Top secret, Veronica. We're going dark, completely covert." My tone was hushed to prevent the patrons of the Camellia Grill from hearing. "It's called Operation Black Swamp."

My best friend and boss laid her Chanel bag on the diner-style marble counter and spun her stool to face me. "This whole situation makes me so nervous."

"How do you think I feel? I'm the one who bears the brunt of it." I peered through the order window at a middle-aged cook in the kitchen, half checking on our food and half checking him out. Given our current predicament, no one in New Orleans was above suspicion.

Veronica chewed her bottom lip. "Do we have a list of names?"

"A *list*?" My head jerked backwards. As owner and CEO of the PI firm Private Chicks, she didn't get much fieldwork, but that was a shockingly novice question. "Any and all discussions of this operation must be spoken, not written. We can't leave a paper trail."

"Gotcha." She fanned herself with a menu. "But with this heat, why are we meeting across town when we could've gone to that new coffee shop by the office?"

"*NOLA Noir?* Does the name alone not explain it to you?"

"Honestly, no."

"It sounds suspect, which is precisely what we don't want." I glanced around to make sure no one was watching and shoved a Nokia Flip into her lap.

She blinked. "A burner phone?"

"Don't use it at home or at work, or even in your car. They could be bugged."

"Oh, Franki. Is this really necessary?"

"How can you even ask that?" I whisper-hissed. "We're dealing with professionals, Veronica. Hardened veterans. By the way," I nodded at a shopping bag on the floor between our stools, "I put together some disguises."

She leaned over and rummaged through the contents.

From the corner of my eye, I spotted the cook watching us. I met his gaze with a stare as steely as his spatula.

The guy didn't flinch. He simply turned back to the grill.

But I had his number.

"No way I can wear this." Veronica raised a black hoodie from the bag. "It's June, and the hottest on record."

I gave her blonde locks and bright look the onceover. "You can't wear that Kelly green dress, either. You stick out like a leprechaun at a funeral, and odds are, we're being watched."

"Here?" She scanned the diner.

"They've got informants everywhere, like a modern-day Black Hand," I said, referring to the extortion rackets run by Sicilian immigrants and Italian gangsters at the turn of the twentieth century. "Hence the 'black' in 'Operation Black Swamp.'"

Her cornflower blue eyes held fear.

My jaw set. I was frightened too.

This operation was the biggest job of our lives, and there was no way to prepare for it. Sure, I'd taken on some criminal masterminds in my PI career and won. But now that my wedding was in the works, those crooks seemed like Sunday School teachers compared to the diabolical duo Veronica and I were up against—Brenda Amato, née Pavan, and Carmela Amato, née Montalbano.

A.k.a., my mom and nonna.

Ever since Bradley and I had picked the church and reception venue, those two had taken their master meddling tactics to mobster level. And according to my father, they'd rewatched *The Godfather* trilogy for pointers. Their intentions were good—get me hitched without a hitch. But like real mob bosses, they thought they called the shots. And I would rather *get* shot with a *lupara*, the Sicilian sawed-off shotgun favored by mafiosi, than submit to their wacky Italian wedding traditions.

A battle-weary sigh escaped my lips. "We'll get through this," I said, more to bolster my own resolve than hers. "All we have to do is neutralize Vito and Michael Corleone and freeze out the swamp animals."

Her lips parted. "The *swamp* animals?"

I didn't disguise my surprise that she hadn't grasped the other part of the operation name. "The ones who'll surface from the swamp's murky depths to darken or derail my wedding festivities."

"That's the list I just asked you for."

"Yeah, but do I really have to tell you who they are?"

Her chin rose. "As your maid of honor, it's my duty to make sure no detail is overlooked, especially not one that could ruin your wedding."

"Fair enough." I held up my hands to tick off the animals on my fingers. "The gator, the snake, the snapping turtle, the black bear, the common loon, and the turkey-necked ostrich, otherwise known as Glenda, Nadezhda, Carnie, Rosalie, Chandra, and Ruth."

"Cute. But ostriches don't live in the swamp."

My lips curled. "The turkey-necked variety does, and she wallows in its muck." I rested my elbows on the counter. "Now, as far as anyone knows, my bridal shower is in November. Our mission is to make sure none of them find out you're throwing me one this Saturday while Bradley's mother and grandmother are visiting."

She massaged her chest, clearly uneasy. "I'm not sure Bradley's family will appreciate the lack of notice, and I don't even want to think about your mom and nonna's reaction."

Neither did I.

"How will you get them to come here from Houston without them suspecting anything?"

"I'll say I've found the perfect wedding dress. My mom will fire up the Ford Taurus and make the five-hour drive in three-and-a-half."

"You do that," her gaze held a warning as she reached for her water glass, "and you'll open the door to more meddling."

"Veronica," I laid my forearm on the counter and turned to face her, "that door is not only open, it's off the hinges. And it's been thoroughly trampled, like my right to plan my own wedding."

She sipped some water. "Weren't you going to hire a wedding planner to help you manage your family?"

"Believe me, I tried. But everyone I've called is either unavailable or too expensive. Do you know what Delilah Delaire costs?"

"Gosh, eight grand, I'd imagine."

"Try twelve. That kind of wedding is out of my league."

"Pardon me, girls." An elderly woman a few stools down

leaned toward us. She wore heavy makeup despite the humidity —foundation with white powder, dark-red lipstick, and black eyeliner on her upper and lower lids. Based on her deep wrinkles and sagging skin, she was ninety if she was a day, and she had the vintage lace-collared dress, rhinestone brooch, and black velvet hairbow to prove it. "I heard you mention Delilah Delaire. Are you talking about the Blain-Adair wedding?"

I shook my head. "Actually, n—"

"Shame they had to call it off," she fretted before I could finish my sentence, "but I can't say I'm surprised. Agata *was* one hundred and two."

And to think my nonna had been calling me a *zitella* since I was sixteen, the so-called "marrying age" back in Dark-Ages Sicily. "Uh, this Agata was getting *married*?"

The woman's watery blue eyes popped. "Heavens no. The bride-to-be is her great niece, Grace Blain. But Agata died the day before yesterday, the morning of Grace's wedding."

Veronica's fingers flew to her lips. "How awful. The family must be devastated."

"About postponing the wedding, yes, but not about Agata's death. They despised her." She scowled. "Agata lorded her wealth over them for decades, always threatening to disinherit them over some foolishness or other."

The waiter rushed up, sweating in his white jacket and black bowtie uniform, and frisbeed our plates—a pecan waffle for Veronica and a Mexican omelet with a side of bacon for me.

He was gone before I could ask for a bottle of Crystal Hot Sauce.

Veronica laid a napkin in her lap and looked at the woman. "By any chance, is Grace Blain the daughter of Edward Blain, the divorce attorney?"

"Why, yes." The woman's face brightened. "Agata was his wife, Lara's, great aunt. Last name was Villeré. She owned that rundown mansion on St. Charles, the one the kids avoid at Halloween."

I knew the place. It made the Munster's' house look inviting. "Not that it's any of my business, but if Ms. Villeré had so much money, why didn't she do the upkeep on her property?"

"She and her older sister, Pia, inherited the place from their parents, and they never took care of it. That was their family home, and they'd lived there together their whole lives." Her sparse brows rose in a panicked look. "Spinsters!"

I'd seen the same stricken stare on the faces of my mom and nonna—every time I had another birthday, and at thirty-two, I was less than one-third the age of Agata. "Their names sound Italian."

"Their mother was from somewhere near Naples. They had a brother, Lara's grandfather. Can't recall his name. There were so many Italians in New Orleans back then."

"And still today." Over three hundred thousand, and it seemed like they all knew my nonna, who'd immigrated to the city with my nonnu and raised my father and uncles in the French Quarter. While I was thinking about it, I took another look at the diner customers.

The cashier passed by, adjusting his bowtie.

"Excuse me, sir." I raised a piece of bacon to flag him down and then, tempted by the sight of it, bit off a hunk. "Have you seen our waiter?"

The man's nostrils flared. "He's back in de damn bathroom. Don' know what he ate las' night, but he's been in dere three times dis mornin'."

The bacon fell from my mouth. *No need for that hot sauce now.*

The old woman spread egg yolk on a slice of toast.

A taste preference? Or does she think it's butter?

She lowered the knife. "What Agata didn't spend on the

house, she made up for in jewelry. Her collection rivaled Elizabeth Taylor's."

Veronica's eyes grew to the size of the Koh-i-nor diamond. "Do you mind if I ask what kind of jewels? My husband's a gemologist, and I'm a fan of gems myself."

"Her most notable pieces were an Art Deco tiara by Cartier, the canary diamond ring Bette Davis wore in the movie *Jezebel*, and the pièce de résistance, Marie Antoinette's pearls. She bought those from the 2018 Sotheby's auction."

My BFF sucked in her breath, transfixed by the mention of the guillotined queen.

Meanwhile, I couldn't get my mind off Bette Davis. I watched *What Ever Happened to Baby Jane?* with my parents around the time I'd graduated from college, and over a decade later the character still creeped me out. The movie was more disturbing than the fairy tales my mother had read to me as a kid. And it didn't help that the woman talking to us had a Baby-Janesque appearance.

Memories of the awful food scenes from the movie and my suspicion of the cook prompted me to look inside my omelet for unwelcome ingredients, even though I had zero intention of eating it.

The woman swallowed some toast. "Agata also inherited all the family jewels after Pia was pushed down the elevator shaft in their home."

The cook shouted.

At first I thought he'd heard the woman's astonishing comment, but a fire had broken out on the grill.

Our waiter ran from the bathroom, as though fleeing a fire himself, and went to help the cook. The two men extinguished the flames, but a bad feeling spread like wildfire in the pit of my stomach.

I looked at the woman. "Did you mean that Pia 'fell' down the elevator shaft?"

"Oh, no." She smiled, revealing long teeth smeared with blood red. "Pia was murdered. Just like Agata."

~

A HUMID HAZE hung over the NOLA Noir sign, which was black except for the white neon outline of a coffee cup and some sort of symbol. *A fleur-de-lis? A puff of steam?* It was hard to tell from the third-floor lobby window of Private Chicks. Whatever the symbol, it was unsettling.

Like that elderly woman at the Camellia Grill.

Was she right that Agata and Pia Villeré had both been murdered? Who is she, anyway?

And why in God's name was she dressed like Baby Jane?

A woman on the street distracted me from my thoughts. She wore all black, including a hat and sunglasses, and walked briskly toward NOLA Noir. She reached the door, pulled her hat brim low, and glanced behind her before slipping inside.

Her dark attire recalled the mourning dresses of my nonna and her nonne friends, who forever mourned the loss of husbands and other beloved family members.

A disturbing thought brought a frown to my lips. *Is she one of my nonna's Sicilian soldiers come to spy on me?*

I turned to Ruth Walker, who sat in the reception desk chair. "Something's not right with that new coffee shop across the street."

She spun, setting in motion the chains on her cat-eye glasses and the folds of her turkey neck. "What's the matter with it?"

"Looks shady, and the 'noir' in the name doesn't help."

Her lips went as tight as her graying brown bun. "You could be describing this office."

Bewildered, I surveyed the exposed-brick lobby and dark décor. "What are you talking about? 'Private Chicks' is a cool name, and this is a historic French Quarter building."

"I'm talking about the stark furniture and frosted glass door with the company name in black letters. Change the 'Chicks' to 'Dicks,' and you've got a detective agency from a 1940s noir movie," she hit me with a hard stare, "where they smoked and drank and got shot."

My index and pinky fingers pointed to the ground in an Italian *scongiuri* gesture my nonna had taught me to ward off bad luck—that Ruth's 'getting shot' remark had cast over me and the office. I doubted it would work, but given the questionable coffee shop, some superstitious backup couldn't hurt.

"Private Chicks has character, Ruth." My tone was defensive because Veronica owned the building as well as the business. "But from what I can see of NOLA Noir, it's sketchy. And in the month it's been open, there have been odd comings and goings."

"Wake up and smell the coffee." Ruth raised her Only-Judge-Judy-Can-Judge-Me mug adorned with the scales of justice. "That's The Big Easy."

I smirked at her—and her mug. "You make it sound as though every place in the city is corrupt."

"Not the buildings, just the people in them."

Good thing Ruth was Bradley's assistant and not a judge like her TV idol. Otherwise, half the town would be in Central Lockup, or the "hoosegow" as she called it.

My gaze returned to NOLA Noir.

A tall, slender man rounded the corner, and I stepped from the window. He wore a dark suit and fedora.

In the dead of summer.

Veronica breezed into the lobby from the hallway opposite the entrance. She went to Ruth's reception desk and picked up the mail. "Any calls?"

Ruth pursed her lips, emphasizing her fuzzy ostrich chin and turkey wattle. "Not even a telemarketer. And instead of going out and hustling business, Ace PI Franki Amato is worrying about that new coffee shop."

If I was worried about anything, it was the conversation with the elderly woman, but I couldn't tell Ruth that. She suffered under the delusion that she, and not Veronica, was throwing my bachelorette party, so word of my Camellia Grill breakfast could raise her swamp-animal sense and clue her in to the wedding planning. "I am *not* worrying about that coffee shop." To prove my point, I turned to face her—and stopped chewing my nail. "As for business, there's none to hustle. There haven't been any homicides in the city lately."

At least, as far as I knew for *certain*.

Nevertheless, my mention of murder brought me back to Pia and Agata Villeré, and I looked out the window.

Ruth harrumphed. "There she goes spying again."

I hated to provide evidence for her accusation, but a suspicious sixty-something male had just left the coffee shop in a round red wig and matching nose. "In my defense, their clientele is sketchy. The Thin Man went in a minute ago, and an old clown just came out. It's like something straight out of a noir film, except for that clown, who is pure horror flick."

Ruth glanced at Veronica. "Or it's a normal day in the French Quarter."

"She's right, Franki."

"About the Quarter, yes." I flopped onto one of the two facing couches in our waiting area. "But the 'no's' in 'NOLA Noir' speak for themselves."

"Anyway," Veronica picked up a letter opener, "since business is so slow, you should take a long lunch. It *is* Restaurant Week, and there are a lot of deals on prix fixe menus."

"Nah. I'm not hungry," I fibbed, hoping no one could hear

my stomach, which was still grousing about not getting that omelet and bacon. Ruth had recently taken to inviting me to take her to lunch, and I wanted to avoid that scenario. "Besides, it's only ten thirty. I'm going to make a shot of espresso and reorganize my office."

Veronica grimaced. "Mr. Coffee died when I turned him on this morning."

"Ugh." I rested my head on the couch. "I need a caffeine boost. All this nothing-going-on has worn me out."

Ruth crossed her arms. "NOLA Noir's right across the street."

My stare was as intense as a triple espresso. "I'll stick with the established coffee houses, like Cici's or PJ's, thank you."

The door flew open, and we all jumped.

David Savoie, our part-time PI, entered with a Tulane backpack and a black go-cup.

Veronica pointed the letter opener at him, and his hands shot up. "David," she said, teeth clenched, "you break that glass, and I'll slice you open like an envelope."

"Sorry, I forgot." He edged his tall, lanky frame around the letter opener and went to his corner desk. "I'm in a hurry. I have to study for an exam."

I sat up. "I didn't know you were in summer school."

"It's not for my Comp Sci degree," he said, sliding the backpack from his shoulders, "it's a course on ethics and the law for my PI license."

"I'm free today, if you need help studying."

Ruth's eyes dropped on me like a gavel. Then she shifted to David, her glasses chains swinging. "I'd think twice before accepting that offer. Every time Franki helps me, I lose a job."

I refrained from comment. The judgmental Judy blamed me for all the ills in her life, and arguing with her was as futile as telling the real Judge Judy that you rejected your court sentence. "Is that coffee from NOLA Noir?"

David flipped his brown bangs to one side. "Yeah, it's the cappuccino the shop is named for."

"Watch out." I eyed the cup and noticed it had the same unidentifiable image as their sign. "No telling what the *noir* refers to."

"Oh, it's liqueur." He paled and gaped at Veronica, who gave him a look as dark as his cup. "Uh, not enough to get drunk or anything."

Ruth tsked in keeping with her I-don't-drink façade. "What kind of liqueur is it?"

"Vick, the owner, called it *nocino*."

"No-CHEE-no?" I repeated. "That sounds familiar."

David removed a black paper bag from his backpack. "You know how Italians drink Limoncello in the summer?"

I puckered—from the irony, not from the memory of the lemon liqueur. "I have some experience with that, yes."

"Nocino is the winter equivalent, made with walnuts."

"Why didn't you say so?" Ruth raised her mug, hoping for a sample. "It's non-alcoholic."

My eyes rolled like an empty liqueur bottle on Bourbon Street. Any alcohol derived from grain, fruit, nuts, or herbs—in other words, all of it—was non-alcoholic to Ruth, which was one of the reasons I didn't want to go to lunch with her. The last time I did, she had so many cherry bounces that she bounced from her chair to the floor.

Veronica scanned the contents of a letter. "'Nocino cappuccino' is catchy. Why doesn't the owner call it that?"

Ruth shrugged. "It's a mystery." She smirked at me. "Or a noir."

I saw her smirk and raised her a sneer. "I think he's just a bad marketer. The indecipherable symbol on the sign is an indication."

"Either way, if you want coffee quick, it's the best option."

"You can stop trying to get me to go there, Ruth. It's not going to happen." I reached for my phone and saw I had a text message.

The contents of which made me shudder.

"What is it, Franki?" Veronica asked.

My eyes were glued to the display. "Delilah Delaire is at NOLA Noir, and she wants me to meet her about an urgent personal matter."

"It has to be your wedding."

"No, I think it's *her* personal matter."

"So?" Ruth shouted. "What are you waiting for?"

I hesitated. The woman at the Camellia Grill had implied that Delilah was the Blain-Adair wedding planner, and I was concerned that she wanted to see me about whatever had happened to Agata Villeré.

Ruth harrumphed. "Franki's probably afraid it'll be a case."

True, but not for the reason she thought. I couldn't explain it, not even to myself, but something told me not to go across the street.

David sat beside me on the couch. He opened the black bag and pulled out a flaky, layered pastry that gave off a heavenly buttery odor.

My stomach roared to life. "Is that...a *sfogliatella*?"

He nodded as he bit off a hunk. "Vick said his Italian grandma makes them."

I catapulted from the cushion. "I'd better go meet that wedding planner."

"Well, well, well," Ruth crowed. "That was such an abrupt about-face, I'm surprised you didn't fall."

Trying to save face, I raised my chin. "It's for investigative purposes."

"Mm-*hm*. While you're investigating the pastries—I mean the planner—get me a NOLA Noir and make it a double." She glanced at Veronica, whose eyelids had lowered. "Since it's non-alcoholic."

Although Ruth didn't fork over any cash, I agreed in hopes the booze would knock her out for a nap.

With my hobo bag in hand, I left the office and bounded down the stairs. The steamy air grew hotter and more suffocating with each flight, as though I was descending into hell instead of the French Quarter. Before exiting the stairwell, I tied my long brown hair into a knot. Then I looked both ways to avoid running into a passing tourist armed with an obligatory Hand Grenade, Hurricane, or Huge Ass Beer, all of which were murder on clothing.

As I stepped onto Decatur Street, the woman in the black hat exited NOLA Noir.

Our gazes met, and she removed her sunglasses.

Definitely not a nonna. "Delilah?"

She stepped into the street.

A black BMW careened around the corner and knocked her from her feet.

Horrified, I screamed as she landed in a crumpled heap a foot away from me. Before my frozen limbs would move, the BMW sped away, and an old black Buick Roadster with tinted windows came around the corner and screeched to a stop.

My traumatized eyes locked with those of a thirtyish woman in the backseat. She was dressed in red—a fitted blouse with shoulder pads and a wide-brimmed hat. Her jaw had dropped.

Mine had too.

Her driver hit the gas, and the car fishtailed.

I pressed myself against the wall of the building as the car swerved, narrowly missing the woman in the street, and sped away.

My limbs shook as I rushed to the woman's disturbingly still body, and when I realized it was too late to save her, my fingers struggled to dial 9-1-1.

But the hit-and-run wasn't the only thing that had shaken me.

It was also the woman in red in the Roadster.

Because she looked like a femme fatale who'd driven in from a 1940s movie.

A *noir* movie.

2

———————

Veronica crouched in front of me on the street outside Private Chicks. "Tell us what you saw, Franki."

Bradley, who sat beside me on the sidewalk, massaged my back as I pressed my fingertips to my temples, trying to force my brain to focus.

My gaze strayed to the chalk outline where Delilah Delaire's body had been and then to the indecipherable image on the NOLA Noir sign. There was an uncomfortable similarity between the two shapes. *Or am I hallucinating?*

Bradley slid his arm around my shoulders. "Did you get a look at the driver?"

My eyes closed, and I tried to think back to the terrible event. The only person I remembered seeing besides Delilah was the woman in red. "I don't know. It all happened so fast, but a femme fatale was following the BMW in a vintage Roadster."

Bradley looked into my eyes. "You're in shock."

"No, I'm all right. Really." Although now that I thought about it, the femme fatale sighting did sound kind of out there. *Did I hallucinate her too?*

Veronica stood and studied the chalk outline. "Who would kill Delilah Delaire?"

Her question echoed in my head. If I didn't know better, I would've suspected my mom and nonna. I mean, the woman *was* a wedding planner, and Lord knew those two wanted total control of my big day. And pretty much everything leading up to it.

The policeman who'd questioned me minutes before exited NOLA Noir, talking on a cell phone. A few officers were still inside. Otherwise, I would've gone in to ask about Delilah's demeanor before the awful incident. But that would have to wait until the police released the crime scene.

"Come on, babe." Bradley rose to his feet and extended his hand. "Let's get you upstairs." He pulled me up, and I was grateful for the assistance. My legs were wobbly as we climbed to the third floor.

Veronica held the door as Bradley helped me into the office.

Ruth's lips wrinkled. "How much of that nocino did she drink?"

Veronica scowled. "She never made it to the coffee shop, Ruth."

As Bradley led me to one of the lobby couches, his cell phone rang. "I'm going to get you a glass of water." He set off for the hallway to the kitchen and pulled his phone from his pocket to answer the call. "Bradley Hartmann."

Veronica sat on the couch across from me. "How are you feeling?"

"Guilty." I pulled a cushion to my chest. "A woman asked to meet me, and it got her killed."

Ruth opened her mouth, but I silenced her with a sociopathic side-eye and then spread out on the couch.

Veronica cleared her throat. "You shouldn't feel guilty, Franki. What happened to Delilah has nothing to do with you."

"Intellectually, I get that. But why did she call *me* and not another PI?"

"Did you tell her what you do for a living when you called about your wedding?"

"Sure did," I rolled my head to look at her, "and she promptly informed me that she was out of my price range."

Veronica's lips retracted as she sucked in a breath. "Yikes. Well, you're probably the only PI she knew of to call."

"Okay," I propped myself on my elbows, "but why would she ask me to meet at a public place like a coffee shop when our office is literally across the street?"

"Maybe she was afraid to be seen entering a PI firm. She was obviously involved in something bad."

"She was." I shot her a look as black as the velvet hairbow on the woman from the Camellia Grill. "The Blain-Adair wedding."

Bradley walked up with the water glass and placed it on the coffee table in front of me. "Blain-Adair? My mother just called about that wedding."

"What?" I sat up. "Why?"

"It was supposed to take place at the Columns Hotel, where she and my grandmother are staying. But a relative of the bride died, Agata Villeré, and the police want to talk to them about that."

Ruth's eyes raked over Bradley. "I didn't know your family was in town."

"Hang on," I gushed, in case she suspected wedding planning. "Bradley, your mother and grandmother are staying at the Hotel Monteleone, not the Columns."

"Evidently I forgot to mention this, but they said it was too noisy in the Quarter, so they moved to the Garden District." He ran his fingers through his hair. "Now they're mixed up in a murder."

I looked at Veronica from beneath my lashes. "We need to

have The Vassal track down the name and address of that woman from the Camellia Grill."

"What woman?" Bradley asked.

"One who told me that Delilah Delaire was Grace Blain's wedding planner and that Agata and her sister, Pia, were murdered. Next thing I know, I get a call from Delilah, who says she needs to see me about an urgent personal matter, and then she's killed outside Private Chicks."

"Outside *NOLA Noir*," Veronica corrected.

"Either way, it's not a coincidence."

Bradley rubbed his chin. "We definitely need to talk to that woman."

Veronica rose from the couch. "I didn't want to say anything this morning, but when I was at the courthouse a few weeks ago, a couple of attorneys were gossiping about Grace's father, Edward, and his law partner. Apparently, their firm is in financial trouble."

Bradley frowned. "They had an account at Pontchartrain Bank while I was working there. I'll make some calls later today to see what I can find out." He pulled his car fob from his pocket. "Are you all right if I run over to the Columns, Franki?"

Reluctantly, I nodded. I would've liked to go with him to check on his mother and grandmother and investigate what had happened to Agata, but I needed to stay behind and wait for the police to clear NOLA Noir. It was imperative to speak to whoever had served Delilah Delaire while the details were still fresh in their mind.

He gave me a peck on the cheek.

As soon as he left, Ruth spun in her chair. "So, you two met up this morning."

The turkey-ostrich's wedding radar was raised. I had to jam the signal. "It was just breakfast, Ruth."

"Was it, now." Her tone wasn't a question.

To hide the fib written all over my face, I went to the office window.

Storm clouds had gathered, casting a dark shadow over the street. Police cars were still outside the coffee shop, and somehow the chalk outline of Delilah's body seemed more starkly white.

My eyes gravitated to the NOLA Noir sign. *Maybe that's what the image is, a dark cloud.*

A noir cloud.

Veronica came up behind me and patted my back.

I sighed. "You know what my nonna's going to say. Delilah's death is a sure sign of *malocchio*, so my wedding is cursed."

"If Carmela thinks it's the evil eye, that's her problem."

I laid a stare as black as the storm cloud on her.

She bit her thumbnail. "You're right. It's *your* problem. So what now?"

"I'll deal with my nonna later. I have to track down an employee or family member of Delilah's. It might be my only way to find out what she wanted to talk to me about." I grabbed my bag and went to my office, where I dialed Delilah's main office number.

The call went to voicemail.

I hung up without leaving a message and opened my laptop to check the wedding planner's website for names of staff members. But all I could find was a generic "Contact Us" form.

Since I had my computer open, I looked up the Blain-Adair law firm. A headshot of Edward Blain appeared, and I shuddered. He had boyish features and reddish hair, but with a low brow and the empty stare of a sociopath.

My cell phone rang, and I started. "Hello?"

"Did you just call Delilah Delaire's office?" a woman asked in a pronounced New York accent.

She must've been outside because I heard traffic. "Yes, I'm Franki Amato, a PI Delilah was supposed to meet. But she's been in an accident."

The woman inhaled so sharply she could've swallowed the receiver.

"Are you okay?" I asked.

"Is Delilah?"

"I'm so sorry... She passed."

"Ohhhh, Moira. We got trouble. That femme fatale was right."

A chill snaked down my spine. I didn't know who Moira was, but the femme fatale had to be the woman in red I'd locked eyes with seconds after Delilah's murder. She hadn't been a hallucination. "Right about what?"

But my question came too late.

The line was dead.

"Moira? Anyone?" I pounded on the door of Delilah Delaire's Decatur Street office and gave the handle another jiggle.

Still locked.

Ignoring the suspicious stares of passers-by, I peered through a window. Everything seemed in order except for an overturned go-cup on the floor. It was black like the one David had earlier. I squinted, trying to make out where it was from.

Then I saw the image from the NOLA Noir sign.

"What the hell is going on with that coffee shop?" I muttered, turning toward the street and slinging my hobo bag higher on my shoulder.

A chubby woman wearing a T-shirt that read "I love serial killer documentaries and Christmas movies" grabbed the arm of a pot-bellied man walking beside her. "Careful, Darren." She shot me a stabby stare. "There are lots of crazies in the Quarter."

"You're telling me," I shouted. She was one to talk in a shirt like that. Watching non-stop Christmas movies wasn't normal.

Leaning against the outside of a souvenir shop, I redialed the number Moira, or whoever she was, had called me from. Based on the traffic I'd heard on the other end of the line, she'd either forwarded Delilah's office phone to her cell, or she'd noted my number and called me as she was leaving the office.

Or maybe fleeing it.

She could be in danger.

Chewing my cheek, I dropped my phone into my bag and headed back toward Private Chicks. My new plan was to try searching social media for names of Delilah's family or staff and, hopefully, talk to the employees at NOLA Noir.

As I walked back up Decatur toward Private Chicks, I spotted a crowd outside the former site of Tujague's creole restaurant across from Café du Monde. They were an unlikely group. Some in linen and pearls, and others in muslin and bones.

And that woman in the Killer-Christmas shirt thought I was the crazy one.

A young guy with white face paint and a top hat à la Baron Samedi, the voodoo loa of the dead, cupped his hands around his mouth. "This is voodoo, not vaudeville!"

"Good things don't always come in pink boxes," a seventyish woman in a peach Chanel skirt suit shouted, waving a handkerchief.

"Make voodoo dolls, not Voodoo Doughnuts," a man with cowrie shells in his graying dreads yelled.

I approached one of the ladies in linen. She was an older Southern woman with a silver-white updo. "What's going on?"

"A *crime!*"

My stomach seized, and I looked for a body.

She gripped her pearls, distressed. "Voodoo Doughnuts intends to open a store right here at this location."

I exhaled, dragon style. But at least finally I understood the woman in the Chanel suit's comment. "Good things come in pink boxes" was the Portland-based company's slogan. Still, the building was across the street from Café du Monde, so if anyone was going to protest the doughnut shop, it should've been the renowned beignet makers. "So? What's the problem?"

She released her pearls and pulled back her chin. "*The problem* is that they plan to take down the old Tujague's sign from 1856 and replace it with their own. I'm with the Vieux Carré Commission." She pressed a haughty hand to her chest. "Since 1936, our mission has been to *preserve* the Quarter, not *destroy* it."

A corner of my mouth tightened, trying to keep me from talking, but I overpowered it. "Is that why your organization worked tirelessly to erase any memory of the Sicilian influence on the Quarter and tells everyone the architecture is French instead of Spanish?"

"I haven't the faintest idea what you're talking about."

My hand went to my hip. "Thanks to the Vieux Carré Commission, neither do most people, including us Italian-Americans."

She touched her updo and turned away. "Save our signs!"

"Preservationists," the Baron Samedi lookalike spat as he eyed the retreating woman. "I don't care about the Tujague's sign, I just don't want the new one. It has that chocolate-frosted voodoo doll doughnut they sell, the one with the pretzel jabbed in it like a pin. Not only is it offensive to my religion, that frosting looks like blackface."

His frustration was understandable, but I kept my mouth

shut. It would've been awkward to have that conversation with a guy whose face was painted white.

He squinted. "I heard you say you're Italian. Are you here to protest the Memphis Mafia doughnut?"

"*Me?* I have no bone to pick with a doughnut named for Elvis Presley's posse." My eyes darted to the bones in his earlobes. "I mean, no beef."

He shrugged and returned to protesting, and I headed for Private Chicks. Of course, I knew what he'd meant by the Mafia comment, but if I protested everyone who misused the word, it would consume my entire life.

The only thing I was upset about was that I now craved a doughnut I couldn't get.

And crawdads. The protest reminded me of old Hippy Pam and her sit-ins to fight boiling them alive.

As I approached the intersection at Governor Nicholls Street, I was glad to be back in my neck of Decatur. Granted, within a one-block radius of the office, there were no less than four witch shops—Cottage Magick, Omen Psychic Parlor & Witchcraft Emporium, Crescent City Conjure, and Hex Old World Witchery. But unlike the ladies in linen and the voodoo practitioners, New Orleans' witches kept a low profile.

A short woman came around the corner and smacked into me, sending me sprawling.

"Franki Amato!"

My spine went rigid—as I lay supine on the sidewalk.

I knew that bellow.

And that blow.

Both were the work of Shona Helper, a loud librarian from Screamer, Alabama, I'd met on Veronica's Venice wedding trip.

"You remember me, right?" she shouted as though I were hearing impaired. "Shona? Like Mona with a *sh*?"

As the pain subsided, I gave her the onceover. She looked

the same—round rosy cheeks, stringy brown hair with bangs. She wore a white T-shirt that said, "Just Row with It" and billowy cargo shorts that accentuated her snowman figure. But she seemed louder than before. "How could I forget?"

She helped me up. "You should really watch where you're going."

Dusting off my backside, I couldn't help but think I'd spoken too soon about those witches. Because Shona materializing in The Crescent City could only be the result of black magic. "Anyway, what're you doing in town?"

"Looking for you." She switched her tote bag to her other arm, and I noticed it was a different color from the romance-writer conference tote she usually carried. Black instead of white. "Veronica filled me in on Delilah Delaire, the femme fatale, and the mystery Moira woman. Did you find her?"

"No," I said, and I refrained from adding, *But when I find Veronica, there'll be a third murder for the police to investigate.*

"Well, she told me you went up the street, so I've been trying to track you down." She squeezed her tote and chuckled. "See what I did there? *Up* the street and track you *down*?"

I glared at the four witchcraft shops. *Which witch had conjured Shona up?*

"To kill time, I got a double espresso at NOLA Noir. And be forewarned, caffeine really amps me up."

That explained the extra volume. "The coffee shop is open?"

"Thankfully, because Café du Monde was too crowded. I think it was spillover from that big brouhaha across the street about Voodoo Doughnuts."

"Yeah, wild, huh?"

"I'll say. And once word gets out that they make a doughnut called 'Diablos rex' with a pentagram on it, the Satan worshippers will be after them too."

And the Alliance Française, who would be as opposed to the

mixing of Spanish and French as the lady in linen from the Vieux Carré Commission.

"But between you and me," Shona said, "I could go for one of Voodoo Doughnuts' wild berry cannolos."

Cannoli with wild berry filling? Now *that* was something to protest.

"Anyhow," she gripped the strap of her tote, "I'll bet you're wondering what brought me to town."

"Yeah, I already asked you that."

"Before I get into it," she bellowed, "don't think I've forgotten that you have a wedding coming up."

My head jerked around, looking for Ruth. "Actually," I said in a hushed tone hoping she'd follow suit, "it's months away. I'm not even thinking about it."

"Well, I told Veronica that if she needs help planning the shower, I'm available. Lucky for you, Screamer is a mere six hours from here."

That wasn't lucky, because the loud librarian would broadcast news of my wedding to all of NOLA, as she was doing at the moment. "Thanks for the offer, but we've got everything under control."

"Just in case you don't, I mentioned it to Bradley's assistant too." Her chin rose. "My last name isn't Helper for nothing."

Alas, it wasn't. Shona was a swamp animal I hadn't taken into consideration, i.e., the Eastern screech owl. If I didn't send her packing back to Screamer, Operation Black Swamp was sunk. "So, you never said what you're doing here."

"Remember, I told you before we left Venice that the Screamer Scullers had a race against the Bayou Rowing Association?"

"Riiiiight." I'd blacked that out—intentionally. "And when is that? Soon?"

"Nah, not for another couple of weeks. I came early to scope out Honey Island Swamp in Slidell where we're racing. Some of our library patrons held a book-and-bake sale to raise the money to send me."

No doubt to get some peace and quiet to read. "When are you headed back?"

Her brows burrowed into her bangs. "I can't leave town. I'm a murder suspect."

She might as well have smacked into me again. "Say what?"

"That's why I was looking for you. This woman I met at the hotel where I'm staying thinks I killed her aunt."

Agata Villeré. The sidewalk tilted, and I pressed my temples to stabilize myself. "Why would Laura suspect you?"

"So you know her. That's great! Because I tried to talk to her, and she told me that if I try to contact her or her family or come within a hundred yards of them, she'd slap a restraining order on me and you too."

"*Me?* What have I done to Laura Blain?"

"Oh, I told her you were super aggressive. A real pit bull." She leaned forward. "And it's not 'Laura.' It's 'Lara,' like Lars with an *uh*."

My eyes went skyward. My brain couldn't take another name comparison. It was too busy reeling from the realization that I'd have to work to clear Shona, in addition to Bradley's mother and grandmother, of Agata's murder, and most likely Delilah Delaire's. "Fine, but you still haven't told me why *Lar-uh* thinks you killed her aunt."

"Because I was admiring her jewelry, and there are witnesses."

A faint ray of hope broke through my black brain cloud. "That's not a crime."

"It is if you *steal* the jewelry."

Whether I wanted to or not, I knew Shona. There was no

way she would steal jewelry, much less kill a woman. "I see. Someone stole the jewels Agata was wearing."

She huffed. "If only. Agata's entire jewelry collection is missing, and everyone thinks I stashed it at the swamp."

My gut lurched. Like me, it was certain that Operation Black Swamp had taken on a whole new meaning.

One I might live—or not—to regret.

3

———

Is this joint for real? The name on the frosted glass door was NOLA Noir, but the black block letters might as well have spelled "Spade and Archer" from *The Maltese Falcon*. The style was unsettling after my encounter with the forties female in her decade-appropriate car, not to mention the murders that had preceded it—Delilah's and, if the Baby Jane lookalike at the Camellia Grill was right, Agata and her sister Pia's.

Then there was the involvement of Bradley's mother and grandmother.

And Shona being a murder suspect.

My head spun from the summary, and I leaned against the wall to collect myself.

"Operation Black Swamp was accidentally prophetic, all right," I grumbled. With each hour that passed, I was slipping further into the murky deep of whatever was going on. And helping Shona Helper could help pull me under for good, which is why I'd given her a research assignment to track down intel on Delilah's staff—while lying low in her room at the Columns.

In theory.

Sighing, I went inside, and my breath caught in my throat.

Instead of a contemporary coffee shop, I'd entered a time warp. Saxophone music played from a stereo, not New Orleans style but the jazz noir of a hardboiled detective soundtrack. And the décor matched the music. Except for a low-hanging lamp over the counter and light streaming through Venetian blinds, the place was as stark and dark as a 1940s black-and-white movie. The only spot of color was a sequined pillow of Nicolas Cage, who seemed all wrong for the noir vibe, unless you counted the pyramid-shaped tomb he'd purchased at the infamously creepy St. Louis No. 1 Cemetery as his final act—or film, as it were.

I looked around for the femme fatale since it looked like a place she'd hang out, but the only person I saw was a man in a trench coat exiting the men's room.

Another shady character. No one who wasn't nefarious would wear a coat in summer. And judging from the way he was clutching his lapels closed, he either had a firearm under there, or he was a flasher.

What was worse, he beat me to the counter.

A door marked *Kitchen* opened, and a fortyish male rushed out. "Hey, welcome. Name's Vick Villano. What can I get you?"

I'd half expected a Humphrey Bogart, but he was a definite Tony Danza—except that his last name meant *villain* instead of *dance*. And he was boyishly boisterous, exuberant even. Probably from a perpetual caffeine buzz.

Trench-Coat Guy leaned forward. "I'd kill for a decent cup of coffee."

"Black?"

"Something a little different." His voice was low, quasi conspiratorial. "To go."

Vick's big brown eyes narrowed, and he pressed a button on an espresso machine. "I'll fix you up. In the meantime, try one of our free chocolate samples. They've got a liquid nocino center."

Trench-Coat Guy pocketed an individually wrapped bon bon and studied a menu. "You serve lunch?"

"We're still waiting on our commercial food license." Vick began steaming a carafe of milk. "For now, we can only make cottage food from our home kitchen, like our pastries. But no animal or fish protein. It's too bad because my nonnina makes the best pasta in Louisiana."

"Nonnina? Is that Italian for 'dame,' or something?"

Vick's eyes widened as though the guy had pulled a tommy gun. "Watch your mouth, eh? That's my grandma you're talking about."

Trench-Coat Guy recoiled. "I didn't mean no disrespect."

"Good. Nonnina means 'little nonna.' It's a term of affection because she's a special lady." He wiped away a tear and poured the espresso into the cup.

I repressed an eye roll. Italian men were notorious mamma's boys, and they were no different with their nonnas. They put them on a pedestal on par with The Virgin Mary, which was one slot below Sophia Loren.

"Hold on a sec." Vick disappeared into the kitchen with the cup.

Was he going to talk to his nonnina? Or put something in the coffee? Trench-Coat Guy *did* ask for "something a little different."

Vick returned, and the contents of the cup were pitch black. "When we get the food license, you come back and ask for my nonnina, Brunella." He added steamed milk to the coffee, finished it off with a twist of orange, and passed it to Trench-Coat Guy. "Her specialties are spaghetti al cognac, penne alla vodka, and scaloppine al Marsala."

Brunella liked the booze, like Ruth.

"You call-a me?" The old woman who emerged from the kitchen was a dead ringer for Strega Nona from the Tomie dePaola children's books. She was 4'10", built like a lump of pasta dough, and had a witchy nose and chin. An unfortunate look for an Italian woman. On the other hand, my Sicilian grandma could've passed for Sophia Petrillo from *The Golden Girls*—down to the black handbag and sharp tongue.

Vick put his arm around his nano nonna and squeezed her in a hug. "I was just bragging about your cooking to our customer."

Her eyes were as hard as black diamonds as she scrutinized Trench-Coat Guy and his go-cup. "That all-a you buy?"

He straightened. "It's a coffee shop, ain't it?"

She pulled a toothpick from the pocket of her apron, which read *Nonna Knows Best*, and slipped it between her lips. "I think-a you want a pastry too."

"Uh, not really."

Vick's boyish face turned bad. He shoved a pastry into a bag and slid it across the counter.

Trench-Coat Guy dropped some bills, grabbed the coffee and the bag, and left before they extorted him any further.

Brunella put her hands on her round hips and looked me in the eye. "You make the big-a order, no?"

She was one tough *biscotto*, and I didn't want to cross her. "Yeah, I'm ordering for myself and a colleague."

She grabbed a broom and went into the kitchen.

And I dropped three free bon bons into my hobo bag, all of which were for me. I'd earned them after that awkward encounter.

Vick flashed a fleshy smile. "Don't mind my nonnina. When it comes to business, she always worries. To use an Italian expression, she 'sees everything black.'"

I could see why in this place.

"When you get to know her, she's a ray of sunshine."

More like a death ray.

He rinsed his hands in a small sink and grinned. "What can I get you?"

"What's in the NOLA Noir?"

His smile faltered, and he glanced toward the kitchen. "Espresso and nocino, a liqueur made from walnuts and coffee beans."

"Two of those to go, and make one a triple—the nocino, not the espresso." Ruth had asked for a double, but I wanted to ensure that afternoon nap happened. I moved to the pastry case.

"I recommend our *babà*. It's on special for Restaurant Week."

Babà was the one Italian pastry I avoided. It looked like a glistening vanilla cupcake without the icing, but it had enough rum to knock out a pirate for his entire Shore Leave. "I'd prefer a sfogliatella. What's the filling?"

One of his thick black brows rose. "You ask a lot of questions."

"I like to know what I'm ingesting. Is that a problem?"

Vick scowled and opened the door to the case. "One is the classic candied orange peel with grappa," he pointed to a sfogliatella topped with a curled orange peel, "and the other has a rum cherry filling."

Forget the coffee, you could get drunk off a pastry alone. "On second thought, just the NOLA Noir, thanks."

He slammed the door, and I jumped because it sounded like a bullet blast. Then he hit a button on the electric coffee grinder.

Despite the tension, I had to get some information. "Tragic about what happened to that wedding planner, Delilah Delaire."

"Oh, yeah." His eyes mimicked his tone—flat. "Sad."

"I saw her come in here right before she was killed. Did you talk to her at all? Or notice anything odd about the way she was acting?"

He attached the portafilter to the espresso machine with an

angry arm jerk, placed two shot glasses beneath it, and punched the brew button. "What's it to ya?"

I shrugged. "I'm just wondering who did that to her."

"Can't help you there." He watched the coffee stream into the glasses but stole a furtive glance at me, as though *I* was the suspicious one.

We'd gotten off on the wrong foot, so I decided to try engaging him on a less confrontational topic. "So, where in Italy is your nonna from? Mine's from Sicily."

He shot me a look as black as the espresso. "Benevento in Campania."

Campania was a region known for the Camorra, a Mafia-type criminal organization that dated to the seventeenth century, which could account for Brunella's brusque demeanor. "Is that near Naples?"

"About forty miles away."

I was pushing it with the questions, but my gut told me to keep going. "How come you decided to use nocino in your coffee? Does it come from Benevento?"

"No, the Emilia-Romagna region, but it's made all over Italy. There's a tradition of collecting the walnuts on the night of San Giovanni, June 24th."

"That's the day after tomorrow."

"Yeah." He poured the espresso shots into go cups. "It's called 'the night of the barefoot virgins.'"

"I'm sorry. *What?*"

"Yo, don't look at *me*. I didn't name it that." He took the cups in the back.

I considered slipping behind the counter to spy on him, but Brunella would have caught me and beaten me with her broom. Or wand.

Thunder rumbled, and I realized the interior of NOLA Noir had grown a shade darker. I peered through the Venetian blinds.

Sudden summer storms were common in New Orleans, but that was fast even for swamp country.

And eerily film noir.

Vick returned with the cups and placed them on the counter.

My gut told me to press him about the bizarre liqueur tradition. "What's the backstory on barefoot virgins and nocino?"

He added milk to the carafe and began steaming. "They dressed in white and climbed the walnut trees to pick the nuts when they were still green. Then they left them on the ground overnight to collect dew. The next morning, they infused them with pure grain alcohol and sugar and left them to ferment until All Saints' Eve."

"Halloween? Why?"

"Both magical and ritual nights." He poured the steamed milk into the cups, added a twist of orange, and slid one toward me. "Try it."

I reached for the cup, but my hand hesitated. The foam looked like a witch's hat.

"What's the matter?"

The lamp over the counter glared in my face like a spotlight. It felt like I was being questioned by police.

Brunella burst from the kitchen. "Is-a there a problem?"

There were lots of problems, but I wasn't going to tell her that. If there was a nonna Camorra, she was a machine gun-carrying member. "Of course not." I took a sip to back up my fib. To my surprise, it was a rich, nutty flavor. "Delicious."

Satisfied, she returned to the kitchen.

I opened my mouth to ask Vick what I owed him, but the words didn't come. Because I was aware of my esophagus in a way I shouldn't have been. It didn't burn. It was lit up in my chest, as though it had been switched on like the hanging lamp. "Um, can I take a look at the nocino bottle?"

His eyes went gemstone hard like his nonnina's. "What for?"

"My throat feels funny. I want to see what's in it."

"I told you. Walnuts, coffee beans, and alcohol."

"Just the same, I'd like to see it."

He produced a clear bottle from below the counter. The liquid was black. *Noir*.

"You didn't use that in my coffee."

"What are you talkin' about." It was a statement, not a question.

I looked at the kitchen door, expecting Brunella the Bully to come out. "You took the cups in the back. What did you put in them?"

The semi-conjoined caterpillars above his eyes lowered. "What did you say you did for a living?"

This was getting weird. "I didn't. Now are you going to tell me what you put in it?"

"You're looking at it." He shook the bottle. Then he put it beneath the counter and began cleaning the coffee machine.

I took the hint and left a ten on the counter and turned to leave—without the radioactive drinks. I wasn't sure what was in them, and I knew he hadn't used the nocino behind the counter. It was possible that he had the same bottle in the kitchen, but it didn't make sense that he would make my drink with that one when he had a bottle at his fingertips.

"Next time you come in," Vick called, "I've got an *ammazza-caffé* with your name on it."

My glowing throat went dry, and I left the establishment. The word meant *coffee killer*, as in a digestif to dull the taste of an after-dinner espresso or its caffeine effect.

But in this case, I was certain it was a threat.

～

"WHY ARE you rubbing your throat, Miss Franki?" Glenda O'Brien, my sixty-something ex-stripper landlady, shouted from the balcony of our fourplex. "Catch the kissing disease from your ex-banker beau?"

I removed my hand from my neck and pulled the keys from the ignition of my 1965 Mustang convertible. A normal person would've asked if I had a sore throat, but that wasn't Glenda. She related everything to sex. Case in point, the ice cream cone outfit she was wearing—a teensy brown waffle skirt, and for a top, cherry pasties on her two scoops of vanilla.

"Hope what little she *does* have on doesn't melt in this heat," I muttered as I climbed from the car.

Glenda descended the stairs in waffle-cone stripper shoes with the words "lick" and "me," respectively. "What did you say, sugar?"

"That I didn't catch mono from Bradley," I fibbed, slamming the car door. "I had one lousy sip of a coffee drink today, and it's like my esophagus is glowing. Not only that, my chest is tight." I scowled and massaged my sternum. "That crazy concoction probably had enough caffeine to fuel my convertible."

She flipped her long, platinum Cher hair. "Sounds like a drink I need to try. Did you get it at Thibodeaux's?"

My gaze shifted to the neighborhood bar and restaurant across the street—then, considering the suspicious coffee situation, strayed to the creepy cemetery next to it. "No, a place called NOLA Noir."

"Vick Villano's new business?"

I turned to face her. "You know him?"

"Intimately." Her tone told me more than I wanted to know. "In fact, I once showed the man a little NOLA Noir in the VIP room at Madame Moiselle's Strip Club." She touched the tip of her tongue to her upper lip and shook her two scoops.

The impromptu ice cream shake put the kibosh on any follow-up questions.

Glenda lit a cigarette holder designed to go with her outfit—a Pirouline rolled wafer. "But I didn't meet Vick at Madame Moiselle's." She exhaled a smoke ring. "He used to own a nail salon next door. All of us dancers went there."

"What happened to it?"

"Went under after a couple of months."

That confirmed my theory that Vick Villano was a bad businessman. "How could a nail salon next to a strip club go under?"

She shrugged. "They only did pedicures."

"Wait." I continued to be confused. "Why didn't they do manicures?"

"Vick was the main manicurist, sugar, and he's got a notorious thumbnail fetish. It's so bad Madame Moiselle's had to ban him."

I couldn't believe I was about to ask this, but given the state of my throat, I had a stake in the thumbnail ban. "What did he do, exactly?"

"He'd hold up dollar bills and make the girls take them with both thumbs. They called him 'Ick Vick.'"

My head recoiled. "Sick Vick" was more appropriate. "I didn't notice him looking at my hands when I paid for my coffee."

"That's odd, sugar, because he made his pedicure clients pay the same way."

The real noir wasn't what Sick Vick had put in the nocino cappuccino, it was why he had a thing for thumbnails—except for mine, apparently. "His grandmother was helping out at the coffee shop. Did she work at the nail salon too?"

"She did. He lives with her over on Walnut Street."

"That's weird, because he made my coffee drink with walnut liqueur."

She took a puff from her Pirouline. "And his house is on the corner across from the Walnut Street Playground."

The guy was nutty for the walnut. "I'm starting to think Vick Villano is a freak."

"A little freak is a good thing, Miss Franki." She batted inch-long false eyelashes. "You should see him in the boudoir."

I'd rather drink an entire nocino cappuccino. I started to tell her about the hit-and-run outside Vick's business, but a vehicle coming up the street caught my attention. Not the killer's BMW or the femme fatale's Buick Roadster, but a black van with a familiar sign and slogan—*Lucky's Liquor and Vaxing—Before you get your drink on, get your hairs in order.* "Someone needs to tell Nadezhda that 'waxing' is spelled with a 'w.'"

Glenda ashed her cigarette. "I've told her, sugar, but that's how she pronounces it with her Russian accent. Plus, the misspelling brings in more clients."

"How?"

"They think 'vaxing' refers to vaccinations. She's thinking about expanding the business to include a clinic."

I had no comment. I'd once predicted the confusion, and a combination liquor store, waxing salon, and shot clinic had real potential in New Orleans.

The van pulled into the driveway and jerked to a stop.

"What's she doing here, anyways?" No sooner had I uttered the question than a fit of panic stabbed my abdomen. "She's not moving in, is she?"

"Relax, Miss Franki. I told you, for the time being, I'm keeping Miss Ronnie's apartment as the headquarters for my Hucci Cucci Hot Couture line."

That was a relief. Ever since Veronica had vacated the apartment next door, I lived in fear of the next renter, especially after a short stint by the Crescent City Medium, Chandra Toccato.

The memory of that experience prompted another round of panic. "What about the apartment upstairs?"

"It's back to being my costume closet. I have more clothes than ever now that I'm a stripper couture designer. Nadezhda's here because we're having dinner at Thibodeaux's for Restaurant Week. Wanna join us?"

Nadezhda Dmitriyeva's personality was as prickly as her spiky maroon-tinted hair, so dining solo in the cemetery would have been more inviting. "Can't." My hand went to my neck. "Gotta take care of this throat."

"What a shame, sugar. After we eat, she's coming to see me rehearse my Hot I Scream Sundae number for Madame Moiselle's summer strip revue this Thursday night." Glenda gave her two scoops a shake. "For the performance, I wear a skirt made from real waffle cone, and I drizzle chocolate syrup on my hot vanilla body and *scream*."

My sweet tooth was notorious, especially for Nutella, but that was one dessert I was happy to miss.

"At least you're getting a sneak peak of my costume." She struck a stripper pose. "I call it 'Hot Stripper Summer,' and I'm selling it on my website. I've already got over a hundred pre-orders."

Wow. She could give Ick Vick some pointers.

Nadezhda kicked open the van door and slid from the seat. If Glenda was Hot Stripper Summer, she was Cold Soviet Winter. She wore combat boots with a black fur-lined stretch minidress that did nothing for her nesting-doll figure.

As she marched toward us, a waft of her perfume set my esophagus aflame, and I clutched my neck.

"Vhy you grab troat?" Nadezhda's lip curled, revealing a missing eye tooth. "You got STD?"

These women needed to get their minds out of the gutter—

then again, I *was* talking to a stripper and a bikini-waxer-liquor-store owner. "It's that toxic scent you're wearing. What is it? Molotov cocktail?"

"*Nyet*," she replied, as though wearing an explosive was an actual thing. "It called Red Moscow."

For once I had no comeback. I hadn't expected such a fitting stereotype.

Glenda blew out a puff. "Miss Franki had a coffee drink at Vick Villano's new place that irritated her throat."

Nadezhda's old-Russian-man brows furrowed. "Zat ick tumbnail guy?"

"You know him too?" I asked.

"*Da*. He come in Lucky's and look at my tumbs like veirdo."

Annoyance pricked my chest. Now that I knew Vick had looked at Nadezhda's thumbnails, I was kind of offended he'd slighted mine. "Was he there for a wax?"

"Not for vax. For booze."

"By any chance, was it nocino?"

Her snake eyes shot to Glenda. "How him know zat?"

My cheeks glowed hot like my throat. Nadezhda persisted in thinking I was a man because the first time I met her I was with a drag queen client—at least, that's the reason I told myself. "Never mind that," I snapped. "What did he want?"

"Vick vant Lucky's to supply nocino to NOLA Noir, but he not have license."

It wasn't like Nadezhda to consider local liquor laws. She was a penny-pinching Communist criminal who'd do anything for a red cent, and Vick didn't sound much more honest. "Are you sure you didn't sell it to him?"

"I give you my toot."

My hands shot up, and I took a step back. I didn't know what was going on, but I wanted no part of it.

Glenda stubbed out her cigarette with the toe of her "Lick" shoe. "She means 'tooth,' Miss Franki."

There was no tactful way to say what I was thinking, so I decided to blurt it out. "You're already down one eye tooth, so you keep it."

Nadezhda side-eyed Glenda. "Frank not have brain."

"It's *Franki*," I ground out. "And I'm not the one offering my teeth to people."

Glenda put a hand on my arm. "It's an expression, sugar. In Russian, 'I give you my tooth' means 'I cross my heart.'"

That made as much sense as Nadezhda's bad business slogan. "Let's get back to Vick, okay?"

Nadezhda's black eyes narrowed, and she gave a signature suck of her eye tooth hole. "Vhy you vant know about Vick?"

"Because a wedding planner named Delilah Delaire was killed in a hit-and-run outside his shady coffee shop today, and he and his nonnina are acting suspicious."

Glenda rested a hand between her two scoops. "Well, that's just awful, sugar, but you can't think they had anything to do with it."

Nadezhda growled. "Vick is crook. I know vone vhen I see."

There was so much I could say to that.

"Now Miss Nadezhda," Glenda admonished, "Vick is different, but that doesn't make him a killer."

She was right about that. "I didn't say I suspected him of the murder. All I know is, Vick didn't like me asking questions about the incident, and then he and maybe his nonnina did something to my coffee that's making my throat radiate." I turned to Nadezhda. "You still haven't told me what happened after you refused to sell him the nocino."

Nadezhda's eyes were as barbed as her spikes. "I not refuse. I not have nocino, so I offer vodka. But him not buy."

That was the Nadezhda I knew. What I didn't know was whether Vick had bought the nocino from another liquor distributor or made it himself. Either way, it raised an unsettling question.

What had Sick Vick put in it?

4

———

"At least you know I didn't poison it," I said to my brindle Cairn terrier, Napoleon, who eyed the breakfast kibble in his bowl with grave suspicion. "I wish I could say the same for Vick Villano and that walnut liqueur cappuccino."

My suspicions of Vick and his nonnina percolated like my espresso maker. A vibrant esophagus was odd, but it was a stretch to think that Vick had poisoned my coffee. Although, it had been eighteen hours since I'd sipped that noxious nocino, and my throat *did* feel phlegmy.

No, my mind was just messing with me after the shock of Delilah's murder—and seeing Shona. "This is one of those times that calls for self-care." I absent-mindedly massaged my neck. "But what *is* that, exactly?"

My gaze swept my furnished apartment—the red-and-gold velvet wallpaper, purple and zebra French bordello furniture, and bearskin rug. Glenda's brothel-chic décor was anything but spa-like.

Still, I could meditate?

Spread out on the chaise longue with an inspirational book?

Relax in a hot bubble bath?

"*Pff!* Who am I? An Instagram influencer? Self-care means food!"

I shot the freshly brewed espresso and glanced around the kitchen. I'd been craving something sweet since the doughnut protest and Glenda's ice cream sundae outfit. But I didn't have either of those things in the house. I opened the pantry door and studied the contents.

"I have all the ingredients to make Nutella s'mores!"

Within minutes, I'd assembled graham crackers, marshmallows, and chocolate-hazelnut spread into double-decker creations that improved my mental state considerably.

After popping the s'mores into the oven, I licked a gob of Nutella from my thumb and took a hard look at the nail. The purple polish was chipped, but there were no unsightly ridges or breaks. "Sick Vick is crazy not to lust after this."

Napoleon settled in on the leopard print linoleum to wait for the s'mores, and I went into the living room and flopped onto the zebra-striped chaise lounge.

The more I thought about Vick's thumbnail fetish, the more I wondered whether his nonnina, Brunella, was aware of it. "Actually, I'm sure she is. While we Italian daughters and granddaughters suffer under the weight of familial expectations, Italian sons and grandsons get away with murder."

Murder.

My hand went to my throat.

The lick of Nutella had given me agita, which had never happened before.

What was in that nocino? And why did Vick Villano dislike me so intensely? Because I asked too many questions?

Or was the real issue that I'd asked him about Delilah?

My cellphone rang. The display showed my parents' number in Houston, which made the tightness in my chest turn hard squeeze. Had I psychically summoned my mom and nonna with the "suffering" comment? Because as sure as my name was Francesca Lucia Amato, Vito and Michael Corleone were calling to meddle in my wedding planning. And given Delilah Delaire's murder, I wasn't ready to invite them to New Orleans, or maybe even have a bridal shower.

There was only one thing to do—use my throat as an excuse to end the call. I tapped *Answer* and forced a cough. "Hi, Mom."

"Francesca?" she shrilled. "It's your mother, dear."

No matter how many times I'd said it was obvious from my greeting that I knew who she was, the woman persisted in introducing herself—either to assert her authority or to drive home the guilt that I didn't call her often enough. Rather than respond, I coughed again.

"What's-a the matter, Franki?" my octogenarian nonna asked in her thick Sicilian accent. "Are you sick-a?"

My thoughts went to Sick Vick. "My throat is irritated from a coffee drink I had earlier, so I can't talk now."

"That's fine, dear." My mother's tone was as radiant as my esophagus. "Your nonna and I will talk for you."

Didn't they always?

"Franki, what-a was in-a the coffee? Grappa?"

"No, nocino."

"*Buono!*"

I rubbed my larynx. "This nocino wasn't good, Nonna. It was acidic...or something. I had it at a coffee shop near the office, but I'm wondering whether it was homemade."

"Surely not, Francesca. That's illegal. And besides, nocino isn't well known outside Italy."

"Yeah, but the owner, Vick Villano, is Italian. His 'nonnina' is from Benevento."

"*È una strega!*" Nonna hissed.

I blinked and stared at the receiver. Hearing her call

Brunella a witch was startling, especially since Vick's nonnina was the spitting image of Strega Nona. "Why would you say that, Nonna?"

"Benevento is-a where *streghe* used-a to meet at an old-a walnut tree."

My head retracted, collapsing my throat and making me cough for real. The walnut kept coming up with Vick and Brunella.

"That's why they make-a that *liquore*, Strega, in-a Benevento."

"She's right, dear, there's even a drawing of witches dancing around the tree on the label."

My hand went to my throat, and I added the liqueur to my new "do-not-drink list," which only had that and nocino on it. Oh, and beer.

"It's quite an infamous tale, really," my mother said. "A priest had the original tree cut down centuries ago, but legend has it that the *janare*—that's what the witches are called in the dialect of Campania—would stand at their windows at night, spread unguent under their arms, and recite a spell that made their brooms fly."

"*Sì, signora!*" Nonna shouted with a smack that was most likely her hand landing on a Bible. "So they could-a dance and-a drink around that-a tree for the Sabbat, a festival for the devil."

I rolled my eyes and reclined on the chaise lounge. The gathering was probably a pagan harvest ritual that had been demonized by the Church. "Well, Vick didn't mention any witches. He said virgins made the nocino on the feast of San Giovanni, which," my hand returned to my throat, "is tomorrow."

Nonna snorted. "He didn't tell-a you the whole-a story, because his-a nonnina is a *janara*. Vick is-a slick."

That was one adjective to describe him—or rather, one of several.

"By the way-a, who is-a his nonnina? Maybe she was-a in-a

New Orleans when I lived-a there with-a your *nonnu*, God rest-a his soul."

"All I can tell you is that her name is Brunella."

My mother giggled. "Reminds me of that comic strip 'Broom-Hilda.'"

Brunella *did* have a broom. Maybe Vick wasn't the one who'd messed with my coffee. "But was it only the virgins who made nocino? Or did witches make it too?"

My mother's giggle had become a cackle. "Why are you worried about that? You no longer qualify to pick the walnuts."

No, but if the witches made the nocino, my mother was more than qualified to brew a batch. "I'm worried about whether Brunella did something to my drink."

"You *should*-a worry!" Nonna shouted. "The janare created nocino. They made-a their own-a pot on-a the night of-a San Giovanni."

"She's right, Francesca. I just pulled up an article on my computer that says the witches have been making nocino since Ancient Rome, when the town of Benevento was known as Maleventum."

"That mean-a 'bad event' in Latin."

Nonna didn't need to translate. Bad events had been happening since I'd sipped that coffee, and they showed no sign of stopping.

"Oh, *thisss* is *interestinggg*." My mother's tone foretold of something boring. "The Romans thought the name Maleventum was a bad omen, so they changed it to Beneventum, or 'good event.' They also believed the walnut tree and its shade were bad omens because of the witches, but they thought the nut was a good omen because it symbolized marriage, fertility, and abundance."

As far as I was concerned, anything that steered our conversations to weddings and babies was actually a bad omen, so I dissolved into a fit of coughing.

My mother let out a sad sigh. "You should really eat some walnuts, dear."

I stood and went into the kitchen. I didn't need walnuts. I needed Nutella, a magical unguent for the tongue that cured family-inflicted ills.

"That's-a not all-a she should-a do, Brenda," Nonna said. "She need-a to put a broom-a at her front-a door to keep-a Brunella out. Those-a janare slip-a through the cracks in-a the frame."

I smirked as I pulled the cinnamon-smelling s'mores from the oven. "We don't need to worry about Brunella slipping into my apartment, Nonna. But, out of curiosity, how could a broom stop her when witches use them to get around?"

"When-a the janare see a broom-a, they must-a count the bristles. But-a they don't-a know their numbers too good-a. So, a broom in-a front of the door keep-a them busy until-a dawn when they have-a to go home."

The legend was laughable. "So, a janara is the uneducated witch equivalent of Count von Count from 'Sesame Street?'"

"This is-a no joke, Franki! The janare do-a terrible things-a. They cast-a spells on-a people and-a sit on-a them while they sleep-a until their chest get-a so tight, they have a heart attack-a."

The janare sounded more like the Italian version of the Cajun *cauchemars*, so-called 'nightmare witches' who rode sleeping individuals like horses until they died. And even though I definitely didn't believe in either kind of witch, something in the coffee drink had caused my torso muscles to contract. I took a couple of deep breaths to expand my ribcage.

"Are you having trouble breathing, Francesca?"

"No, my chest feels tight."

My mother's laughter bubbled from the phone like steam from a cauldron. "Of course it does. You're a hypochondriac like your father."

Time for that unguent. I bit into a s'more that was so hot I had to spit it back onto the pan and fan my face. Between my glowing esophagus and freshly scalded mouth, I'd probably get an infection.

"Just-a be careful," Nonna warned. "The janare are evil."

The burn had shocked some sense into me, making me realize how silly I'd been to suspect Brunella of being a witch. If anything, she was Camorra. "I appreciate the advice, but witchcraft is just plain BS."

"Listen to-a me, Franki," nonna chided. "This is-a no old-a wives'-a tale. The janare are real-a women who know-a the herbs-a."

Herbs.

My chest grew so heavy that I would've sworn a janara sat atop it. I'd had a few encounters with a local witch named Theodora, and even though I didn't believe she had magical powers—much less that she was three hundred and one—she made herb spell kits.

And Vick had bragged about Brunella's cooking, not to mention the fact that Italians had used herbs to make digestifs for at least as long as the witches of Benevento had been making nocino.

Grabbing my phone and the tray of s'mores, I returned to the zebra chaise longue with Napoleon in tow. It was time to take my mom and nonna up on their offer to talk for me. They were freaking me out. And agita or no, the s'mores looked too good not to eat.

As my mom and nonna yammered on, I placed the s'mores on the coffee table and read a text message I'd missed from Bradley.

. . .

On my way to Pontchartrain Bank to see what I can find out about Edward Blain's finances. My mother and Grandma are expecting you at the Columns for breakfast at nine. Love you, B

Disappointed, I looked at the gooey deliciousness I'd prepared for myself. Then I shrugged. I could eat again. The s'mores were self-care, not a meal.

"Carmela!" My mother's shout held a note of hysteria. "This article says Delilah Delaire was killed by a car."

"*Mamma mia, che disgrazia!*"

They knew her? I dropped the s'more and grabbed the phone. "Mom, I'm working on that case. How did you know Delilah?"

"Your second cousin Giada used her for her wedding some years ago."

"*Madonna mia*, Brenda! We don't-a talk about that-a side of-a the family."

I had no idea who Giada and her side of the family were, but if my nonna invoked the Virgin Mary and didn't talk about them, they were either Mafia or mortuary people. "Who is she, again?"

"Surely you remember *Giada*, Francesca." My mother emphasized the not-to-be spoken name because she took great pains to point out that my eccentric relatives came from the Amato side of the family. "She majored in bioarchaeology like her father. It's the study of human remains found at excavations."

"She's a grave-a digger!"

Ah. So, mortuary people. "And when did I meet her?"

"Oof! You're as forgetful as your father."

My dad wasn't forgetful. He didn't listen to my mom to begin with.

"You met her at your cousin Paul's wedding."

Didn't remember Paul, either. But in my defense, I came from a big family.

"Brenda, that's-a the wedding where Franki ate-a so many rum-a desserts, she got-a drunk and-a passed out."

If I had a dollar for every time someone in my family brought up that incident, neither Bradley nor I would have to work for a living. "Um, I was twelve, and no one told me Italians douse their pastries in rum."

"True," my mother sing-songed, "but gluttony is another trait you share with your father."

On that note, I huffed and stuffed a s'more into my mouth. But the rum pastry reminder did make me feel better about not remembering my cousins.

"Anyway, dear, Giada's married to a prominent New Orleans attorney, and they live in a fabulous home on St. Charles. But..." She gave a soulful sigh. "they're childless."

"Another reason to eat-a the wal-a-nuts, eh Franki?" Nonna prodded.

Not walnuts. More s'more. I crammed another into my mouth.

"I'll get you some at Costco, Francesca. But you might've heard of her husband's law firm from Veronica, because they're quite prestigious. Blain Adair?"

My cough was genuine because I was shocked—and choking on the s'more.

Blain Adair was the same name as the wedding.

Do I have family connected to this case?

∽

"THE COLUMNS IS CERTAINLY dark and disturbing," I said aloud in the empty entryway. Compared to the hotel's white exterior with its majestic columns and lush green veranda, the interior of the Italianate mansion was a mood—*murderous.*

It didn't help that it was storming out.

Pretty Baby, the Brooke Shields movie about a child raised in New Orleans' Storyville red-light district had been filmed in the hotel, and it showed. Like my apartment, the décor was brothel chic, mahogany wood with ornate chandeliers, soft furnishings in velvet and silk, and flowery flock wallpaper. A hallway ran the length of the house to a reception desk by a grand staircase. On the left side of the mansion was a long parlor with a sitting area in front of a fireplace and a billiard table. On the right was a coffee shop at the front of the house, a stunning bar and adjoining lounge, and in the rear a tearoom across from the reception desk. The kitchen was in the back of the house.

No one was around, so I entered one of two doorways to the parlor. The bulbs in a chandelier flickered on and off.

"Must be a leak," I muttered none-too confidently. "Water from the storm affecting the old wiring."

From the corner of my eye, I saw a middle-aged man in a Columns Hotel uniform standing in the doorway closest to the reception desk. He didn't seem alarmed that I'd been talking to myself. Instead, he seemed alarmed by the chandelier.

"That flickering happen often?" I asked.

He gave a half shake of his head and backed from the room.

"On that note..." I hoofed it from the parlor and crossed the hall to the lounge. As I passed two pale green couches in the middle of the room, my attention lingered on an old piano covered with lit candles and a curtained dining alcove with a red velvet booth and a stained-glass window reminiscent of a chapel. "Not comforting, either."

The adjoining breakfast room was less spooky thanks to peach-colored wallpaper and light from large windows. I was heartened to see a professional espresso machine—and no nocino.

A thirty-something male employee exited a door behind a counter.

As I approached, I made eye contact—not with the employee but with a man in a powdered wig on an oil painting behind him. The canvas had been punctured on either side of the man's head, so I scrutinized his eye sockets to check for spy holes.

"Kitchen's closed," the employee said. "All we have are muffins."

My gaze dropped to the tattoo on his neck—flames. Given what my throat had been through, I could relate. "Did you work this past weekend?"

"Nah, I was in jail."

Airtight alibi. "Is your manager around?"

"That's why the kitchen's closed. He's at the police station."

"Then nothing for me, thanks." I wasn't about to eat the food after that revelation, but I might visit the bar. I could use something strong in light of the light flickering.

Bradley's mother, Lillian, entered followed by his grandmother, Cordelia. They were Northeastern versions of the Southern women I'd seen at the Voodoo Doughnuts protest—pearls but paired with white summer silk instead of linen.

"Francesca," Lillian circled me in an embrace, "it's such a relief to see you."

Over her shoulder, I saw Cordelia press a handkerchief to her mouth. I went to hug her. "Are you all right?"

"A bit discombobulated," she gave a wan smile and caressed my cheek, "but otherwise fine, dear."

Lillian led Cordelia to a table. "I'm afraid Mother and I are still in shock. First we found out Agata Villeré was murdered, and then Bradley told us the wedding planner was run down. You're lucky you weren't killed, Francesca."

My fingers formed the scongiuri gesture behind my back. With comments like that, I was as good as dead. "Bradley said the police questioned you." I sat across from Cordelia. "Was there a problem?"

"Nothing of the sort." She checked her sterling-silver hair. "Something isn't right in this old house. I can feel it."

"You mean," I side-eyed Powdered Wig Guy to check again for eye holes, "you think the murderer is still on the premises?"

Lillian shook her ice-blonde side lob. "It's because the hotel is eerie. The Blains and the other guests checked out after Agata was found dead, so Mother and I are here alone with a librarian."

Knowing the librarian was Shona, that was more than eerie. It was flat scary.

"We're not alone, Lillian." Cordelia placed her palms on the table. "I told you, I feel a presence. It's strongest in the ballroom on the third floor."

Lillian's lips folded. "Why don't you go lie down, Mother? I'm worried about you."

"Don't treat me like a doddering fool." Cordelia's gray eyes went steely. "I might be getting on in years, but my instincts are solid."

"Of course, Mother."

Powdered Wig Guy and I exchanged an "Awk*ward!*" look.

Lillian rose. "I'll get the three of us skinny lattes."

"None for me, thanks." While I didn't share her choice of coffee drink, I did share her concern about Cordelia—albeit for a different reason. Cordelia's maiden name was Toccato, as in

Chandra, the kooky Crescent City Medium. Granted, she was related to Chandra's husband Lou, but I was starting to suspect that all the Toccatos were susceptible to psychic silliness.

Cordelia rummaged in her Lady Dior bag. "Lillian and I should've stayed at the Hotel Monteleone."

"I'm surprised you were able to get a room here at the Columns. Most people rent the entire hotel for weddings, and a family as wealthy as the Blains can afford it."

"Evidently, their money has run out." She placed a pill box on the table. "During the rehearsal dinner, Agata humiliated the bride's father by interrupting his speech and saying she was forced to foot the bill for Grace's wedding."

"You heard her?"

"We were on the balcony, so we saw her too. She said he didn't even have the money to pay for his daughter's dress." Cordelia's brow furrowed. "You should have seen his face, Francesca. Pure hatred. And the bride went as white as the pantsuit she was wearing."

"What about her mother, Lara? How'd she react?"

"She tried to quiet her aunt, but Agata was not one to be silenced. She said this was the last money they'd ever get from her. She'd make sure of it."

Sounded like Edward and Lara had a motive for murder. Too bad I couldn't contact them thanks to that restraining order. "I'm sure Bradley mentioned that their wedding planner, Delilah Delaire, asked to meet me hours before she was killed."

Lillian gasped as she placed two glasses of water on the table. "Did she want to do your wedding?"

The Hartmanns couldn't have been more different from my family, but when it came to Bradley's and my wedding, they were astonishingly like-minded. "Uh, no. I think Delilah knew something about Agata's murder and needed my help."

"Shame she didn't survive that hit-and-run," Lillian drawled. "You could've traded your services for hers."

My mother couldn't have said it better.

Lillian returned to the counter for their coffee, and I turned to Cordelia. "I need to figure out what Delilah knew. Any ideas?"

"None. She was in the kitchen during most of the rehearsal dinner."

Interesting detail. Could be the reason the kitchen manager was at the police station. "I asked to speak to the kitchen manager, but I think he's being questioned. Did you see anything the morning Agata's body was discovered?"

Cordelia washed down two aspirin with water. "We weren't allowed to go near her room. It's on the second floor at the front of the house, and the police cordoned off that end of the hallway."

"Is it still blocked off?"

"I'm not sure. We're on the third floor."

"While you and Lillian have your coffee, I'm going to take a peek." I pushed back my chair and slipped into the hallway.

The reception clerk wasn't at the desk, so I hurried to the mahogany stairwell. It rose in a square formation for three stories, culminating in a domed stained-glass skylight.

As I climbed creaky stairs to the second floor, Shona awaited me on the landing. Her black tote was from the mystery writer organization Sisters in Crime.

Not an auspicious sign.

"How come you didn't answer your phone?" she shouted. "I just called you."

I'd never given her my number, but she *was* a librarian. "Sorry. It's on silent."

"Well, I found Moira on social media. She's Delilah Delaire's assistant, and her last name is Mulligan, like the stew."

"Great. That'll help me track her down."

"Speaking of stew, I talked to a consultant I hired to help me prepare for the race. He lives at Honey Island Swamp and goes by the name Swamp Sasquatch, not to be confused with the skunk ape of the Southeastern swamps, and he needs to meet with us about my case."

Two more swamp animals I never would've anticipated, and I had no intention of meeting either. For one thing, I didn't want to get involved in Shona's rowing training. And for another, I had no desire to know why she'd related the Swamp Sasquatch and whatever a skunk ape was to stew. "That'll have to wait. I've got to visit a cousin and find Moira after I check out Agata's room."

"Oh, Agata stayed in the Premier Avenue Suite at the end of the hall. I'll show you." Shona led me to Room 10. "It's locked, but you can see inside through a window on the balcony."

The suite was across from a study with red walls covered in mirrors and old photographs of long-dead people, which did nothing to reduce the mansion's creep factor. Although, it smelled divine—sensual and earthy thanks to the "Per Fu Mes Tabaco" room diffuser. "Where did the rest of the family stay?"

"The bride—who does *not* deserve the name Grace—demanded Agata's suite. But Agata made her stay in a small room two doors down."

So Grace also disliked her aunt. "Who was in the room next to Agata?"

"The Double Queen Chambre?" she asked—to display her knowledge. "Edward and Lara. And both beds were slept in, know what I'm sayin'?"

Shona might've been carrying a mystery tote, but her romance-tote roots were showing. "Let's go check that window."

We exited a door to a huge balcony with gray wicker

loveseats, antique wooden cabinets, and various tables. There was also a small bar.

The balcony overlooked St. Charles, a stately avenue known for its grand Queen Anne-style houses, but the view was obscured by a massive oak tree with Mardi Gras beads and a strand of fake pearls hanging from its branches. A streetcar came up the street packed with people avoiding the rain. It would've been a gorgeous scene from a time gone by...

...*if* the hotel hadn't been the site of a murder.

I peered into the window of the suite where Agata had died. The room was spacious with a king-sized bed surrounded by gold Tiffany lamps, a salmon velvet settee, and a small fireplace. A crystal chandelier hung from a coral-colored ceiling, and the wallpaper depicted a pastoral landscape in mint, maroon, and white. A deceptively serene scene given what had happened in the suite.

On a whim, I pushed up the window, and it opened a few inches.

A strange odor wafted out.

A young male employee, maybe eighteen, came out on the balcony holding a serving tray. He was pale and thin with ginger-brown curls. He nodded, embarrassed, and began stacking dirty glassware that had been left on the bar.

Shona sniffed the air. "Do you smell raisins?"

"Yeah." I looked at the window. "And maybe vinegar?"

Glass shattered behind me. I spun and saw the employee collecting the pieces of a champagne flute.

He stood and backed away, just as the reception clerk had done after seeing the flickering bulbs on the chandelier.

"Wait." I read the kid's nametag. "Ethan, do you know what that smell is?"

His gaze shifted to the window. "T-tobacco, ma'am."

"Holy smokes!" Shona bellowed. "Agata smoked at the age of one hundred and two?"

Ethan took a step back—or he was propelled backwards by the force of Shona's lungs. "The Columns doesn't allow smoking, and Miss Agata didn't smoke."

My ears pricked up. "Then...who was in her room?"

His lips pressed together, trembling. "M-Mr. Hersheim, ma'am."

Shona's eyes bulged, and her head tilted forward. "*Simon Hersheim?*"

He nodded.

"Who's he?" I looked from Shona to Ethan.

He didn't answer.

Shona pressed a hand to her chest. "Simon Hersheim is the tobacco magnate who built this mansion for his family in 1883 with the money he made from his company, La Belle Creole Cigar Factory."

"Um, *1883*?" I half-laughed. "Don't tell me you both think the ghost of the owner lit up a cigar in Agata's room?"

Ethan chewed his lip.

Shona shrugged. "It could happen."

"*Please*," I practically spat. "If ghosts existed—and they don't—I think we all know they wouldn't smoke."

Music began to play.

Our heads jerked toward the window.

The source was an old-timey radio next to Agata's bed.

My lips pursed, and my pulse picked up. "That radio had better be controlled by the front desk, Ethan."

He hung his head. "It's nooot," he wailed, pressing the tray to his chest. "It's maaanually operaaated."

"Hey." Shona pointed at the window. "I know that song. It's Herman's Hermits, the British band from the Sixties."

"So?"

"It's called 'The Man with the Cigar,' Franki." Her eyes were as big around as Ethan's tray. "If that's not proof Simon Hersheim is among us, I don't know what is."

Despite my skepticism, the hair on the back of my neck rose. I didn't know what was going on in the mansion or in the city, but my instincts screamed one thing.

Real or imagined, the swamp animals, witches, and ghosts promised terror.

5

———————

"Holy. Cash. Cow." I gaped at Giada's mansion through my Mustang windshield, struggling to believe that someone who shared my DNA lived in such splendor. "This place could give the Columns a run for its money."

"Where are you?" Bradley's voice came from my phone on the passenger seat.

The size of the house had so startled me I'd forgotten I was talking to him. "At my second cousin Giada's in the Garden District."

"I didn't know you still had family in New Orleans."

It was tempting to reply, *Neither did I*, but I kept that quiet. Being oblivious of one's relatives wasn't a good look for a soon-to-be bride. "We're not close. But in an odd twist, her husband works at the Blain Adair Law Firm."

"Seriously? Were they at the rehearsal dinner?"

I glanced at the front door. "That's what I'm here to find out."

"Well, I found out that the firm has a mere six grand at Pontchartrain Bank."

The balance didn't square with its prestigious reputation—

or with Giada's palatial digs. "Do they have another account somewhere else?"

"As far as my ex-colleague knows, they don't. He said they applied for a business loan a few months ago, but it was declined because they didn't have enough collateral."

"What about their office building?"

He sniffed. "Turns out, they sold it last year and rent from the current owner."

My fingers squeezed the steering wheel. "Then they could use a windfall, like an inheritance."

"And old Aunt Agata Villeré was worth a cool five million."

My eyes darted to Giada's mansion. *What are the odds that my cousin's husband—or my cousin, for that matter—had something to do with Agata's murder?*

A beep on the other end of the line startled the thought from my head.

Bradley exhaled. "That's my mother, but I'll call her back."

"You should answer, babe. Your grandmother wasn't doing so well at breakfast."

"Then I'd better take it. Love you."

"Love you too."

He hung up, and I climbed from the Mustang. The storm had cleared, and the manicured lawn glistened in the sunlight. A squirrel was perched on a mosaic-tile bench beneath a magnolia tree, and a cardinal drank from a marble fountain. "Even the animals are living high on the hog."

The eerie tones of a pipe organ erupted on the street.

My head turned so far on my neck that an owl would've been proud. I didn't know where the sound was coming from, but I saw why it was happening.

The music was a horror soundtrack.

Because my parents' Ford Taurus station wagon had pulled up.

The organ stopped as abruptly as it had started, which didn't seem right. The unexpected arrival of my mom and nonna warranted Bach's "Toccata and Fugue in D Minor," or at the very least the theme from *The Godfather*.

My mother shoved open the driver door and looked in the side mirror at her dyed-brown hair, which had grown so big that it was approaching bouffant. Or porcupine. "Good timing, Francesca."

Hotly debatable.

She exited the car in a billowy blouse and palazzo pants. "Your nonna and I thought you might be here."

"That's interesting, because I didn't think you two would." I gave her a quick hug. "How'd you get here so fast?"

She opened the door to the back seat. "Desperate times call for drastic speed, and we had emergency bags packed in case you needed help planning the wedding."

"Okay, but I don't." My hand went to my hip. "And what's the emergency?"

"We *had* to get you some walnuts, dear. Remember," she sing-songed, "marriage, fertility, and abundance." She pulled a five-pound bag from the car and shoved it into my stomach.

A tough nut to swallow.

"Plus," her tone dropped to a whisper, "we wanted to check on Giada."

"Why?" I glanced at the mansion. "Did something happen?"

My mother bounced backwards on the defensive. "Well, I'm sure she's in shock over her wedding planner's murder. We can hardly leave her alone in her time of need."

The woman was really scraping the bottom of the excuses barrel to cover her intent to wedding meddle.

Nonna shuffled up in her basic black mourning dress and pinched my cheek. "*Quanto sei bella!*"

My face burned, not from the how-beautiful-you-are compliment but from her dough-kneader grip.

She released my throbbing skin and wagged a finger. "I don't-a like-a this-a business with-a the wedding-a planner. Why did-a she call-a you and then-a die?"

Even though I had the same question, the implication that I was connected to Delilah's death made me uneasy. It spelled trouble, and more than just the malocchio. "I'm trying to find out, Nonna."

The front door opened, and a fortyish woman waved.

Giada. I could see the family resemblance. Dark eyes, high cheekbones, medium mouth—which seemed out of sorts with her bleached blonde hair and lady-in-linen outfit.

"Franki, is that you?" Giada's palms pressed to her cheek. "How nice to see you all grown up and not drunk on rum!"

My smile took a dive. I could also *hear* the family resemblance. I tossed the walnuts into my Mustang and slammed the door to relieve my displeasure.

"Welcome, Amatos! Come in!" Giada ushered us into a sumptuous entryway that smelled of fresh flowers. After a round of hugs, she gestured to an adjoining room. "Please, make yourselves comfortable in the parlor."

An impossible order. There was so much money in the room, the Louis XIV furniture had probably come straight from the Palace of Versailles. Giada might resemble us physically, but financially, she came from other DNA.

"The décor is not my style," she said, as if reading my mind. "It's my husband's. Or, I should say, his mother's."

"Isn't that-a nice-a, Brenda?" Nonna asked in a not-a-nice tone. "She decorate like-a her hus-a-band's mamma."

My mother froze in mid-sit. She had the wild-eyed look of a trapped animal. And the hair to match.

As much as I hated to ruin my nonna's fun, I had homicides

to investigate. I took a seat between my mom and nonna on the settee across from the throne-backed chair where Giada sat. "I'm not sure if my mother mentioned this, but I'm investigating a complicated case. By any chance, is your husband related to the groom's father in the Blain-Adair wedding?"

Her face fell. "That's Wolf's older brother, Bear. The groom is our nephew, Lion."

"I see," I said, even though I couldn't comprehend the family's fixation on animal names. "Were you at the rehearsal dinner at the Columns Hotel on Friday night?"

"No, we were only invited to the wedding. Wolf and Bear don't get along."

"Wolves and bears *are* natural predators," I joked.

An awkward silence ensued.

"So, uh," I glanced around, and my gaze landed on an antique sword on the wall, "why don't they get along?"

Giada massaged the back of one hand. "Their mother raised them to compete with each other. And right now, there are two Adairs at the firm, but only one of their names is listed as a partner."

The whistle of a tea kettle stopped me from pointing out the obvious—the name belonged to both brothers.

She leapt from her chair, clearly glad for an exit from the conversation. "I'll be right back with tea. Oh, and some rum pastries for Franki." She grinned. "Just kidding!"

Everyone burst out laughing, except me. Unlike my predator joke, Giada's wasn't funny. But I *did* make a mental note not to serve rum at my wedding.

Or walnuts.

And certainly not nocino.

"Oh, FranCESca." My mother sucked in an awe-inspired breath and picked up a bridal magazine from a stack on a marble-and-gold-leaf table. "This WEDDING DRESS."

The corners of my mouth fell. The dress was a Southern-belle style that reminded me of a hoop skirt Glenda had once loaned me for Pirate Week—sans the "porthole" caused by her lit cigarette.

Nonna gazed at the magazine over my mother's shoulder. "*Uffà!* It look-a like the dress-a Bette Davis wore in-a *Jezebel*."

The reference was as jarring as the organ music, especially since Agata owned the canary diamond ring Bette Davis had worn in the movie. A ring Shona had supposedly stolen, among other items. Which was ridiculous. Agata was murdered for her money and jewels, most likely by a family member and possibly one from the Blain Adair Law Firm.

Giada returned with a tea service.

"Is someone getting married?" I asked, nodding at the bridal magazines.

"No," she placed the tray on the table, "those belong to my friend Moira."

The name sent a shockwave through my chest. "As in, Delilah Delaire's assistant?"

Wary eyes met mine. "We met when she arranged the catering for my wedding. Do you know her?"

"No, but I spoke to her on the phone after Delilah was killed by a car. I need to find her. Moira could be in danger."

Giada dropped to her throne. "I don't know where she is."

"That's not good," my mother exclaimed.

Nonna's brow knit. "Is-a she on-a the lam-a?"

"Not exactly..." Giada picked up the teapot. "She's in hiding, afraid for her life."

Organ music exploded in the room.

We all jumped.

"Sorry about that." Giada began filling our teacups. "The organist at the church behind us practices at this time."

My nonna mimed drinking. "I think he's-a been hitting the communion wine-a."

Quite possible. The guy couldn't get through an entire song. But at least I had an explanation for one of the spooky soundtracks. Now I just needed to crack the mystery of the Herman's Hermits song on the radio at the Columns.

And find Moira.

"If you hear from her, Giada, please let me know."

"Of course." She handed me a cup of tea.

I blew on it before taking a sip. I didn't want to burn my s'more-scalded mouth.

My phone vibrated in my bag. I put down my cup and checked the display. The Vassal. "It's the office. Excuse me for a minute." I tapped *Answer*. "What's up?"

"The elderly woman you spoke to at the Camellia Grill is Janine Crawford."

"Crawford?" I echoed, thinking of Bette Davis's nemesis, Joan. And Janine meant "little Jane." "What is this Baby Jane theme going on?"

"Pardon?"

"Nothing. Good work, Vassal. See you at the office tomorrow."

My mother reached for her tea. "Who's Crawford, dear?"

I dropped my phone into my bag. "A woman I met at the Camellia Grill who told me about Agata Villeré's murder."

Nonna crossed herself. "She was-a killed?"

"Carmela," Giada lowered her teacup, "did you know her?"

"Nah. When-a she and-a her sister, Pia, were kids-a, they were local stars in a vaude-a-ville show."

The organ music blared again, and I was fully supportive. Vaudeville was not only creepy, but Bette Davis's character in *Whatever Happened to Baby Jane?* was a child vaudeville star.

My mother looked from Nonna to me. "How is Agata associated with the Blain-Adair wedding?"

"The maternal great aunt of the bride. She was murdered at the rehearsal dinner, and the woman said her older sister, Pia, was murdered years before."

"Good heavens." My mom's hand went to her heart. "Did the wedding go on?"

She *would* ask that. "No, Mom. The family called it off."

Nonna's beady black eyes were wider than if she'd seen an apparition of the Virgin—or Simon Hersheim from the Columns. "A murder at a rehearsal dinner, and-a then the wedding-a planner who called-a you was-a killed too?"

I nodded.

"*Malocchio!*"

My mom threw back her head and let out a shrill note that rivaled the organ, causing me to spill scalding tea on my thigh.

I shot from the settee.

Nonna pointed a crooked finger at me. "Your wedding is-a cursed!"

Giada hopped from her throne and handed me a napkin. "Everyone stay calm."

"Well, I was," I dabbed at my wet pants, "until Nonna and Mom started screaming about the evil eye."

"Hold tight." Giada rounded a corner to the kitchen and returned with a bottle of olive oil and a cup of water that she placed on the table. "There's one way to find out if malocchio is involved."

Everyone leaned in, and I followed suit, even though I had no clue what we were doing. "What are we looking at?"

Giada put a drop of oil in the cup.

It elongated.

Like an eye.

A *side*-eye.

I recoiled. I didn't know what was going on, but that was bizarre.

"Oh my." Giada pressed a finger to her lips.

My mother flounced backwards into the couch cushion, and my nonna pulled a rosary from her purse.

"What?" I scanned the stunned faces of my family members.

Giada swallowed. "You've got the evil eye."

Organ music exploded.

I threw up my arms. "Is that freaking organist spying on us?"

"Whyyy?" my mother wailed. "She was almost at the altar, Carmela. What do we dooo?"

"I tell-a you what-a." Nonna pushed herself up and pried the sword from the wall. "We slice-a some-a heads like-a we do the prosciutto."

"Now, Carmela." Giada wrestled the weapon from Nonna's dough-kneader fingers. "Violence isn't the answer."

"Non-a-sense. It always work-a."

"This time calls for a different strategy." Giada took my hand. "Excuse us for a moment." She led me to a baroque dining table in an exquisite room off the kitchen. "Have a seat, Franki. We can fix this."

"Don't tell me you believe in the malocchio. You have an archaeology degree."

"With a minor in Art History, and both taught me that all cultures and religions believe in the evil eye." She shrugged. "There must be *something* to it."

If Giada was trying to comfort me, it wasn't working. What I needed was a rum pastry. "You got any babà?"

She patted my scalded thigh. "You like the jokes, don't you?"

Yeah, except that I was serious.

"Let's focus. Do you feel unwell? That's one of the symptoms of malocchio."

Apart from the wear and tear, I felt good. "Nope. Totally fine."

"Headache?"

I shook my head.

Her brow arched. "Excessive yawning?"

A yawn escaped my lips. *The power of suggestion.*

I yawned again.

And I straightened in my chair. *A second yawn* was *excessive.*

"Mm-hm," Giada said. "Have you had a financial setback lately?"

"No, surprisingly."

"Bad luck?"

My eye strayed over my shoulder in the direction of my mom and nonna.

"There you go." Giada tapped my chest. "Someone is either jealous of you, or they admired you without taking the proper precautions."

"Um... precautions?"

She nodded. "After they pay you a compliment, they have to spit three times. If they don't—unintentional malocchio."

"Well, that's a problem," I crossed my arms, "because I discourage any and all spitting in my vicinity. But again, I don't really believe I have the evil eye."

"You'd better be sure. In severe cases, you could end up poor—"

"Already there."

"Injured—"

"That too."

"Or dead."

My lips pursed, and I shifted forward. "Let's say someone *did* put the evil eye on me. What's the remedy?"

Giada's gaze was flat. "There isn't one."

"Wait. What?" I flailed an arm in the direction of the parlor. "Then how do I call off my mom and nonna?"

She crossed her legs and gripped her pearls. "You don't."

I fully expected the organ music to start, but apparently, even the organist was stunned by Giada's response.

"The key is to prevent whoever gave you the evil eye from continuing to do it. Besides wearing a horn amulet and doing the scongiuri, a common Sicilian method is to sprinkle salt inside your front door." She released her necklace and flicked her fingers. "All those granules confuse the evil spirits."

Granules. Like the broom bristles the janare had to count when a broom was at the front door.

A gasp came from my still-phlegmy throat.

Did Vick's nonnina give me the malocchio?

"GLAD TO BE GETTING AWAY from that nuthouse." I climbed into the Mustang and slammed the door. "Telling me I have the evil eye, and my wedding is cursed." I shoved the key into the ignition. "My whole family is nuts." I paused and glared at the five-pound bag of walnuts on my passenger seat. "And you're the proof."

Despite my conviction, my eye strayed to the rearview mirror to check my complexion. A little peaked, but nothing out of the ordinary. "Malocchio, shmalocchio."

As I pulled the seatbelt across my chest, I yawned.

Again.

And the organ started up.

Whatever was going on with the spooky soundtracks, I'd had enough. I started the engine but waited for a car rounding the corner to pass.

My jaw dropped.

It was the Buick Roadster I'd seen following the black BMW that had struck and killed Delilah Delaire.

The driver and I locked eyes. He hit the gas and sped down the street, but not before I'd spotted the femme fatale in the backseat.

"What are you waiting for?" A woman screamed—

From right behind me.

In the back of my car.

Her index finger shot into the front seat. "Follow that femme fatale!"

My foot floored the gas pedal, while my brain tried to decide whether I should follow the woman in red or flee from the one in black in my backseat. I hooked a U-turn and stared at my stowaway in the rearview mirror. She wore a hooded cape and sunglasses, so the only things I could make out were her oval face and fleshy lips. "Who the hell are you?"

"Moira. I came to see Giada but saw she had company."

My body relaxed, as much as it could during a high-speed chase. "I'm Franki, the PI who called you yesterday after Delilah was killed."

She removed her sunglasses, and revealed the oversized brown eyes of Judy Garland, but with a tougher, born-in the-Bronx edge that went with her accent. "I know who you are. You think I'd get into a complete stranger's car with all the maniacs out there?"

If a maniac was anywhere, she was right behind me.

"Speaking of maniacs, you should lock this thing when you leave. There are a lot of creeps and killers running around."

Although I was focused on the Roadster, I shot her a pointed look over my shoulder. "Uh, you're telling me. And while we're on the subject, would you mind explaining why you got into my unlocked car?"

"I'm afraid for my life after what happened to Delilah, so I could hardly walk up to Giada's front door and knock. Besides, I didn't know if I could trust those women with you."

"Ha!" I slapped the dashboard. "That makes two of us."

"Then what were you doing with them?"

"They're my mom and nonna, but I often ask myself the same question."

The Roadster swerved through traffic, and I did my best to follow, speeding around a Jeep.

"Hey, you need to allow at least a car length before you pass. You could've clipped that guy's taillight."

Great. Moira's not only a maniac, she's a backseat driver. "Despite what you may have seen on TV and in the movies, high-speed chases aren't a regular feature of my job, okay?"

"No, it's not okay." She catapulted over the seat and kneed my tricep.

"Ow! What the—?" I jerked my arm, causing the Mustang to swerve onto the median. I righted the car and glared at her. "Are you trying to get us killed?"

"Actually, that's what I'm trying to avoid." She latched her seatbelt. "I got in front in case I needed to take over the driving, and it's looking like I will."

"Just sit still, and we won't have any problems." I hunkered over the steering wheel, both to keep her from grabbing it and to keep pace with the Roadster. The driver had skills. "Now, what did you mean on the phone when you said, 'That femme fatale was right?'"

"She came to the office an hour or so before you called, looking for Delilah. I told her she was out, and she said Delilah was in danger. Then she left without telling me so much as her name."

Mysterious. "Did you mention that Delilah was meeting with me?"

"Are you out of your mind? Our motto is 'discretion is our

business,' and even if it wasn't, the woman looks like she stepped out of a 40s crime flick. No way I'd tell her Delilah was meeting a PI."

She had a point, so I overlooked the "out of your mind" comment. For now. I had bigger problems at the moment—namely, traffic lights, and making it through any red ones alive. "What did she say, exactly?"

"She pressured me to tell her where Delilah was. Said if she didn't find her, Delilah could end up a stiff."

Very 1940s of her. "And she didn't explain why?"

"She didn't have to. I already knew the reason Delilah was in danger, and Delilah did too. That's why she asked you to meet her at NOLA Noir. She couldn't risk being seen at a PI firm."

At the mention of the coffee shop, I had to harrumph. "Since you brought it up, I went by your office earlier and saw a go-cup from NOLA Noir on the floor. Was that yours?"

"Yeah, I must've knocked it over when I rushed out of there. I'm the one who told Delilah that coffee shop would be a good place to meet you, but I was wrong on a couple of levels."

My gaze darted from the Roadster to the rearview mirror. "A couple?"

"Her murder, for one. And their walnut cappuccino. Made my throat burn."

A lump rose in my throat—a combination of empathy and the conviction that something was up with that nocino coffee. I wanted to ask her if Sick Vick had ogled her thumbs, but it didn't seem the right time. Moira might think I was a kook and take the steering wheel from me.

"So, I realize 'discretion is your business,'" I said, blowing around a Toyota Corolla, "but are you going to tell *me* why she was in danger?"

"Not to be rude, but you're kind of pushy."

This from a woman who entered my car uninvited and told me how to drive.

The Roadster hooked a last-minute left on Calliope, and I jerked the steering wheel. The Mustang fishtailed into the turn.

"Whoa!" Moira braced herself on the dashboard. "Mind taking those corners a little slower? I could get whiplash the way you're driving."

"How about you do less complaining and more explaining, starting with why Delilah was in danger?"

"Fine. While she was at the rehearsal dinner, she overheard a plan to kill the quote 'old battleax.'"

Agata Villeré. I'd suspected as much. "How did she hear this? Where was she?"

"Outside a second-floor study overlooking a balcony."

Had to be the red room with the old photographs and mirrors.

Moira gripped her seatbelt. "Delilah went looking for the bride's parents to tell them about an issue with the food, which is normally my job, but we had two weddings that weekend, so she had to handle the catering."

"And the parents weren't with their guests?"

"No, and neither was the bride, Grace, which is odd. But then again, Delilah said the whole family had the manners of boors." Moira elbowed my side. "Can you believe Grace called me yesterday for the day and time of a bridal swap? Her great aunt was murdered, and she wants to trade in her back-up dress."

That was pretty shocking, as was the elbow to my ribs. "Where and when is this swap?"

She huffed. "Oh, jeez! You too?"

"Uh... I *am* planning my wedding, but this is for the investigation."

"In that case, it's at Wedding Belles—that's b-e-l-l-e-s, as in Southern. Tomorrow at ten."

The name reminded me of the godawful plantation gown my mother had shown me, a sure sign that I shouldn't invite her dress shopping.

The Roadster rocketed around a pickup and turned right on red under the highway.

I skidded to a stop behind the truck.

"They're going into the Warehouse District!" Moira gestured for me to follow. "Go around this guy, or we'll lose them." She reached for the wheel, and I jerked it before she could and took the turn.

We drove a couple of blocks, but the Roadster was gone.

Moira lowered her cape hood, revealing short dark curls. "I'll bet they drove into one of these warehouses." She sighed. "We'll never find them now."

"Something's bothering me." I pulled to the side of the road. "If the femme fatale came and warned you about Delilah, why's she running from us now?"

"Maybe she can't be seen with a PI, either."

Could be, which made me wonder what she had to hide, and whether she was connected in some way to the killings. "Did Delilah give any details about who and what she overheard outside the study?"

"It was definitely a man discussing the plan to murder Agata."

"Any idea who?"

"She thought it was the bride's father, but the door was closed so the sound was muffled. She didn't know whether he was on the phone or talking to someone in the room, and she didn't have time to find out. All of the sudden, the door started opening, so she ducked onto the balcony and hid behind a bar."

That had to be the one where the Columns employee, Ethan, dropped the champagne flute. "Did Delilah hear anything else?"

"She did, but it didn't make sense. The man went onto the balcony because she heard his footsteps. He grumbled something under his breath, and before he left, he said the oddest thing, 'black swamp.'"

Organ music echoed in my head.

And the trill of an Eastern screech owl.

Moira's dark eyes bore into mine. "I don't know what it means, but the derelict probably meant it as a threat."

There were only two things I could think—the swamp was where Shona was accused of stashing Agata Villeré's missing jewels, and black swamp was the code name of my wedding-planning operation.

6

"Open up, Glenda." I pounded on her apartment door. "This is urgent. Mission critical."

After my conversations with Giada and Moira, I was desperate. I didn't know what the father of the bride had said when Delilah hid on the Columns balcony, or whether my wedding-planning operation name played into it. What I did know was that my family could inflict more harm with the malocchio marriage malarkey than all the swamp animals, witches, and ghosts combined. I had to do something to stop them. Something drastic.

A yawn escaped my lips.

My fingers gripped the second-floor railing. *The evil eye? Or just everyday exhaustion?*

The door opened, and I got another shock.

Glenda's normally platinum-colored Cher hair was actual Cher-hair color, and she wore what looked like a pared-down peasant version of the infamous black Bob Mackie Oscar dress. "Are you rehearsing for a 'Gypsies, Tramps, and Thieves' number?"

"No, sugar." She looked at her outfit. "This is my Wanton Witch costume."

I should've known better than to think she'd impersonate Cher. By Glenda's standards, her outfits were far too concealing.

Glenda took a drag from a broomstick cigarette holder, and my mind conjured an image of the janare counting its bristles. Then I stole a glance at the cemetery across the street to check for Vic's nonnina, Brunella. And that weird witch, Theodora.

Not to mention my mom and nonna.

The cemetery looked dead, so I turned back to the business —or rather, the wantonness—at hand. "Why are you wearing a witch costume in June?"

"Hucci Cucci Hot Couture is going to capitalize on Halloween," she said, smoke wafting from her mouth like steam from a cauldron. "It's right around the corner."

And right around the time the janare's nocino would be ready to drink.

"I'm also doing a Vampy Vampire, a Naughty Nurse, and a Provocative PI." She winked as she took another drag. "I designed one with you in mind."

"So I gathered."

"How?" she huffed a smoke puff. "I haven't said it yet."

"It's not Provocative PI?"

"No, Nasty Nun."

My jaw snapped shut. I didn't know whether to complain or cross myself. I opted for neither since I was in a hurry. "Listen, I'm hoping you can bail me out of a jam with my family. Any chance I could rent Veronica's old place for a week?"

"I told you, Miss Franki, it's now my business headquarters."

"You started Hucci Cucci upstairs in your costume closet. Can't you go back there for a few days?"

"My sewing machine is downstairs, sugar, with all of my material."

Since her clothes consisted of fabric swatches, that couldn't have amounted to more than a yard. "I'll move it all for you."

Glenda's eyes narrowed, and she rolled the cigarette holder between her fingers. "That's only part of the problem. How would it look if I used a closet as my business headquarters?"

It was my turn to narrow my eyes because her costume closet was one of the apartments in the fourplex. "The same as it would look to use Veronica's old place, so I can either rent that or the closet."

"Why don't you just crash in my champagne flute?" She gestured to the giant dance prop in the middle of her white living room.

I'd spent some hard times in that glass and had no desire to go back. "I've been renting from you for years. Can't you do me this favor?"

"I suppose, sugar. It's going to cost you, though."

It always did. But staying with my mom and nonna in a one bedroom would cost me so much more. "Name your price."

"A month's rent."

My body went rigid. *Is this the financial setback Giada had asked about as proof of the evil eye?*

"Take it or leave it, Miss Franki."

"Send me an invoice," I hissed through my teeth. "Now I've gotta run, so when my mom and nonna get here, you'll have to explain the situation and let them in."

Glenda thrust a bony hip in my direction. "First we need to settle some unfinished business."

"What? A rental agreement?"

"No, sugar. If I'm going to deal with your hair-puller mother and the Catholic cover-up artist, I'm going to need a tip."

Couldn't argue with that. I pulled two twenties from my wallet, but we both knew hundreds were in order.

Glenda held out the side of her sequin spiderweb G-string.

With a sigh, I slid the bills under the strap.

She let the G-String snap back into place. "Where are you off to in such a rush?"

"To pick up that librarian, Shona, I met in Venice. Believe it or not, she's been implicated in Agata Villeré's murder, and she wants me to meet some swamp consultant who has information that could help clear her."

"Oooh," she ran a palm over her pentagram pasties, "*do* tell me more."

Judging from her lusty reaction, she wasn't interested in Shona. "The guy calls himself the Swamp Sasquatch, Glenda. He's hardly date material."

"Speak for yourself." She gave a saucy wink. "But for the record, I was talking about an idea for a costume." She slid her hand across the sky like a director painting a vision. "Swampy Sexpot, or Swampy Siren."

Glenda could call the costume whatever she liked, but all I saw was Swampy Stripper, a whole new breed of swamp animal.

"Speaking of sexpots, Miss Franki, I ran into Maybe Baby today."

I hadn't thought of her in ages, since she'd ended up the House Mom at a fraternity I'd investigated. "What's she up to these days? Did she go back to stripping?"

"She's studying to become a nurse."

"That's...wow." I was happy for her but concerned for her future patients. Maybe Baby wasn't the sharpest syringe in the box. Truth was, she made dumb blondes seem smart—like surgeons. On the flip side, she would've been a great fit at Nadezhda's future booze, waxing, and vaxing clinic.

"Anyhoo," Glenda flipped her black locks, "Maybe Baby asked about you, and I told her about your encounter with Vick Villano. She was a regular at his nail salon. Always got her toes done in Promiscuous Pink, until the incident."

"'The incident?'"

"Mm-hm. Vick was obsessed with her thumbnails. They're short and squat like he likes them."

The corner of my mouth twitched. So were mine, and they hadn't garnered a glance.

She blew out smoke. "However, his grandmother doesn't approve of strippers, so she took over the pedicure. You'll never believe what happened."

Since I had an Italian nonna, I could hazard a guess. "She painted her toenails black with the letters v-a-f-f-a-n-c-u-l-o?"

"Close. The nails got infected and fell off. Poor Maybe Baby couldn't strip for weeks. All she could do was lap dances."

So many things about that made me squeamish. But I wasn't thinking about thumbs, or even toes.

Only my throat.

Because "the incident" was proof that Vic's nonnina, Brunella, had harmed at least one person on purpose.

Had she tried to harm me too?

And what about Delilah?

THIS SWAMP TREK is really making the case for the evil eye, I thought, as I followed Shona through trees and moss and grass. Humid steam mingled with sweat ran into my eyes. Nevertheless, I kept one eye fixed on her fishing waders while the other watched for unwelcome visitors. I'd grabbed my galoshes and a mosquito net hat from my apartment to protect me from water and insects, but I had deep concerns about the swamp animals. I still wasn't sure I wanted to meet the Swamp Sasquatch, and I definitely didn't want to run into whatever a skunk ape was.

To be honest, I wasn't too psyched about being with Shona either. I didn't believe she'd killed Agata, but under the circumstances, a Sisters in Crime mystery tote paired with a *Never Underestimate a Woman with Oars* T-shirt was a bad look. I knew from my experience with her in Venice that she used oars called "cleavers."

Shona paused and shot me a dark stare over her shoulder. "We're almost at the Swamp Sasquatch's house. Try not to look alarmed when you meet him."

Evidently, the fact that his name alone was alarming had escaped her librarian logic. "Care to elaborate?"

"He's a big bear of a man, and he wears a nutria fur."

"In this heat? I mean, the humidity out here makes a hot tub seem refreshing."

Shona shrugged and resumed walking. "The fur keeps the mosquitoes from biting."

I scratched my neck, wishing she hadn't said that. The power of suggestion with yawning also applied to mosquito bites. But I reminded myself that there *was* one positive to this sweltering swamp excursion—I wasn't going to Mambo Odette's voodoo shack. Anywhere had to be better than that scary place.

We came to a dingy gray trailer home near the water decorated with skins, bones, and possibly dried animal parts.

When would I learn not to think-speak too soon?

An enormous man with gray hair emerged from inside, carrying a knife. And a squash. "Miss Shona, you got my message."

"And as instructed," she gestured to me, "I brought my PI friend, Franki."

He switched the knife to his left hand and extended his right for a shake.

Reluctantly, I shook it but kept my gaze glued to the blade.

"Sylvain Fontaine's de name. Hauling cypress is my game."

Shona nodded. "His name is French for 'forest fountain.'"

And yet he lives in the stinky swamp. My eyes rose to the nutria fur hanging around his neck and shoulders. It reminded me of the fox stole Bette Davis wore in *What Ever Happened to Baby Jane?*, which made the encounter even more unsettling.

He followed my gaze and chuckled. "De ladies *do* love Nute. Dat's the name o' my fur friend." He tugged on the dead nutria's tail, and it raised its glassy eyes. "He looks purdy aroun' de neck, don't he?"

"MMMmmm," was all I could get out. Because Nute looked like he had rabies and an oil gland issue, and he stunk so bad, he made the sulfur-sewage smell of the swamp seem pleasant.

The Swamp Sasquatch tapped his surprisingly full head of hair. "What de ladies *don't* like is de gator head hat I wear when I work in de water, cutting de cypress."

"The *bald* cypress," Shona said, unable to resist the urge to be specific.

"It's de best wood dere is." He took a seat on one of the stump stools. "Native Americans made canoes wit' it 'cause it resists everthang—moisture, rot, and insects."

As if on cue, a huge flying creature landed on my arm, and I flung it off.

Oblivious, the Swamp Sasquatch put the squash on a stump and began slicing. "De cypress trees got one root dat go as deep as dey is tall, and roots dat shoot out horizontal around de tree twenty to fifty feet before dey go down vertical in de ground. De roots send up *boscoyos*."

"Cypress knees," Shona said, interpreting his Cajun.

The Swamp Sasquatch used Nute's tail to dab sweat from his brow and continued slicing. "It's dangerous work. Animals swim up in dose roots, and I never know when I'm gonna meet me a snake or a gator."

The mention of swamp animals made me shudder. It was hard to know which was worse, the real thing or the people version.

Shona pulled up a stump. "The Ancient Greeks and Romans called the cypress the 'mournful tree,' and it was sacred to the Fates and Furies and the rulers of the underworld."

Although I hadn't a clue who the Fates and Furies were, it struck me that both "fate" and "fury" applied to Shona, alias The Wise Old Eastern Screech Owl, launching into a library lecture in the middle of a murder investigation.

She opened her arms in full tell-you-what-I-know mode. "They planted a cypress by a grave or in front of a vestibule to warn outsiders that the space had been corrupted by a dead body. And the Romans put bodies on cypress branches before interment. To this day, it's the principal cemetery tree in Europe and the Muslim world."

"Miss Shona is right." The Swamp Sasquatch whacked a squash in two. "Dey saw it as a symbol of death and de underworld 'cause it won't regenerate if you cut it back too much. Dat's why a lot of caskets are made from cypress."

My alarm was growing, not because of Nute or the knife, but because the Swamp Sasquatch was strikingly similar to Shona when it came to sharing knowledge.

He paused and added the squash to a frying pan. "By de way, you ladies got good timin'. I'm cookin' up a late lunch."

It was two o'clock, and I hadn't eaten. But I wasn't hungry after the mournful history lesson, and certainly not for swamp food.

A fly dive-bombed my net. I shooed it away and heard a clipping sound. I turned to the source, and my stomach jumped.

The Swamp Sasquatch was cutting the legs off dead frogs.

With wire-cutting plyers.

He put the pan on the ground, picked up a blow torch, and turned it on. Flames shot at least a foot.

And my alarm shot at least two. "What're you doing with that thing?"

"Cookin' de frog legs. It's faster 'n lightin' a fire. Easier too." He lowered the flames to the pan and torched the contents. After less than a minute, he shut off the blow torch and knelt over the pan. "Dis is what you call blackened frog," he said pointing to the scorched legs and squash. "Wait till you curl your lips up on dat."

My lips were curling up, all right. Potentially permanently.

"Time for de finishing sauce." He rose and carried the pan to the swamp, dunked it under water, then stood and swished it around.

My involuntary swallow was an act of resistance from my throat, which had already been through so much. "*That's* the sauce?"

The Swamp Sasquatch gave a satisfied grin. "Cools 'em down and gives 'em dat extra flavor."

Yeah, that extra flavor of cholera, dysentery, and Hepatitis A.

He stuck his unwashed hand into the pan and stirred the frogs and squash. Then he picked up a leg and bit off a hunk. "Mm-MM-*MM*, chères." He wiped his mouth with Nute. "Dat's some good eatin' right dere."

My head spun, and I fanned myself with my hat. The heat had taken a toll on me, and the finishing sauce had just about finished me off.

He plunked the pan onto a stump. "You ladies help yourselves."

Shona dived right in, and my stomach gave a frog-sized leap. I didn't know how she could even *think* of eating after what we'd witnessed, much less put those legs in her mouth.

My phone vibrated, and I was immensely grateful to have something to do with my hands other than reach for torched frog. The caller was Bradley's mother.

"Hi, Lillian."

"Francesca? It's Mrs. Hartmann, dear."

Her greeting was not unlike my mom's, which was another odd similarity between the two women. "Is everything okay?"

"Perfectly fine," she drawled. "I thought you'd like to know that the kitchen manager has returned to the hotel. She's British."

An odd detail, but okay. "Thanks for letting me know," I said, and I meant it. Because after my swamp experience, I not only needed to question the kitchen manager about Agata, I also needed some disease-free lunch. "Be there within the hour."

I hung up. What I needed now was to get the Swamp Sasquatch to talk about something other than trees, cemeteries, and recipes. "Shona said you wanted to talk to us about an urgent matter."

"Dat's right." He swallowed some frog. "She said you was helping clear her name in de murder of dat lady, Miss Villeré, and I found something dat might help."

"What is it?"

"Dis mornin' I came upon some tire tracks. Ain't no one come out here widout me knowin' about it, so I set to trackin' 'em. Where dey stopped, I found dese invites." He pulled ivory-colored cards from his shirt pocket and handed them to Shona and me.

My fingers might as well have been scorched by the blow torch. "Invitations to the Blain-Adair wedding?"

Shona pushed sweaty bangs from her face. "The only people that would have a stack of these invitations is the Blains."

I gave a lopsided nod because that was only half right. "They could have been planted out here to connect the Blains to the crime. Or you, for that matter."

"How?" she howled. "I wouldn't have these invitations."

"You would if you got them from the Blains at the hotel and put them out here to throw the police off your trail."

Her round face deflated. "I hadn't thought of that."

Funny, because she thought of literally everything else. I looked at Swamp Sasquatch. "Can you show us the tire tracks?"

"Sorry, *chère.*" He sucked a leg bone and tossed it into the grass. "I got a company expecting a load of cypress in an hour. I can take you ladies over dere tomorrow."

"That'll work," I said, even though I didn't relish a return to the swamp—or his gory trailer. "But did you notice anything else?"

"Dere is one thing. Dese invitations coulda been left by whoever was drivin' a car I heard come out here early Sunday mornin', 'round three a.m."

My mind went to the black BMW that hit Delilah Delaire. "Did you see the car?"

"Never could find it, but I smelled cigarette smoke."

I glanced at Shona, who, regretfully, was stress-eating a fistful of frog. "That could've been anyone."

"Nah, not dis kind of tobacco."

Shona stopped in mid-chew. "You recognized the scent?"

"Sho' did. It's a fermented tobacco. Smells like rotten fruit and vinegar."

I locked eyes with Shona. We were both thinking of the smoke odor in Agata Villeré's room at the Columns.

She pointed a chewed-clean bone at the Swamp Sasquatch. "You've got a good nose."

He blushed. "Aw, dat ain't de reason. But a strong smeller *do* come in handy in dese parts."

Based on his trailer décor, I hoped he didn't explain how.

"Dat tobacco is one of de rarest in de world. Choctaw and Chickasaw tribes grew it out here. Dey put it in hollow tree trunks and sealed it wit' stones to ferment it. Den in de 1700s, de Acadians adapted de process to wood boxes instead o' dem trunks. To dis day, it's only grown by a couple dozen people in St. John's Parish."

That was right next to Orleans parish, where New Orleans is located. "What's the name of this tobacco?"

"Perique."

Shona gasped. "The tobacco magnate!"

My lips, which were still curled from the leg lunch, curled further. "Don't tell me you think the ghost of Simon Hersheim was smoking at the swamp too?"

"Okay." Her eyes bulged from the effort to repress the comment. "But after you left the Columns this morning, I looked up Simon Hersheim's cigar factory, La Belle Creole. And he used perique."

Despite what I would call a "pending belief" in the evil eye, there was no way I was buying a cigar-smoking ghost with a penchant for Herman's Hermits. For one thing, if the ghost of Simon Hersheim existed, he could float anywhere for a smoke, so why the hell would he come to the swamp?

And for another, I had a plausible explanation for the perique odor.

The swamp smoker was Agata and Delilah's killer.

But did he—or she—bury Agata's jewels out here to frame Shona?

Or merely to throw us off the scent?

7

"Ingrates!" The Columns kitchen manager brought her knife down with a *thwack*, sending red juice squirting from a tomato. "The whole lot of them!"

Shona took a step backwards that spanned the three feet between her and the exit. "If you'll excuse me, I have some research to do in my room."

She turned and fled so fast I was surprised her fishing waders weren't still standing in the doorway.

But I couldn't blame her for bolting. Anyone who said the English were mild mannered hadn't met Edith Cook. In the past ten minutes, the stout sixtyish redhead had not only slaughtered an innocent tomato, she'd punched down bread dough with the skill of a pro boxer and deboned a chuck roll one-handed.

Even more disturbing, the dish she was making called for a fresh chicken and an ox kidney. And I had the distinct feeling she'd done the killing herself.

Edith pointed the knife at my chest, and my hands surrendered. "The father of the bride thinks he's King Charles. The man barged into my kitchen and looked down his conk at my cooking. Then he had the gall to lecture me about organic farming and composting."

Guessing that a "conk" was a "nose," I decided to keep mine out of her spat with Edward Blain—mainly because I wanted to keep it.

"Had me banished from my own kitchen, he did!" She tossed the tomato flesh into a bowl and stabbed another. "To add salt to the wound, he had the wedding planner cater the rehearsal dinner."

Moira mentioned that Delilah had to handle the catering. "So you weren't here that night?"

"No, and I was chuffed to bits to have a break from that family, especially the bride-to-be, Grace." She picked up an onion and ripped off the skin. "That one walks around the hotel with such a smirk on her gob. She handed me a list of demands for her meals as long as her pins, and it was evident from reading them that she'd never so much as boiled water for tea."

"Gob" was evidently a "mouth." But "pins"? Were they a body part?

"And don't get me started on her mum, Lara." She began violently dicing the onion. "It's clear from the name she gave her daughter that the woman wouldn't know 'grace' if it hit her in the bonce."

Although I wasn't sure I'd grasped the whole conversation, I was confident in a couple of assumptions. One, there was a lot of tomfoolery going on with the English language in Great Britain. And two, if Agata Villeré had died from knife wounds, Edith Cook would've been my number-one suspect. "What about Lara's aunt, Agata? Did you interact with her?"

"*Oof!* Did my best to avoid the old woman. She seemed to think the Columns was Downton Abbey, and I was her lady's maid. Ran me right ragged, that one."

"So you *did* talk to her?"

"Only to take her orders. Reminded me of her food allergy every time, as if I were a proper dunce." The knife came down in rapid succession.

And I took another Shona-step back. Edith had just sliced the tops and tips off carrots without looking down. "What was Agata allergic to?"

"French sorrel, deathly so."

"And you're certain she didn't eat any?"

Edith raised her chin—according to what we called it in American English, at least—and picked up a meat mallet. "It's an herb used in French cooking. Wouldn't have either in my kitchen."

"Certainly not," I gushed to save face, and possibly my fingers. "By the way, I went up to Agata's room earlier, and I smelled tobacco smoke. Do you know whether she or any of the Blains smoke?"

"That would've been the last straw, now wouldn't it have?" She proceeded to pound the beef chuck.

The woman was destined to be a cook, and not just because of her last name. She had a violent streak. Compared to her, the Swamp Sasquatch was a gentle giant.

"If I were you, I'd stay far from Room 10. There are cold spots, the toilet flushes on its own, and we've had guests who claim they awoke to a middle-aged woman sitting on their bed or sobbing on the side of the tub in the bathroom. Others have seen a ghost staring in the windows."

"Was it Simon Hersheim?" I joked.

Edith scowled, unamused. "No, the Woman in White. She floats across the third-floor ballroom in a white gown. We don't know her name because she doesn't speak."

"It's best that way," I said, dead serious. "But speaking of women and monochrome clothing, did you see a woman dressed like a Forties femme fatale, maybe in red, among the Blain's guests at the hotel?"

"What guests?"

Stunned, I took a step forward. "The Blains didn't have any guests staying here?"

"Who in their right mind would want to spend time with that lot?" Her rage renewed, she grabbed a knife and made mincemeat of the ox kidney.

I took that step forward right back. "Then why rent rooms at the Columns? They live in town."

"The bride thought she should have a suite at The Roosevelt, but Agata told her she'd have a room here and be grateful for it. Evidently, Agata had a personal connection to the hotel."

I added that to a list of questions I had for Janine Crawford, the elderly woman from the Camellia Grill. "I heard Lara found her aunt's body. Can you tell me anything about the crime scene?"

"Well, I can do you one better than that." She washed and dried her hands and glanced at the closed kitchen door. Then she pulled a phone from her apron, tapped a couple of buttons, and held up the display. "I snapped this photo of Agata," she said, her voice low, "after Lara left the room to inform the family that her aunt had passed."

I scoured the image, unprepared for what I saw.

Agata was on her back in the king bed, eyes wide open, her long gray hair disheveled around her. The covers were tangled, as though she'd thrashed around, and she had a hand on her throat. When I saw what was on the nightstand, my chest tightened.

An oversized mug, and beside it, a plate with an uneaten sfogliatella topped with a curled orange peel—that was disturbingly familiar. "Did this food and drink come from the coffee shop downstairs?"

"No, it was closed, so Agata must've had it delivered. The mug isn't ours either." Her lips tightened. "Apparently, she was too good to drink from a paper cup."

Was it a NOLA Noir cup? "Did the night clerk see who delivered it?"

"He left early for a doctor's appointment, so no one was on duty."

A perfect opportunity for the killer. "Did you find a go-cup? Or the bag the food came in?"

"The police asked after them as well, but there was no cup or bag in her room. I told the officers that Agata was such a fusspot, I wouldn't be surprised if she'd taken it outside to the street bin herself. But they didn't find it there either." Edith picked up her knife. "Highly suspicious, if you ask me."

It was indeed.

"I'll tell you this, though." Edith began massacring some unidentified organ meat. "There was a bit of coffee left in that mug, so I took a good sniff."

My heart beat hard. Edith was a cook, so she would have a "strong smeller" like the Swamp Sasquatch. "Did you detect anything unusual?"

She sniffed as if to demonstrate her nasal prowess. "Walnut, as plain as the conk on me face."

"This case gets more horrifying by the hour," I told myself as I turned the Mustang onto Maple Street and hit the gas. I couldn't get away from the Columns fast enough after what I'd learned in Edith Cook's kitchen. "Wringing a chicken's neck is bad enough, but plucking it with her teeth? What kind of animal *does* that?"

Shuddering, I turned my thoughts to the walnut odor Edith had smelled in the empty mug at Agata's bedside. The coffee had to be the nocino cappuccino from NOLA Noir. Based on my throat's reaction to a single sip, I would've sworn that an entire mug of that noxious coffee had killed the elderly woman. But a more likely scenario was that the drink had been poisoned.

Or seasoned with an herb Agata was deathly allergic to. Although, that didn't seem plausible. She would've tasted an herb in her coffee, especially one she'd been so worried about consuming.

A bigger question was whether Vick or Brunella had killed Agata. The fact that the NOLA Noir cup and bag had disappeared sure made it seem as though they'd tried to cover their tracks.

On the other hand, a member of the Blain family could've disposed of the packaging to cast suspicion on them. Edward certainly had motives to get rid of his wife's aunt—chief among them, money. And he might have threatened Delilah Delaire on the Columns balcony. Because he and the rest of the family would've been the first to come under police scrutiny, the obvious thing to do would be to frame Vick or his nonnina.

Or hire them to do the killing?

And who was the femme fatale in all of this?

"*Ugh.* I don't know." Rounding a curve in the street, I passed the cemetery across from the fourplex and shot the scongiuri. Then I screeched to a stop.

The driveway was overflowing with FIATs.

"*Mannaggia.*" I squeezed the steering wheel. Nonna had convened her Sicilian nonna friends to save me from the malocchio. The irony was that the gathering itself was a sure sign that I not only *had* the evil eye, but that it had hit me as hard as a blow from Edith cook's kitchen mallet.

"No worries. This is why I rented Veronica's old apartment."

Edith's imagined mallet struck me again—Glenda hadn't given me the key.

My eyes darted to the second floor. Her lights were out, and it was only seven p.m. "Now what am I going to do?"

Thibodeaux's across the street was open until two a.m. *Then what? Tiptoe into my apartment and sleep in the tub?*

My eyes moved to the cemetery. "Not on your life."

I parked in front of the fourplex and dialed Bradley.

"Hey, babe," he answered. "I was about to call you."

"Are you at home?"

"No, the lobby at the Columns, waiting for my mother and grandmother to come down. I'm taking them to dinner for Restaurant Week."

And I was in my car waiting for a dinner invite—that didn't come. "Cordelia must be feeling better."

"So-so." He cleared his throat. "That's what I was going to call you about. It's silly, I know, but she's worried sick about the fact that a wedding planner contacted you and was killed."

So that was the reason Cordelia had looked ill at breakfast—me. I slouched in my seat. My family was hard enough to manage. Now we had to deal with Bradley's too? It was too much.

Tears pricked my eyelids.

Bradley chuckled. "My grandmother thinks it's the evil eye."

The tears dried up. "I thought you came from a sensible family."

"What's that supposed to mean?" he asked decidedly sans chuckle.

"It means I expect that kind of nonsense from my nonna." I glanced at my apartment door. "She was raised on superstition in Sicily. But your grandmother is upper-crust Boston society."

"Don't forget, before she married my grandfather and became a Linde, she was a Toccato."

Which meant "touched," as in "crazy," and Cordelia was starting to show it. Much like Lou Toccato's psycho-psychic wife, Chandra.

"Franki," he exhaled my name, "don't let this upset you. We'll straighten it out."

"How?" I huffed. "I'll solve the case, but it won't change the fact that Delilah Delaire called me and died."

"We'll just have to convince our families that their concerns are irrational."

"That's like trying to convince Catholics that they're Baptists," I snapped. "It's never going to happen."

"Listen," his tone had lowered, "they're coming downstairs now, so we'll have to figure this out later. Love you."

"Yeah." I hung up and studied my dejected face in the rearview mirror.

And yawned.

"O.M.G." I straightened in my seat. "*Did* someone put the evil eye on me?"

No, I had to resist that notion. Otherwise, I'd turn into my mom and nonna and, apparently, Bradley's grandmother.

Still, the yawning was excessive. *Or was it?* I'd been through a lot in the past couple of days, i.e., Delilah's murder, the shock of seeing Shona, watching my mom and nonna pull up in front of Giada's mansion. And on top of all that, there was the Swamp Sasquatch's blackened frog legs and Edith Cook's chicken. "It's just as well that Bradley didn't invite me to dinner. I need a good night's sleep."

But sleep wasn't going to happen in my apartment—or in Veronica's. I flashed back to Giada asking if I'd had any bad luck. This was that bad luck. "Maybe I do have the malocchio."

I grabbed my bag from the passenger seat and turned to reach for the door handle. And screamed.

Evil eyes peered into my car window!

Then I spotted a toothpick protruding from an eye-tooth hole. Clenching my intact teeth, I pushed open the door. "Nadezhda, what are you—"

Leaves rustled in the cemetery.

My head jerked toward the sound.

A grotesque figure with long white hair and broken black bones covered in cobwebs emerged from the graveyard gate.

I pulled the car door shut, locked it, and started the engine. Before I could back out, the figure limp-ran beneath a streetlight.

It was Glenda looking like she'd been in a car accident—or looking like a *car* that had been in an accident. The heel was missing from one of her black-and-white-checked stripper shoes, and what I'd thought were bones were bent windshield wipers, circling her bosom and waist like broken feather plumes. The cobwebs were actually ignition wires holding the whole outfit together.

Without so much as a glance in our direction, Glenda climbed into the back of Nadezhda's black van, which was parked near Thibodeaux's, and slammed the doors.

At that point, I rolled down my window—because I had to ask. "Hey, Nadezhda, could you get the key to Veronica's apartment from Glenda?"

She removed the toothpick. "Nyet. I have message. You pay but not get key."

I narrowed my eyes. "What're you talking about, Russki?"

"Baby babushkas catch Glenda vit net. Ruin vindshield viper outfit."

Glenda's look suddenly made sense. It was Hucci Cucci Hot Couture—or rather *Car*ture—made from auto parts, and she'd apparently had a run-in with the nonne, who were forever trying to clothe her. "Where are you taking her?" I half-laughed. "To the mechanic?"

Nadezhda wasn't amused. "She spend night vit me. Tomorrow she have Hot I Scream Sundae dance. She not vant baby babushkas break vaffle skirt."

Glenda had mentioned wearing real waffle cone for the performance, and as the windshield wipers attested, the nonne were nothing if not destructive. "Surely she can't expect *me* to stay with the baby babushkas?"

"You strong man. You can take." Nadezhda spat through her eye-tooth hole.

I recoiled, and Giada's words echoed in my head, *After they pay you a compliment, they have to spit three times. If they don't— unintentional malocchio.* Of course, Nadezhda had insulted me by calling me a guy, but she'd also called me "strong," which qualified as a compliment. "You'd better spit two more times."

She complied.

That was surprisingly easy.

Nadezhda went to the van and drove away.

Steeling myself for wailing, clacking rosaries, and tearful prayers, I exited the Mustang and entered my apartment.

Nonne were wiping down the walls and furniture with bowls of water. I would've been excited that they were cleaning except that they were using rock salt. A tall nonna whose name I never remembered was also pouring the salt into little red bags that reminded me of voodoo gris gris.

Even more bizarre, no one looked at me, not even Napoleon. But in his defense, someone had filled his dog bowl with chopped veal cutlet.

My nonna shuffled from the kitchen with a bowl of water.

"Nonna, did you throw a net on Glenda?"

"*What*-a? She fell-a."

I had my suspicions about that, but there was no point in arguing with her.

My mother emerged from the kitchen. "The nonne were carrying the net to my car, Francesca, and Glenda accidentally got tangled in it as she was coming downstairs. It's for collecting walnuts."

"Wait. Why do you need a walnut net?"

Nonna put the bowl on the coffee table. "Young-a people today! You put-a the net-a under the tree and-a give it a shake-a."

"No, what I meant was, why are you picking walnuts? You brought me that five-pound bag from Costco."

My mother dried her hands on a dish cloth. "Given the complex nature of your condition, we spoke with a consultant from Benevento."

"Hang on," I said, grabbing hold of an armchair. "What do you mean 'complex?'"

Nonna tapped my chest. "You have-a the malocchio, and-a you drank-a the nocino of a janara. A double curse-a."

Leave it to my family to make the situation out to be worse than Cordelia. "You don't know for sure that Brunella is a janara."

"We can't take our chances, dear." My mother twisted the dish towel. "The consultant said the best antidote is to make nocino and drink a cup. Luckily, tomorrow *is* June 24th, the night of San Giovanni, so the timing is perfect."

I considered pointing out that no one in the room was a virgin who could pick the walnuts, but that would've gone over as big as calling us all atheists. "Who is this consultant?"

"Giada called your cousin Sofia, whose grandmother was born in Benevento."

I had a cousin Sofia? I'd probably met her at Paul's wedding too—post rum pastries. "But the nocino won't be ready until November."

"And-a you get-a married in-a January." Nonna wiped her hands, problem solved.

Over four months was a long time to wait. But what did I have to lose—except possibly my throat?

A knock interrupted my thoughts.

The nonne stopped cleaning and cast concerned looks at my nonna.

Santina Messina, a long-time friend of the family, nodded in the direction of the door. "Nonna Nunzia."

"*Avanti*," Nonna called, instructing this new nonna to come in.

The door opened with a creak, which it didn't normally do. From out of nowhere a wind kicked up and blew through my living room. I half-expected a Sergio Leone spaghetti-western soundtrack to play.

What I didn't expect was the woman who entered.

I was used to little old Sicilian ladies draped in black, but this one was the Italian Christmas witch, La Befana, in the flesh. She had a hooked nose complete with wart, arthritic fingers, and skin so shriveled it made apple-head dolls look like they'd had Botox.

Black eyes peered from sunken sockets semi-obscured by a black scarf.

"I...is she a janara?" I asked no nonna in particular.

My mother shook her head. "A *majara*."

The term was unfamiliar. "Is she here to pick the walnuts?"

"No, dear. Nonna Nunzia isn't the consultant from Benevento. She's originally from Sicily, like your nonna, and she's come to check on your malocchio."

Like an evil-eye doctor? Funny, given her grim reaper demeanor.

Nonna Nunzia approached and shoved her palm on my forehead.

Tears sprung from her eyes.

And she yawned.

Twice.

"*L'ucchiatùra*," she pronounced like a death sentence.

"Il malocchio," Nonna interpreted.

Nonna Nunzia removed her hand from my head as wails and cries erupted in the room—multiple "*O, Signores*", a few "*Santa Vergines,*" and a "*Gesù bambino.*"

For my part, I'd uttered a mental "Holy Hell."

Nonna Nunzia pulled a bottle of olive oil from a bag on her arm and placed it beside the bowl of water on the coffee table. She crossed herself three times, closed her eyes, and spoke in an unintelligible hiss.

Sidling up to my mother, I covered my mouth. "Why is she whispering?"

"So no one can steal the secret rite. The majare pass them down to their daughters, and there are only two nights a year they can do it. Christmas and tomorrow night."

The feast of San Giovanni was full of surprises.

Nonna Nunzia added rock salt to the water and a few drops of the olive oil. She made the sign of the cross three more times over the water and inserted her thumbs.

I leaned forward to see if the oil had elongated, as it had done at Giada's.

Her knobby fingers reached for my face—and yanked open my eyes.

"Ow." I tried to pull away, but the woman had hold of my eyelids. "Can you let those go?"

Ignoring my request, she rubbed the mixture around my temples and jammed a hand into my stomach. Then she pointed to the chaise longue.

"Sit-a, Franki," my nonna ordered.

Reluctantly, I obeyed.

Nonna Nunzia pulled a red cloth from her bag and used it to cover my head. Next, the weight of the bowl was on my skull. I had a bad feeling about where this rite was headed—pun intended.

The nonne gathered around me to watch whatever Nonna Nunzia was doing.

"Um," I held up a finger, "the bowl is hurting my brain."

Oddios and *Mamma mias* ensued.

"Franki," Nonna said, "if-a your head-a hurt, it's a bad-a sign."

"*Or*, my head hurts because you put a heavy bowl of water on it."

Silence.

The bowl was removed, and then the cloth.

Nonna Nunzia eyed the other nonne. "*Nu casu difficili.*"

That Sicilian I understood. "Why am I 'a difficult case?'"

She didn't answer.

Nonna shuffle-ran the dish into my bedroom. Moments later, the toilet in my bathroom flushed.

Nonna Nunzia packed up her oil. She pulled a piece of paper from her bag and gave it to my mother.

Then she gave me a zucchini.

The door creaked open, something else it didn't do, and she left.

Personally, I didn't know what was more perplexing—the opening and closing of the door or the vegetable. "Is Nonna Nunzia coming back?"

No one answered.

Which I took as a "yes." I looked at the paper in my mother's hand. "How much did her visit cost you?"

"Majare don't charge for their services, Francesca."

This experience kept getting crazier. "If that's not a bill, what is it?"

"An incantation you say in your head when a woman looks at you sideways, or when you meet a man with a unibrow—they can provoke the malocchio unintentionally."

I'd always thought unibrows were strange, but I had no idea how much.

Next, I opened the paper. The words were in Sicilian with a handy English translation.

FÈMMITI, *fimmina juràta*
  Ca sì peju d'un serpenti
  La to lingua mi la mettu
  Mmenzu e denti
  Quantu tu a mia nun mi fai nenti.

STOP, *irate-angry woman*
  You're worse than a serpent
  I'll put your tongue
  between my teeth
  So to me you can do nothing.

"TOO BAD I didn't have this twenty minutes ago. I could've used it on Nadezhda," I said, following my mother into the kitchen.

She tightened her apron. "I read somewhere that only twenty majare are left in Sicily, so it's a good thing we found one here in New Orleans."

Good wasn't the word I would have used.

"At any rate," she arranged arancini on a plate, "I'm sure you're glad your nonna and I came. The emergency was so much bigger than we'd thought."

Glad wasn't the word I would've used either. In fact, I had no words, so I decided to eat. I put the zucchini on the counter and reached for an *arancino*.

My mother slapped my hand. "*You're* having walnut pesto for dinner. Remember," she sing-songed, "marriage, fertility, and abundance."

I'd set myself up for that. When I'd come home earlier to get my mosquito hat and galoshes, I'd tossed the five-pound bag of walnuts on the counter instead of hiding it or giving it to squirrels.

"The zucchini reminds me," she said, putting it in the refrigerator vegetable bin, "I had to run to Rouse's Market earlier to get fresh basil. That's an herb you could grow yourself."

Who had time to grow things? "I guess."

"Herbs are easy, dear. They don't take up much space. You could grow them in a small patch of the yard or even in a pot."

With a sigh, I sunk into a chair at my kitchen table in preparation for a "tip tirade," i.e., when my mother had what she believed was a helpful suggestion, and she aggressively drove it into my head to drive me into doing it.

"Fresh herbs really dress up a dish. You'll want to have them at hand when you and Bradley are married." She choked back a sob and gripped the counter. "That is, *if* you get married."

This tip tirade had dragged on long enough. "Mom, have you ever heard of French sorrel?"

She perked right up. "Of course. It tastes like bitter greens and lemon."

"*Shht!*" I waved my arms. "The nonne can hear you."

"So?"

"*Sooo*, there could be some ridiculous lemon tradition related to undoing the malocchio, and if so, I want to avoid it."

"Francesca Lucia Amato," she drawled, "I don't know where you come up with this stuff."

"Uhhh, *Mom*," my eyes bulged from the shock of that statement, "the two of you forced me to steal a lemon from a St. Joseph's Day church altar to land a marriage proposal, then you hired that creepy cape-wearing Sicilian marriage broker, and now you've called in a malocchio diagnoser. So I think you *do* know where I come up with this stuff."

She shook her head, convinced that *I* was the out-there one in the family. "I was just talking to your nonna about lemons because you add a teaspoon of the juice to walnut pesto, and she didn't say a *word* about..."

My mom continued with her lecture, but I'd stopped listening after "lemons" and "walnut." She was right. The two flavors went well together, which meant that the lemony herb flavor of French sorrel wouldn't be out of place in nocino.

It was time for an incognito visit to Walnut Street.

Not to look for a walnut tree.

But an herb garden.

8

———————

"This is a Hansel and Gretel situation waiting to happen," I grumbled, staring through the windshield of my Mustang at Vick and Brunella's house. "It's even got a ready source of children from the Walnut Street Playground."

Sure, they didn't live in the forest, but Audubon Park was close enough. And the place was New Orleans shotgun style, which, compared to gingerbread, made for a way scarier fairy tale.

I parked around the corner and got out of the car. It was five a.m., so I had about thirty minutes to find out whether they had an herb garden before the sun came up. First I checked the sidewalk mailbox to make sure I had the right house. A piece of junk mail was addressed to Brunella Pagano.

My eyes widened. *Pagan?*

Is Brunella a witch?

A large gray dog in the front yard of the house next door growled and hiked his leg on a For Sale sign. Then he trotted to the wrought-iron fence and stuck his muzzle through the bars.

I smiled. "Good dog."

He let out a bizarre bark that sent me dashing to the park, where I crouched in some bushes. I didn't know his breed, but he must've had a throat issue too because his bark sounded like a donkey being murdered.

"Bad dogkey," I whisper-shouted.

The door of the house opened, and the traitorous animal went inside.

In case anyone else came out to investigate the noise, I stayed hidden a little longer. As I sat waiting, I yawned three times in succession. But not even Nonna Nunzia could blame that on the malocchio. I'd had a bad night thanks to sleeping upright on the chaise longue—and that veal cutlet Napoleon ate.

A pair of headlights came around the corner, and a white truck stopped in front of Vick and Brunella's place.

What do we have here? I crouched lower.

A tall, thin guy in a white uniform got out with a small paper bag, looked from side to side as he walked up the sidewalk, and deposited the bag on the porch. As he got back in the truck, he scoured the street again and drove away.

"Suspicious behavior." Then again, it was dark, this was The Big Easy, and he was making a delivery to a witchy woman who looked like she'd stepped from the pages of a Tomie dePaola book and into a setting straight out of the Brothers Grimm.

It was tempting to run to the bag, but I didn't in case Vick or Brunella came out to retrieve it.

What could be inside?

Milk didn't come in paper bags, and neither did the newspaper.

Could be some kind of herb. French sorrel?

Or walnuts.

It *is* June 24th, the day of San Giovanni, when nocino is made in Campania. On the other hand, the street was named after the nut, so surely some were around. I pulled my phone from my bag to google whether Audubon Park had any walnut trees and saw a text from Bradley.

Hey, babe. I feel bad about our call earlier. Why don't you and I sneak off to dinner at Copper Vine tomorrow night? They've got a special menu for Restaurant Week, and I'm craving a piece of their black walnut pie and you.

I almost dropped the phone. "What the hell is going on with the walnuts?"

"There are no walnut trees here, only Southern Live Oaks," a male voice said.

From beside me.

In the bushes.

Terror shot through my body, and I erupted from my hiding spot, braying like a donkey being murdered. The encounter made Moira Mulligan popping up in my backseat seem normal.

A man emerged from the leaves, which didn't help the alarming situation. He had a fleshy face, maybe sixty-five years of age, and a protruding belly. His clothes were worn, and he smelled of BO. He chuckled and gave a wink. "You've got a healthy set of lungs on you."

I wished I could say the same for my battered esophagus and burned mouth.

He flashed a one-toothed smile and held out his hand. "Willie T."

"Uh, Franki." I gave him an extended-arm handshake to keep some distance between us. Anyone that cheerful at five a.m. had to be deranged. "What's the *T* stand for?"

"It's not the initial. It's t-e-a, as in the beverage."

Well, it clearly wasn't for "teeth." But judging from his breath, his last name should've been a different drink. "Do you come here often?"

"Certainly do. I've lived here for years." He gestured to the expanse of the park. "Since you're interested in walnuts, I would imagine you came to see the Tree of Life. Or perhaps you know it by its Live Oak Society name, the Etienne de Boré oak?"

This guy really needed to meet the Swamp Sasquatch for a round of tree talk. "No to both."

He smacked his teeth—er, tooth. "Shame. It's at the opposite end of the park by the Audubon Zoo, but well worth the walk. The tree was once part of Jean Etienne de Boré's sugarcane plantation, hence the name, and it's a popular site for weddings."

Willie was a walking Wikipedia article. He'd probably get along great with my mother. But given the wedding venue reference, I wouldn't want them to meet. I would, however, introduce him to Shona. "No offense, but I'm not here to tree watch...or get married."

He kicked at a lump of dirt. "This is a delicate matter, but I simply must ask. Do you need a place to stay?"

I glanced at my hobo bag. I really had to get a better purse. "Thanks, but no."

"Well, I do have plenty of room for guests, but that's not what I meant. I thought perhaps you were interested in the house that's for sale?"

"Actually, I have a question about the people who live in the one on the corner."

"Ah, a jilted lover."

Given Vick's weird thing for thumbs, I didn't want Willie to think we'd been together—even though I was confident my nails would've made the cut. "A private investigator."

His eyes took on a sly slant, and he folded his hands in front of his belly. "Then you'll be pleased to learn that I narc for notes, as in cash."

"Pleased" wasn't the adjective I would've chosen, but since Willie appeared to be homeless, I wanted to help him out. I opened my wallet.

"A C note, to be specific."

"A hundred bucks?" The price of info was steep in the park. "I don't carry that kind of money."

"I'm a businessman, so I'll give you a discount." He bounced onto his tiptoes and flashed a lone-toothed grin. "All you've got."

I gave him a hard stare and handed over fourteen dollars. "Do you know if the owners have an herb garden?"

"Indeed I do, and they do not. The backyard is a junk heap. Full of nail salon stations from the grandson, Vick's, former business."

Creepy that Vick couldn't even part with the equipment. "Do you know if either one of them smokes or owns a black BMW?"

"No to both."

This was getting me nowhere. "What else do you know about them?"

"Let's see..." Willie tapped his tooth. "Vick's forty-two, never married, and lives with his grandmother, Brunella. She's eighty-three, widowed, and loves reruns of *Sex in the City* and *Hannibal*."

I didn't know which was more disturbing—the thought of Brunella watching a show about a sex columnist or one about a serial killer who ate his victims. "You got all that from living across the street?"

"No, from looking in windows and trashcans." He pulled up his pants. "I'm in data collection, and I dabble in waste management."

That was like saying Glenda worked in public relations. But I had to give Willie Tea credit—the guy had a future in résumé writing. "About the waste management, I could use your help with that paper bag at the door."

"Gotcha." His eyes glowed like the moon—and my esophagus. "It's got poo in it, and you want me to light it on fire."

For the second time since meeting him, I jumped back. "What do I look like? Some kind of freak?"

His lids lowered. "You *are* spying on a house from the bushes at 5 a.m. How do I know you're not up to mischief or out for revenge?"

"Because I'm a PI," I whisper-huffed. "Now go find out what's in the bag, okay?"

"That'll cost you a C note."

I put my hands on my hips. "You already took all of my money."

Willie did another bounce-and-smile combination. "Lucky for you, I also deal in trade. What do you have in that bag?"

Me, lucky? Yeah, to leave the park with the shirt on my back. I rummaged in my purse and found the bon bons from NOLA Noir.

"Don't mind if I do." He snatched the chocolates from my hand and tore into a package. "Being on a former sugarcane field has set off my sweet tooth."

Probably not a phrase he should use.

"Mmm, positively scrumptious." He gummed the chocolate and shivered. "A liquid center to boot."

Liquid? That's right—Vick said they had a nocino center. "Hey, I just remembered. It's a liqueur that lit up my throat, so I'd stop there, if I were you."

"Nonsense." He opened a second package. "I haven't had bon bons this good since the EuroChocolate Festival in Perugia last October." He popped the chocolate and crossed the street.

The man went to Italy? Forget the new purse, I needed a new job—park narcing.

Willie bounded up the sidewalk and stooped over the bag.

The sound of a car engine sent me back to the bushes, and I watched in shock as the 1940s black Buick Roadster slowed to a stop in front of Vick and Brunella's.

Because it was dark and the car had tinted windows, I

couldn't see inside. But I had no doubt the mystery woman was in the backseat.

Who is she? And why is she surveilling Vick and Brunella—like me?

I emerged from the leaves to get a license plate number, but the Buick sped around the corner. I turned to the porch.

And I gasped.

Willie Tea was flat on his back, and yet the car hadn't come close to him.

An awful thought struck me.

Did the NOLA Noir bon bons *kill* him?

I rushed across the street and knelt at his side. A whiff of his breath practically punched my head backwards, and my eyes began to water. "Okay, wow. That's potent." I put my hands on my thighs, struggling to recover. "It's a good thing you're breathing, because mouth to mouth is off the table."

The paper bag was beside him, so I checked the contents. And I knew what had happened to Willie.

He'd fainted, and I'd darn near joined him.

Inside the bag was a quart-sized plastic container.

Full to the brim with blood.

"LIKE, DID I HEAR YOU RIGHT?" The police tip line operator was incredulous—and a female who sounded all of eighteen. "A quart of blood in a paper bag?"

I made sure I was out of earshot of the tourists at Café du Monde. The sun had barely come up, and the line was already spilling onto the sidewalk. "Yeah, it's insane."

"Totally. I mean, how come the paper didn't dissolve in all that liquid?"

My lips tightened against my teeth. It wasn't comforting that the New Orleans PD had this woman taking anonymous crime information. "No, the blood was inside a plastic container in the bag."

"Oooh, now *that* makes *sense.*"

Does it? No matter how I looked at the blood delivery, there was no logic. "Just have someone pay a visit to that address, and to NOLA Noir."

I closed the call and picked up my Café du Monde to-go order of half a dozen beignets. After my experience with the nocino cappuccino, I didn't want any Italian pastries filled with liqueur. Just plain dough and plenty of powdered sugar.

Munching on a beignet, I set off on the four-block walk to my office. The protesters were still outside Tujague's creole restaurant, and the obvious divide between the two sides was starting to show. A middle-aged woman in a *tignon* headwrap typical of voodoo mambos was arguing with an elegantly updoed lady in linen who held a sign that read, *Sacrifice Voodoo Doughnuts, not our city's history!* Since I was already wrangling with the nonne over my double-cursed state, I made it a point to stay on the opposite side of the street.

After taking another bite of beignet, I googled "nocino" on my phone with my free thumb—and noticed that the morning light really set off my nail.

The first link that came up was to a drink article. Apparently, the Italian liqueur was known on the American cocktail circuit. There were recipes for a Nocino Sour, a Milk Punch, which I staunchly avoided after my last case involving a murderous Mardi Gras krewe, and the Walnut Manhattan. The last one prompted me to google the walnut tree, and the sentence that appeared onscreen brought me to a halt.

The Black Walnut tree is native to Louisiana.

My feet began to move, and my mind raced with questions.

Is it a coincidence that it's the black walnut, as in noir?

And is the tree the reason Brunella left Benevento for New Orleans?

If so, does that mean there's a black walnut tree in town where witches gather? "If there is, it's definitely not in Sick Vick's backyard."

At the intersection of Decatur and Governor Nicholls Street, where my office was located, I shoved the beignet bag into my purse. I'd ordered exactly enough for myself and had no plans to share them with the likes of Ruth. I stuffed the last bite of beignet into my mouth and, on instinct, glanced up the street at Hex Old World Witchery.

And I sucked in a breath of powdered sugar.

Brunella had just come out of Hex, and she was headed my way.

I ducked around the corner and coughed. A white puff of powdered sugar came out, and I went flat against the side of the building.

It was in the shape of a witch's hat!

Not only that, on top of the damage to my esophagus and mouth, I now had my lungs to worry about.

There was only one course of action. I hurried up the next block and took the long way around to Hex. I'd been to the witchery before, and it wasn't your typical tourist shop. Women who identified as witches ran the place, and its headquarters was in none other than Salem, Massachusetts.

No one was at the counter, so I browsed the merchandise. Some coffin nails, a green bar of soap labeled "Wicked Witch Wash," and a bottle of Pure Magic Grave Spirits Room Spray, which probably explained the store's musty decay odor.

A middle-aged witch with high cheekbones and teased black hair reminiscent of Elvira exited a door behind the counter. She wore a red peasant blouse, a black maxi skirt, and a look of pure suspicion.

"I'm Madge," she said in a voice suited for a cackle. "Let me know if you need any help." She gestured to a wall display. "And be sure to check out our new ritual tools and witch wear."

"Actually, I work at Private Chicks up the street."

She crossed her arms. "What are you implying? That a witch can't be a PI?"

"Not at all," I said, taken aback. The last thing I wanted to do was to irritate a witch. "With access to spells and potions, witches would make great PIs."

Her heavily lined eyes narrowed. "Because our intellect alone wouldn't suffice."

I took a deep breath. This witch was kind of a bitch. "All I meant was that I'm not here to shop. I came to ask about a woman who just left the store. In her eighties, four-feet-ten?"

"You mean, Strega Nona from the Tomie dePaola books?"

"*Tombola.*"

"What's that?"

"Sorry, the Italian version of 'Bingo.'"

A half-smile snaked across her cheek. "Don't apologize. It's got 'tomb' in it."

I'd never made the connection, and now that I had, I didn't want to play it again.

"Strega Nona bought two items." Madge led me to a rotating display. "An oil and a spice from our 'Herbs from a Witch's Garden' collection."

My glowing throat went dry at the herb reference, and I spotted a bottle that reminded me of my nonna's insistence that the Benevento witches worshiped Satan. "Was it French sorrel?"

"Whoever heard of a witch using that?"

She didn't have to be rude about it. "Okay, then. The ground Devil's Claw Root?"

"No, that's used to bring back a lover." She held up a liver-spotted hand. "Not that an eighty-year-old woman couldn't have a love life."

Especially if she watched *Sex in the City* like Brunella.

Madge picked up two items. "She bought this nutmeg essential oil and our ground cloves."

A relieved sigh escaped my lips, and maybe some powdered sugar. "Those are typical Italian nonna cooking ingredients."

"Not this nutmeg oil." She put her hand on her hip. "It isn't fit for consumption because it's pure, from the plant. You use it to conjure money, luck in gambling, or psychic awareness because it's ruled by Jupiter, and its element is Fire."

Fire? My hand went to my neck. *Was the nutmeg oil what had lit up my esophagus?* "And the clove?"

"Put some in a red bag, and it'll stop the gossipmongers."

Madge ought to do that herself. After our initial impasse, she'd turned out to be fairly loose-lipped. "So, do you think Strega Nona is a witch?"

"Hard to say, but I'll let you in on a secret." She motioned for me to approach with a knobby finger, and despite all of my childhood fairy-tale training, I drew near. "The most dangerous people aren't us witches," she said, "but the wannabes."

"How so?"

"Listen to me, hon." Her tone was as dry as the Graveyard Dirt Ritual Incense. "You can't imagine the crap those posers will throw into a spell."

"Crazier than, say, human or animal blood?"

"*Pff!* That's old hat."

I assumed she was referring to the witch variety.

Madge waved off the notion. "Witches have been using blood for good and bad for centuries."

"As have vampires," I said, not because I believed in the supernatural creatures, but because New Orleans had a community of real people who lived like them, including the blood-drinking and even the coffin-sleeping.

"No doubt." She toyed with her pentagram necklace. "But these witch wannabes come in here complaining that they put all this natural stuff from their kitchens in a spell, and all their hair fell out. And I'm like, what'd you expect? A perm?"

I touched my hair. I had to be careful because I'd put olive oil and baking soda in it a few days ago. "So, what should I do if I think I drank one of her potions, maybe with that nutmeg oil?"

"Uh," she rotated her eyes as hard as Linda Blair's head, "go to a doctor?"

My stomach, which had resisted the adverse effects of the nocino cappuccino, started to bubble. "While I'm here, what do you suggest for the evil eye?"

"Today is St. John's Day, so there's some herbs you could gather, but you'd have to hurry because they need to be bathed in dew."

It was telling that the witches celebrated San Giovanni too. "Which herbs?"

"St. John's wort, mugwort, lavender, rue, garlic, sage, and rosemary. You tie them with a string, knot it seven times, and place it in front of your door. They're known as St. John's herbs, and they'll take care of that evil eye."

My lips tightened. Naturally, my mom and nonna had called that majara instead of picking the herbs. Those witches delighted in torturing me.

"Of course," Madge pointed to a package, "you could always just get this Demon-Be-Gone smudge stick."

The stick name sounded like it could not only handle the malocchio, but also my mom and nonna. "I'll take it. Actually, two."

Madge pulled the sticks from the rack and led me to a shelf lined with candles and handsewn poppets. "After you see the doctor for that nutmeg oil you drank, you should light this Uncrossing candle from the Marie Laveau New Orleans Voodoo Spell collection. It'll undo most root and herb hexes, but since Strega Nona is an Italian witch, I can't guarantee it."

I was all ears. "Why? Because it's a different culture?"

"That and they don't usually belong to a coven."

Not liking the turn the discussion had taken, I reached for the candle, just in case. "What does a coven have to do with it?"

Madge swirled her hand, as though conjuring something. "Think of them as non-profit organizations."

I'd try, but I couldn't promise anything.

"If a coven witch is going to put a spell on you, she has a code of ethics to follow, and a board that ensures she does so." She gave a curt nod. "Not the witches from Italy, though. A lot of them are rogue."

This wasn't good news. As I was all too aware, a regular Italian nonna was already rogue by definition. A rogue witch nonna was a foe I was powerless to fight, not to mention that the conversation had raised a broader concern.

What sort of witch's brew had Agata and I drunk?

9

"Yo, Franki!" Vick raised his arm in a Fascist salute-style greeting as I came up the street from Hex Old World Witchery.

Keeping my gaze neutral, I gave a curt nod. He was unloading boxes from an unmarked truck parked in front of NOLA Noir. I squinted to try to see whether the delivery consisted of more containers of blood, and I spotted something that made the breath catch in my still-sensitive throat.

Vick technically had a unibrow—the cause of unintentional malocchio—and I hadn't memorized Nonna Nunzia's incantation.

In my defense, however, her protective spell was about an "irate-angry woman," which clearly didn't jive with a unibrowed male situation. Now that I thought about it, that majara really needed to update her handout. *But what can you expect from a free service?*

"Don't forget," Vick flashed a Tony Danza smile, "that ammazzacaffè is waiting for you!"

My lids lowered to a glare. How could I forget his offer of a 'coffee killer,' especially after discovering that he and his nonnina had potentially axed Agata with a cappuccino? And even if they weren't the murderers, their noxious nocino had probably permanently altered my throat's cellular structure.

Without a word, I entered the stairwell to Private Chicks, thinking of the toxic nutmeg oil Brunella had purchased from Madge at Hex. It was San Giovanni's Feast Day, so the old witch was probably whipping up a batch of her nasty nocino.

Maybe for me.

My phone vibrated in my bag, and I fished it out. I'd missed several calls from Shona and a text from Moira.

I'LL PICK *you up outside your office at 9:45 this morning to go to Wedding Belles. I'll be in disguise, and so will the car.*

"WOW. THE CAR *TOO*?" The woman was in serious hiding.

I pocketed my phone and opened the office door, coming face to face with Ruth.

The chains on her readers were in full swing, and one of her Keds was hopping. "You finally get some work, and you can't be bothered to make yourself available to the client?"

"It's nine o'clock, Ruth. It's not like I'm late."

"Tell that to Shona." She flailed her arm—and her turkey waddle. "She called twice to ask for updates because you didn't answer your cell."

Grimacing, I closed the door behind me even though I already wanted to leave. Shona was probably stressing about the wedding invitations the Swamp Sasquatch found. "The next time she calls, tell her I've been working on her case since five a.m."

"I've been here since seven, and this is the first I've seen of you." Ruth gestured to her reception desk. "So where, pray tell, have you been working?"

"In the bushes outside a suspect's house, that's where."

She hissed, ostrich style. "That's not working. It's just a regular night out for you."

I'd offered her that jab on a silver platter. Good thing I hadn't mentioned my bush companion, Willie Tea. "Since we're talking about work, why aren't you ever at your part-time Mardi Gras krewe job?"

Her turkey waddle went taut. "Because I've got to hold down the fort here and field your client calls."

"As I just pointed out, I'm doing my job. So do us all a favor and slack off." I'd wanted to use a stronger word than "slack," but the weak word worked—Ruth's beak had snapped shut.

Bound for Veronica's office, I stopped by David and The Vassal's corner desk. The former had his nose in a book, and the latter in a computer monitor. "David, can you work your hacking magic and get me cell phone records for Agata Villeré and Edward Blain? I need to know who he called after Agata insulted him at the rehearsal dinner and whether she phoned in an order to NOLA Noir the morning she died."

He gave a signature flip of his bangs. "According to my ethics class, you need a warrant for that kind of information."

"Don't bite the hand that feeds you, son, particularly when *this* hand," I wiggled my fingers, "has just been shopping at Hex Old World Witchery."

The Vassal's already lens-magnified eyes grew wider behind his glasses. "Can I do anything for you?"

"How kind of you to ask." I shot a reproachful stare at David. "Find Janine Crawford's contact info and get me an appointment to speak to her. She's old-school, so she's probably in the phone book."

His big eyes blinked. "The 'phone' *what*?"

Despite The Vassal and David's intelligence, I often wondered how they made it through life. "Look it up. And when you call Janine, remind her that we met at the Camellia Grill and explain that I'm a PI."

The Vassal went to work, and I headed up the hallway to Veronica's office.

My BFF looked up from papers spread across her desk. "I was just about to call you." She grinned. "I have news."

"So do I, and you'll want to brace yourself."

"Uh-oh." She gripped the arms of her fuchsia leather chair. "Okay, shoot."

"Based on my conversation with the Columns kitchen manager," I took a seat across from her desk, "Agata Villeré most likely died after drinking a mug full of nocino cappuccino from NOLA Noir."

Her head tipped forward. "So her death was accidental?"

"I didn't say that. The go-cup and paper bag were missing, which makes me suspect foul play. The coffee could've been doctored with an herb Agata's allergic to, but I think Vick's nonnina, Brunella, used a toxic nutmeg oil from Hex Old World Witchery in the same batch of nocino Vick served me."

Veronica leaned back in her chair. "Why would Vick and his grandmother want to kill Agata?"

"I'm still not sure they did. But here's the kicker—Glenda told me that Brunella once put something in Maybe Baby's toenail polish that made her nails fall off, as a warning to stay away from Vick."

"Ick." She stuck out her tongue. "That's a kicker, alright."

"Except that Maybe Baby couldn't walk for weeks," I added with a pointed stare. "Brunella is clearly dangerous, even though she looks like Strega Nona." I paused. "Hey, while we're talking witches, do you still have your old apartment key?"

Her brow hiked up. "Mind explaining that connection first?"

"Glenda's designing a witch costume, and she's acting like one too. She's refusing to give me a key to your old place because of a run-in she had with Nonna and the nonne."

"Your *Nonna's* in town?"

"Didn't I tell you to brace yourself?" A long-suffering sigh escaped my lungs. "Turns out I have a second cousin Giada, who's married to one of Edward Blain's law partners, and he's the uncle of Grace Blain's intended groom. And Giada's best friends with Delilah Delaire's assistant, Moira. Not only that, my mom and nonna showed up outside Giada's house, and then Nonna brought in a Sicilian majara to diagnose my malocchio. And guess what?"

"Franki," she said, her tone tense, "after the series of events you just laid out, there's no way I can guess what you're going to say next."

"Then I'll tell you. I've got it."

"Oh, well." She straightened in her chair. "I could've guessed *that*—I mean, that she'd *tell* you that."

My lips folded, but there was no time to respond. A whoosh of wind made the hair on the back of my neck stand up.

Nonna Nunzia?

My head snapped around to the door.

Nope. Just The Vassal, mouth-breathing.

"Sorry to interrupt." He pushed up his glasses. "Janine Crawford wants you to meet her at Galatoire's for Friday lunch today at five."

"Um, five o'clock is dinnertime, and today is Wednesday?"

"I pointed that out, but Ms. Crawford said, and I quote, 'I've been retired for so damn long that the day and time is whatever the hell I say it is.'"

Veronica huff-laughed. "You can't argue with that logic."

"Not to be disagreeable," The Vassal clasped his hands, "but I can."

I shook my head. Just another indication that the kid would have trouble in life.

"One more thing." He turned to me. "Ms. Crawford asked me to convey a message—she likes champagne, and you're paying."

My lips pursed, but I wasn't surprised. I'd been paying ever since I moved to New Orleans. "I'll be sure to bring my least maxed-out credit card."

He retreated down the hall, and I turned to Veronica. "So, what's your news?"

The grin returned to her face. "I booked a table at Copper Vine for your shower this Saturday."

The room tilted. "Black Walnut, Veronica!"

"Huh?"

In the chaos, I'd confused my operation name with Bradley's reference to the Copper Vine's pie. "I meant, 'Black Swamp.' And ixnay on the ower-shay!" I hissed à la Ruth. "The turkey-necked ostrich is lurking."

She waved off my concern. "Ruth's in the lobby. She can't hear us."

I rose and checked the hallway before closing the door. "Don't confuse her species with common poultry," I warned, returning to my seat. "The turkey-necked ostrich has the sonar of a bat, and the last thing I want is for her to pick up on the restaurant name and gobble-hiss it to the other swamp animals."

"Sorry. That was careless of me." Veronica began stacking the papers on her desk. "Let's talk about Shona's case. What's on today's agenda, besides buying Janine Friday lunch on Wednesday at dinner?"

"An appointment at Wedding Belles—"

She squealed. "To find your *dress*?"

If my BFF couldn't contain her excitement, I was going to have to cut her from the wedding planning. "Can you please stick to the operation protocols?"

"Right." She nodded to show she meant business. "Burner phones and disguises."

It was tempting to believe she was back on board, but I remained skeptical. Veronica was exhibiting the characteristics of a swamp animal—the largemouth bass. "To answer your question, I'm going to a bridal swap because Moira said Grace Blain will be there to trade in her wedding dress."

"So soon after the murder of her aunt?"

"Exactly. Something's up with that."

My phone vibrated, and I checked the display. "It's Lillian. Bradley's grandmother hasn't been herself lately, so I need to take this." I tapped *Answer*. "Hello?"

"Francesca, this is Cordelia." Her voice was so vibrant she practically crowed. "Are you free this evening?"

It was a relief to hear her in good spirits—and to get a dinner invite. "As a bird. What's up?"

"Bradley said he told you that I have deep concerns about the death of the wedding planner and what it means for you."

My abs went on the defensive. "He did, but—"

"That's not the only thing weighing on my mind. Something is going on in this hotel, and I'm determined to get to the bottom of it. I've contacted an expert to perform a séance in Room 10."

White hot fear seared my skin. *Did Cordelia hire—*

"Chandra Toccato," she replied, reading my unthought thoughts.

Something *was* wrong with Bradley's grandmother. She was as "touched" in the head as the so-called "expert" she'd hired. If I didn't know better, I would've bet Cordelia was related to Chandra instead of her husband, Lou.

Veronica mouthed, "Is everything okay?"

My head jerked in a hard hell-no. "Cordelia, maybe you should cancel the séance," I cast a desperate look at my BFF, "with Chandra."

Veronica buried her face in her hands.

"Why on earth would I do that?" Cordelia asked. "I want answers about what's going on, for your sake as well as my grandson's."

And I wanted to steer clear of Chandra. I would've gladly endured malocchio treatments from all twenty of Sicily's remaining majare rather than spend a night listening to the sham psychic schmooze with fake ghosts. "The Columns management probably won't appreciate the spectacle."

"Nonsense." Cordelia's conviction was as firm as her voice. "I rented the room today, so I'm free to use it however I wish. Plus, I want to meet the psychic. Toccato is a rare name in Italy, so I'm certain we're related."

The skin-sear sensation shifted to a flayed-alive feel. "I wouldn't rush to any conclusions. Maybe there's a Spanish branch of Toccatos."

"I've researched the name, Francesca, and I know my own heritage. It's as Italian as Amato."

If I didn't know I had the malocchio, I would've sworn that I'd been struck by a spell kit from Hex—one that dooms the victim to lifelong connections with kooks from her old cases.

"My mother was from near Naples," Cordelia announced. "Benevento."

The name made me shiver. I couldn't understand why the infamous town with the janare and the walnut tree kept coming up in conversation, but at least I knew how Bradley came by his love of black walnut pie.

"Francesca?" Cordelia asked. "Are you still on the line?"

"Yes, I'm here." Although, in truth, I was barely hanging on.

"The séance is at ten p.m. in Room 10 of the Columns. Don't be late."

"*Mm-mm*" was all I could force from my traumatized throat. Then I hung up.

Veronica exhaled. "How can I help?"

"You can't, but maybe Janine Crawford can." I went to the window behind her desk. "Cordelia just revealed that Bradley's great-grandmother was from near Naples. Benevento, of all places."

She spun her chair to face me. "What would Bradley's great-grandmother have to do with Janine?"

"Nothing, I hope." I gave another shiver. "But remember when Janine said that Agata and Pia's mother was from 'somewhere near Naples?'"

"Vaguely."

"Well," I looked down at NOLA Noir, "Vick's nonnina, Brunella, is from Benevento, and I'm willing to bet their mother was too."

Veronica ran her fingers over her chin. "Even if their mother *was* from Benevento, she wouldn't have been alive during Brunella's lifetime."

"True, but you know old-world Southern Italy and vendetta. There could've been a longstanding family feud. Or..." My gaze shifted to the undistinguishable shape on the coffee shop's sign, and I flashed back to the plastic container on Vick and Brunella's porch. "...a history of bad blood."

"When you said the car would be disguised," I shot a look as black as the paint job at Moira who was squeezed between me and the burly Uber driver in the front seat, "I didn't envision this."

Phil Redman, the merry crypt keeper from Saint Cecilia Cemetery, leaned around Moira to look at me. "She's on the downlow, Franki, so a hearse is the ideal vehicle." He belly-laughed Santa style. "See what I did there? *Downlow? Hearse?*"

My lower lip tried to push the upper into a polite smile, but it didn't work.

Moira shook her curls. "I can't get over the fact that you two know each other."

Honestly, I couldn't either.

Phil twisted his bushy brown beard with one hand as he steered the funeral car with the other. "Franki's consulted with me on two homicide cases. However, business at the cemetery has been slow, so I'm moonlighting for Uber. I'm about to pitch an idea to them for a new ridesharing service called Uber Undertaker—When you need a body buried fast."

"Given New Orleans' murder rate," Moira groused, "I think it could work."

And I was starting to think my suspicions of a spell kit that doomed its victim to lifelong connections with kooks from her old cases was spot on—and that Madge from Hex had cast it on me.

Moira checked her watch. "The bridal swap is underway. Can you pick up the pace?"

"Your wish is my command." Phil pressed a Croc to the gas pedal.

I wished she hadn't asked him that. He was already driving like a bat out of hell. If he didn't slow down, he'd get us killed— and take us straight to the cemetery.

Moira's oversized brown eyes swept over my clothes. "We need to do something about your outfit."

"It's a disguise." I looked down at the Saints football jersey I'd pulled from my Operation Black Swamp bag. "What's wrong with it?"

"You look like a thug. Bridal swaps are *events*, the same as wedding dress appointments. Women dress up, drink champagne." She eyed my Yankees baseball cap. "Not Mad Dog 20/20."

"Ah." Phil smiled fondly. "The Blue Raspberry flavor was Flat-Footed Don's favorite. Landed him an early grave at Saint Cecilia."

Not a good advertisement, but it did make you wonder, *Did this Don guy have collapsed arches? Or was he caught flat-footed by the drink?*

Moira rummaged in her bag. "As a caterer, I keep a spare dress on hand in case of spills."

"That reminds me." Phil reached across us and popped the glovebox, revealing a charcuterie board that could've come from a coffin. "Might I tempt you with some homemade *salumi*?"

My lips retreated from my teeth. Phil's cured meats were courtesy of unwitting critters that roamed the cemetery. "I don't have an appetite."

Moira shoved a wad of fabric at me. "Put this on."

The dress was as unappetizing as Phil's salumi. It was flesh-colored with pink flowers that resembled a psoriasis flare. "This will clash with my black sneakers."

Phil gazed into the rearview mirror and stroked his beard. "A previous client left a black number in the back that would be perfect for you."

"Uh..." I looked in the back—where the deceased were kept. "I don't know."

He winked. "I'm in the business of body measurements, so I can guarantee it would fit you like a custom casket."

If the cemetery went under, Phil had best become a butcher, because his future as a tailor was dead on arrival.

A high-pitched beeping came from my bag.

Moira recoiled. "What've you got in there? The bat phone?"

Annoyance flitted through my chest. She'd already insulted my disguise, and now she was attacking my ringtone. Nevertheless, I pulled out a Nokia Flip.

"A burner phone!" Phil had a gleeful twinkle in his eye.

Moira didn't. "Is this related to Delilah's case?"

"No, a personal matter."

She pulled her handbag to her chest. "I'm starting to wonder if that thug outfit *isn't* a disguise."

Since Moira was getting on my nerves, I wasn't going to calm hers. I flipped open the phone. "Yes, Commissioner?"

"It's the turkey-necked ostrich," Veronica gushed.

"Who's calling?" Moira asked. "The Penguin?"

"Hoo!" Phil slapped the steering wheel. "That quip was right on the money, Moira."

Yeah, but she had the wrong habitat. "Sorry about the interruption," I said into the receiver. "Go on."

Veronica sighed. "You were right about the turkey-necked ostrich eavesdropping on us. She called the black bear and told her you're enroute to Wedding Belles."

The news that Ruth had blabbed my whereabouts to my mom's busybody friend Rosalie confirmed my worst suspicions. My breath came in fits, and I feared I'd become Uber Undertaker's first client. "How..." I huffed, "How long ago?"

Moira pulled the dress over my head, and I shoved my arms through the sleeves to regain phone access.

"Six or so minutes," Veronica said. "It took a while to get my burner phone on."

By now, Rosalie would've called my mom, who would've fired up the Ford Taurus. Luckily, we were on Magazine Street, where the boutique was located. "Okay. I'm on it."

I dropped the phone in my bag. No disguise was going to fool my mom and nonna, so I hoped to get the job done quick. If not, I'd leave Moira to investigate. The caterer was a natural-born homicidal-maniac hunter.

Moira nudged me. "Phil's going to wait for us and take you back to the office."

While I didn't relish the idea of a second ride from hell, it was hotter than Hades out, so walking would've been worse.

Phil eased the hearse to a stop beside cars parked along the street. "Wedding Belles is on the corner. I'll drop you here to be discreet."

There was nothing discreet about a car that carried corpses. Speaking of which, thanks to the flesh-and-pink dress, I climbed from the hearse looking like I'd come from a casket. I opted to leave my bag with Phil and followed Moira to Wedding Belles.

One look inside the boutique's bay window almost sent me running to Phil's funeral car. Women attacked dress racks—and each other—like wild animals. "So much for champagne."

Moira clenched her jaw. "The wedding business is getting more cutthroat."

Exactly what I was afraid of.

"Over there." She pointed to a short, slim blonde holding two wedding gowns at the counter. "That's Grace Blain."

Grace appeared to be waiting for a bridal consultant. I scanned the store layout for a better vantage point. "There's a dress rack behind her. If we follow the ones along the wall, we can listen in on the transaction."

Moira nodded and opened the door. We were hit with a blast of squeals, cries, and the odd obscenity. Not only that, the room reeked of too many perfumes and small wedding budgets.

Resolute, we stooped and began skirting the racks. As we approached the one behind Grace, Moira stopped short, and I slammed into her.

Next thing I knew, a big burly body rear-ended me.

Fists clenched, I turned expecting Rosalie, who was as big around as the black bear I'd nicknamed her for.

Instead, the merry crypt keeper flashed a set of teeth that rivaled those of any skull at Saint Cecilia Cemetery.

"Whoa! Jeez, Phil!" I shouted. "What're you doing in here?"

"Taking a peek at the bridesmaid section." He fluffed his mustache. "Given the nature of Uber Undertaker, it would be good to have nice dresses at the ready."

To quote Veronica, I couldn't argue with that logic. But I really wanted to.

"Aren't you double parked?" Moira asked, ever mindful of the law.

Phil chuckled. "A benefit of driving a hearse in a voodoo-centric city—no one will go near it, not even the police."

I sure as hell wouldn't.

Moira motioned for us to duck.

We did, and the three of us peered through the dresses on the rack. An attractive forty-something female whose professional demeanor and sleek ponytail were clearly under duress had come to the counter.

Grace scowled. "Finally. I don't have all day."

"I'm sorry. Your credit card was declined."

"That's impossible. It's a Black Card."

The consultant's smile showed signs of strain. "Yeees. I'll need another form of payment to cover the difference—preferably one with your name on it?"

Given the Blains' money problems, the card must've belonged to Edward or Lara.

"Uh," Grace shifted to one leg and sized her up, "how about you run the card through again?"

Additional cracks appeared in the consultant's smile and in the pancake makeup on her forehead. "Nooo. I got a message to call the credit card company, and they told me to cut up the card."

"Don't. You. Dare." Grace leaned over the counter. "My father is an attorney, and he'll have this two-bit boutique shut down *stat*." She pulled her phone from her Birkin bag, tapped a button, and pressed it to her ear.

The clerk opened a drawer and drew a weapon—a pair of scissors.

"Heavens," Phil whispered. "This is more fun than the cemetery and Uber combined. Perhaps I should moonlight here."

I didn't know what was creepier—the thought of a crypt-keeper bridal consultant or the fact that he'd referenced "fun" and "cemetery" in the same sentence.

"Daddy?" Grace's high-pitched whine rivaled my bat phone ringtone. "This awful woman at Wedding Belles is going cut up the credit card you gave me."

As I'd suspected, the card was Edward's.

"Can't you stop her?" Grace shouted.

The clerk smirked and smacked the scissors against her palm.

Grace's face went from red to purple. She hung up and grabbed one of the dresses. "You'll regret this, even more than that messy ponytail and makeup that highlights your wrinkles."

The clerk's wrinkles were glaringly evident as she began hacking the card.

Grace stormed from the store right as my mother's Ford Taurus screeched to a stop out front and nonne began piling out.

Phil clasped his hands in wonder. "Goodness me! Is it a *funeral* wedding?"

The clerk's head jerked up, further fraying her ponytail. She dropped the card on the counter and rushed toward the elderly women in black mourning dress flooding into the store.

Capitalizing on the chaos, I dashed to the counter, scooped up the credit card pieces, and escaped through a door marked *Private.*

Moira caught up with me and helped fit the credit card pieces together. But the name on the bottom wasn't Edward Blain.

The Black Card belonged to Agata Villeré.

I shouldn't have been surprised since Lillian and Cordelia overheard Agata say that Edward couldn't afford to pay for Grace's dress.

Moira glowered. "Why did the man give his daughter a dead woman's credit card?"

The answer to that was obvious. What I wanted to know was how Edward had gotten it. *Did Agata give him the card for wedding expenses? Or...*

Did he kill her for it?

10

——————

"It's a warzone out there." Moira peered from the door of the storeroom at Wedding Belles. "Operation Boutique Storm."

"Sounds about right." I pressed *Send* on a text to David, telling him to get me Agata's Black Card bill and skip the ethics lecture or risk unethical harm to his person. "Those brides are worse than bridezillas. Each one could command her own army brigade."

"Who's talking about the brides? It's those Italian grandmas. They're running women out of dressing rooms."

The nonne were either looking for me, or chasing out the brides' whose dresses weren't church appropriate, as in white versions of the black mourning dresses they were wearing. *Actually, probably both*, I thought, as I opened a cabinet in search of a bag to hold the credit card pieces.

"Hey, your nonna is one of them." Moira looked over her shoulder at me. "So is your mother."

I didn't call them Vito and Michael Corleone for nothing. "Why do you think I ran in here?"

She peered through the door. "You'd better keep running. Your mom just pulled a plantation-style dress from the rack."

"Yeahhh," I sighed the word and opened another cabinet. "I've been ignoring her Southern Belle fixation."

"You can't afford to any longer. Check this out." Moira stepped aside.

As a precaution, I threw a veil over my head before peeking into the boutique. Not only had my mom put on the plantation gown, she was carrying a parasol—and twirling. "Tell Phil to get the hearse."

"Gladly," Moira said. "Your family is scaring me."

Not the first time I'd heard that.

"Meet you out back in five." She slipped out the door.

In a cabinet drawer, I found a paper bag and dropped the credit card pieces inside. Then I headed for the exit.

A scream stopped me in my tracks, followed by "*Dio mio!* You can't-a go in a church-a like-a that."

It was my nonna, and I sincerely hoped she was scolding my mother for dressing like Scarlet O'Hara. Against my better judgement, I turned around and took a look.

A nonna with a full mustache and sideburns held up a cut-out wedding gown as a slender brunette looked on in distress. "Madonna mia, Carmela! What would-a the priest-a say about-a these holes?"

"*Sacrilegio,*" Nonna cried, raising a fist.

The brunette, whose face matched the fuchsia bridesmaid gowns Moira was dragging Phil from, balled her fists. "It's no one's business if I want a dress with 'holes,' not yours or my priest's."

Nonne throughout the boutique stopped reproaching young women and crossed themselves.

A portly nonna in a too-tight mourning dress put her hands on her rotund hips. "You want a dress-a wit-a holes?!" She grabbed the scissors the clerk had left on the counter. "I give-a you holes!"

The clerk, who'd been standing as rigid as Lot's wife after she turned into a pillar of salt, sprang to life and dived for the dress—

—just as the nonna took a snip.

Gasps and groans erupted, and the brides blanched in horror.

Because the clerk's ponytail was no longer semi-sleek. It was snipped. Sans body on the black-and-white marble floor.

On that note, I dashed for the exit. There was no way I could afford to foot the damaged dress bill because, unless Shona's library patrons held another book-and-bake sale, I was working her case pro bono. Come to think of it, the financial setback Giada referenced as a sign of the malocchio wasn't the grand I'd paid Glenda to rent Veronica's old apartment, it was Shona.

Gritting my teeth, I pushed open the heavy metal door and turned around to prevent a telltale slam.

As I turned to look for the hearse, I was knocked upside the head.

By a mystery tote.

Full of books.

"Owww!" My hand massaged my skull. "Have you lost your mind?"

Shona was as hot as the bride with the cut-out gown, and I don't mean sexy—although her white skorts were showing a lot of leg. "Ruth called and said you took the day off to shop for your wedding dress," she scream-shouted, "when I'm out here sweating bullets over those wedding invitations the Swamp Sasquatch found."

The next time I saw the turkey-necked ostrich, *she* was getting a knock upside the head for deliberately feeding the Eastern screech owl inflammatory information. "Tone it down and hold your tote. I'm trying not to pay for a dress I didn't damage."

She hiked the tote on her shoulder, revealing her white "Rowing is an oar deal" T-shirt. "When I'm anxious, I can't tone it down."

Super.

"Listen, Shona, I came here to investigate Grace Blain, and I got evidence that could help clear you." I held up the bag with the cut-up credit card.

The hearse careened around the corner and screeched to a stop, billowing smoke from the back like a mobile crematorium. The culprit was burning tire rubber.

But still.

The tinted window rolled down, revealing first Phil's ghoulish grin and then his forearm tattoo of a cat in pajamas. "Your carriage, miladies."

Shona leaned forward, clutching her maniacal mystery tote. "Hey, can you take us to the swamp? We're supposed to meet a cypress hauler."

"Delighted to! I'm a salumi maker myself, and I've been hankering to try some swamp animals in my recipes."

Phil, like Willie Tea, would get along swimmingly with the Swamp Sasquatch.

Shona hopped into the hearse beside Moira.

"Uhhh," my eyes darted to the back of the corpse car, and I stooped to look in Phil's window, "*I* ride shotgun."

She huffed. "Not when I'm having to help *you* investigate. Now take your purse," she handed my hobo bag to Moira, who gave it to Phil, "and jump in back quick. I don't want to pay for the damaged wedding dress, either. You know the library patrons had to foot the bill for this trip."

More proof I wasn't getting paid. *And* that I was sitting in back. Controlling my anger, I took my purse from Phil and straightened.

And I froze like Lot's wife and the clerk.

The barrel of a gun was pressed between my shoulder blades.

"Franki!" Moira pointed around Phil. "The femme fatale!"

The Buick Roadster zipped in front of the hearse and slammed on the brakes, and my assailant ripped the paper bag from my hand.

The woman in red—disguised in bridal white—darted from behind me still holding the gun. She hiked her wedding dress and jumped into the backseat.

As I ran toward the classic car, it sped away.

"Phil!" Shona shrilled. "Follow that femme fatale!"

My ride from hell took off like a devil rocket firework—without me in it.

"*Bienvenue, chère!*" Sylvain Fontaine stood outside his trailer home, stirring a pot over a fire that smoked like the tires on Phil's hearse. "C'mon round over here to de campfire."

The so-called campfire was the size of a bonfire, but it was preferrable to his blow torch. Too bad the swamp was already as sweltering as a sauna in the Sahara Desert, and my mosquito hat didn't help. "Has Shona been here today?"

"Haven't seen hide nor hare o' her."

She was probably still chasing the femme fatale to find out who she was and why she'd taken Agata's cut-up credit card. Personally, I didn't know what to make of the mystery woman's grab-and-run. All I knew was that I hoped Shona stayed gone. After the stunt she'd pulled outside Wedding Belles, I wanted nothing to do with the loud librarian.

Or her mystery tote.

What was more, the next time I saw her, I had every intention to fire her as my client. I was still sweating from my walk back to the office from Wedding Belles, and the huge campfire wasn't helping.

"Speaking o' hide," the Swamp Sasquatch wiped his hands on Nute, his nutria fur-piece, and gestured to the pot, "I whipped up a batch o' summer stew."

Operation Black Swamp came to mind—certainly not because I planned to serve the stew at my wedding, because I would've sooner served one of Chef Mel's roadkill recipes from the Bayou Cuisine cooking school. The issue for me was that the stew was the color and consistency of tar, and it had large chunks of animal in it—possibly the skunk ape Shona had referenced. "Oh, I couldn't possibly."

"Ya sure? Dere ain't nuthin better dan a meal you catch off de swamp land and cook up fresh."

I nodded hard to leave no doubt. After seeing him dunk blackened frog legs in the bacteria-infested water, I could think of countless better meals. Hell, even Phil's cemetery salumi.

My phone rang, and it was Bradley. "Excuse me for a minute. I need to take this."

"You do whatcha need to, chère."

What I needed to do was escape his scary summer stew. I slipped the phone under my hat net and pressed it to my ear. "Hello?"

"Hey, babe. You never answered my text about dinner tonight at Copper Vine. I was hoping we could sneak away from our families for a couple of hours and get some alone time."

"You have no idea how much I'd love that," I said, eyeing the Swamp Sasquatch and that bubbling pot. With him in the vicinity, I couldn't tell Bradley what had happened with the femme fatale outside the bridal boutique. "But, I have to interview

Janine Crawford at Galatoire's at five, and then I need to shower and change before the séance. By the way, are you going to that?"

He half-laughed. "I wouldn't dream of missing a chance to get to the bottom of whether I'm related to Lou Toccato."

My fingers squeezed the phone. "That's not funny, Bradley. Chandra can't ever even *suspect* the two of you are related. Otherwise, she'll show up at every family function with her charm bracelet, and you know what'll happen next."

"Yep. Her arm will shoot up, the bracelet will jangle, and she'll channel a spirit conveniently linked to your current homicide investigation."

A memory of Bradley's mother, Lillian, wearing a charm bracelet strikingly similar to Chandra's hit me like one of Chandra's uninvited spirits. But the women's shared taste in jewelry was only a bizarre coincidence. Bradley was related to Lou, not Chandra. If there was one consolation in the family connection, it was that. "Don't forget that she also charges me for those spirits she channels."

"Oh, I haven't. But it's not like we'll invite the Toccatos for Christmas, Franki." He paused. "Just the non-gift-exchanging holidays, like New Year's, Memorial Day, July 4th..."

Fireworks exploded in my head. "Bradley—"

"...and weddings, showers, and special events."

An image of Chandra jangling that charm bracelet over me in the delivery room caused me to break out in sweat as thick as the Swamp Sasquatch's summer stew. "BRADLEY!"

"I'm *kidding*, babe."

Sighing, I wiped the fear from my forehead. "That's a relief, because after tonight, I want to be done with her psychic shenanigans."

"Then you can rest easy. We don't have any contact with my mother's side of the family. I never even knew my grandmother's maiden name until that PI Veronica hired figured it out. I only knew her as a Linde."

I wouldn't have said this to Bradley, but I had a feeling that Cordelia had kept her maiden name quiet, and hence her Italian origins, to fit in with upper-crust Boston society. Why she now embraced being a Toccato, I didn't know. But I needed her to go back to hiding it.

Before the séance.

Chandra was a swamp animal, the common loon. And if Cordelia told her that Bradley and Lou were related, that cuckoo bird would show up at my shower and every family function thereafter, invite or no, spewing spirit schmatter and billing me for it.

A beep sounded on the other end of the line.

"Duty calls," Bradley drawled. "Why don't we just shoot for dinner tomorrow?"

"Sounds good. See you at the séance." I hung up and immediately felt bad for not telling him I loved him. But not that bad. His Chandra jokes had left a sour taste in my mouth.

But not as sour as the thought of the summer stew.

The Swamp Sasquatch took a slurpy sip of the black goo, tilted his head, and smacked his lips too many times. "Dang, dat's good. You're gonna want a bowl o' dis, Franki." He returned the wooden spoon to the pot. "I was afraid de rat would overpower it, but you can really taste de spider."

My hands shot up in a stop gesture. Those weren't ingredients I'd put together.

Or apart.

"Maybe some other time." I flashed a smile. "I've got an early dinner. I came out because I was hoping you'd show me those tire tracks where you found the Blain-Adair wedding invitations."

"Sure thing, chère. Jus' give me a minute to close up de

kitchen." He put the pot on a stump stool and poured a bucket of swamp water on the fire. Then he retrieved a board from the ground and used it to cover the pot. "Gotta keep dem bugs out."

He should've thought of that before he'd added the spiders.

The Swamp Sasquatch led me to an old blue Chevy truck that looked like the brides from Wedding Belles had used it on a dress reconnaissance mission and been caught in a siege with a warring bridal-boutique faction. On top of a rusted frame and a battered front end, the windshield was shattered, and the driver door was missing.

I removed my mosquito hat and climbed into the passenger seat.

And I flattened against what remained of the back-rest cushion.

A snake as thick as a fire hose was coiled around the rearview mirror.

"Aw, that's jus' Puppy." The Swamp Sasquatch stroked the snake's skin. "He don' bite. He's a python, so he swallows his food whole."

As if on cue, Puppy raised his head and stared straight at me.

A fresh round of sweat broke out on my lip and forehead—over the pre-existing layer of perspiration. "J-just the same, could he please stay here?"

"Let's go, Puppy." He grabbed the snake. "The lady wants ta ride in peace."

That's p-i-e-c-e, I mentally corrected, *as in, one.*

Outside the snake's insides.

The Swamp Sasquatch carried Puppy to a grassy spot near the pot and pointed at the python. "Don' even think 'o eatin' my summer stew, now." Grinning, he bounded back to the truck and slid into the driver seat. "Cain't trust no one around a rat stew, especially not a python."

"You can trust me," I said earnestly.

He started the engine. "Dem tire tracks are a mile or so up de road."

I was happy to hear it. Sylvain's things were full of unpleasant surprises, starting with Nute and hopefully ending with Puppy the python. And honestly, the hearse was more comfortable than his truck. Something pricked at my bottom, and I was praying it was a protruding cushion coil.

We drove in silence as swamp smells invaded the open truck. Salt, sulfur, something dead. We came upon a marshy area with a yellow reed-like plant. "Dey call dat smooth cordgrass. It grows up ta seven foot."

All I could think of was what might be hiding in it.

A gator.

A body.

A killer.

"Dis is it." He turned into the grass, and I found out what lurked inside.

A gray Mercedes—with Edward Blain beside it.

The picture I'd seen online hadn't prepared me for his size. The man was massive. He carried his weight in his upper body, and he was almost as tall as the smooth cordgrass.

"Wonder what dis fella is doing," the Swamp Sasquatch muttered, parking behind the Mercedes.

My first thought was, *Looking for the wedding invitations he dropped?*

"Bad thing is," he shut off the engine, "he parked on dem tire tracks."

Which prompted my next thought, *Is Edward literally covering his tracks?*

The Swamp Sasquatch slid from the seat. "Can I help ya, mister?"

Beneath Edward's low brow, his gray eyes turned black. "Who are you?"

"Sylvain Fontaine. I live out here."

Edward shot me a questioning stare.

"I'm a PI, investigating the murder of your wife's great aunt and Delilah Delaire, the wedding planner—"

"I know who Delilah Delaire is," he interrupted with a hard stare.

Undaunted, I stepped forward. "Because she planned your daughter's wedding? Or because you threatened her after she overheard your phone call in the study at the Columns? Something about a 'black swamp?'"

His body tensed, but his stare relaxed. "Because I paid the wedding bills."

"That's not what Agata told the guests at the rehearsal dinner."

"The woman was a hundred and two. She wasn't in her right mind." He'd uttered that information in the rehearsed tone of a defense lawyer.

The guy was despicable. "Actually, she *was* in her right mind. Because today your daughter, Grace, tried to use Agata's Black Card to upgrade her wedding dress, and she called you to complain when the clerk said she had to cut it up."

His brow dropped further, and every one of my cells went on alert. My body recognized what my brain already knew.

Edward Blain was fully capable of murder.

His face went flat, as though controlling his expression. "I see you're willing to lie to cover for your client. Speaking of Ms. Helper, I came to look for the jewels she hid after she killed Agata. But since you're out here, I'm guessing you already know where they are."

I looked him in the eyes. "Shona didn't kill anyone or steal those jewels. But since *you're* out here, I'm guessing *you* did."

"Remember who you're talking to, lady. You'd best watch what you say and steer clear of my family, or I'll see you in court." He spun and climbed into the Mercedes, slamming the door.

A familiar scent wafted from the car.

The perique tobacco I'd smelled in Agata's room at the Columns.

Edward backed the Mercedes from the cordgrass, glaring at me before turning the vehicle and speeding away.

"Well, looky here." The Swamp Sasquatch squatted and pointed to the ground. "You can still see de old tire tracks beside de new ones."

I stooped to study the tread patterns.

They matched.

Edward Blain's car had been here before. *Had Edward?*

If so, why?

He certainly could've been searching for Agata's jewels, but there was another possibility I couldn't ignore.

Edward had hidden the jewels himself, and he'd come to make sure they were safe and sound where he'd left them.

Rising to my feet, I gazed at the smooth cordgrass.

Had it been hiding a killer?

11

———

"*That's* what you wear to Friday lunch?" Janine Crawford's watery eyes registered their disapproval of my Saints jersey from beneath the hood of her vintage white gown.

Resisting the urge to point out that it was Wednesday dinner, I nodded at her attire. "That's what *you* wear to Friday lunch?"

"I look like Marlene Dietrich," she said, looking every bit like Yoda in blood-red lipstick. "You look like a hooligan."

Better than a "thug," to quote Moira, but Janine was one to talk with her hoodie dress. I took a seat at the corner table and winced at the bottle of Dom Perignon on ice. My ego could withstand her critical eye, but my least-maxed-out credit card might not survive her expensive taste.

"See that woman?" She pointed at a costumed figure heading for the stairs. "She's dressed nice."

The woman was clearly a member of the Merry Antoinettes because she was in full Marie Antoinette mode from the pouf down to the pannier and the pearls in between. It wasn't Mardi Gras, but the krewe was known to participate in charity events year around. And based on the ruckus coming from the second-floor dining room, there was either a party going on or another French Revolution in progress.

I glanced at Janine, questioning the state of her eyesight. "Eighteenth-century court clothes are exaggerated even for Galatoire's."

"It's always better to be overdressed than underdressed."

Overdressed was one word for it. The hips on the Merry Antoinette's getup were as wide as my Mustang. "I'll remember that."

I poured myself a full flute of the champagne I was paying for, because I was going to need it. "I asked you to meet me today to find out more information about Agata Villerè and her sister, Pia. You said their mother was Italian. Do you know if she was from Benevento?"

"The infamous witch town? Possibly. Thanks to the way she pitted her daughters against each other, they had a Blanche-Baby Jane relationship."

The frightful film reference prompted a mental replay of the organ music from the church behind Giada's mansion. It was disturbing that *Whatever Happened to Baby Jane?* would keep coming up. "What did their mother do to them, exactly?"

"She forced those girls into vaudeville and paraded them around town like dolls. Every Sunday, she made them wear their finest clothes, then she sat them on the front porch of the Columns and kept track of who got the most shouts from passersby on the streetcar. The winner got to eat an ice cream sundae while the other watched." She smacked her lips. "The winner was always Pia."

That explained Agata's personal connection to the hotel—and why she might've hated her sister enough to kill her.

Janine picked up the salt shaker and dropped it into her handbag.

My head cocked to the side. *Did she just...?*

The pepper shaker joined its mate.

She did.

"Um," I scratched my neck, "the salt and pepper *inside* the shakers is free, but not the shakers themselves."

"Oh, foo. They're included in the price of the bill."

The one I was paying.

A man sitting alone at the table next to us rose to take a phone call.

Janine reached over and swiped his knife and fork, adding them to the clandestine collection.

My head snapped around to make sure no one saw her put them into her bag. None of the other diners seemed to be staring our way, but regardless, I was sweating worse than I had at the swamp. Friday lunch on Wednesday at dinner with Janine Crawford was seriously stressful. "Listen—"

"Your order, ladies," a dour-faced waiter interrupted, holding a tray of food.

Janine cleared space for plates. "I took the liberty of ordering appetizers."

And a hundred-dollar bottle of Dom.

The waiter placed the food in front of her. "Shrimp cocktail, oysters Rockefeller, escargot, and fried eggplant."

This meal had all the makings of the financial setback related to my malocchio, but at least the eating would keep Janine's thieving hands busy. Nevertheless, the waiter had left, so I decided to get on with the questioning before she stole the table and chairs out from under us. "When we met at the Camellia Grill, you mentioned Agata's jewelry collection. Did you hear that it's missing?"

"No, but I expected as much."

Funny, because I hadn't. "Why would you say that?"

"Edward killed Agata to pay off his debts and live high on the hog." She swigged champagne, leaving a gory lipstick print on the flute. "He'll want to sell those jewels, but Lara and that greedy Grace won't hear of it. They've been waiting all their lives to see and be seen in those gems."

"Why are you so sure Edward killed Agata?"

Janine's stare was pointed. "When you're as old as I am, you know the obvious."

After my encounter with Edward at the swamp, I thought he'd killed Agata too. But neither my instinct nor the wisdom of Janine's age constituted proof.

"Another thing that's obvious," she picked up a shrimp, "others will come for those jewels."

The "others" startled me, especially since Shona was accused of stashing Agata's jewelry at the swamp. "Do you mean other relatives?"

"Maybe." She dipped the shrimp into her champagne instead of the cocktail sauce, which was weird, but at least she hadn't stolen the cocktail glass.

Yet.

Following the shrimp spectacle, I bypassed my champagne in favor of water. "Who else would try to get the jewels?"

"Anyone Agata cheated to get her hands on them, like the rightful heir to Bette Davis's canary yellow diamond ring from *Jezebel.*"

Gasps erupted in the restaurant.

"Off with her head," a woman cried.

Is management coming for Janine? Surveying the scene, I spotted the reason for the bizarre cry.

A four-foot guillotine held by a gaggle of Merry Antoinettes.

The murder weapon wasn't merry. It was scary. And I was starting to wonder whether I'd been right about a French Revolution underway upstairs.

Janine swallowed and watched the self-described "scandalous party queens" carry the guillotine upstairs. "Some people will call me an old fool, but I know Marie Antoinette's pearls are the reason Agata was killed."

That comment was as surprising as her kleptomania. "The pearls? Why?"

"Marie Antoinette wore them with the Hope Diamond. You familiar with that?"

"Vaguely," I said, pretty sure Veronica had mentioned it.

"It was a big blue diamond that a 17th-century French gem dealer stole from the eye of a Hindu statue. The priests then put a curse on anyone who had the stone, and the dealer up and died from a fever. That diamond has caused death and destruction ever since. Suicides, murders, cars going over cliffs."

I shuddered. Not from the story. Janine had dipped fried eggplant in the cocktail sauce, but that wasn't the gross part. The eggplant was covered in powdered sugar like a beignet. If I were French, I'd stage a revolution over a crime like that.

Janine took another slug of champagne. "Louis XIV bought the diamond from the gem dealer before he got the fever, and then he died from gangrene." Her lips puckered. "Had a touch of it once myself. My toes began to rot, and I lost the nails."

I chugged my champagne, trying to kill the images of Janine's feet, not to mention the one of a toenail-less Maybe Baby doing lap dances. "I take it Marie Antoinette inherited the diamond?"

She nodded. "And we all know what happened to her."

Not least because of the guillotine the Merry Antoinettes had carried into the restaurant.

"After that, the diamond went to her closest confidante, the Princess de Lamballe, who died right away. Then it passed through a series of owners, killing pretty much all of them. If you ever want to see the diamond, it's on display at The Smithsonian."

Not a chance. Given my malocchio, a cursed eye jewel could

be my death knell. "Surely Agata didn't own the Hope Diamond?"

"No, but Marie Antoinette used it as a clasp for her pearls, so they're cursed too. And if you ask me, the curse is the reason those pearls hadn't been seen in public for 200 years until Agata bought them at the Sotheby's auction for 2.5 million."

"Wow. I knew Agata had money, but that's a lot to pay for pearls."

Janine shrugged. "She used the life insurance payout from Pia's death. Why do you think she killed her?"

My jaw dropped, both because of the revelation and because Janine was salting the escargot with the shaker she'd stolen.

She opened her handbag, and the shaker was stolen again. "Agata was obsessed with jewels, and Pia wasn't the only one she murdered to get them. That Bette Davis ring belonged to her maid, who told Agata that she'd inherited it from her movie-producer uncle and needed to sell it. Then out of the blue the poor woman falls ill and dies. The next day, Agata produced a newly signed will from the maid bequeathing the ring to her."

If Janine's assertions were true, then the phrase "only the good die young" explained how Agata had lived to be one hundred and two. "Did this maid have family?"

"Sure did." Janine rubbed a pat of butter on her hands, which now seemed normal. "They went to the police but that got them nowhere, even though the doctors never could diagnose the cause of the maid's death. I wouldn't be surprised if one of them comes for that ring now that Agata is dead."

As I digested the news, along with an oyster, I wondered whether one of the maid's heirs already had.

❧

"THE FEMME FATALE pulled a *gun* on you?" Bradley's voice erupted in my ear.

Wincing, I switched the call to speaker and put the phone on the console. The last thing I needed was to crash the Mustang and have to rely on rideshare drivers. Like Phil. "She obviously wasn't out to kill me, or she would've pulled the trigger."

He gave a sharp exhale. "Still, it's not good that she's armed."

My back and I were well aware of that. So aware, in fact, that I pressed the spot between my shoulder blades into the seat to check whether it was bruised.

Yep.

I turned onto St. Charles Street. "The only thing she wanted was Agata's credit card, which makes me think she's investigating whoever killed her and Delilah too. She might even be the Bette Davis ring heir that Janine Crawford mentioned."

"Or she wanted to destroy the credit card because she's Edward's accomplice in the murders. For all we know, he stashed the jewels at the swamp so the two of them could run off together."

An entirely plausible scenario.

A high-pitched beep sounded, and I shot a side-eye at my bag.

What now?

"Bradley, Veronica's calling. I've got to go."

"She is? I didn't hear a beep on the line."

I froze. For security reasons, I hadn't told him about the burner phone or Operation Black Swamp. "Uh… I meant that I have to call *her* about the séance."

"Okay, but let me know when you get to the Columns, and I'll come out to meet you. I don't want you walking in the dark alone."

"K. Love you." As I hung up, I felt guilt about the fib but there was no time to wallow in it. If the burner phone was beeping, it meant a swamp animal was on the move. I dug the Nokia Flip from my bag. "What's going on?"

"The turkey-necked ostrich is tailing me," Veronica paused, "in a *hearse*."

Ruth hired Phil too? Forget Uber Undertaker, the guy should rebrand as Uber Underground—When you need to stalk a live body on the downlow. "It's that cemetery caretaker I know. He's driving as a side gig."

"Well, what should I do? I'm almost at the Columns."

I glanced in the rearview mirror to make sure they weren't behind me. "You've got to lose her. It's bad enough that the common loon is holding the séance. I can't have any other swamp animals in attendance. They'll start chittering, and before you know it, their animal instincts will figure out that the bridal shower is this Saturday."

"I'll do my best."

"Do better than your best," I said, a tad testy. "Put your race-car-driving skills to work, and hurry. The séance starts in fifteen minutes."

"Fine. But watch out, Franki, because you're starting to sound like a bridezilla." She hung up.

"At least I'm not one of those brides from Wedding Belles." I shoved the phone back into my bag and focused on the task at hand. I'd arrived at the Columns, but because Ruth was on the hunt, I passed the hotel and turned down a side street to park out of sight.

As I searched for a space, I couldn't help but admire the old mansions. A two-story Italianate house caught my eye, and I slowed to a stop. It had arched windows and doors reminiscent of a Tuscan villa and a magnificent old tree in the yard. The only thing I didn't appreciate were the oddly placed bushes that dotted the lawn.

"Wait. Is it my imagination, or are those bushes moving?" I

don't know why, but I thought of Willie Tea. Then I squinted and saw a sight almost as terrifying as Glenda emerging from the cemetery in her Hucci Cucci Hot *Cart*ure.

Those weren't bushes.

They were women in black dresses.

Surrounding the tree!

"*Janare*," I whisper-breathed.

My foot floored the gas pedal, and I steered out of there Daytona-500 style. "Uh-uh. No. Not happening," I said to myself. "I've already got the malocchio, my family, and swamp animals to contend with. I simply cannot afford to attract the attention of rogue witches."

After a few seconds, I rounded the block. It wasn't every day you saw witches gathered around a tree, so they had to be connected to the case.

I pulled up next door to the mansion and took a closer look at the scary scene.

"Oh, God." The back of my skull pounded the headrest.

Because the women in black weren't janare.

They were nonne.

And up the street was the Ford Taurus.

"That explains why no one was at my apartment causing double, double toil and trouble when I went to shower," I grumbled, shutting off the engine. I got out of the car and walked up the sidewalk.

My mother stood on the edge of the yard in one of nonna's mourning dresses, staring up at the tree. Next to her was a large bowl filled with salt, or maybe sugar.

"Uh, Mom?"

She jumped and pressed her hand to her heart. "Good heavens, Francesca! What are you doing lurking around like that?"

The irony of the question was completely lost on her. "I'm

going to a séance." My pitch rose with every word. "What are *you* doing lurking around in someone's yard?"

Irritation flickered across her face. "Keep your voice down, dear. The homeowners are out of town, and we don't want the neighbors to know we're out here."

"You haven't answered my question."

"Uffà!" Nonna shuffled over, holding a bottle of pure grain alcohol. "It's-a the night of-a San Giovanni. We've gotta pick-a the walnuts to make-a the nocino for your malocchio."

I yawned.

Twice.

Psychosomatic much?

Two nonne in mourning veils approached, and I was shocked to see the faces of Giada and Moira behind the tulle. "What are you two doing in nonna clothes?"

Moira's lids lowered. "I'm in hiding from a killer, remember?"

"Also," Giada raised her veil, "we didn't want anyone to see us and call the cops. But don't worry. The people who live here are friends of mine, and they won't mind that we're taking some walnuts. They never pick them."

Which raised the question of who *was* picking them—in accordance with the terms of the tradition. I surveyed the unlikely crew. Not a virgin among them, much less one in white. I looked up at the tree to see who they'd rustled up to do the picking, and a walnut cracked me on the forehead. "Ow!"

"Stop standing around," a voice boomed from high in the tree—alerting neighbors in a three-block radius, "and pick up those walnuts."

The virgin walnut picker was Shona. In her white skorts and "Rowing is an oar deal" T-shirt.

Given this intimate revelation, I was surprised she'd abandoned her romance tote in favor of the mystery one. There was only one thing left to ask. "How the hell did you all end up together?"

Moira checked for onlookers before raising her veil. "When Shona and I went after the femme fatale, your Mom and nonna and a whole lot of FIATs followed us."

My mother shook her head. "Unfortunately, the femme fatale gave us the slip, dear, and you did too because you weren't in the hearse like I'd thought. It's a shame because I'd found the perfect dress for you. It had a hoop skirt and seven petticoats."

From the sound of things, I'd not only dodged a bullet from the femme fatale, I'd also dodged one from my mother—in the form of a dress that would've killed my wedding dead. Even so, I was still going to fire Shona for leaving me to walk back to the office in the heat of summer.

"Like I told-a you, Brenda," Nonna's eyes gleamed in triumph, "my *nipote* knows-a better than-a to ride in a hearse when she's-a gotta the double malocchio," she jerked a thumb at Giada, "and the bad-a luck of-a this-a one-a here, who is-a the daughter of a bone-a collector."

"A bone *biographer*," Giada corrected.

Either way you defined bioarchaeology, it was a bummer. "Actually, Nonna, I should've been in that hearse, but someone left me behind, which brings me to my next point." I glared up at the tree. "You're fired."

Shona leaned out from a limb. "You can't do that! You work for me."

"Have you paid me for my services?"

"No."

"Then I don't work for you."

Shona scrambled down the tree trunk and trotted up to me, her round chest puffed. "So you're going to desert me in my time of need?"

"You don't need me. You've got your mystery tote."

She gasped and leapt back.

Turning to head to the Columns, I ran smack into the turkey-necked ostrich.

Ruth's turkey-neck contorted in the moonlight. "Did I hear you right? You just fired a paying client?"

"She's not a 'paying client,' Ruth. She didn't even pay for her trip to New Orleans. Her library patrons held a book-and-bake sale to cover the costs."

Ruth spun on Shona. "You're *fired*, missy."

Silence ensued.

A woman's scream sliced through the night. Actually *two*.

One came from Shona.

The other came from the Columns—where my fiancé was.

"Bradley!" I broke into a run.

12

My breath was failing as I ran up St. Charles, but I wouldn't stop. I couldn't. I had to keep going until I found Bradley and his family safe and sound.

Hopefully.

Pulse pounding, I hurdled the steps to the Columns porch, threw open the door, and raced up the long entryway. Apart from the glow of the candles on the old piano by the chapel alcove in the lounge, the hotel was ominously dark. Even scarier, the bar was closed, which didn't happen in New Orleans. Not even during a hurricane.

Or after a murder.

Passing the unmanned reception desk, my feet pummeled the grand staircase.

But I felt as though I was moving in slow motion.

And seconds seemed to take minutes.

One...

Two...

Three...

Meanwhile, I didn't hear a living soul.

Except for me.

I reached the second floor-landing and doubled over. Not from grief, but relief.

Bradley and his mother, Lillian, were helping Cordelia down the stairs from the third floor.

Gathering my wits about me, I straightened. "I heard a scream. Is everything alright?"

Lillian gripped Cordelia's arm as they went down a step, failing to meet my gaze. "Mother saw the ghost of the Woman in White."

"I'm sorry I caused such a fuss." Cordelia's gray eyes were haunted. "But she startled me. She was so real…"

Bradley shot me a skeptical look as he eased his grandmother to the landing.

I took Cordelia's hands. They were ice cold. "Where did you see her?"

"In the ballroom."

"What were you doing in there?"

"The air-conditioning gave me a chill," she pulled her wrap tighter, "so I went to get my shawl before the séance."

Lillian gestured up the stairs. "You have to cross the ballroom to get to our hallway, but it's really just an open space in the middle of the floor."

Cordelia looked at her diamond watch. "It's almost ten. Chandra should be arriving for the séance."

Exactly the motivation I needed to drive me to hunt a ghost. "Y'all go ahead to the room. I'm going to take a peek upstairs."

"Franki, wait." Bradley put his hand on my shoulder. "I'll go with you."

"Stay with your grandmother. This will only take a minute."

He nodded, but his eyes were guarded.

Gripping the railing, I started up the stairs. I understood why Cordelia needed help coming down. The steps leaned inward, as though the house was beginning to collapse in on itself, which did nothing for the butterflies in my stomach. Because the Columns had a creepy side, and even though I didn't believe in ghosts, I did believe in homicidal maniacs.

Like Edward Blain.

Maybe Vick and his nonnina, Brunella.

And definitely that bloodthirsty kitchen manager, Edith Cook.

Arriving on the third floor, I saw what Lillian had been talking about. The so-called ballroom was nothing more than a small dance floor in the middle of the house with black columns running down the center. Along one wall were two chairs positioned around a marble coffee table and a black vanity with an oval mirror. On either side of the space were hallways.

One of which glowed red.

"Interesting color choice." It was probably an homage to the film *Pretty Baby* and the Storyville Red-Light District it depicted. Nevertheless, I entered the hallway to investigate.

As I'd expected, there were doors to the rooms, but there was one thing I hadn't anticipated. At one end of the hallway, a half dozen steps led to a black door. Directly above it was the red light, illuminating odd messages painted in gold on the front of each step. They were disconnected phrases, semi-disappearing in the harsh red glare, like fragments of thought from people who'd departed and were suspended between this world and the next.

...day to create...

...more ways...

...to love your...

Goosebumps pricked my arms. It was exactly the kind of place a ghost would haunt, but that wasn't the issue. The door was just plain weird, and I wasn't sure I wanted to know what was behind it.

Nevertheless, I crept closer. The butterflies in my stomach

had grown bat sized. Buying time, I paused to check the handles of the other doors lining the hallway.

All locked, dang it.

Reluctantly, I tiptoed up the steps and read the messages on the door.

Bain de Sousse

Sun-bathing

Soon to be rest stop for the dreamers

"Ah. A harmless rooftop area." Still, my hand trembled as I gripped the handle.

Locked too.

"Well, whatever's going on at the Columns, it's not a ghost."

Retracing my steps, I re-entered the ballroom and almost jumped from my skin. No Woman in White. Just my reflection in the vanity mirror.

Apparently, I wasn't entirely convinced of the not-a-ghost bit.

Taking a final look around the ballroom, I spotted an open book on the marble coffee table. "Better to flip through that than listen to Chandra's psychobabble."

Taking a seat, I checked the cover. Volume XXIX of *The Encyclopedia Americana*. Returning to the page, my eyes landed on an entry for *werewolf*. I was surprised to learn that people in the Middle Ages believed witches turned themselves into werewolves and other animals by anointing themselves with ointment and putting on an enchanted girdle.

The legend reminded me of the janare and the unguent they spread under their arms to fly. If I believed in such things, I would've sworn the swamp animals were greased-up witches in magic girdles. But there was a big problem with that theory—Glenda would never wear such a garment. Now, an enchanted *thong*? Absolutely.

With a sigh, I rose and went downstairs to Room 10.

Chairs were positioned around the bed where Agata had

died. Giada, Moira, Shona, and Ruth, sat on the bathroom side, and Cordelia, Lillian, Bradley, and Veronica sat on the balcony side. The only open chair was at the foot of the bed.

Veronica spotted me in the doorway. "Franki, take my seat next to Bradley."

I strolled over to her. "You keep it." I looked at my fiancé. "No offense, babe, but I want to be close to the exit in case Chandra brought her charm bracelet."

He half-smiled. "None taken. Did you see anything suspicious upstairs?"

"Yes, a lone-wolf volume of *The Encyclopedia Americana.*"

His brow arched in confusion, but under the terms of Operation Black Swamp, I couldn't explain why that was unsettling.

"Excuse us for a second." I pulled Veronica to a corner of the room. "You were supposed to lose Ruth."

"I tried, but she lost *me.*" She folded her arms in defeat. "She's crafty."

"Like a turkey-necked-ostrich fox." I glared at Ruth, whose sonar was up like a turkey-necked-ostrich-fox bat. "Speaking of crafty, where are my mom and nonna?"

"They went back to your apartment. Your nonna and the other nonne refused to come because séances are against the Catholic religion."

And yet they'd enthusiastically participated in a pagan walnut-picking tradition.

Shona's gaze locked onto mine. "Apparently, supporting one's friends in their time of need is against the Catholic religion too."

Ruth glowered at her. "Pipe down, freeloader."

"*Freeloader?*" Shona blew out a breath. "I guess you didn't study Latin, because it's called 'pro bono.'"

Ruth tipped her head forward like a turkey-necked-ostrich

bull about to charge. "And I guess you didn't study Spanish, because it's called 'no bueno.'"

I watched the know-it-all-off enrapt. In an unexpected séance development, someone else was the target of Ruth's wrath.

Moira raised her veil. "Don't worry, Shona. I've got your back. It's a rough world out there, and we women have to stick together."

"Oh," Giada's eyes widened, "I'm sure Franki feels the same. Right, cousin?" she prodded with a nod. "Given your *predicament*?"

My "predicament" was a clear reminder of my malocchio—as if I could forget it at this godforsaken séance. "No, because they didn't stick with me at Wedding Belles."

Moira and Shona dropped their jaws in shock.

Ruth snorted at the supportive duo. "There you have it. If you two want camaraderie, we're going to need cold, hard cash."

Another unforeseen séance development—I agreed with Ruth Walker.

Veronica tapped my arm and pointed at the door.

A pudgy hand with paddle nails was feeling around the wall. The fingers found the light switch and shut off the chandelier. Then the hand slid from sight, and the door slammed shut.

Shona spun in her chair. "Who did that?"

"The Crescent City Medium," I said with dread, "in preparation for her grand entrance." I turned to Veronica. "Time to get this Chandra show on the road."

We took our seats.

Light streamed in the window from the streetlamp below, so I took a moment to survey the room, remembering the guest complaints Edith Cook had rattled off—cold spots, mysterious toilet flushes, an apparition of a middle-aged woman sitting on the bed or sobbing on the side of the tub, a ghost staring in the windows.

Despite my odd experience on the third floor, I still wasn't worried about a spirit showing up. The only thing that spooked me was Chandra finding out Bradley had Toccato blood.

I shuddered. That was a haunted house and horror show all in one.

A dull thump interrupted my awful thought, and another came to me—Maybe we *were* being watched by a shadow of a human, i.e., Edward Blain.

My eyes shot to the window overlooking the balcony.

No one was there.

The door opened, and everyone jumped.

A glowing orb appeared, surrounded by a sparkling shimmer.

And a huge alien head?

"Everybody take cover," Shona bellowed and dropped low. "It's a spirit!"

The orb—a.k.a. Chandra's light-up crystal ball—hit the floor, and Chandra herself leapt into my lap. "Oomph!"

"Is it Agata?" she shrieked in her Boston accent. Her moon-pie face, made even larger by her teased brunette-and-blonde bob, peered fearfully from the Esmeralda-from-*Bewitched* collar of her silver sequin dress. "Or the Woman in White?"

A deep regret overtook my soul. I should've thought to bring the Demon-Be-Gone smudge stick and Uncrossing candle Madge had sold me—not to ward off an evil spirit, but an ersatz psychic. "Chill out, okay?" I unwrapped her arms from around my neck, relieved she wasn't wearing her charm bracelet. "Shona thought *you* were the spirit."

"Yeah," Shona barked, "your crystal ball lit up the sequins on your dress and made you look mystical."

Chandra rolled her eyes. "*That* was the idea."

Given her attitude, I pushed her off my lap. Clearly, Chandra wasn't a weightless ghost, and her Pillsbury Doughboy body type wasn't light and airy like a pastry, either. Plus, I had no time for a snarky psychic.

She checked her crescent-moon earrings and then gathered her crystal ball and her composure. "Evidently, we need a lesson in séance etiquette before we start." Her tiny mouth puckered. "First, no talking and no shouting. Otherwise, you'll spook the spirits."

All eyes went to Shona.

"Second," Chandra ticked a paddle nail, "take pictures and post them on social media with #CrescentCityMedium #Stellar-Psychic #AllPaymentMethodsAccepted."

Ruth cocked her jaw. "Since when does etiquette involve pushing someone's services?"

"Strictly verboten at Delilah Delaire," Moira said.

Chandra gave her behemoth bob a bump, revealing a flash of tiara embedded in the teased hair. "What I do is a public service. It's not about money."

A male groan came from out of nowhere, followed by a thud.

Chandra spun and stared at the bathroom, her paddle nails pressing her chest.

We all looked at Bradley, who shook his head. Then we eyed each other, wondering the same thing. *Was Chandra's statement so outrageous that an actual spirit had weighed in?*

Nahhh, she probably recruited her husband, Lou, to play the part of the spirits.

"Well, then," Chandra walked to the side of the bed where Cordelia sat and bowed as though she were royalty, "let's summon the spirit of Agata Villeré."

Everyone nodded, eager to shrug off the unexplained occurrence.

She placed the crystal ball on the bed, and its glow made me wonder yet again what Sick Vick had put in my nocino to make my throat radiate—and whether he'd conspired with Edward to poison the cappuccino that killed Agata. One thing I was sure of was that we weren't going to find that out from the séance—if the Chandra sham even happened. She was having trouble climbing on the bed.

Chandra raised a chubby leg, but the bed was too tall for her to slide on. She took a step back, leapt forward, and just missed the top. Determined to conquer the uncooperative bed, she leaned over the side, dug her elbows into the mattress, and serpentined toward the center, her legs sticking straight out. The decorative blanket bunched up, and she slid backwards. In desperation, she gripped the duvet cover and pulled it and the crystal ball to the floor with her.

"For crying out loud." Ruth rose to her feet. "I need to get home in time to catch up on *Dr. Pimple Popper*. Lean over the bed and put your arms over your head."

Chandra, whose face was as red as someone who'd had a laser peel, complied.

Ruth yanked her to the middle of the mattress, tossed the now dark crystal ball after her, and sat down.

Cordelia cleared her throat. "Is there a problem with your crystal ball?"

"Of course not," Chandra scoffed, eager to keep the job she was doing so selflessly in service of the public. "It's a sign from the spirits that they'd rather speak to us directly."

Or a sign that the light was damaged after falling repeatedly on the wood floor.

"I'll channel Agata through her spot on the bed." Chandra adjusted her Esmeralda collar, lay against the salmon-colored pillows, and spread her arms at her side. "Agata," she said in a low, summoning voice, "are you among us?"

Ruth hmphed. "How much is she getting paid for this alleged public service?"

Chandra rose on her elbows. "Did you listen to the séance etiquette lesson?"

"I did, but I spent a small fortune on an Uber to get here, so I expect a little theater."

It pained me, but I agreed with Ruth again, which made me question who and what I'd become and whether malocchio was a factor. "Honestly, she's got a point, Chandra."

Giada clapped to get our attention. "Silence! Mrs. Toccato is trying to work."

Chandra contemplated Giada. "Who are *you*?"

"Franki's second cousin."

"You might want to check your genealogical tree, because Franki and her family aren't even slightly considerate."

My gaze ricocheted from Chandra to Bradley's taken-aback mother and grandmother and back to the mouthy medium. She was lucky the bed was surrounded by witnesses. Otherwise, I would've shoved the burned-out ball into her 'bonce.' *Or is it 'gob?'*

Chandra returned to her supine position and closed her eyes. "Come to us, Agata. Tell us who murdered you in cold blood."

The door opened.

Everyone gasped, and Chandra shot up.

The specter of Agata didn't enter. Glenda did in a sheer white G-string and bralette so tiny it was essentially two pasties attached by a thread. She dragged off her cigarette holder and exhaled a ghostly smoke ring. "My favorite kind of audience. Awed and slack jawed."

Bradley stood and gestured to his seat.

"Mr. Hartman, honey," Glenda licked her lips, "you *do* know how to treat a lady."

Lillian paled and coughed, and Cordelia patted her back.

Glenda flicked her cigarette into the fireplace and settled in beside Lillian and Cordelia, who were as white as if they'd seen a stripper ghost. But the truth was they'd just seen Glenda's lady parts up close.

"*Ahem.*" Chandra scowled at Glenda. "I'm trying to work."

Glenda turned to Veronica. "You didn't tell me this was a sexy séance, Miss Ronnie."

"What?" Moira ripped off her veil. "Is *that* why she's on the bed?"

Chandra's arm shot up. "Stop right there."

"Hey, no judgement." Glenda crossed her legs, showcasing a shoe with a skull platform and a bone heel. "If I'd known, I would've brought a date, that's all."

"To be clear," Chandra said to Cordelia, "this is a clean séance."

Glenda winked at Bradley. "It doesn't have to be."

Lillian moaned and fanned herself with the edge of Cordelia's shawl.

Chandra shot Glenda a glacial glare and flopped backwards. "Agata, are you with us? Give us a sign of your presence."

A woman wailed.

Chandra's eyes popped, and the hair on the back of my neck stood up.

The wail hadn't come from Lillian, but from the bathroom. *Was it the middle-aged woman sobbing on the side of the tub?*

Swallowing hard, I went to the bathroom and peered in.

Empty.

Maybe it is *Lou in the next room, mimicking a woman.*

All eyes were on me, including Chandra's, as I returned to my seat. "If there *is* a ghost in there, she's invisible."

"They usually are," Shona said.

Chandra glanced at the bathroom, then lay back and closed

her eyes. "Is that you, Agata? Or are you the Woman in White? Make yourself known. Come to us."

The door opened.

Everyone gasped, and Chandra rocketed upright.

Nadezhda entered with a glass of champagne and a vodka martini.

Everyone gasped again.

And I couldn't blame them. Nadezhda *was* wearing white—snakeskin, to be exact—and she cut a frightful figure with her spiked maroon hair, sneer-smile, and eyetooth hole. But my focus was on her drinks. "Is the bar open?"

"Nyet. I help self."

Bummer. I could've used a stiff one to get me through this spectacle, but I didn't want to steal the booze like that Communist criminal.

"Giada," Chandra glared at the ceiling, "could you please recap the séance etiquette lesson for Nadezhda and Franki?"

"Vhat her problem?" Nadezhda asked as she handed Glenda her champagne. "She got girdle in vad?"

In light of the *Encyclopedia Americana* entry, "girdle" got my attention.

Glenda sipped from her flute. "She's sexually frustrated, Miss Nadezhda."

"Excuse me," Chandra huffed. "I don't need a girdle, and Lou is a superb lover."

An image of Lou Toccato nude except for his toe shoes leapt into my brain. *You know, I could make a drink and leave cash on the bar.*

Cordelia tightened her shawl. "It's getting late. Perhaps we could continue?"

"Yes, let's." Chandra lay back.

The raisin-vinegar scent of perique tobacco wafted into the room.

Has to be Lou.

"Glenda," Chandra ground out, "are you smoking again?"

"I'm smoking *hot*," Glenda ran a hand over her bralette, "but not a cigarette."

Shona scanned the room. "Simon Hersheim, the original owner of this house, smoked that tobacco."

Chandra's hands trembled.

Which made me doubt that Lou was behind the smoke.

"Is...?" Chandra's voice trailed off. "Is that you, Simon?"

"Yes," Chandra replied in a deep man voice.

Okay. The smoke is totally the work of Lou.

"But that's not me smoking," Chandra-as-Simon said.

Chandra gripped the sheets. "Then who is?"

"The killer."

My lips wrinkled. A sham psychic séance prediction. Still, Edward *did* smoke that tobacco, and in my gut, I knew he'd murdered Agata, and most likely Delilah.

"Simon," Chandra said, "can you tell us the name of the killer?"

Cordelia leaned forward, fully taken in by the Chandra charade.

Silence ensued.

"Simon?" Chandra repeated. "Are you there?"

Feet pounded the grand staircase, going down.

"Welp," I slapped my hands on my thighs, "I guess he's leaving."

Chandra's eyes opened, and she scanned the guests, as if she was checking to make sure we were all present.

Suspicious, I turned and looked at the door.

The piano downstairs began to play random notes.

Chandra bolted from the bed, taking the sheet with her. "What's going on in this hellhole hotel?"

I had the same question, almost verbatim. Chewing my lower lip, I got up and went into the hallway.

The scent of perique tobacco was strong, and the door to Room 9 was open. Not only that, the light was on and so was the radio.

"Franki," Bradley pulled me from the doorway, "let me go in first."

Too late.

My eyes had seen the unforgettable sight.

Edward Blain lay face up and fully clothed on one of the two queen beds.

Dead.

13

―――――

"Chandra, could you get off my back?" I wished I'd meant that figuratively, but the phasmophobic fraud had jumped on me in the doorway of Room 9, after seeing Edward's body in the bed. The worst part was, her legs were cutting off my circulation above *and* below the waist.

"I... I can't... He's dead."

"Which means he can't hurt you, so get off."

"Maybe he can't, but his killer could still be in the hotel."

"And with you on my back, we're both sitting ducks."

Her ankles locked at my abdomen.

Maybe I should've thought before I'd said that. "If you don't climb off me right now, I'm going to do something drastic."

She tightened her arms around my neck, irritating my already damaged throat.

The absurd scene captured the essence of our relationship. She'd first latched onto me while I was investigating a homicide at a haunted plantation, and ever since then she'd been slowly cutting off my life blood, like a hoop skirt.

Which reminded me of my mother in that Southern belle

wedding gown. I tried to shake off the image—as well as Chandra—but no such luck.

"All right," I anger-hummed, "don't say I didn't warn you." I did a couple of 360s to try to fling her off, but she didn't budge. I considered shearing her off via an antique buffet, but I didn't want to damage the two art deco lamps on top. Instead, I hobbled to the wall and knocked her back into it. Each time I did, her legs splayed open and closed.

Someone clapped and whistled.

It was Glenda, but I couldn't fathom the reason.

She sashayed over, bit the tip of her cigarette holder, and sized up Chandra and me. "You two do that number at Madame Moiselle's in thongs and pasties, and you'll triple what you're earning doing PI work and séances."

"Nyet." Nadezhda curled her lip. "Frank keep clothes."

"For the last time, Nadezhda," I growled, "it's *Franki*, as in, *Francesca*."

"Da, da." She sneered and sipped her martini.

The snarky Soviet was lucky Chandra was on my back. Otherwise, I would've forced her to eat her words—and her martini glass.

"Well," the spooked psychic cleared her throat and released her hold on mine, "as the saying goes, 'there's safety in numbers.'" She lumbered to the ground, almost taking me with her.

Finally free, I launched into a round of shoulder rolls and hip-flexor stretches to get the life back in my limbs.

Veronica exited Room 10. "The police are on their way, and Lillian is looking after Shona."

"Did she finally come to?"

"For a few moments." She paused to tie her hair into a bun. "But then she remembered what happened to Edward and fainted again."

At least she was quiet.

Bradley came out and wrapped me in his arms. "How're you holding up, babe?"

"Better now," I said, not so much because I was nestled in his chest but because the mad medium was off my back. I pulled away and looked into his eyes. "How's Cordelia?"

He grimaced. "Pretty shaken up. After the police come, I'm moving her and my mother to my place. I never should've let them stay here after the murder, but my grandmother insisted on having this séance."

I squeezed his hand. None of us could have predicted that a Chandra séance would end in another murder—actually, maybe Chandra's, but not anyone else's.

Bradley returned to the room, and Moira stepped into the hallway. Her veil was lowered, but her hackles were up. "Giada's on the phone with her husband, Wolf. When she's done, we're getting out of this place."

"You can't." I shrugged. "None of us can."

"Franki's right." Veronica rubbed her biceps. "A man died, which means we're all potential suspects. We have to stay until the police have questioned us."

"It's a fine time to tell us that," Ruth barked from the doorway of Room 10. "The show was so bad, I texted my Uber driver to pick me up." She raised her phone. "He's already outside."

Veronica shook her head. "You're going to have to tell him the situation."

"Uh," I raised a finger, "if the driver is Phil Redman, leave out the part about the dead body." After all, the guy needed a test case for Uber Undertaker, and Ruth would've gladly given him Edward if it meant getting her home sooner to watch *Dr. Pimple Popper*.

"Attention, sexy séancers!" Glenda raised her arms and

shook her gauzy bits. "Since we're stuck waiting on the fuzz, y'all come on back into Room 10." She shoved Moira inside. "I'll give you a sneak peek of the Hot I Scream Sundae number I'm performing at Madame Moiselle's tomorrow night."

I shot a panicked look at my BFF. "Bradley's family is in there."

"On it." Veronica made a beeline for the door.

From the corner of my eye, I caught sight of Chandra who was pressed against a wall, making like a Pillsbury Crescent Dough Sheet. "Is Lou here?"

Her head moved from side to side, but her eyes remained fixed on the doorway of Room 9.

"Seriously, Chandra, if Lou was helping you with the séance behind the scenes, it's time to come clean. Otherwise, the police will consider him a suspect."

Chandra stayed silent and slid along the wall to the study.

I hadn't selected the common loon as her spirit swamp animal for nothing, but the behavior was odd even for her. "Why are you sliding?"

"Because I... I need my bag, but I don't want to turn my back on a spirit." Her eyes darted around. "Or a murderer." She slid into the study doorway, backed in, and disappeared.

Suspicious, I entered the study.

Chandra was stooped over a couch, rummaging through a crescent moon-shaped clutch. I figured she was looking for her phone to call Lou—until I heard a tell-tale jingle. "Give me. That. Bracelet!"

"Back off." She hit me with her hip. "I need this."

"Well, *I* don't." I tried to twist the spirit-channeler from her grip, but her paddle-nailed fingers were as strong as her pudgy legs. "Drop it!"

"Not on your life, sister."

There was no way I'd let go either. If I did, she'd channel the ghost of Edward and further enmesh herself in my case—and continue her slow kill of my vital organs.

We were both stooped over from the effort. Chandra kicked out a leg, causing me to trip. And I brought her down with me.

She landed on my rib cage and bounced.

Naturally.

Once again trying to shake her, I rolled, and she rolled with me, into the hallway.

"Oooh," Glenda cooed from the doorway of Room 10. "You should do this number in a pool of Cool Whip."

I couldn't comment. Not only was the lunar lunatic crushing my lungs, we were locked in mortal combat—brides-from-Wedding-Belles style.

The charm bracelet inched closer to me, and so did Chandra's piranha teeth.

Inspired by the bracelet, I channeled my inner thug-hooligan *and* my hair-puller mother. And I yanked her huge bob with all my might.

The maneuver worked. I got the bracelet.

And the top of Chandra's bob!

Chandra turned lunar white, as though she'd seen a ghost *and* a murderer. She snatched the hairpiece, ran past dead Edward, and locked herself in the Room 9 bathroom.

Evidently, her fear of being seen with small hair was greater than her fear of running into a killer.

Glenda inserted a fresh cigarette into her holder. "I should've stayed out here with you and Miss Chandra, sugar. There are some real party poopers in Room 10. They didn't even want a preview of my show, if you can believe that."

"Gee," I pulled myself to my feet and pocketed the charm bracelet, "you'd think they'd be in the mood to let loose."

Nadezhda exited Room 10, sipping her martini through a

straw she'd inserted into her eyetooth hole. "You check Edvard's vallet for grandmas?"

My head retracted. "Grandmas? What?"

Glenda flicked her lighter shut. "It's Russian slang for money, sugar."

"Da. Like 'lemons.'"

My head retreated further into my neck. I wasn't the least bit surprised the penny-pinching Communist had asked me if I'd rifled through a murdered man's wallet for money, because God knew she'd take cash from a collection plate in the hands of a dead priest. But given my storied history with "grandmas" and "lemons," the association of the two in any context was too much for me to bear.

A force bounded into the hallway and bowled me over.

Not a spirit.

Shona.

"Whoopsy!" Her stringy hair framed her face as she leaned over me, and it took everything I had not to pull it. I'd recently read that people inherit more DNA from one parent than the other, and it was becoming pretty obvious who the majority of mine had come from.

"Franki," she boomed, "with Edward dead, I'm the main suspect again. You can't abandon me now."

Since she'd knocked me on my backside, I really wanted to. But I couldn't. "I'll help you. Just let me get up so I can check out the crime scene before the police arrive."

Shona used her rowing muscles to pull me to my feet, and I limped to Room 9. It was huge with high ceilings and ornately carved mahogany furniture. A wooden shelf with mirrored panels hung above the fireplace. It held glassware as well as complimentary bottles of water and wine, courtesy of the Columns. There were no signs of a struggle, and nothing looked out of place.

Except for Edward.

Chandra was taking her time in the bathroom, so I knelt on the floral rug to check underneath the beds. There were no surprises under Edward's, but I did find something under the other.

A whiskey glass on its side.

The groan we'd heard had been followed by a thud. *Was it the source?*

"Vhat you see?" Nadezhda asked.

"A vhiskey—I mean, a whiskey glass. Edward must've dropped it."

Glenda exhaled a cloud of smoke. "I'll bet his drink was poisoned, sugar."

Was the drink the murder weapon? That was how Agata had died, but not Delilah.

"Go on, Franki," Shona shouted. "Get the glass."

"And ze vallet," Nadezhda urged.

By now it was apparent that if I wanted to solve the case and stay out of jail, I needed to tune out more than one member of the peanut gallery.

Not wanting to leave my fingerprints on potential evidence, I turned on my phone light and aimed it at the glass. There was a dark amber residue, which could've been from any number of beverages. I slid halfway under the bed and got a whiff of the contents.

The odor was unmistakable.

Walnut.

Edward was drinking nocino?

"IN A STUNNING DEVELOPMENT," the morning news anchor seemed to stare right at me from the TV atop Veronica's office file cabinet, "local attorney Edward Blain was found dead last night at the Columns Hotel. Police haven't ruled out foul play."

Unnerved, I pulled my feet into Veronica's desk chair and tucked the throw around me. I was positive Edward had killed Agata and Delilah. *Was I wrong?*

Or are there two killers on the loose?

"In other news," he shifted his gaze to a different camera, "chaos broke out at Wedding Belles yesterday when an unruly gang of Italian grandmothers descended on the boutique dressed entirely in black."

The corners of my mouth twitched as I reached for my cappuccino. I came by my thug-hooligan look honestly.

"According to management, the gangster grandmas didn't steal anything, so their motive is unclear. Lyle LeLeux is live on the scene." His jaw hardened. "Lyle?"

The camera cut to an already sweaty thirty-something reporter on the street outside the boutique. "Thanks, Steve. I'm at Wedding Belles with one of the brides affected by yesterday's incident. Can you tell us what happened?"

A tiny blonde leaned into the microphone. "I came to buy my dream Vera Wang dress. It's got a plunging V bodice and see-through lace that hugs your curves. But a group of grandmas shamed me into getting this final-sale dress I can't return." She held up a gown that could've doubled as a parachute and burst into tears. "Nooow I'm going to walk dooown the aiiisle looking like a giiiant marshmaaallooow."

I felt for the girl, but the truth was, she'd gotten off easy. Those of us who had nonnas knew from hard-lived experience that they had artillery far more destructive than Catholic guilt, including heavy Bible-laden handbags, holy water guns, and citrus fruit.

Veronica entered the office.

"Oh!" I jerked and balanced my coffee to keep it from spilling.

"Sorry to scare you." She placed her Chanel bag on the desk. "But I couldn't sleep. Every time I closed my eyes, I saw Edward on that bed."

I could relate.

"Did you spend the night here?"

"Yeah, Glenda's still refusing to give me the key to your old place, so it was either camp on the lobby couch or fight Napoleon for the chaise longue."

She half-smiled and glanced at the television. "Any updates on Edward?"

"Nothing we don't already know."

Her mouth twisted. "I don't understand what he was doing in Room 9."

"Edward and Lara stayed in that room the night of Agata's murder, so he knew he'd be able to eavesdrop on the séance from there. And since no one was at the reception desk, he would've had easy access to the key."

"But why drink nocino, of all things?"

"Beats me." I contemplated my cappuccino, which was admittedly a poor caffeine choice given the circumstances. "But if that *is* what killed him, the killer must've taken the bottle when they ran out of the hotel."

She sighed. "What a night."

"Right?" I drained my mug. "Remind me to never be stuck with that crew at a murder scene again. It was bad enough that Glenda offered to strip, but when Nadezhda started showing off her eyetooth-hole tricks, I almost joined Dead Edward on the bed."

"Me too." She gestured for me to follow her. "Come on. Let's get some coffee."

"As long as it's not from NOLA Noir."

"Nope, the Private Chicks percolator."

I rose and gripped my side. "Ow, ow, ow…"

"Do you have a cramp?"

"No, two pains. Chandra and Shona." I launched into a side stretch, and a jingle came from my pocket.

"What's that?"

"Chandra's charm bracelet. I'm going to bury it at the swamp, just like Agata's jewels, only I'm going to leave it there."

She smirked and left, but I hung back and looked out the window at the coffee shop sign. I still couldn't decipher the image above the cup, but I'd come back around to thinking it was steam.

Or perique smoke?

I gathered up my mug and phone and went down the hall. "You know," I said, entering the kitchenette, "I saw Edward at the swamp yesterday morning."

Veronica looked up from the can of espresso she was holding.

"He claimed he was looking for the spot Shona had hidden the jewels, but he was lying."

"What do you think he was doing?"

"Covering his tire tracks, for one thing." I pulled out a chair at the two-top. "He'd driven out there before, and when he did, he dropped some wedding invitations that Shona's race consultant found."

"Hm. Makes me think *he* hid Agata's jewels at the swamp."

I nodded. "I accused him of that very thing, which he aggressively denied. Then as he was leaving, I smelled perique in his car."

"Do you think he was smoking the perique we smelled during the séance?"

"If he was hiding in Room 9 to eavesdrop, you'd think he'd be smart enough not to give himself away with tobacco smoke."

She inserted the portafilter into the espresso machine. "Chandra looked really scared when Glenda said she wasn't smoking."

"Because Chandra is a ghost-fearing con. She probably did her research on the Columns history, and when Shona mentioned Simon Hersheim, she ran with it, never expecting smoke to make a ghostly appearance."

"That reminds me," she said, spooning sugar into her cup, "we know the groan came from Edward. But what about the woman wailing?"

"It definitely wasn't the ghost of the Woman in White."

Veronica pressed the brew button. "It could've been Vick's nonnina or Lara or Grace."

"Don't forget the femme... Wait." My palm hit the table. "The wedding dress!"

The espresso machine stopped, as if it too was shocked.

"What wedding dress?" Veronica asked.

"The femme fatale disguised herself in one of the gowns at Wedding Belles yesterday, and she was still wearing it when she sped away in the Buick Roadster. I'll bet she was the Woman in White Cordelia saw upstairs in the ballroom. Cordelia said she 'looked so real.'"

Veronica took a seat. "If she *was* in the hotel, she could've killed Edward."

"Sure, but it's hard to pin anything on her without knowing who she is." I drummed my fingers on the table. "Although, she might be a relative of Agata's maid."

"Why would you think that?"

"Janine Crawford told me that Agata's maid inherited Bette Davis's canary yellow diamond ring from a relative in show business, and she said Agata killed her to get it."

Her blue eyes darkened. "That's awful."

"Believe me, I know. Bradley thinks the femme fatale was Edward's lover. If he's right, maybe they had a falling out, and she killed him. Or, it was Lara, because she found out he was having an affair."

Veronica shot her espresso. "We need to find out who this mystery woman is. Any idea where to start?"

"Not yet." I leaned my head against the wall. "In the meantime, I'm going to find out where perique is sold in New Orleans, starting with the smoke shops here on Decatur Street. Maybe I'll get lucky and connect it to one of our suspects."

The door to Private Chicks slammed, and our eyes met.

"No." Veronica shook her head. "I know that slam."

Just in case, I peered into the hallway. Sure enough, it was David. "You're here early."

"Yeah, got an exam, but I heard about Edward on the news." He unzipped his backpack. "So I wanted to get you his phone records."

A twinge of excitement ran down my spine. I was finally going to find out who Delilah Delaire had overheard Edward talking to when she hid on the balcony.

He pulled out a sheet of paper. "The number highlighted in red is the only one he called the night of the rehearsal dinner."

Veronica came out of the kitchenette. "That makes it easy."

"Not really." He flipped his bangs. "The number's unlisted, and I can't trace it."

"Then let's call it." I grabbed my phone from the table and dialed as Veronica and David looked on.

Someone picked up on the second ring.

"Hello?" The voice belonged to a woman.

One I knew.

I hung up. "This is why you use a burner phone."

"Why?" Veronica asked. "Who was it?"

There was no easy way to say this, so I decided to just come out with it. But when news of this went public, the ramifications would stretch far beyond the confines of the case.

"Giada."

"Francesca Lucia Amato!" My mother's shrill drill-like voice held a distinct note of jackhammer. "How could you ID your second cousin in a murder?"

From my living-room-armchair hotseat, I looked to Nonna and Giada on the chaise longue for support. After all, we were talking about a crime. But their stares were so hostile they verged on homicidal—while my nonna worked a rosary.

Even Napoleon glared from his spot on the bearskin rug. Although he was just mad that the uproar I'd caused was interrupting his all-day nap.

"Well, Francesca?" My mother jackhammered, pacing in front of the fireplace. "What do you have to say for yourself?"

I tugged at the neck of my T-shirt. As I'd predicted, the ramifications of Edward Blain calling Giada's house the night of the murder had indeed extended far beyond the confines of the case.

To me.

"It's not like I did this, Mom."

She stopped pacing and shot me a semi-crazed side-eye. "Well, the NOLA PD didn't do it."

True, but she was missing the point—by a long shot. "Okay, but keep in mind that Giada isn't the suspect here. It's her husband, Wolf. He *is* one of Edward's law partners."

"Since when is being an attorney a crime, Francesca?"

A leading question if there ever was one.

Giada sniffled and dabbed a tissue at her nose. "And I thought you were so cute when you got drunk on those rum pastries at my wedding."

"I *was*," I protested. "I mean, as cute as a drunk twelve-year-old could be."

My mother gulped from the glass of wine she'd poured herself. "How could you even *suspect* poor Wolf?"

The name made it easy, but I couldn't say that. "Because he didn't deny it when Giada asked him about the call, *did* he?"

Nonna clacked her rosary beads, and Giada started ugly crying.

"Good Lord, Francesca!" The wine glass came down on the coffee table with a whack. "Would you stop tormenting your second cousin?"

I knew better than to answer. My mom was judge, jury, and, if I so much as uttered a word, executioner. But if anyone was being tormented, it was me.

She resumed pacing, hands on hips. "This is worse than the time you abandoned Bradley at baggage claim like an old suitcase."

Proof positive of that torment. "For the last time, Mom, I didn't abandon him. And this isn't worse than that."

"How do you figure?" she huffed.

"Because that could've cost me a husband, and Giada still has one, even if he does wind up—" I came to an abrupt halt. In the heat of the moment, I'd talked myself into a corner. There was nothing to do but go forward with metaphorical guns blazing. "—living in prison."

A wail escaped Giada's lips that was oddly similar to a police siren, and my mother reached past her wine glass and went straight for the bottle. She took a hard swallow and pointed it at me. "I knew your malocchio was going to be a problem, but I had no idea it would be this bad."

"What does *that* have to do with *this*?" I practically screamed.

"Your bad business affects the family, Francesca."

"Malocchio isn't even a real thing!"

"Then how do you explain this murder mess?"

"Why don't you ask Wolf?"

Giada's tear ducts opened and produced full-on waterfalls. "I can't. He's in jaaail!"

My mother put her hands on her hips. "There you go again, tormenting your second cousin." She looked at the ceiling. "Where did I go wrong?"

"Don't-a get-a me started." Nonna returned her rosary to her handbag. "And it's-a not all-a Franki's-a fault. Giada's got-a that bone-a-digger father. *Porta iella!*"

Giada lowered her tissue. "He's a bioarchaeologist, Carmela, and that doesn't bring bad luck."

I didn't see how Giada could justify that statement when she believed in the malocchio, but there was no way I was going to argue with her. I didn't think she was involved in the murder, but she was a Montalbano like my nonna, which meant she was unpredictable. And probably dangerous.

A knock echoed in the apartment.

"It's-a for me." Nonna rose and shuffled to the door.

A nonna with skin the color of Parmigiano Reggiano entered with a pan of Sicilian pizza known as *sfinciuni*. "*Condoglianze*, Carmela."

Nonna nodded, and the woman cast a look of sadness at Giada and my mother before proceeding to the kitchen.

More nonne entered, one after the other, commiserating and carrying dishes that smelled of garlic, rosemary, and regret.

It was Phase One of a familiar mourning ritual that I called *Condolences and Comfort Food*. No one had died, but Italian nonne the world over treated the news of a potential criminal husband like a family death, and the reigning matriarch was the rightful recipient of the grief.

An extremely wide nonna wriggled through the doorway. "Eh, what're you gonna do, Carmé? You lost Big Joe twenty-three years ago, and now this."

Big Joe was my nonnu, and as far as I was concerned, two-plus decades between misfortunes was a really great stretch. But the nonne saw life through black mourning veils, and they collected tragedies like Girl Scout badges.

Nonne continued to arrive, and ten or so had gathered in my kitchen.

A thought struck me as I watched them lay out the food on the table (and jockey for the primo spots for their dishes)—*It's probably not an ideal week for a surprise bridal shower.*

Nonna closed the front door, raised her chin, defeated but still dignified, and processed to the kitchen. She took her designated place at the head of the table, signaling she was ready to commence with Phase Two.

The Suffering Stories.

A nonna with bags under her eyes the size of two Gucci Jackies rested a hand on my nonna's arm. "Tough break about Giada's husband, Carmela, and I know about those. Just this week Nicky Junior got laid off, and Nicky Senior got the gout. You think I was waiting on them before, you should see me now. *Uffà!*"

"My Maury spent my collection plate money for the year on lottery tickets," another said. A pained look crossed her sagging face. "He only won two dollars."

A nonna with a neck the length of a ciabatta crossed herself, probably as a reaction to the disastrous winnings rather than the theft from the church. "Speaking of money, the IRS is auditing my cousin Tina's husband, Sal, for embezzling."

"How about Lina's grandson, Lino?" a nonna with a profusion of chin hair asked. "He got a girl pregnant and announced they're going to live together." Her gaze swept the table to make sure she had everyone's attention. "In *sin*."

A cacophony of *Maria Vergines* and *Gesù mios* came from the kitchen. Living in unholy matrimony with a baby on the way was the Catholic equivalent of committing a murder.

A sob sounded from a nonna with a facial mole shaped, fittingly, like a teardrop. "I thought I had it bad with Dom's diabetes, but I feel for you, Carmela, what with Giada's husband and Franki's never-ending engagement."

My head jerked back so hard it hit the wall.

"Watch out, Carmé," Wide Nonna warned. "Mary's granddaughter was engaged so long, her fiancé married someone else."

That scenario called for more information, but I didn't dare open my mouth.

"You know what I always say, Carmela," Chin-Hair Nonna cast her a pointed look, "long engagement, quick divorce."

"Which doesn't bode well for Franki," a nonna with a serious nose said, "especially after she got the malocchio and went to a séance."

On that note, I grabbed matches from the fireplace mantle and lit the Uncrossing candle in front of my mother. Then, for good measure, I lit the Demon-Be-Gone smudge stick and waved the smoke around.

Nonna emerged from the kitchen. "Is-a that-a some of-a your séance-a sacrilege?"

The sad, suffering looks of the nonne had turned to suspicious stares.

I didn't need a mirror to know that my eyes glowered. Giada's husband was a possible accomplice to murder, and yet somehow my engagement was the tragedy. "No, I didn't get this stuff from the medium, Nonna. I bought it from a witch in the Quarter."

Gasps and cries of horror erupted from the table. Some nonne wobbled, threatening to fall from their chairs, and those who retained their balance reached for their rosaries. Meanwhile, Ciabatta-Necked Nonna bit into a piece of sfinciuni in a culturally appropriate display of eating her feelings.

"Francesca!" My mother gripped the mantle for dear life. "What in the name of Sam Hill has gotten into you?"

Yes, it was wrong to speak to my nonna that way, especially in front of guests. But how much could one woman in a never-ending engagement take?

Another knock rang out in the apartment.

This time I went to answer because I was on my way out. I opened the door to a late nonna with a lazy eye and a lasagna. Her eye led my gaze over her shoulder, where I spotted Glenda coming down the stairs holding her real waffle cone skirt. She must've forgotten it when she'd moved to Nadezhda's place to escape the nonne.

"Come in." I ushered the nonna inside. "The suffering stories have started, and you don't want to miss your slot."

I closed the door behind me and met my landlady at the base of the stairs. She was wearing two coconuts, a palm leaf, and platform stripper flip-flops. "I need that key to Veronica's old apartment, Glenda."

She *pff*ed a puff of smoke. "Not until you pay me two grand for the Hucci Cucci outfit the Lilliputians ruined."

"Two *grand*? How can you justify that?"

"It's couture, Miss Franki."

"It's *car*ture. You got those parts from the junkyard, and that price is highway robbery, no pun intended."

She exhaled a cloud of smoke like a bad car exhaust. "You're paying for my artistic input."

"I'm not paying you for anything else. I already gave you a grand in rent."

"Then no key for you." She dragged off a cigarette holder that resembled a tropical cocktail straw. "It's just as well because I'm going to let Miss Shona stay in the apartment. She's out of funds, and the police won't let her leave town."

So, not only was I working Shona's case for free, I was also putting her up. I had half a mind to call her library and suggest that they hold another Book and Bake sale. Otherwise, Shona would be going home to Screamer, and all reading, studying, and researching would cease.

An old GTO convertible pulled up in the driveway. Behind the wheel was a bleached blonde in oversized pink sunglasses and a halter top that consisted of two pink ribbons running down her breasts.

Maybe Baby.

"There's my ride." Glenda sashayed to the car.

"Love the summer stripper look, Miss Glenda," Maybe Baby squeaked in her high-pitched voice.

I knew what she meant, but technically, all stripper clothing was summer wear.

"Hi, Franki!" Maybe Baby waved, which didn't work so well with those ribbons.

Casually, I strolled to the driver side and stole a glimpse of her thumbnails on the steering wheel. I could see what Sick Vick saw in them. They were nice, but I wondered how those toenails had grown back after the "incident." "Hey, Glenda tells me you're studying to be a nurse."

"A nurse*maid*."

My gaze fell again to those ribbons. "As in, a wet nurse?"

"I don't give baths," she squeaked. "I'm studying to stripe candy."

"Ah, a candy striper, like a nurse's assistant." That was a far better fit for her, as was a candy *stripper*. "You *do* know that's a volunteer position."

She lowered her sunglasses. "Not at this hospital. I get tips and inheritances."

"Uhhh... Come again?"

"That's right, Miss Franki." Glenda gazed at Maybe Baby with pride. "The male patients have been giving her tips, and an older gentleman with a heart condition named her the heir of his estate."

The reading of Agata's will! I made a mental note to have Veronica find out the date. From what I'd learned about Agata, that document promised to be a riveting read.

Glenda positioned the seatbelt between her coconuts. "I told Maybe Baby that if she stripes her candy right, she could set herself up for life."

Based on her ribbon-style blouse, I'd say she was striping her candy really well. "Listen, Glenda said you know Vick Villano and his grandmother."

Maybe Baby frowned and pulled her feet into the seat, then hugged her legs.

I couldn't see her toenails in the shoes she was wearing, but evidently, they were still a sore subject. "Anyway, I was wondering, do you remember whether Vick or Brunella smokes?"

"Vick does."

My pulse picked up. "Perique?"

She blinked. "No, just brisket."

My hand braced my forehead. I'd been through a lot, and this conversation was proving to be too much. "I was thinking cigarettes or cigars?"

"Oh." Her eyelashes batted. "I didn't know you could eat those."

I sucked my teeth. Probably best to stick to my original plan to visit the smoke shops on Decatur.

Glenda adjusted a low-hanging coconut. "I hate to be rude, Miss Franki, but we've got to leave. My Hot I Scream Sundae skirt is wilting in this humid heat. Which reminds me, don't miss my performance tonight. It's going to be a *scream*." She winked. "See what I did there?"

I did. I just didn't plan to see it at Madame Moiselle's.

Maybe Baby lowered her feet and backed from the driveway. As the GTO drove away, a wind kicked up.

One I recognized.

Nonna Nunzia was behind me, holding a basket and standing next to a nonna I didn't know. And I wasn't sure I wanted to. She was big and boisterous, with a bouncy brown wig and lipstick and blush the color of tomato sauce. She reminded me of an Italian Julia Child.

She bounded up and pulled my face into her enormous bosom. "You must be the one who got the malocchio, God love ya."

Once again, I hedged on my earlier conviction that the evil eye wasn't a real thing. Because, apparently, it was written all over my face.

The woman pressed me even harder. "You haven't been around a man with a unibrow, have you? Because you've got a strong case."

I tried to say Vick Villano, but since my mouth was smashed into her breastbone, it came out a moan.

"There, there." She patted my back with a hand the size of one of Shona's rowing oars, knocking what little breath I had left from my lungs. "Don't worry, *bella mia*. Like my shirt says, '*Never fear, Nonna is here!*'"

I had fear. And lots of it. Because my oxygen was gone.

She released me with a shove, and I stumbled backwards, gasping for air. She elbowed Nonna Nunzia, who took the hit like the stoic Sicilian grandma she was. "It's a good thing you brought me, Nunzia. The girl's got the malocchio so bad she can barely breathe."

Before I could point out that my oxygen deprivation was her doing, she slid an arm around my shoulders and slammed me into her side. "I'm Nonna Titti, the consultant from Benevento."

Titti was the accepted Italian nickname for Tiziana, and based on where my face had been, it was a perfect fit.

"So tell me, *cara mia*," she squeezed me as though I were pasta dough, "why haven't you taken the malocchio cure?"

Breath surged into my body, as did a rage, and I broke free of her grip. "There's a *cure*? My second-cousin Giada said there isn't one."

"We nonne always have a cure!"

I was tempted to glare at Nonna Nunzia for not telling me about that, but I didn't want to rile her. I'd already taken a beating from the consultant, and the majara was just as much a manhandler.

Titti smashed my cheeks between her oar-paddle palms. "What're we nonna's for, if not to relieve pain and suffering?"

Given my personal experiences, that question was as confusing as the story of Mary's granddaughter being engaged so long that her fiancé married someone else.

She let go of my face and stroked my hair with the gentleness of a sumo wrestler. "As I told your nonna and mamma, all it takes is a prayer and the sign of the cross."

First I'd found out that my mom and nonna could've gathered the herbs of San Giovanni rather than call the majara, and now I learn that something my nonna did twenty times a day could've relieved me from my malocchio misery? From the sound of things, I was going to need something stronger than the Demon-Be-Gone smudge stick and Uncrossing candle to handle the women in my family. "Is there a cure for the NOLA Noir nocino I drank?"

Titti clucked and clapped my bicep. "Unfortunately, no, which is why you'll have to wait and drink the nocino your nonna and mamma made you. The janare of Benevento were ruthless. Did you know they were the inspiration for Strega liqueur?"

I didn't, but I did want to know why she'd brought up the witches. "Are you saying that Brunella Pagano is a janara?"

"My family left Benevento when I was a baby, so I can't confirm it. But the symbol on the NOLA Noir shop sign suggests so."

The excitement made me slightly dizzy—or it was brain damage from the lack of oxygen. "Are you talking about the steam?"

"What else?" She thumped my chest, which hurt. "That cup of coffee is topped with the canopy of the infamous Benevento walnut tree."

The one the janare danced around during their festival for the devil.

"BRUNELLA MIGHT LOOK like a fairy tale witch," I said into my cell phone and stepped around a suspicious substance splattered on the Decatur Street sidewalk, "but she's a real one."

Veronica was silent on the other end of the line. "You *do* realize how that sounds?"

"Hear me out, okay?" I glanced behind me at Hex to make sure Madge wasn't lurking. "Women who think they're witches perform spells with things like blood and nutmeg oil and

French sorrel, so it doesn't matter whether they're technically 'real' or not."

"Does it matter that French sorrel is a harmless spice?"

"Uh," I dropped my voice an octave to make it grave, "Agata was deathly allergic to it, so yes."

"Well, whatever Brunella is or isn't, I agree she and Vick are prime suspects."

Finally, some consensus. "After I finish my tour of the smoke shops, I'm going to stake out their house again to see whether I can spot one of them smoking—tobacco, not meat."

"Yeah," her tone was as arid as dry rub for brisket, "I got that."

"Sorry, I'm fresh out of my conversation with Maybe Baby."

"What about Lara and Grace and the femme fatale?"

"That's why I'm calling. Since I can't go near the Blains for fear of a restraining order, I need the details on the reading of Agata's will." I walked around a herd of tourists pausing to gawk inside every shop. They were drinking from fish bowls on lanyards around their necks, so maybe I should've called them a school. "I have to know whether Lara and/or Grace inherit the money and the jewels, or whether Agata left it all to someone else."

"I'll get on that today."

"I'm almost at the Ra Shop, so I've gotta run. Text me the minute you find out anything."

"You know it."

We hung up, and I spotted a crowd of protesters outside the corner smoke shop. As I passed Omen Psychic Parlor & Witch-craft Emporium, something jingled in my bag. I looked inside.

Chandra's charm bracelet.

Coincidence?

Surely, because Chandra was no psychic, and her bracelet wasn't magic. Although, like witches, the woman could inflict a lot of damage, so there was no way she was getting the bracelet back. I tucked it in the pocket of my jeans to keep it quiet and made my way through the crowd in front of the two-story white building that housed the Ra Shop.

The protesters appeared to be the voodoo crew from outside Tujague's creole restaurant. I surveyed the building exterior to see if I could figure out what they were upset about.

The top story had a wrap-around balcony with an *Available* sign, so they had to be protesting the smoke shop. I scanned the products in the window that spanned the front of the store. Bongs, face glitter, and something called "The Gotcha! Belt." Curious, I leaned in to read the package. *Great party joke! Big fun! Contains 3.5 ounces of novelty urine.'*

I jerked back.

"Frustrating, isn't it?" a fortyish blonde in a cute short set and sun visor asked.

"I wouldn't call it 'frustrating.'" I looked again at the box. "Maybe 'freaky?'"

She flipped her long braid behind her back and squared her hips like she was ready to fight. "You don't find it frustrating that this company is exploiting, not one, but *two* religions to make a profit?"

"Uh, I was talking about the urine."

She grimaced. "Do you need to pass a drug test, or something?"

"No." I pointed to the box. "It says it's a party favor."

"Oh. Now it makes sense."

Did it? Because I still couldn't fathom what "novelty urine" was or why a belt was involved and how any of that made for "big fun" at a party.

She pointed to the smoke shop's yellow sign. "I was talking about the Egyptian god thing the shop's got going on—the name and the eyes on their branding. The right one is the Eye of Ra, and the left is the Eye of Horus. Ra gives you protection, and Horus deflects the evil eye."

I made a mental note to see if the Eye of Horus was for sale inside the shop. Based on what I'd learned from the Benevento consultant, my mom and nonna had no intention of helping me cure my malocchio, whether it too was real or not.

"Hey, I remember you." The guy with the top hat and painted white face from the Voodoo Doughnuts protest walked up.

At least, I thought it was him. In New Orleans, a lot of people dressed like the voodoo god of the underworld.

"Brandi," he nodded in greeting at the blonde, "this is that Italian lady I met outside Tujague's I was telling you about." He gave me a wary onceover. "Are you here to join the protest?"

"No, she's here for party urine." Brandi shot him a knowing look.

"Gotcha," he said in keeping with The Gotcha! Belt theme.

Since neither of them had a problem with party urine, I didn't bother to set the record straight. "So, what happened with the Voodoo Doughnuts protest? Did you win?"

"Nah." Baron Samedi twisted a bone in his earlobe. "It's still going on. Would you believe they offered to replace that chocolate-frosted voodoo doll doughnut on their sign with their company logo?"

Sounded like a win to me. "What's wrong with that?"

He gave a start, and I would've sworn his face paled beneath the white makeup. "It's Baron Samedi."

So was he, but I didn't want to point that out. Something about these two was a tad off. "Why are y'all protesting the Ra Shop, anyway?"

"Mainly because of their voodoo cigars."

The cigar got my attention. "What's that?"

"Exactly." Brandi resquared her hips. "Why do companies have to drag religion through the mud to make their money?"

Fair question. "But doesn't Baron Samedi smoke cigars and Pall Mall cigarettes?"

"So do I," the Baron Samedi lookalike said, "but that don't make it voodoo."

I wondered about that.

Brandi adjusted her sun visor. "In voodoo, the only time we use a cigar is to cleanse a space. That's it."

Baron Samedi nodded. "And we sure as hell wouldn't use one that had a face on it like Mr. Bill from that old *Saturday Night Live* skit." His mouth formed an O, as though he were afraid. "'Oh no!'"

"What?" I spun around.

"No," he shook his top-hatted head. "'Oh no!' is what he said."

"Who?" I turned around again.

"Mr. Bill!"

The guy might look like a voodoo god, but inside he was basically Maybe Baby.

Brandi huffed and wiped sweat from her upper lip. "Those voodoo cigars aren't the only product I take issue with. They sell tobacco with a voodoo queen on the package. It's disrespectful to us voodoo queens."

My mind reeled at that revelation. She could've been the granddaughter of one of the ladies in linen, and the guy who dressed like Baron Samedi was offended by people using his image. *What world was I living in?*

Oh, yeah. New Orleans.

Baron Samedi's eyes hardened. "You wanna talk about disrespectful. They also sell a tobacco called B. Frog's VooDoo Tour."

"Oh, yeah." I winced in mock sympathy. "The 'voodoo tour' is a problem."

"No, it's the frog on the package. He's wearing a seersucker suit and playing a damn banjo. Makes us look like a bunch o' bumpkins."

I wanted to ask his views on Kermit the Frog, but the timing was all wrong.

"The worst part is," he scratched his neck, "it's good tobacco. Virginia cavendish and perique."

My ears pricked up. Maybe I'd found the shop. The problem was, I had to cross protest lines to go inside. Voodoo-practitioner protest lines, at that.

But I had murders to investigate. "Well, I'm just going to pop in for a box of that party urine."

"She's going in," a voice shouted.

Angry cries came from the crowd.

And some curses. Voodoo curses.

"Tobacco traitor," a female yelled.

"No," Brandi held up her arms, "she's buying the party urine!"

"Oh, well," a guy with a live snake bigger than Puppy the python waved his hand, "at least it's not the cigar."

Taking advantage of the momentary lull, I yanked open the door.

Something hit the back of my head, and I looked down.

A gris gris bag.

Not wanting them to think they'd gotten my goat, I grinned. "Green is money, and I could use that!" Especially since I had the malocchio and was supporting Shona.

As I knelt to pick it up, something that might've been a crow hit my forehead. I checked for blood and looked down.

A voodoo doll with a pin in the chest.

It had a mass of brown yarn for hair and was swaddled in black cloth, like a cross between my mom and nonna.

"This will come in handy too," I said, and I totally wasn't kidding. I dropped the doll in my bag and dashed into the store.

"Welcome to the Ra Shop." The voice came from a cloud of smoke, which cleared to reveal a man behind the counter with glasses and a bushy beard that rivaled Phil the Uber Undertaker's.

Now that was a great party trick.

He lowered his vape pen. "Sorry about the chaos outside."

"No worries," I replied. Although, truth was, I had plenty, i.e., pains in my chest where that pin was located.

"Can I help you?"

"Hang on." I reached into my bag and removed the pin from the doll. "Okay, now I'm ready. So, you sell perique tobacco, right?"

"Pure and in blends."

"This is a long shot, but have you ever sold it to a woman who looks like she stepped out of the 1940s?"

"Yeah, she came in a week or so ago with a real chooch."

"Chooch" was a word I knew well. It was from the Italian *ciuccio*, which meant "dummy," as in a baby's pacifier, and it brought to mind someone I knew. I pulled out my phone and googled an image. "Did he look like this?"

The guy puffed on his vape pen and scrutinized the photo. "Tony Danza? Yeah. Real similar."

Vick Villano and the femme fatale knew each other.

This put a whole new spin on things, and so did whatever I was inhaling from the guy's vape pen. When the haze dissipated, the question in my head was clear.

Are Vick and the femme fatale the killers?

15

———

"Hush! Bad dogkey," I whisper-shouted from the bushes on the Walnut Street Playground across from Vick and Brunella's corner house.

The dog next door with the donkey-bray bark continued to woof-haw.

If that mad mongrel didn't stop, he'd out me to the whole neighborhood. It was seven p.m., so most people were home.

Desperate to silence him, I opened the takeout bag from Taceaux Loceaux—Spanish for *Crazy Taco* but spelled the Cajun French way—and debated between the ones with meat, i.e., Messing With Texas, Carnital Knowledge, and Seoul Man. I didn't want to give the damn dog any of them, but I'd gotten the assorted five-taco order, so I could sacrifice one in the interest of the investigation.

Hoping Korean barbecue would suit his fancy, I hurled Seoul Man into the yard.

He sat and began to eat.

So did I. Tortilla chips and queso fundido. "Melted cheese with garlic, onions, and peppers." I opened the container. "Fun indeedo."

Chips weren't the smartest choice for a stakeout, but no one was on the playground to hear me crunching.

As I chomped a cheese-dipped chip, I scanned Vick and Brunella's place for signs of life. The shotgun-style house was dark, and there were no cars out front. Even though Willie Tea had told me that Vick didn't own a black BMW, I couldn't rule out a connection between him and the car that had killed Delilah Delaire.

But if Vick *was* the one who'd run her down, something struck me as odd—the femme fatale following behind his car in a Buick Roadster, with a driver no less. After all, Moira said that the femme fatale had come to Delilah's office just before she was killed to warn her that she was in danger. *So why would the woman turn right around and be involved in Delilah's murder?*

Or was she trying to stop Vick from killing Delilah? If it was even him...

The bushes rustled, and I spilled queso on my shirt.

Willie Tea's face emerged through the leaves, and he flashed his toothy—as in, one—grin. "Thought I heard you in here."

So much for the no-one-could-hear-me-eating-chips theory. And for the "fun" in "fundido."

"Suppose I'll pull up a seat." He moved some branches and sat cross-legged beside me. "What's the latest on the investigation?"

Unsure whether to spill the tea to Willie Tea, I contemplated him for a moment. I'd never told him the details of the case, but I *had* revealed that I was a PI. And he was a park narc with solid information, so I decided to trust him. "I'm trying to find out whether Vick and Brunella are involved in a series of murders—Agata Villeré, Delilah Delaire, and Edward Blain."

"Dear me." He pressed a hand to his T-shirt of the Patron Saint of Go Cups, St. Togeaux. The Cajun French spelling of "to go" reminded me that I should've gotten a margarita with my Taceaux Loceaux.

"You know," Willie wiped sweat from his brow, "they do seem rather shady, but I never would've expected them to be involved in homicide. Petty theft, certainly. A burglary, yes. Perhaps even armed robbery. But never this."

Somehow that wasn't comforting. "What I need to know from you is whether either of them smokes, specifically perique tobacco."

"A fine product. Love the raisin notes."

"You know it?"

He reached for a chip. "I've done some work in horticulture."

Based on what I knew of his résumé, that probably meant he'd pilfered the tobacco from a grower. "Have you ever smelled it coming from their house?"

"That kind of information is going to cost you."

"Sorry, but I wasn't expecting you to drop by the bushes tonight. I didn't bring a C note, or any cash for that matter."

He interlaced his fingers. "Then I shall have to accept my payment in tacos."

Since he was homeless, I couldn't refuse him food. But it pained me to agree because my version of sharing was buying the other person their own portion. And it was far too late to do that. "Help yourself."

Willie grabbed the Messing With Texas, which messed with me. It was the one I'd most wanted to eat.

He gummed the taco for a few seconds, and it was gone. The guy might have a sole tooth in the front, but he could put away food faster than a person with a full set.

He wiped his hands on his baggy pants. "I've never smelled perique tobacco coming from their home. However, I have seen both Vick and Brunella smoke on their front porch. Cigars."

My stomach lurched at the news—or because of the peppers

in the queso. I still suspected that Edward Blain was the one who'd smoked perique in Agata's room the night he'd killed her and then again in Room 9 next door during the séance. But, since Vick and Brunella smoked cigars, who was to say that one or both hadn't been there helping Edward?

"By the way," I dipped a chip, "if anyone asks, we've never met."

Willie lowered his lids. "I don't bite the hand that feeds me."

"No, you only bite my tacos."

"You had four." He raised his nose. "You could certainly spare a couple."

My forehead tilted forward in a warning in case that was a weight comment. Willie could spare a couple of pounds, himself. But I couldn't afford to offend an informant, so I held my tongue and reached for another chip. And cheese. "The 1940s Buick Roadster that pulled up the last time I was here, had you ever seen it before?"

"That's going to cost you as well."

I held up the chips.

He bypassed the bag in favor of the Carnital Knowledge taco, leaving me with only two—the All Hat, No Cattle and the Basic B, which stood for "Basic Breakfast" and also something else that captured my current mood. "That Roadster has been here at least three times that I've seen, and each time there's a woman in the backseat who looks like a 1940s film star."

"That femme fatale is also a suspect. Why didn't you tell me about this last time?"

He pursed. "I passed out, remember?"

Oh, I remembered, despite the fact that the booze on his breath had killed more than a few of my brain cells. "I stayed until you woke up. That would've been the ideal time to tell me all of this."

"I'm a professional, and I expect to be paid for my work." He held up the Carnital Knowledge as evidence. "However, you'd run out of cash and boozy bon bons."

"And I'm going to run out of tacos if you don't stop eating them."

"You still have the All Hat, No Cattle and the Basic B."

Apparently, Willie had been to Taceaux Loceaux, which was way more believable than that EuroChocolate Festival he'd mentioned in Perugia, Italy. "You said you were in data collection, so tell me what you know about the femme fatale."

His head didn't move, but his eyes lowered to my takeout.

"All right, take another damn taco," I snapped. "But the last one is mine, *capisci*?"

He passed me the Basic B.

And I had the distinct feeling he'd picked it on purpose, and not because it meant Basic Breakfast.

"She and Vick are an item, but they fight quite often. She might look like a femme fatale, but she's insecure, and he's devoted to his nonna. It doesn't help that Brunella doesn't care for her."

Brunella didn't care for anyone, from what I could tell. "Anything else?"

"Mm-hm." He gummed the All Hat, No Cattle. "Vick and the femme fatale have been on edge lately. For instance, when they're on the front porch, they often scan the park as though they're worried about someone eavesdropping."

Because someone was.

Him.

I grabbed a couple of chips. "Has the guy in the van made anymore deliveries? Or has anyone else come by the house?"

"Not that I've seen." His forehead wrinkled, and he paused to wrest off a piece of taco with his lone tooth. "Although..."

I passed him the Basic B.

"...about an hour or so ago," he said, resuming playing like a jukebox that had been fed more coins, "Vick drove up in a black van. Brunella came outside loaded for bear, barking orders at him in Italian. He went inside and brought out empty cardboard boxes that he loaded into the back of the van. Then they left."

A chip went down sideways and got caught in my still-Nocino-scarred throat. *Were they packing up NOLA Noir so they could skip town after Edward's murder?*

Or were they up to something more sinister?

THE STREETLAMP REFLECTED off the thick humidity, casting a hazy pall over NOLA Noir. Although I couldn't confirm Vick and Brunella's whereabouts from the third-floor window of Private Chicks, I was certain they were inside the coffee shop. What they were doing, I didn't know.

But one thing was clear. The Feast of San Giovanni had passed, so they weren't in there making nocino. Not to mention that we were in the French Quarter, where there was nary a chance that they would've found a virgin to pick the walnuts.

The clock by the door read ten thirty p.m. If my instincts were right, Brunella and Vick had come to clear out the shop after Edward's death. It was possible that they'd gotten a surprise police visit after I'd called the tip line to report the bag of blood, so they were most likely fleeing before the cops came calling again.

Anxiety chewed at my gut, and I chewed a nail—but not one of the undeniably attractive ones on my thumbs. *Had the police discovered the source of the blood?* The delivery guy seemed cagey when he dropped off the bag, but surely it was animal. Pig's blood was used in traditional Italian cuisine, and Brunella *was* a cook.

But she was also a Benevento witch, and their recipes were spells.

And nocino for their Sabbat ceremony to celebrate the devil.

I leaned against the wall and wondered for the nth time what Brunella had put in her nocino. *Did she add the blood, nutmeg essential oil, and cloves to the walnuts and alcohol? Some French sorrel to kill Agata?*

Madge at Hex had said that cloves in a red bag could stop people from gossiping. *But what if someone drank them in a witch's walnut potion?*

My hand clutched my throat. *Is that why my esophagus glowed? To keep me from talking?*

"Your mind is pranking you, Franki. Get a grip." But the cloves raised the question of why pure nutmeg oil wasn't fit for consumption. I grabbed my phone and googled it.

NUTMEG CONTAINS MYRISTICIN, *a compound that, in excessive quantities, can cause convulsions, organ failure, and death.*

MY ENTRAILS SEIZED, and probably my liver. "My mother doesn't know what she's talking about. I'm not a hypochondriac like my dad." The phone dropped from my hand, and I slid down the wall to the floor. "I've been poisoned."

Is that how Vick and Brunella had killed Agata Villeré and Edward Blain? That is, if they were the murderers. I was almost positive that Edward had killed Agata and Delilah, but he could've had help from Vick and Brunella, and from Wolf Adair, my second cousin Giada's husband.

And what about the femme fatale? She had to be the supposed ghost of the Woman in White that Cordelia saw in the Columns ballroom, which meant she could've killed Edward while he was eavesdropping on the séance. And since she'd gone to the tobacco shop with Vick, she could've even been the perique smoker. Because it sure as heck wasn't the ghost of Simon Hersheim.

But why would the femme fatale and Vick want Edward dead?

My head hit the wall. The case was complicated and getting more so.

Meanwhile, three people were dead.

Are more to come?

The door to Private Chicks swung open, and the light came on.

I was paralyzed from surprise—and possibly the toxic effects of the nutmeg oil—as Ruth Walker glowered in the threshold.

Like the Grim Receptionist Reaper.

She slammed the door, causing the frosted glass to rattle. "What're you doing here at this hour? Did your landlady finally kick you out?"

This from a woman who'd lost free housing on the Galliano steamboat when she was fired from her cruise director job. But I didn't dare mention that. Not only had she blamed me for her firing, she'd gotten revenge by moving into my office. It had taken five weeks and a deposit on an apartment to get her out. "If you must know, I'm staking out NOLA Noir."

Ruth shook her head. Her bun didn't budge, but her turkey wattle swung. "When I told you to hustle business, I meant a *paying* case."

"It's not my fault the main suspect is a free-loading librarian." My tone was taut—unlike her neck. "That reminds me, Shona has been awfully quiet today. Did she call you again?"

"No, but I'd wager she's hiding from me." Ruth slammed a

desk drawer. "I told her last night that I am personally going to see to it that she coughs up the cash she owes this company."

"And I would like nothing less. Now, would you please shut off that light? It could blow my cover."

"Not until I find my readers. I forgot them, like you forgot my nocino cappuccino the other morning, and I need them to see."

Ruth might not be able to see, but I saw one thing quite clearly—I didn't only need the Demon-be-Gone smudge stick and Uncrossing candle at my house to ward off my family. I also needed an extra set at the office to ward off *her*. "Couldn't that wait until tomorrow?"

"N to the O, missy," she said, rummaging among some papers on her desk. "Without my readers, I can't watch my pre-bedtime episode of *Judge Judy*."

Some people were lulled to sleep by soothing sounds, but Ruth drifted off to court sentences.

She straightened and pointed at me. "Speaking of that cappuccino, I want a refund."

"Uh, you didn't pay me, remember?"

"Good thing, because I didn't get any coffee."

And because I'd given all my money to Vick, Shona, and Willie Tea, who'd also taken my tacos. "You should thank me after what happened to Agata and Edward. Whatever mystery ingredient they put in their nocino lit up my throat and probably killed them."

"The only mystery is how you still have a job."

I hopped up and hiked my bag on my shoulder. I already had toxins in my system, so I didn't want to work in a toxic environment. "I'm off to investigate whatever's happening across the street."

Ruth's eyes drew into fissures. "You should put those ace PI skills to work finding a psychiatrist, because there's no funny business going on at NOLA Noir. Those murders have something to do with the Columns Hotel and those highfalutin families."

"If I use my ace PI skills for anything," I opened the door, "it'll be to find a new receptionist who minds her business."

I left and descended the three flights of stairs, hoping my hunch was right about the criminal activity at the coffee shop. Otherwise, Ruth wouldn't let me live it down until her dying day, and she'd live another four decades to make sure I suffered.

As I exited onto the street, the hot summer air coated my face like a warm, wet washcloth. When this was all over, I didn't need a bridal shower. I needed a vacation to Iceland.

NOLA Noir was dark, so I decided to check around back for a window. Brunella and Vick might've been working via candle-light—perhaps even a candle from the Marie Laveau New Orleans Voodoo Spell collection.

In the event I was being watched, I stayed on my side of Decatur Street and crossed the intersection at Governor Nicholls. And I ducked into the doorway of a corner grocery.

A black NOLA Noir van with the image of the coffee cup and walnut canopy-shaped steam from the company sign was parked on the side of the business.

My mouth was agape—not because of the van, but because Ruth's ruthless rudeness had helped me with a case.

Before leaving my hiding spot, I scanned the vicinity for Brunella or Vick. A sign in the grocery window beside me caught my attention.

Due to the *high summer temperatures, we will NOT be accepting* "boob" *or* "sock" *money. It is unsanitary.*

Sorry for the inconvenience,

Management

THE POLICY CHANGE WAS SERIOUS. If all the grocers adopted it, half of New Orleans would go without food.

Crouching low, I turned my attention to the van. The street was quiet, so I darted to the driver door and pulled the handle. Locked. I turned on my phone light and peered into the back-seat window. On the floor was a box of unlabeled green bottles with cork stoppers. The liquid inside was black.

Noir like nocino.

Shining the light on a bottle, I got a catch in my battle-scarred throat.

The black brew *bubbled*.

Brunella appeared in my head in a swirl of smoke, cackling like my mother while pouring nutmeg essential oil and cloves into a boiling cauldron.

Of blood.

My body began to tingle, and I backed from the window.

A strong coffee odor assailed my nostrils, and a burlap sack whooshed down over my head and torso.

A hand clamped my mouth shut, preventing the scream that wanted to erupt from my lungs like a volcano, and a stout body with arms of steel dragged me backwards.

Amid the struggle, I heard the latch of a car door opening.

The rear of the van?

Fear surged throughout my body, but I had to remain calm.

Using a trick I'd learned from my short stint in Austin as a rookie cop, I threw my head back to deal a blow to my attacker's face.

But I caught wind.

Whoever had a hold of me was short, and that could only be one person.

Or rather, one witch.

A hard shove launched me forward like a broom taking flight. I landed in the back of the van and hit my forehead.

The last thing I saw was black.

Noir.

16

Tiny rays of light stabbed at my brain. *Are they coming through the NOLA Noir Venetian blinds? Is that why I smell coffee?*

No, I'm moving, and I hear an engine.

Am I in a car?

Panic gripped my gut. Is it the mystery woman's black Buick Roadster from the 1940s?

The vehicle turned, and I rolled into a wall.

Whatever I was in, it was too big to be a trunk.

Hold on. I remember flying.

On a broom?

The memory rushed back—I was pushed into the NOLA Noir van, and the tiny rays of light were coming through the weave of the burlap sack that had been thrust over my head.

Anxiety churned in my stomach like coffee beans in a grinder. I'm in a real-life noir film, a Big Easy version of *The Blue Dahlia* complete with a femme fatale. But this movie has a paranormal horror twist—Brunella is a witch obsessed with a TV show about a serial killer.

Not to mention Sick Vick and his thumbnail fetish.

Oh, God. What are they going to do with me?

My stomach stopped churning and went into a freefall.

Maybe Sick Vick wants to cut off my thumbs as a creepy keepsake. He'd probably gotten the idea while watching *Hannibal* with his nonnina. I wriggled my thumbs to make sure I still had them.

Wait. My hands are free.

Vick and Brunella hadn't tied me up. Not only were they bad businesspeople, but as kidnappers went, they were freaking terrible.

Slowly, I eased the burlap sack from my head. I'd expected to see bags of coffee beans and creepy thumbnail photos taped to the walls.

But a mobile waxing table and booze boxes?

Bile began to bubble in my belly, much like the liquid in the green nocino bottle. This was no noir flick with a horror twist. It was a bad B movie with characters in desperate need of development. Because the van I was in didn't belong to NOLA Noir. It was the Lucky's Liquor and Vaxing van, the very vehicle Nadezhda had once screwed me out of a two-thousand-dollar down payment to buy.

And all I'd gotten in exchange was a lousy Tic Tac.

I sat up.

Nadezhda and Glenda were in the front seats, and on the dash between them was the light source—a GPS screen that lit up the silver-sequined tracksuit of my matryoshka manhandler.

The rage reached a rolling boil, and I popped my cork. "You freaking kidnap me and don't say anything?"

Glenda spun in her seat, and I screamed louder than I had when I'd first met Willie Tea in the bush. A false eyelash hung from her eye, and her platinum Cher hair had been reduced to the haywire gray locks of Phyllis Diller. Not only that, she was dressed in a tragic terrycloth bath wrap.

"Miss Franki," she used the edge of the wrap to dab sweat from her brow, "that scream is the reason Miss Nadezhda had to ambush you. We knew you'd make a big fuss and tip off the enemy to our presence."

Nadezhda stopped the van at a red light and cast a look at Glenda that was harder than a hammer and sickle. "Vat I tell you? Frank is veak."

Her *man*sult shook me from the shock of my landlady's missing hair, and I noticed that the spikes on her maroon 'do were drooping. I didn't know what was going on with the two of them, but they needed to take a cue from the Lucky's Liquor and Vaxing slogan and get their hairs in order. "I'm not weak, and I wouldn't have screamed if you'd pulled up like normal people and asked me to get in."

"There was no *time*, sugar," Glenda said, verging on hysterical. "We're on a mission to find Ick Vick."

"Da." Nadezhda growled. "Zat pee hole dandruff."

"Uhhh…" I cocked my head. "What?"

"It Russian insult." She shot me a bewildered look. "You never hear?"

No, but now that I had, I didn't feel so bad that she'd called me weak—or a man. "I know why I'm looking for Vick, but why are you?"

Glenda fanned her chest with a flyer from Madame Moiselle's. "Last night Miss Nadezhda and I got NOLA Noir coffees before my Hot I Scream Sundae number, and awful things have been happening ever since."

"Like what?" I looked from my landlady to Nadezhda. "Your throats are glowing?"

"Nyet." She hit the gas, and the van lurched forward. "Zat coffee eat lipstick and veneer off teet."

My hand went to my breast. If she hadn't referenced lipstick with the word veneer, the story would have been even more concerning.

Glenda lowered the air-conditioner temperature to harsh-Russian-winter. "And I broke out in a sweat that hasn't stopped. During my performance, it caused my cherry pasties to slide off."

So she *had* melted after all.

"The crowd went wild, understandably," she opened her towel and leaned into the A/C vent, "until my wig went the way of the pasties. Now I'm not only hot in *two* senses of the word, I'm bothered, sugar."

I thought of the boob and sock money sign. The management was right to change their policy. "If you're after Vick, I think he's back at NOLA Noir with Brunella."

"We'll deal with him later." She adjusted her eyelash in the passenger mirror. "Right now, our main priority is to find out what's in that nasty nocino."

There was no way I was going to tell them the ingredients. I wasn't sure I had the entire recipe, and the mention of the blood could lead to a blood-letting.

Glenda lit a cigarette sans holder—another heretofore unseen sight—and huffed out the smoke. "Miss Nadezhda contacted some liquor distributors and found out that Vick ordered a case of pure grain alcohol from a place in Slidell."

Nadezhda wrung the steering wheel as though it was Vick's neck. "After I offer him real Russian vodka. Vould you believe?"

I "vould" because that stuff was as toxic as she was. "Did he have it delivered?"

"Sure did, sugar. To a commercial kitchen here on Frenchmen Street."

"So, he and Brunella have another rental space?"

"With a big coffee roaster, apparently. We're wondering whether they have a liquor still to make the nocino."

Or a cauldron.

Nadezhda slowed the van to a stop, and the side door opened automatically. She turned and gave me a pointed stare, which was in stark contrast with her droopy spikes. "Vell, vat you vait for?"

"I'm going in alone?"

She bared veneerless teeth. "Vat you do for living?"

Nadezhda had a point, but she could've said it more nicely. "Fine. I'll take a look." I climbed from the van, eager to escape another showing of the black nubs in her mouth. "I'm going to need one of you to guard the entrance, and the other needs to check for an exit."

"I'm sorry, Miss Franki. I truly am." Glenda pulled on her platinum wig as the van door began to move. "But I have an urgent score to settle with Ick Vick."

The door clicked shut, and the van sped off.

"I knew I couldn't count on the two of them," I grumbled, "and not just because of the kidnapping."

As I walked to the commercial kitchen, I kept an eye on my surroundings. Frenchmen Street was known for its live music and late-night eateries, but not the section I was in. There were sketchy vacant lots and rundown buildings that had never been restored after Hurricane Katrina. It didn't help that the street-lamp was out.

I switched on my phone light and tried the door handle.

Unlocked.

The windows were dark, so I opened the door a crack and shined my light inside. The place looked less like a commercial kitchen and more like an old warehouse with gray walls. To my left were bags of coffee in the same burlap sacks I'd been kidnapped with, and against the back wall was an old Formica table and a gas range with a huge stainless steel stock pot. Not a cauldron, but alarming nonetheless.

I shifted the light to my right and gasped.

Naked mannequins—with their hands missing.

"It's worse than I thought," I whispered. "Vick's not just after the thumbs. He wants the whole hand."

A creak made me jerk the phone light to the far-right corner.

There were stairs, and the figure on them was no mannequin.

The glint of a pistol caught my attention first.

Then I looked into the fox eyes of the bearer.

The femme fatale.

KEEPING the pistol aimed between my eyes, the femme fatale descended the steps and switched on a light. "Who sent you?"

I raised my hands, speechless. And not only because of the gun. I hadn't expected her Lauren Bacall voice and ability to walk in the black form-fitted dress. Plus, against the gray-wall backdrop, it was as though I was watching a live-action film noir.

"Go on." She waved the pistol. "Make like a canary and start singing. Who's paying you?"

"No one." And that was the truth because Shona sure wasn't. "I'm a PI, and I'm investigating the murders of Agata Villeré, Delilah Delaire, and Edward Blain."

"Why are you tailing me?"

"Actually, I was looking for Vick and Brunella."

She semi-lowered the pistol. "Did Tricky Vick double-cross you too?"

Another Vick nickname—or Vickname, as it were. And it reminded me of a bad dog I'd once met during Mardi Gras. "'Double-cross' isn't the word I'd use," I said, both because he hadn't cheated me, and because it sounded like something from an old movie. "Maybe 'double-dose.' My involvement in the case started when he served me an alcoholic coffee that lit up my esophagus."

"You've got moxie to drink his java. That yuck has no business being in business."

The "yuck" threw me, but I didn't show it. "We agree on that."

A corner of her red-lipsticked mouth rose. "Name's Hedy, like Lamarr."

"Mine's Franki, like, uh, *Frankie and Johnny*."

She lowered the pistol to her side and smoothed her Rita Hayworth hair. "Until Tricky Vick conned me, I'd planned to open my own retro boutique, a competitor to Trashy Diva in the Quarter, called 'Forties Femme.'"

I pointed to the naked handless mannequins. "So, these belong to you?"

"Nope, not mine."

Vick was definitely ick and sick.

And Hedy was still armed, so I had to be careful with the questioning, and let her talk.

She glanced around the dingy room. "This warehouse and the NOLA Noir space were on the rental market as a package deal. I had a verbal agreement to lease them for peanuts, but when I went to sign the papers, someone had beat me to it."

"Tricky Vick?"

She nodded. "It's my fault for spilling the beans."

A coffee beans pun came to mind, but I didn't mention it. Hedy had about as much humor as a, well, femme fatale. "You told him about the deal?"

"I never could resist a ducky shincracker."

The mystery woman was no longer a mystery, but her language was. Kind of like Edith Cook's, the Columns Hotel kitchen manager. "What's that? Some kind of gangster?"

Hedy shot me a look similar to Nadezhda's when I'd asked the meaning of pee hole dandruff. "No, a jive bomber."

"Is that a fast talker?"

Her flawless face tensed. "They both mean 'good dancer,' all right?"

I gave up. She had a gun, and the Forties were confusing.

"Anyways, I was sitting at a night club with a chrome dome drip—"

"Wait." I raised a finger. "Is that a type of coffeemaker?"

"No. A boring bald guy." She put her hands on her hips, accentuating her linebacker-sized shoulder pads. "Sheesh. Are you from Mars?"

This broad had hutzpah. If anyone was an alien, it was her.

"As I was saying," she took a seat at the Formica table and crossed Betty Grable legs, "I ditched the chrome dome drip when I saw Vick come into the club with those big eyes and that thick head of hair."

"Yeah," I checked the pot for nocino before taking a seat, "he reminds me of Tony Danza from *Taxi*."

"Is he the cabbie that Vick got to drive me home?"

I was starting to think Hedy really was from the Forties. "No, a different guy."

"You talk a lot of gobbledygook, you know that?"

I had to bite my lip. After all, she *was* packing heat.

Hedy draped an arm over the back of the chair. "Anyway, Vick and I danced, and he bought me a drink. That's when I told him my plans for the boutique, and how I was going to get the clams to pay for it. I was supposed to inherit a ring worn by Bette Davis in a movie, but Agata Villeré nicked it."

"Then, you *are* related to her maid."

"So, you know the sordid story about my Aunt Ella." Her face turned hard, and she rested a hand on the gun. "Agata deserved what she got for dusting her off."

I presumed "dust off" was a euphemism for "murder," and a darn good pun since her aunt was a maid.

Her fox eyes sought mine. "But Vicky didn't kill Agata. When I confided in him about what she'd done to my aunt, he offered to help me get back the ring. He recognized Agata's name because he'd gotten an online order to deliver java and a pastry to her the next morning."

"Quite a coincidence," I said skeptically.

"It *was*. Square." She gave a decisive nod. "When he delivered her order to the Columns, he tried to get her to return the ring. They argued, and Edward Blain heard them and saw an opportunity to frame Vicky."

"Edward? Are you sure?"

"Flat." Another decisive nod.

I didn't know what "flat" or "square" meant, but she definitely did.

She spun the gun on the table. "When Vick got to the Columns, no one was at the front desk, but he heard a man's voice coming from the parlor. He said, 'The wedding planner overheard the plan.'"

Then Edward *did* know Delilah had been eavesdropping on his conversation with Giada's husband, Wolf, the night of the rehearsal dinner. "Did Vick actually see Edward say that?"

"No, but when he left Agata's room, he noticed Edward spying on him through a crack in his door. Later, I did some gumshoeing of my own and found out the reception clerk was a no-show at work that morning, so the guy in the parlor had to be Edward. No other man was staying in the hotel."

That aligned with my understanding of the events, but one detail didn't. "If Edward wanted to frame Vick, he would've left the NOLA Noir bag and go cup in Agata's room. But it was gone, which makes it look like Vick took it to cover his tracks."

"Because Agata told Vick to take the trash with him."

Agata was allegedly uppity, but the story was too convenient. "Let's say Vick is innocent. Why were you following the black BMW that killed Delilah Delaire?"

"Because I was trying to tip the dame off. I even went to her office."

That lined up with Moira's version of the events.

"Afterwards, I went to Edward's law firm. I saw a big man in a hat and long overcoat that I think was him get behind the wheel of a black BMW parked behind the building, and I tailed him." Her jaw clinched. "To NOLA Noir where he ran down Delilah."

The story was plausible, but I couldn't rule out her involvement in Edward's murder, especially since she'd been defending Vick, even after the dope had "double-crossed" her. "Okay, but what were you doing in the Wedding Belles dress at the Columns the night of the séance?"

"The same thing I was doing when I put the gun to your back and took Agata's credit card from you—trying to find out who killed Agata so I can find my Aunt Ella's ring. I didn't plan on anyone ratting me out."

No, but thankfully, Cordelia had. "Incidentally, I didn't appreciate the gun stunt, then or now. That aside, none of this addresses the real issue of what killed Agata. Vick brought her a nocino cappuccino, and she died after drinking it."

"Edward must've poisoned the java."

"You mean, the nocino. That's what he was drinking when he died."

She gasped. "He *was*?"

I nodded. "Most likely made by Brunella. The witch."

"Don't talk about my nonnina like that." Vick's voice cracked through the room like a bullet, and his gaze was murderous. Based on the weapon he was holding, he hadn't come to share his side of the story.

But to kill me.

VICK CLOSED the door behind him. Unlike Hedy, he didn't have a pistol. He held a strange stick—purple with gold swirls.

Some kind of coffee-bean poker?

Or one of Brunella's wands?

He looked from me to Hedy. "Which one of you called the cops?"

Her luscious lips parted. "You think I'd rat you out?"

"Someone did. While my nonnina and I were out, a detective left his card in the door."

So Vick and Brunella *hadn't* been questioned about the blood.

Hedy stood and took a step toward him. "I couldn't do you dirty, Vicky. You know I'm head over heels for you."

Apparently, she hadn't gotten the film noir script. Femme fatales were supposed to use their feminine wiles to gain power over men, not kiss up to them.

Vick turned to me and sneered. "I should've known. You're ATC."

"What does that stand for?" I looked at my hands. "Attractive-Thumbs Chick?"

"Pff!" His face contorted. "Alcohol and Tobacco Control."

I didn't appreciate the "pff," but I had bigger things to worry about. "You think I'm a liquor inspector?" I asked, incredulous. Although, I was kind of kicking myself for not considering it as a career. "I work across the street from NOLA Noir, at Private Chicks."

His semi-unibrow went angular. "The escort service?"

I didn't know what irritated me more—the fact that he thought my PI firm was a front for prostitution or his disbelief that I could work there. But one thing was certain—Vick was too much of a chooch to give me the malocchio. "It's not an escort service, but with thumbs like these," I flashed my nails at him, "I'd make a fortune in the profession."

He showed no reaction. *Bupkis*, to use a Forties term.

Another -ick word described Vick Villano, and, ironically, it was old-fashioned slang for "detective."

I rose from the table. "I came to find out what you put in the nocino. That single sip I took ravaged my throat. It also made my ex-stripper landlady sweat and ate the veneer off her friend's teeth."

His eyes popped. "Your landlady is Lorraine Lamour?" he asked, using Glenda's stage name. "I heard about what happened during her Hot I Scream Sundae number, but I didn't know it was from the nocino."

"Everyone knows you can't refreeze melted ice cream, so thanks to you, she could be ruined." I lowered my lids in contempt. "Even worse, your nocino killed Agata Villeré and Edward Blain."

Vick dragged his hands down his face. "*I'll* be ruined if this gets out."

My blood went cold. He hadn't tried to deny that his nocino had killed two people.

"What're you going to do, Vicky?" Hedy asked.

"I can handle Lorraine, and I already got rid of the nocino. I just came back to make sure I didn't miss anything." He looked at me. "And I did." He pointed the stick at the stairs. "Go."

I turned to Hedy, expecting her to show him who was the boss.

"You heard the man." She turned the pistol on me. "Upstairs."

My hands went up, but my stomach dropped. "We're on the same side, remember?"

"Sorry, doll." She shrugged. "When it comes to that dreamboat, I'm done for."

Hedy was no femme fatale. She was a full-fledged Forties floozy.

With her pistol pressed into my back once again, I climbed the stairs to a wood-paneled room with an old desk and more bags of coffee beans stacked beside a commercial grinder.

Vick entered and picked up an empty burlap sack.

Hedy shook her head. "It would have to be something larger, like a 50-gallon trash bag. She's at least a size 16."

I didn't know what was worse—the fact that she'd suggested how to dispose of me, or that she'd upped my clothing size.

He rummaged through a desk drawer. "I don't got a bag that big."

A flash of irritation interrupted the fear. He didn't have to rub it in.

"Well," she surveyed the room, "the only other option is the grinder."

His eyes darted to the machine. "Can we do that?"

My head jerked to the grinder in horror. The opening was small—but big enough. "You're really going to off me over liqueur ingredients?"

Vick began to pace, his hair bouncing with each step. "When I opened the coffee shop, I didn't know how hard it was to get nocino in the U.S. So I had to use my nonnina's family recipe to make my own, against liquor laws."

He made the nocino? I flashed back to accusing him of not using the bottle behind the NOLA Noir counter, and it all fell into place. "You thought I was an ATC inspector who planned to shut down the shop."

"That can't happen, you hear? NOLA Noir ain't doing too good, so I need to sell. Restaurant Week is my chance to showcase the place and find a buyer. Otherwise, I'm bankrupt." He leaned in. "This will surprise you, but I'm not so hot at business."

I added "pitiful bad guy" to his résumé. No self-respecting villain, especially one with the last name Villano, would admit to that kind of weakness. If he hadn't been about to kill me, I would've introduced him to Willie Tea for some self-promotion pointers.

Hedy rubbed his shoulders. "Don't be so hard on yourself, you silly lug."

My lips pursed. She was a failed femme fatale, but she was straight from a movie.

Trying to buy time to plot my escape, I turned to Vick. "What did you put in the nocino that made it bubble?"

"It was an honest mistake, okay?" He ran a hand through his hair. "The recipe calls for nutmeg, so I used my nonnina's nutmeg essential oil. Then I saw her rubbing it on her wrists for high blood pressure, and she told me it wasn't safe to eat."

I was starting to wonder if I'd been wrong about Brunella. Instead of a witch, she might've been a homeopath. "Since you mentioned blood, did you put that in the nocino too?"

He blew out a breath and looked at Hedy. "Is this chick from Mars, or what?"

"Either that," she said, "or she's off the cob."

Despite their decade difference, these two were made for each other. "Don't play dumb, Vick. A paper bag of blood was delivered to your house."

"Paper?" he echoed. "Wouldn't that fall apart?"

Too bad Vick was a criminal, because he could've had a future as a police tip line operator after the coffee shop closed. "Okay, so you aren't playing dumb."

A snort from behind me made me look over my shoulder.

Brunella.

Her doughy Strega Nona face was as hard and black as the rolling pin she smacked against her palm. "I wish you hadn't-a said-a that."

17

"Thanks for sticking up for me, Nonnina." Vick sniffed and shifted his wounded-puppy gaze from me to his grandmother. "You know I'm not dumb."

Brunella gave a dry grunt. "You're dumb as a walnut, which is-a why we're in this mess." Her beady eyes locked on mine. "I was talking about the blood. She knows because she give-a me the tail."

"You mean, she's been tailing you, Nonnina."

"*Zitto.*" She silenced her grandson and shuffled toward me.

And I backed against a wall. I was more afraid of her rolling pin than Hedy's pistol and Vick's stick. Italian nonne could wield the utensil like samurais did swords and inflict just as much damage.

"This-a one here follow me when I buy nutmeg oil. Then I find-a police at the house. I have-a to hide in the park bushes."

Those bushes are a popular hangout. I wonder if she met Willie Tea.

Brunella smacked the rolling pin against her palm. "Now we must resolve-a this *problema.*"

If she isn't a witch, she's definitely Camorra.

As if to confirm my suspicion, Brunella took a seat behind the desk to conduct her nefarious business like Don Corleone—and my mother. "She knows."

Vick eyed her uncertainly. "You said that already. But so what if she knows about the blood? It's for your *sanguinaccio dolce*, right?"

Hedy leaned closer to her dreamboat. "What's that, Vicky?"

"Italian for 'sweet blood pudding.'"

Her lips went askew. "Crummy."

I would've said "yuck," but Hedy was committed to her Forties take on English vocabulary.

"You have to try it." Vick grinned and put his arm around her, as though they were on a date instead of a hostage-taking. "It's delicious, and it looks really cool too. It's black because of the blood and the dark chocolate and cacao. She puts it in the rind of half of a hollowed-out orange."

Nonnina nodded, satisfied. "It's-a Hannibal Lecter's favorite."

Not what I wanted to hear at the moment.

Hedy blinked. "Who's Hannibal Lecter?"

And she accused *me* of being from Mars.

"He's a character," Vick said.

Like you, Forties Floozy, I wanted to add. Instead, I took a cue from the serial killer reference and moved an inch toward the door.

Brunella leaned back in her chair and rested clasped hands on her round belly. "The sanguinaccio dolce is not-a why we get investigated." She raised her chin. "I have a side gig-a."

Vick jerked, releasing Hedy. "Doing what?"

I wanted to know myself. "Selling witch walnut potions?"

Her beady eyes reduced to pinpoints. "What do you mean, 'witch?'"

"You shop at Hex. It's a witch store?"

Brunella blinked. "It is-a?"

Since she looked like a witch herself, she apparently thought Madge and the others looked normal.

"I do sell-a something, but not-a potions." She looked at Vick. "I make-a food for people when you work at NOLA Noir."

"Oh, jeez. Catering from the house?" He threw up his hands. "Nonnina, that's against Health Department regulations. They'll fine you and shut down the coffee shop." He rubbed the back of his neck. "How am I gonna get us out of this?"

Hedy grabbed Vick by the shoulders. "We have to find the Bette Davis ring, Vicky. That canary yellow diamond is worth quite a few clams. Then we can run away together. Start fresh in Reno."

"Or Casablanca," I offered.

Vick looked stricken. "And leave my nonnina?"

Who's the boss? Brunella is.

"You can't live with her forever, Vicky."

Brunella jerked forward and grabbed the rolling pin. "Sure he can."

"Nonnina's right." Vick shrugged off Hedy, and she stormed to a corner to sulk. He paced and wrung his hands. "There has to be another way to fix this... I know." He snapped his fingers and pointed at Brunella. "We could ask your customers not to talk."

"There's another problema." She spun her rolling pin. "I've-a been cleaning the money at the coffee shop."

His brow furrowed. "Washing it? In our sink?"

Vick was a himbo. "She means laundering money, through NOLA Noir."

"What money?" he asked.

"*Mamma mia!*" Brunella raised a hand to the heavens. "From-a my catering. What else-a?"

I was with Vick on this one. How much money could anyone make off boozy pasta? Scratch that. In The Big Easy, a small fortune, especially during Mardi Gras season. "Forgive me for intruding in a family matter, but you've got a coffee shop and a commercial kitchen. Why not cook in one of those?"

Brunella recoiled. "How you gonna make-a food with-a love in a work kitchen?"

Her response hit me like a rolling pin. Everyone knew Italian nonne cooked with love, but Vick's nonnina didn't strike me as one of them.

She rose from the desk and shot a look at Vick. "You know what this-a means."

His eyes darted left to right. "Can you give me a hint?"

I halted my inching toward the door to shake my head.

Brunella looked from her grandson to me and back.

"Nonnina," he leaned close to her ear, "we can't kill her."

She whacked his bicep with her rolling pin. "What-a you thinking?" she asked as Vick rubbed his arm. "I mean, we gotta pay her off. She's-a IRS."

It was a wonder that Vick and Brunella had managed to start a single business, much less several. "I'm not IRS or ATC." Sticking with the acronym theme, I added, "I'm a PI. And the only reason I came here is to find out the ingredients in the nocino."

Brunella's face glowed like oiled pasta dough. "In that-a case, you come to the house and have a nice-a meal. Then I give-a you an ancient recipe." She waved the rolling pin at Vick. "Get-a the van."

These people weren't the killers, but they weren't well—and they had weapons. There was no way I'd go willingly to their fairytale house of horrors. "Thanks, but it's late. I need to get home and let my dog out."

"We stop there on-a the way." Her lips spread into a sneer that may or may not have been intentional. "Then you try my sanguinaccio dolce." She jutted out her chin and made an awful slurping sound.

The same one Hannibal Lecter made when describing how he'd eaten a guy's liver with fava beans and Chianti.

THE SLURP WAS my cue to escape this treacherous trio. I had to think of something to save my skin—because Hannibal Lector.

Frantic, I glanced around the room and grabbed the closest thing. Coffee beans.

And I threw them at Brunella.

She started so hard that her big nose bounced. "What did-a you do that-a for?"

"Yeah, Franki," Vick whined. "Coffee is expensive."

So, maybe the janare counting thing only worked with broom bristles. But if nothing else, I still had hope they'd slip on the beans.

When I ran.

I dashed down the stairs to the first floor and began dodging behind mannequins in case Hedy started shooting. Sensing Vick hot on my heels, I turned around to look. My foot caught on something, and I stumbled, losing precious seconds.

Vick headed me off at the door. "What're you doing?" His tone was one of bewilderment. "We're just going for dessert, and it's an offense to my nonnina to dodge her invitation."

Given his Tony-Danza demeanor, I couldn't get a read on whether he was for real or conning me. But in light of the ammazzacaffè threat he'd made on two separate occasions, I settled on the latter. Because even though the word meant *digestif*, under the circumstances, I couldn't afford to ignore its literal translation—*coffee killer*.

Vick unlocked the door, pushed it open, and turned to extend a hand to Brunella. "Watch your step, Nonnina."

A burlap sack came down over Vick, who let out a muffled shout.

Glenda and Nadezhda?

Rolling pin in hand, Brunella stepped into the street, giving me a clear view of the scene.

Glenda was dragging a writhing, screaming Vick toward the back of the Lucky's Liquor and Vaxing van. She might've been sixty-something and scrawny, but she'd been pole-dancing for decades, and she was still raging-sweating.

Hedy pushed past me and Brunella and pulled her pistol. "Let him go."

Glenda's eyes were as hard as bullets. "Not on your life, sister."

"Lorraine, baby," Vick said, using her stage name, "is that you?"

Hedy lowered her weapon and scowled at Brunella. "Who *is* this broad?"

"My ex-stripper landlady," I said.

"You got the *ex* right, Miss Franki." Glenda glowered at the burlap sack.

"If this is about Agata," Vick whined, "I didn't do it. I delivered the coffee and a pastry, and then I had a talk with her about Hedy's ring. But that's it, I swear."

For some reason, I believed him.

Glenda continued dragging Vick to the van. "This isn't about Agata, but it is about that coffee. Thanks to whatever you put in it, I had a literal meltdown during my Hot I Scream Sundae number."

"I'm sure you were a sensation, Lorraine. You're still the hottest dancer at Madame Moiselle's."

"Well!" Hedy shoved the pistol into her purse.

Glenda dropped Vick at the back of the van. "I'm hot, all right, Ick Vick, you Sick SOB. And you're about to take some heat too. In a couple of senses of the phrase."

Brunella raised her rolling pin and went on the offensive.

Glenda stepped on Vick's back with the waffle-cone stripper heel that said *Me* and deployed her only weapon.

The terrycloth bath wrap she'd been wearing.

For the first time in my memory, my landlady didn't strike a pose or shimmy. She just stood there stark naked, sweating.

Brunella stopped and stepped back.

Understandably.

Glenda dropped into a stripper squat and bound Vick's hands and feet with strips of burlap sack.

Vick tried to resist, but he was powerless in that position. "You've got to listen to me, Lorraine. It wasn't intentional. We had a little accident with the recipe, that's all."

"That's *all*? My days of doing the odd performance are over, and I'm sweating so bad I can't wear my wig." Glenda stood and pulled the sack from Vick's head.

He took one look at her sweaty birthday suit and sparsely haired head and swooned.

Glenda gritted her teeth and knocked on the back of the van.

The doors burst open to reveal a second horrifying sight— Nadezhda sneering sans veneers and holding her waxing pot.

"Vick," she nudged him with the shoe that said *Lick*, "this is my Russian bikini-waxer friend." Glenda flailed an arm—and a breast—at Nadezhda. "She's going to help you get your hairs in order."

"Nooo!" He rocked back and forth rocking-horse style, trying to flee. "Nonnina! Hedy! Help me!"

Brunella waved off his plea. "I'm-a not touching-a that. I make-a food with these hands."

Hedy gave her Forties hair a bump. "You're done for, Vicky."

"Why?" he cried, bewildered. "You've got a gun. Shoot!"

"Not after you two-timed me with this cheap chippie. And besides, my bean-shooter doesn't have bullets."

I should've known. On top of being a failed femme fatale, she was a fraud too.

Nadezhda hopped from the van and helped Glenda lift a hog-tied Vick inside.

"Strip him bare," Glenda spat. "Top to bottom."

Vick's semi-unibrow popped. "B-bottom?"

Nadezhda grinned, showing her nubs. She smeared wax on Vick's head, applied a strip, and ripped it off.

Vick screamed bloody hair murder.

Police lights flashed, followed by a short siren blast.

"The fuzz!" Glenda slammed the van doors and climbed into the front seat. The tires squealed, but not as loud as Vick.

Hedy and Brunella took off in the NOLA Noir van, abandoning the soon-to-be chrome dome dope.

And me.

The siren resumed, and the police car gave chase.

Stunned by the turn of events, I made like one of the mannequins.

Tires screeched, and another van came around the corner.

With a flaming toilet on top.

It was Lou and Chandra's company van, Crescent City Plumbing and Palmistry.

Chandra hopped out looking like a Sixties alien from a *Star Trek* episode with her huge head of hair, silver mini dress, and moon boots. She held up one of Lou's signature tools—that also reflected her Crescent City Medium moniker—a crescent wrench. "Hand over the charm bracelet, Amato."

"How'd you know I was here?"

"Glenda told me. I've been looking all over town for you. Now stop stalling and hand over the goods."

Very femme fatale of her. "Maybe I don't have it with me."

"Maybe you do."

"Either way, you're not getting it. That bracelet is the bane of my existence."

She whacked her palm with the wrench. "If you don't hand it over in the next thirty seconds, this baby will be the bane of your existence."

Slowly, I backed away. Chandra not only prided herself on being Boston Strong, but she was also a Cancer. And in my experience, those born under the moon sign were more than a little moody.

"Twenty seconds..."

As I debated how to disarm her, a tow truck with tinted windows pulled up.

With a six-foot-long crawdad perched on the boom.

Chandra glanced over her shoulder. "We don't need a tow."

The driver, who looked none too friendly and vaguely familiar, exited the vehicle, squared his hips, and crossed his muscular arms across his chest. "I ain't here to tow nobody."

"Listen, mister, I'm in a mood," she growled, and began turning to face him, "so if you don't mind..." She completed her turn and lowered the wrench. "...I'll just be going."

The driver and I both watched as Chandra moon-walked to the van, got in, and sped off.

He resquared his hips and zeroed in on me.

And I swallowed. We were alone in the Warehouse District.

In the dead of night.

"So... Can I help you?"

"You can." He pointed to the truck. "Get in."

"Big Chuck says you two know each other," Shona shouted from beside me in the backseat of the tow truck, making me *really* regret its tinted windows.

Moira leaned around Shona as Giada looked on from the passenger seat in front of her. "From Crawfish Fest?"

The driver, aka Big Chuck, eyed me via the rearview mirror. "You questioned me about a case, remember?"

Oh, I remembered. I was at the festival investigating an ax murder, and Big Chuck was waving his pincers and raving that a fellow crawfish colleague who'd no-showed was making him miss his baby brother's jail-release party. He also claimed the colleague's behavior was a violation of the Crawdad Code of Conduct.

Which made me wonder whether forcefully taking a woman from a warehouse was a violation of the same. I would've been grateful that they'd picked me up, but they were just as unstable as Vick, Brunella, and Hedy. And Big Chuck had the jarring habit of anger-asserting his words. "How'd you all know where I was?"

Shona semi-turned, shoving her mystery tote in my side and pushing me into the door handle. "We didn't. I called Glenda to get the key to Veronica's old apartment, and she filled us in on what was happening. Since we were out doing some investigating of our own, we decided to come by."

I'd have to talk to my landlady about sharing my whereabouts—after she stopped sweating and put her clothes and hair back on.

Moira leaned around Shona. "Did you find out anything from Vick, Franki?"

I shoved the mystery tote back at Shona. "He claims he accidentally put pure nutmeg oil in a batch of nocino. It's toxic, but I don't know if that killed Agata."

"Why not?" Shona's question hit my ear drum like an arrow.

"Because," I pointedly rubbed my ear, "several of us have had his nocino cappuccino, and despite some nasty side effects, none of us have died."

"But Agata was elderly." She glanced at the others for support. "It could've taken more of a toll on her."

"Dat's right." Big Chuck aimed the mirror at me. "When my Ne Ne was eighty-five, she ate a fried gator po-boy Peacemaker style over at Mahony's and had a stroke."

As a connoisseur of the sandwich, I was surprised I hadn't heard of that one. "Sorry to hear that. But what's 'Peacemaker style?'"

"Peacemaker is the name of their fried oyster, bacon, and cheese po-boy. But Ne Ne swapped the oysters for gator."

It should've been called the *Rest In* Peacemaker based on those ingredients—and Ne Ne's unfortunate demise. "I think Edward added something to the coffee to make sure it killed Agata, just like whoever used nocino to kill him."

The tow truck went over a pothole, bouncing me between Shona and her mystery tote and the hard door handle. I couldn't believe I was thinking this, but the hearse was more comfortable. "Just out of curiosity," I leaned around Shona to talk to Moira, "what happened to Phil?"

"Oh, it's exciting." Her eyes lit up. "He has his first Uber Undertaker client."

Giada smiled. "Someone needed a body buried fast."

Leaning back to ponder that, I caught Big Chuck staring me down. *If I don't watch out, I could become Phil's next assignment.*

To evade his hostile gaze, I checked my phone. I'd missed a text from Veronica about the reading of Agata's will. It was at eight-thirty a.m., nine hours away.

"Anyone want a daiquiri?" Big Chuck anger-asked, making all of us jump.

"Let's get a round," Shona shouted.

Once again, I lamented that I hadn't been able to get a preview of the tow truck's passengers through the tinted windows. Between Big Chuck and Shona, I was getting a headache. Although, a daiquiri would help.

Big Chuck pulled into the drive-through of New Orleans Original Daiquiris, which, despite decades of anti-drinking-and-driving campaigns, had been a local institution since 1983. It was one of the many ironies of The Big Easy, and possibly the origin of one of its lesser-known nicknames, "The City of Yes."

"We need five of the forty-four-ounce size," he anger-asserted into the speaker, "all Crawgator."

Given his crawdad side gig and the news of Ne Ne's final fried-gator sandwich, none of us dared ask for a different flavor.

While we waited for our drinks, Giada rested a hand on Big Chuck's shoulder. "I don't mind saying this in front of you." She turned to look at me, and tears threatened to spill. "The police are questioning Wolf as we speak."

Big Chuck handed her a napkin from Willie's Chicken Shack.

"Before he went to the station," she dabbed at her eyes, "he admitted talking to Edward the night of the rehearsal dinner. He swore they only talked about a plan to save the law firm." She crumpled the napkin. "But I don't know whether to believe Wolf or not."

Apparently, Giada trusted Chuck more than her husband, which was kind of understandable. After all, Wolf was a lawyer at a sketchy firm linked to two murders, while Big Chuck lived by the honorable Crawdad Code of Conduct.

Moira pulled a couple of twenties from her handbag and passed them to Big Chuck. "Well, I got some gossip from a former client of Delilah's. Apparently, a week before Agata died, Lara was notified that she'd changed her beneficiary in the will. No one knows who the new heir is."

The will promised to be a riveting—and revelatory—read. "Maybe that was Edward's motive, kill Agata and contest the change. Then he would've had the money to save his firm, which is probably why he called Wolf when he did."

"Solid theory," Shona said, as though she was the PI on the case. "Edward was the only Blain who stayed at the Columns the night of the rehearsal dinner. Lara and Grace left soon after Agata's awful speech."

That was news to me. "Who told you they left?"

She shot me a self-important side-eye. "Adonis from the Columns coffee shop."

"The one who had a flame neck tattoo and did jail time?"

"Mh-hm."

Because of her former romance tote and her ability to pick walnuts in accordance with the San Giovanni tradition, I had to ask for a clarification. "Is Adonis his actual name? Or are you calling him that for some other reason?"

"It's his name." Her side-eye narrowed. "What are you insinuating?"

"Nothing. It's just that he didn't give me that information when I questioned him."

"*You* didn't pay him."

The drive-through window opened, and a young girl in a Daiquiri-Is-My-Favorite-Fruit T-shirt handed Big Chuck a tray of drinks.

"So," I half-turned to confront Shona, "you can pay Adonis, but not me?"

"Sure. With your credit card."

"Come again?" My tone was hot, like our driver's.

"Dat ain't cool, Shona." Big Chuck shoved a drink at me.

That Shona swiped.

"Why not?" she huffed. "Franki's working my case, and she pays people for information all the time."

Any doubts I'd had that the malocchio was a real affliction vanished like my Crawgator daiquiri. And I intentionally looked at Shona with envy—or maybe more the cup—to give the evil eye to her. "I pay informants when it's *my choice*. How'd you get my card number, anyway?"

"I'm a librarian." She adjusted her collar. "I work in data acquisition."

Shona was starting to remind me of Willie Tea. Like him, she drained my money and dabbled in padding her résumé. "Do it again," I took a drink from Big Chuck, "and no one will have to investigate your murder."

She scooted toward Moira, relieving my middle of her mystery tote. "Someone's moody."

I'd learned from the Madame of Moody, i.e., Chandra. "On the subject of credit card theft, which *is* a felony, don't forget that Edward gave Agata's Black Card to Grace to use at Wedding Belles. And I'm sure he used it himself to place an online order for Agata from NOLA Noir, maybe even from a computer at the Columns."

"Ooh!" Shona shoved the mystery tote back into my middle. "That jives with something the night clerk said. He told me Edward was creeping around the hotel, watching him. I'll bet he was waiting for him to leave the reception desk so he could use the computer."

Big Chuck slapped the steering wheel. "Dat's how I see it too, Shona."

My eyes met his in the rearview mirror, but his hard stare discouraged any question I had about his ongoing participation in the case discussion.

Moira leaned around Shona. "One thing that's got me worried, no one's seen Lara since the rehearsal dinner. She's not answering calls or texts."

That wasn't terribly surprising. "Maybe she's in hiding, like you. In the span of a few days, she's lost two family members."

Giada turned around. "Do you think Edward did something to Lara before he was murdered?"

"It's possible." Moira pulled her handbag to her chest. "Men are maniacs."

Shona scowled. "*My* money's on Grace."

"You mean, *my* money," I anger-asserted à la Big Chuck. "And the police haven't identified Lara as missing. Before we jump to conclusions, I say we wait to see if she shows up to the reading of the will in the morning."

Big Chuck nodded. "Good point, Franki."

Shona took a long drink. "Speaking of Grace, the night clerk also overheard her argue with Agata about the Bette Davis ring. She wanted to wear it at the rehearsal dinner, but Agata said she was hardly diamond material, more like cubic zirconia. Edward was there, and he agreed. Her own *father*."

Moira tsked. "It was well known in social circles that she despised him for spending all their money and making her reliant on Agata."

So Grace had a reason to hate Edward.

Big Chuck gave a snort of disgust. "Sounds like his daughter done him in."

Since he'd agreed with me earlier, I was now more inclined to include him in the conversation. "Maybe, Big Chuck. But Lara could've hated her husband for the same reason."

Giada looked at me. "What about the femme fatale? She had a gun."

I shrugged. "Turns out she's the rightful heir to the Bette Davis ring, but I don't think she killed Edward."

"Why not?" Moira asked. "That certainly gives her a motive."

"Yeah, but the ring is missing with the rest of Agata's jewels, so she would've wanted Edward alive to find out where they are.

Plus, she didn't even have bullets for her pistol. Despite her femme-fatale flair, she doesn't have the killer instinct." I took another slug of daiquiri and flashed back to the shock on Hedy's face after the black BMW hit Delilah.

Where is that car?

Did Edward hide it in the cordgrass?

Or— I glanced out the window at St. Charles Street. I knew where we were. "Big Chuck, could you pull a U-turn?"

He yanked the wheel, and we did a wild 180.

Either he was still angry about me asking for Phil, or he was offended that I'd dissed his investigative skills.

Giada turned in her seat. "Where are we going, Franki?"

"Just up the street." I peered out the window, watching for the house the kids avoided at Halloween. "Stop here."

Moira looked out. "What're we doing at Agata's mansion?"

I was asking myself the same thing, because it looked like a place Baby Jane and Blanche would have lived. It was a two-story moss-covered mansion with eroding gray paint, dilapidated shutters, and attic windows with broken glass. The house resembled a gated mausoleum, which was fitting, because it was located beside one of the city's most infamous cemeteries, Lafayette No. 1.

Where *Interview with a Vampire* and *Dracula* were filmed.

"Are we breaking in?" Shona asked.

Not without the Demon-Be-Gone smudge stick and Uncrossing candle. I pointed to a carriage house to the right of the mansion. "We're going to look in that building."

We climbed from the tow truck, except for Big Chuck who was doubling down on his Crawgator daiquiri and approached the gate.

It was padlocked.

Moira dug in her bag. "I have a nail file."

Big Chuck exited the tow truck. Holding his Crawgator drink

in one hand, he pulled the chain from the boom and hooked it to the padlock. "Move out the way, ladies."

We certainly did.

He got back behind the wheel and hit the gas, ripping off the entire front gate.

So much for the Crawdad Code of Conduct.

I went to the carriage house and tried the handle. "Locked too."

Big Chuck backed the tow truck to the door.

Using my drink straw, I shoveled daiquiri into my mouth while he ripped the door off the building.

As I'd suspected, a tarp-covered vehicle was inside.

Before I could remove the cloth, Shona yanked it off with the flourish of a true mystery-tote sleuth.

Beneath it—the black BMW.

18

———————

The head lights of the black BMW came on, lighting up the carriage house.

A driver was inside?

Shocked, I looked at Giada, Moira, and Shona. "Who would hide in a car that was covered with a tarp?"

They didn't respond, but I already knew the answer.

Edward's killer.

The BMW began backing out, taillights glowing demon-eye red. The windows were tinted darker than the ones on Big Chuck's tow truck, so it was impossible to see who was driving.

The car cleared the building and stopped.

And the trunk popped.

Two strong arms scooped me up.

Stunned, I gaped into the angry eyes of Big Chuck—and the googly ones of his crawdad costume. "What're you doing?"

"Makin' damn sure you don't get back in my tow truck."

"Why? What did I do?"

"You wanted to ride with Phil, so here you go." He tossed me in the trunk as nonchalant as Edith Cook tossing a manhandled chicken into a pot. His googly eyes bounced to and fro as he gripped the trunk lid with his pincers and slammed it shut.

I felt around in the dark. The space was narrow and had...

Satin-lined padding?

A pang pierced my chest.

Not only was I in a trunk, I was also in a coffin. "Dear God," I whispered, "I'm Phil's Uber Undertaker client."

The black BMW began to move.

Despite the trauma of finding myself in a trunk tomb, I had to admit that the coffin was more comfortable than Big Chuck's tow truck. Besides the satin cushions, there was no hard door handle and, best of all, no Shoutin' Shona with her mystery tote.

The BMW picked up speed, and Phil was doing his bat-out-of-hell driving. The car twisted and turned so violently that I literally rolled in my grave.

Is he taking me to Saint Cecilia Cemetery?

Or Lafayette No. 1?

It was hard to say which was worse. Phil once told me that the crypts of Saint Cecilia were crawling with grave grasshoppers known as *chevals-diable*, and then there were the critters he used to make his salumi. But Lafayette No. 1 was so macabre that Anne Rice had a horse-drawn hearse pull her through it in a glass coffin to publicize her book *Memnoch the Devil*. Not the kind of place I wanted to spend eternity.

The BMW braked, and the engine shut off.

My ears pricked up.

Silence.

The coffin lid opened.

Phil flashed a cheerful grin. "Time to get out, Franki. You're not dead..." His eyes sparkled like Santa's. "...yet."

Refusing his extended hand, which, oddly, was clad in surgical gloves, I climbed from the coffin. We were in a park surrounded by cordgrass, and in the middle was the Tree of Life, the one Willie Tea had told me was popular for weddings. *Am I getting married?*

The tree *had* been decorated with some sort of ornaments.

Wait. No. They're...

Walnuts the size of oranges?

Women in black emerged from the tall grass cackling and swigging from bottles of nocino.

Janare?

Majare?

No, the gangster grandmas.

And—zero surprise—my mother.

Phil pulled a stack of gowns from the trunk. "Time to put on your dress." He rifled through the black number his previous client had left, a couple of bridesmaids dresses he'd bought from Wedding Belles, and the flesh-and-pink floral number Moira had loaned me. Then he held up the plantation wedding dress my mother had tried on. He kissed his fingertips. "This one is *bellissima!*"

A blood-chilling scream escaped my lips. "Over my dead body!"

Phil tapped his fingertips together and licked his lips like Hannibal Lector. "That can be arranged."

Why? Why had I said that to a cemetery caretaker?

The nonne forced me into the huge dress, including a hoop skirt, seven petticoats, and a corset for good measure. They stepped back, and I discovered they'd finished the look with a bonnet and parasol.

Nonna Nunzia stepped forward with a bowl of water. She added a drop of olive oil, and it morphed into the face of Strega Nona.

Or was it Brunella?

My mother poked me in the side, where the tow truck door handle had been. "Drink it, Francesca."

"Go on-a," Nonna urged. "This is-a the cure you ask-a for."

"For my malocchio?"

My mother threw back her head and cackled. "No, dear. For your never-ending engagement."

Chin-Hair Nonna leaned in so close I could feel her whiskers, and then she transformed into Ruth Walker. "Long engagement, quick divorce, missy."

The nonne began to chant the saying, and the Voodoo Doughnuts protestors materialized and joined in. Their pitch reached a frenzy, and the Baron Samedi lookalike raised a voodoo doll of me.

And it had a cappuccino mug.

Frightened, I looked at the bowl.

It was now a NOLA Noir cup. Only it wasn't filled with nocino cappuccino.

But novelty urine.

"I'm not drinking that."

"Why not-a?" Nonna cried. "It's-a big-a fun at-a parties!"

"Nonna, nothing's going to make this party fun."

The crowd turned nasty, and the protesters and the nonne took turns sticking a pin in the Franki voodoo doll's throat. Her mouth formed an O.

Like the voodoo cigar.

And Mr. Bill.

"Trust us, Franki." Titti threw open her arms. "What're we nonna's for, if not to relieve pain and suffering?"

Glancing around for an escape, I spotted something odd. The walnuts in the Tree of Life had turned into Mardi Gras necklaces.

My hand moved to my neck, and I looked down. I was wearing Marie Antoinette's pearls. Not only that, my plantation-style wedding gown had become the black mourning dress Scarlett O'Hara wore in *Gone With the Wind*.

Or was it Bette Davis in Jezebel?

Titti grabbed my face with her oar-paddle hands, and I glanced around looking for the Merry Antoinettes with the guillotine, convinced I was about to be beheaded. But instead, something more terrible happened.

She pressed my head between her breasts.

And I couldn't breathe.

A horn honked.

"Hurry up," Phil called in a merry voice. "We've got to get this girl buried!"

Buried? I thought I was getting married!

Panic set in as I realized what was about to happen. Titti was going to ease my pain and suffering by suffocating me. Because this wasn't my *wedding* party—it was my *funeral* party.

In desperation, I used precious oxygen to scream into her bosom, "This dress is so *big*, it won't fit in a mausoleum!" But it came out, "Mih meh mih muh *mihhh*, mm muh mih mih mm muhmuhmmihmuhm."

The crowd went silent.

Did I get through to them?

The nonne crossed themselves and parted to reveal a horse-drawn hearse with a glass coffin, the one that had carried Anne Rice through Lafayette Cemetery No. 1.

Phil was at the reins, beckoning to me. "Franki!"

That's funny... He sounds like Bradley.

"Franki," he called again.

I squinted. *It* is *Bradley.*

That was galling. Now I had to survive, if for no other reason than to give that man a piece of my mind.

Summoning the combined lung-strength of Shona and Big Chuck, I inhaled. And opened my eyes.

Bradley knelt beside me, his brow wrinkled, and kissed my

hand. "I've been trying to wake you up, babe. You stopped breathing."

"Yeah," my tone was as acid as a woman who'd drunk novelty urine. "Thanks for not rescuing me from my funeral party."

His expression went from startled to amused. "Were you having one of your elaborate nightmares?"

I didn't answer. Because I'd figured out that I was lying on one of the two couches in the Private Chicks lobby, and according to the clock above the door, it was already ten thirty.

The events of hours before rushed back. Getting kidnapped by a melted Glenda and nub-toothed Nadezhda, having a gun pulled on me by a femme fatale in a warehouse full of mannequins, and then a coffee stirrer and a rolling pin by Vick and his nonnina. Vick getting waxed. Chandra showing up with a crescent wrench, getting abducted by a man with a crawdad on this tow truck, and drinking forty-four ounces of a daiquiri flavor called "Crawgator." The discovery of the black BMW at Agata's mansion. And, of course, Big Chuck dropping me off at the office—and not in a coffin in the BMW's trunk.

"Bradley," I rolled to my side and took his hands, "once we're married, we need to consider leaving New Orleans... Start over someplace where normal people live."

"You mean, you want to live close to your family?"

I dropped his hands. "I said 'normal,' Bradley. Not neurotic."

Veronica cleared her throat. "Well, I, for one, hope you don't leave. You might feel differently once you're married and in your own home."

"And out of the fourplex funhouse." I sat up. Bradley moved beside me, and I snuggled into his side.

Veronica took a seat on the couch across from us. "I take it Glenda never gave you the key to my old apartment?"

"Uh, no. She gave it to Shona, and I didn't want to stay with her." That leech librarian had done a lot of damage to my finances without even having my credit card. No way I was giving her easy access to my wallet and phone.

"While Bradley's hosting his family, why don't you stay in my guest room?"

"No, I've been coming in at all hours because of this case. Besides, my mom and nonna will head home the day after tomorrow when Bradley's family leaves."

"If you change your mind, you know the address. By the way, does tomorrow still work for our lunch date?"

She was talking in code about the bridal shower. The timing was inconvenient, but I had no intention of being the subject of another Suffering Stories session. They were already the stuff of nightmares without an actual nightmare thrown in. "Yes. Come hell or high swamp water."

"Good. We have a noon reservation at Copper Vine."

Bradley looked down at me. "Will you bring me a piece of their black walnut pie?"

"Of course," I agreed. But I would do no such thing—not after the way he'd betrayed me in my dream.

"Now that we have that settled," Veronica's eyes grew serious, "Glenda called and told me what happened last night, and I filled in your fiancé."

Bradley gave me a squeeze. "Why didn't you call me, babe?"

"When? I never got a break. It was one sideshow after another complete with clown cars."

He chuckled, but I didn't. Instead, I grabbed my bag from the coffee table to check for Chandra's charm bracelet.

Still there. But what to do with it?

Veronica glanced at Bradley. "I have two pieces of news. First, Vick and Brunella were questioned in Agata's murder but released. Then Glenda and Nadezhda got a visit from an officer because Vick reported them for abducting him and waxing off his body hair... and I mean all of it."

Bradley blinked. "You didn't tell me that part, Veronica."

And I wished she hadn't told him now. The mental image of a hairless Vick was ick. And sick. I got a visual of the chicken Edith Cook had plucked with her teeth, but in place of a beak, it had big Vick lips. "What happened?"

"The police aren't pursuing charges because Nadezhda lied and said Vick had broken into her van and used her wax to change his appearance."

Bradley arched a brow. "What about his... *other* hair? Why would he wax that?"

"Babe," I widened my eyes in a come-*on* look, "this is New Orleans. The police aren't going to think anything's off about a guy who waxes his privates to evade arrest."

He cocked his head. "You're probably right."

Veronica scooted forward. "And for the second piece of news, I got the scoop on Agata's will."

I cast off Bradley's arm and leaned in. "Well?"

"Agata didn't leave a cent to her family. Her last words to them were something along the lines of 'That's what you get for biting the hand that feeds you.'"

A recurring theme lately. "Who was her beneficiary?"

"The Vieux Carré Commission."

That was a punch in the gut. Since her mother was from Benevento, she could've at least given half to the American Italian Cultural Center.

Bradley rubbed his chin. "I wonder if the Blains knew that before she died."

I was sure Edward did. *But who killed him?* "Do you know whether Lara was there?"

"Actually, she wasn't, which I found odd. It was just Grace."

That *was* odd. And concerning. *Was Moira right?*

Did something happen to Lara?

I picked up my phone, and it rang in my hand. The number was one I didn't recognize. "Franki Amato."

"Yeah, I know," Swamp Sasquatch said. "Miss Shona gave me your number."

And probably my credit card information.

"How's your day going, chère?"

"Can't complain." Although I certainly could have.

"I'm callin' because I found a little somethin' you're gonna wanna see."

My lips pursed. "Is it alive?"

"Why, no." He sounded surprised by the question, but given the case, his trailer décor, and his cooking, it was the obvious thing to ask.

"Was it ever?"

"Nah, it's a lady's earring. Real fancy too."

Agata's jewelry?

"JUST IN TIME, CHÈRE." Sylvain Fontaine smiled and wiped sweat from his brow with Nute. "I made us a batch o' Italian weddin' soup."

I stopped short. The reference to the soup reminded me of my nightmare and the nagging sensation that I might not get married without a hitch.

He swallowed a bite of the soup. "Mm-mm-*mm!*" He dropped the spoon into the pot. "Dis ain't de one your mawmaw makes."

It sure ain't, I thought. My mawmaw's, aka nonna's, smelled like meatballs and delicious spices. His smelled like dirty socks and sulfur, and I had no doubt the broth was pure swamp water. And believe you me, the name Honey Island Swamp was a misnomer, because there was nothing sweet about the place or its water.

"I got de idea to make it when I found me a carrot by de water. Somethin' must o' carried it to dese parts, 'cause it had some chaw marks on it. But it was still good for cookin' and eatin'."

Was it, though?

He grinned with pride. "Den I went to de store and got me some maccheroni and a container o' Kraft real parmesan cheese."

"You should do more of that." I mustered an encouraging smile. "Not cheese called 'parmesan,' maybe, but the store part."

The Swamp Sasquatch scratched his head. "What for? I got me nature's bounty at my fingertips!" He spooned a meatball from the pot and sprinkled it with cheese. "Jus' taste dis right here. Gator and wild pig. It's yum yum for de tum tum."

He held out the spoon, and I flashed back to the fried gator po-boy with bacon and cheese that had done in Big Chuck's Ne Ne. The meatball wasn't fried, but it contained enough bacteria to wipe out half of New Orleans.

And I was not only sweating from the stifling heat, but I was also sweating how to get out of this situation. "Uh, it's awfully hot out for soup."

"Hurry up, Willie," the Swamp Sasquatch said. "Soup's on!"

Startled, I turned to see Willie Tea coming around the side of Sylvain's trailer. He was sporting the same dirty shirt and baggy pants, but he'd added suspenders. The only thing his outfit was missing was a handkerchief tied to a stick.

"I'm famished." Willie rubbed his hands together. "Good day, Franki."

The greeting was irritating. We'd agreed not to tell anyone we knew each other, or so I'd thought. Served me right for trusting a park narc. "How do *you two* know each other?"

Willie hooked his thumbs in the suspender straps. "We're members of the same non-profit organization."

"Let me guess. A tree society."

"Why, no," Swamp Sasquatch jutted out his lower lip, "but dat's not a bad idea."

Willie released a suspender to point to the spoon. "Are you, perchance, going to eat that?"

Unlike my money, the meatball was one thing I was thrilled to give Willie. "Would *you* like to?"

"Happy to oblige." He took the spoon from the Swamp Sasquatch, sank his lone tooth into the meatball, and wolfed it down.

Good riddance.

Willie took a seat on a stump near the fire, pulled a handkerchief from his pocket, and tucked it into his collar in anticipation of more meatballs.

As I moved to join him, a bird with a five-foot wingspan swooped down.

"Holy crow," I shouted and jumped back as it landed on my stump.

"Dat's an osprey." Swamp Sasquatch shook his finger at the creature. "Now, Maxime, you know better'n to take a seat from a lady."

The bird shot him a piercing stare but hopped to the next stump.

Apparently, Maxime was another of Sylvain's peculiar pets, and he wasn't leaving without his wedding soup.

"Go on and sit, chère, while I serve up de grub."

My stomach sank to the bottom of the swamp, but I did as I was told and sat next to Willie. "You still haven't told me the name of the organization."

"The Vieux Carré Commission."

My jaw dropped in shock. Ladies in Linen they were not.

"That's weird. This morning I found out that Agata Villeré bequeathed her fortune to the Commission."

"Indeed?"

"My, oh my." Swamp Sasquatch handed me a bowl. "Dat's somethin', ain't it?"

Willie eyed my bowl. "It's hardly a surprise. The Villeré family are long-standing supporters."

"I heard it was jus' Pia." The Swamp Sasquatch poured Willie a bowl.

Interesting that Agata would leave her money to an organization supported by the sister she allegedly murdered. "Did either of you ever meet Pia?"

"Nah." Sylvain shook his head. "She died about ten years ago, before I became a member."

Willie downed a meatball. "I never made her acquaintance, either. I rarely have time to attend the meetings, what with my busy schedule."

Doing what? I wanted to ask. *Park narcing and dabbling in professions?* "What about Agata? Did she attend the meetings?"

"Not dat I'm aware of."

Something about this was off. If Agata wasn't an avid supporter of the Vieux Carré Commission, it didn't make sense that she would leave her entire fortune to them. "What about the Blains? Are they members?"

Willie shook his head, too busy swilling swamp soup to speak.

"Nah." Swamp Sasquatch ladled another bowl. "If de rumors are true, dey don't have any money to donate."

It was hard to believe that Willie and the Swamp Sasquatch had the money, either. But then again, hauling cypress could be lucrative, and Willie had his hand in all kinds of things, including people's wallets.

The Swamp Sasquatch placed a bowl on the osprey's stump. "Dive in, buddy."

Maxime dipped his head into the bowl and fished out a meatball that he promptly dropped. He pecked at it a few times and swallowed it.

The whole scene was proof that not even a fierce predator could put away food like Willie Tea.

"Eat up, Franki!" The Swamp Sasquatch slapped my shoulder, causing me to spill a quarter of the broth—thankfully. He watched and waited for my reaction to his recipe.

Which just wasn't going to be positive.

Or maybe even sanitary.

Like the soup.

The heat was on in both senses of the term. Sweat trickled down my neck, and my eyes darted around, looking for a way out of the impending disaster. Because if anything was going to prevent me from getting married, it would be me eating the Swamp Sasquatch's cooking.

"Hey," I half-screamed as a solution came to me, "what about that earring you wanted to show me?"

"Oh, dat's right." He pulled it from his pocket and handed it to me, which was the perfect opportunity to ditch the bowl.

The earring was magnificent—a large square-cut emerald on gold backing. Something Queen Elizabeth would have worn to a party, or even her coronation. "I'm not a gemologist, but this looks expensive."

Willie looked up from his soup. "It's Cartier. I used to work in fine jewelry."

Maybe when he was stealing it from a house. "Where did you find it?"

"Where de marsh meets de swamp."

"They meet?"

"Sure do." The Swamp Sasquatch made himself a bowl of

soup. "A big ol' cypress marks de spot. A gator stores its food under de roots."

Of course one did.

Willie used the handkerchief to dab his lips. "Sylvain asked me to tell you about an interesting encounter I had with someone in a long overcoat and hat in the area of that cypress."

The femme fatale's description of Edward.

"Tell her what dey was drivin'."

Willie's eyes resembled Maxime's. "A gray Mercedes."

The color and make of the car Edward drove to the marsh. "Was he a big man, like Edward Blain?"

"Nothing of the sort," Willie said. "Short and female, I'm certain of it."

The Swamp Sasquatch sat on a stump. "It was dis morning, bright an' early."

My stomach shifted, queasy. Shona was short, and she *had* been accused of stealing Agata's jewels. "Willie, was this woman, by any chance, built like a snowman?"

"Fairly fit, I'd say."

My eyes darted to the murky swamp beyond the Swamp Sasquatch's trailer. I was relieved the woman wasn't Shona, but I had the sinking feeling I'd been wrong about at least one aspect of the case.

If I was right, my prediction about the code name for my wedding planning taking on a dark new meaning was about to come true.

And maybe, just maybe, so was my nightmare.

19

T he phrase "dark night of the soul" was forefront in my mind as I stared at the Mississippi from a Moonwalk bench, the river walk named after former Mayor Maurice "Moon" Landrieu. I was living the anguish of that expression, except that it was day. Two o'clock, and hotter than Dante's Inferno.

Although I'd been tempted to go to the "big ol' cypress" where the Swamp Sasquatch had found the emerald earring, I'd investigated enough cases to know that was a job best left to the police.

Because *swamp animals*, the critter kind.

And because the cypress symbolized death and the underworld.

What I had to find was Edward's killer.

But how?

And where?

"Ugh." I threw my head back. "I don't *knooow*."

At an impasse, I did what I always do.

Lunch.

In the form of the All That Jazz po-boy I'd bought at Verti

Marte. It wasn't Peacemaker style like the one that had done in Big Chuck's Ne Ne, but it was close. A footlong loaf of seeded bread, grilled ham, turkey, and shrimp, sauteed mushrooms, two kinds of cheese, sliced tomato, and topped off with their mustard-based Wow Sauce.

The first bite sent streams of sauce and grease down my chin. "'Wow,' indeed." I dropped the sizeable sandwich on the to-go bag and reached for a napkin. "Definitely enough to give me a stroke."

But death by decadent po-boy wasn't a bad way to go, especially when one alternative was being struck by a car like Delilah Delaire.

The memory made me shudder. To console myself, I grabbed a couple of Zapp's potato chips—the Evil Eye flavor with bloodshot eyeballs on the package. Fitting for obvious reasons.

The Creole Queen passed by, its paddle churning the brown river water. The Mississippi wasn't the black swamp, but it was dark nonetheless. And muddy, like my thoughts.

About the figure in the hat and long overcoat.

The femme fatale had watched "a big man" in that outfit climb into the black BMW that had killed Delilah, but Willie had seen a "short" and "fairly fit" woman wearing the same in Edward's gray Mercedes at the swamp.

And that meant Edward had most likely been killed by his wife or daughter.

But which one?

Lara? Or Grace?

The latter fit Willie's description. And based on the pictures I'd seen on Grace's Instagram page, Lara was short and fairly fit too. And she loved the color green.

Did they both conspire to kill him?

Still at an impasse, I picked up the po-boy and glanced at the

Verti Marte brand on the bag. The 24-hour corner store and sandwich shop had once been Leon's Grocery, named for the Leone family from Sicily back when the lower French Quarter was known as Little Palermo.

Until the Vieux Carré Commission worked their black magic to erase that history.

I crunched another chip. "Why would Agata Villeré leave everything to the VCC?"

It was a mystery.

Like the murder of her older sister, Pia.

My phone rang. A number I didn't recognize. "Hello?"

"Franki, it's Shona. Like Mona with a *sh*?"

My eyes rolled so hard they could've outchurned the Creole Queen's paddle. "Yeah, I know how to say it."

"I'm a librarian, okay? My middle name is Detailed."

And also Deafening. "What's up?"

"Moira and I are at Agata's mansion. We followed Grace here."

It occurred to me that I ought to let *them* solve the case so that I could get on with my wedding planning. "So? Maybe she's picking up something she left there before the place goes on the market."

"Riiight. And I've got a first edition Gutenberg Bible to sell ya."

"Thanks, but my nonna's got a collection of Bibles that could rival the Vatican Library's, so I'm covered."

"Grace is looking for the jewels, as sure as my name is—"

I waited for her to complete the sentence, but she didn't. And because Grace was in the vicinity, I had to make sure nothing had happened. "Shona?"

"—like Mona with a *sh*."

The woman really needed to see somebody about her name-clarification condition, because it bordered on pathological.

"While we're on the subject of Agata's jewels, do you remember seeing anyone wearing square-cut emerald earrings at the rehearsal dinner?"

"Yeah, I do. But I can't remember who."

"Uh, apparently Detailed *isn't* your middle name."

She huffed. "For your infor—"

The sound of a struggle ensued.

My gut tensed. "What's happening?"

"Moira here, Franki. I had to commandeer this conversation because Grace just broke a window and went inside."

Breaking and entering? Something was up, possibly a hunt for the jewels. I rose and began to run—begrudgingly—to the office to get my car. I crossed Decatur Street and saw the voodoo practitioners and the Ladies in Linen protesting in front of the old Tujague's.

The woman from the Vieux Carré Commission was on her phone. Her face was red—from rage, not the summer temperature.

And my gut told me to investigate. After all, Moira and Shona were on sleuthing duty with Grace, so I could spare a few minutes.

The Lady in Linen left the protest with the phone pressed to her ear and walked briskly toward Jackson Square.

Throngs of tourists helped me to pass unnoticed.

She entered the main gate to the park in front of St. Louis Cathedral and took the walkway to the equestrian statue of General Andrew Jackson in the center, where she turned and went to a bench in the South corner.

Meanwhile, I skirted the wrought-iron fence around the park and crouched behind the pedestal of a statue not two feet from where she sat.

"All right, I can talk now." Her tone was as hard as the

coating of hairspray that held her updo intact in the intense humidity. "Have the police arrived yet?"

To make sure I didn't miss a word, I leaned from behind the statue.

"Then there's no time to waste. I know for a fact that Agata was selling the jewels to keep the Commission from getting them." Her hand went to her neck. "Marie Antoinette's pearls may be the only thing left."

I blinked. If that was true, it called into question whether any jewels had been hidden at all, especially since Lara or Grace could've lost the earring that the Swamp Sasquatch found.

"Well, if she does find them in the mansion, we tell her that she either gives them to us, or we'll sue." She glanced around.

And I ducked.

"But there is an alternative." Her voice was low and lethal. "We threaten to go to the police and tell them the whole sordid truth—that *she* killed Pia. We merely neglect to mention the part about Agata tampering with the elevator in the first place."

The cathedral bell tolled, but it might as well have been a bomb exploding. Because the Lady in Linen had just revealed that Agata Villeré set up a family member to kill her sister, one who had gone on to kill Edward.

And I knew who she was.

~

"Grace?" I called through the broken window of Agata's mansion. "Are you in there?"

Silence.

Chewing my cheek, I surveyed the unkempt yard. Shona and Moira were nowhere to be seen, and I'd not only circled the property, I'd also checked the carriage house to make sure the black BMW was still there. The only thing I could think was that Grace had left, and they'd followed her.

But I couldn't shake the feeling that something bad had happened.

To be on the safe side, I dialed Shona's number. No answer, and her voicemail was full.

Naturally.

My stomach in knots, I turned back to the window. "Anyone home?"

A loud thump came from upstairs.

"That's a yes." I clinched my jaw and climbed through the window into a dilapidated French neoclassical-style dining room. The place had been ransacked.

Violently so.

Nothing was left untouched. The dining table was over-turned, the stuffing ripped from the chairs. Even the chandelier had been damaged.

What struck me most, though, was that the dark green velvet walls had been slashed, and an oil painting of a middle-aged woman, undoubtedly Agata, had a pair of scissors stuck in the canvas.

Right through the throat.

My fight-or-flight response fully activated, I walked among the scattered contents of two French commodes into the adjoining entrance hall, where statues on either side of enor-mous columns lay broken. I stopped to read spray-painted graf-fiti lining the walls of the rotunda staircase. Despicable messages calling Agata every kind of vile name imaginable.

The kind of hate that was decades in the making.

Beside the stairs was the elevator that had sent Pia plum-meting to her death.

Muffled footsteps crossed the second floor, precisely in the area where the elevator would've been.

And I knew who'd made them.

Pia and Edward's killer.

The runner on the stairs absorbed the sound of my shoes. But I was confident that she knew I was coming. What worried me was the kind of reception I'd get.

When I got to the top of the landing, I knew where to go.

The boarded-up elevator was in a mauve bedroom that resembled something out of a 1940s Hollywood movie the femme fatale would star in, except that it had been ransacked like the rest of the mansion.

She was sitting on the end of the canopy bed. Her head was lowered, and beside her was a wheelchair that I knew had belonged to Pia. And she looked as rough as the room. Her ivory linen jumpsuit was rumpled, her shoulder-length blonde hair hadn't been washed, and she was pale with smeared mascara beneath her wise green eyes.

"I know you felt you had no choice, Lara."

A sob escaped her throat, followed by a cascade of tears.

And I waited in the doorway while she cried it out.

After a few minutes, she raised her head, meeting my gaze dead on. Her eyes were flat, expressionless. "All my life, I did what was expected of me. I was a good daughter, a good wife, a good mother. And where did that get me?"

My lips pressed tight. Lara sounded like my mother, and that was a question you did *not* want to answer. I knew from hard-learned experience, as in a summer of being grounded with no TV—or Nutella.

"Figures you wouldn't say anything. You've got a PI career, so what could you know about my plight?" She shot me a sideways stare.

And I mentally kicked myself for not getting around to memorizing Nonna Nunzia's incantation, because I now had triple malocchio.

"I'll tell you where my devotion to my family got me." Lara twisted her emerald engagement ring, staring at a spot on the floral rug. "Dependent on people who don't give a damn whether I live or die. I was supposed to keep house, keep a social calendar, and keep up appearances. I did that to perfection, and here I sit. Alone, with nothing."

"You've got Grace."

"Ha!" She shook her head. "My daughter only comes around when she wants something. And now that the money and the jewels are gone, I won't see her again. Her father raised a narcissist, just like himself."

From what I'd sensed, Grace was an entitled brat, but she hadn't been involved in Edward's murder. "Do you mind if I ask what happened with Pia?"

Lara put her head in her hands. "Edward and I needed money, so I asked her for a loan. She blamed our financial problems on me and said I needed to get a job." She looked up. "Can you imagine?"

Honestly, I could. My mother had put me to work in the family deli at the age of fourteen, and when I'd informed her that child labor was illegal, she made me work overtime.

Lara stroked the arm of the wheelchair, almost affectionately. "We argued, and I kicked the footrest. It rolled backwards into the elevator," she gazed at the boarded-up doors, "and the carriage just…fell."

How awful that must've been.

"Apparently, Agata had told Pia she'd cut the cable, but I didn't know that at the time. She hated Pia for being their mother's pet, and she paid her back by trapping her here in this room like a caged animal."

Goosebumps rose on my arms. Janine Crawford was right when she'd said that Pia and Agata had a Blanche-Baby Jane relationship. Agata's actions were eerily similar to what Bette

Davis had done to Joan Crawford's character in *Whatever Happened to Baby Jane?*

Lara sat up and rubbed her thighs. "Pia didn't have access to a phone, so she wrote a letter explaining what Agata was doing. The problem was, she needed someone to take it to the police. Then one day when Agata was out, Yvette Lirette from the Vieux Carré Commission dropped by unannounced to find out why Pia hadn't been attending their meetings."

There was no need to ask who Yvette was. She was the Lady in Linen. "I know the rest of the story. Yvette never gave the letter to the police. Instead, she held onto it, and when Pia died, she used it to blackmail Agata, forcing her to make the VCC her beneficiary."

Lara nodded. "Leaving me high and dry, which is what Edward intended to do."

"Did you know he was going to kill Agata?"

"No, but I knew he'd done it as soon as I walked into her room at the Columns and smelled his tobacco."

The raisin-vinegar odor of perique was unmistakable—and definitely not the work of the ghost of Simon Hersheim.

"I confronted him, and he said he killed her to save our home and the law firm. We already knew we weren't getting a dime from Agata, so I asked him if he'd taken her jewelry collection. He said Agata claimed she'd sold most of it. She told him he'd never find what was left." Lara's gaze grew hard. "But I didn't believe him because I'd followed him out to Honey Island Swamp, and then he tried to frame that librarian for hiding the jewels."

Lara was as good a sleuth as Shona and Moira. Too bad she was on the wrong side of the law.

Her lips twisted. "I'd long suspected that Edward was having an affair with one of his clients, so I followed him, not knowing that he'd killed Agata hours before."

"And while you were at the swamp, you lost an emerald earring that you went back to look for early this morning."

She nodded. "And to try to find the pearls. They belonged to Marie Antoinette." She cast me a look of desperation. "You haven't found them, have you?"

"Honestly, I've been focused on finding you."

She sighed and massaged her forehead. "Right."

Lara seemed reasonable, the calmest killer I'd ever confronted. So I decided to press on. "Did you kill him at the séance because he was going to leave you and take the jewels?"

"Yes. It turns out that he was at the séance hoping to get some information that would lead him to the jewels. And he was livid that I'd followed him. We argued, and he admitted that he planned to sell Agata's jewelry and leave me—not for another woman, but because he couldn't stand the sight of me. After I'd sacrificed my youth for him." She clenched her fists and punched the bed. "So I waited until he pressed his ear to the wall, and then I picked up his drink glass and hit him in the back of the head. He groaned and collapsed. Dead."

That was the thump I'd heard.

Tears streamed down her cheeks. "I didn't mean to kill him. When I realized he was dead I cried out."

And Lara had made the wail that had seemed to come from the bathroom in Agata's room.

She wiped her wet face. "Then I panicked. I ran downstairs and played that old piano to make it seem like one of the Columns ghosts. After all, that's what the séance was for, to summon the spirits."

Well, that and summoning money to Chandra's wallet.

"But even though it was an accident," her face went flat, "I'm glad Edward's dead. Now I can search for the pearls without worrying about him finding them first."

Not exactly, but it wasn't yet time to remind her of her fate. "How are you so sure Agata didn't sell the pearls?"

"It has to do with her mother. She hated her and everything she represented."

"You mean, her Italian heritage?"

"Precisely. Agata wanted to be pure French like her father. And in this town, Marie Antoinette is still the reigning queen."

The Merry Antoinettes were proof of that. Because the VCC had rewritten history.

"So, when Agata learned Sotheby's was putting some of Marie Antoinette's jewels on auction, she used the insurance money from Pia's death to buy the pearls."

Even though Janine Crawford had alleged as much, the confirmation was as jolting as the elevator carriage drop.

Lara's green eyes turned dark. "And since the old bitch got that money by setting me up, those pearls are mine, regardless of what she put in the will."

The venom in her voice caught me off guard. It was out of sync with Lara's cool, calm demeanor. "Except that...you're going to have to turn yourself in."

"I know." She bowed her head. "But I need the money from the sale of the pearls to settle my debts and pay for my legal defense."

Whatever Lara had done, she had the right to an attorney. "One last question. What did Edward put in the nocino cappuccino that Agata drank?"

"A quadruple dose of the heart medication she'd recently started taking. I have the bottle." She reached into her back pocket and pulled out what appeared to be a large tube of lipstick.

Which was weird.

And then it hit me—at the same time as the electrical current—that the lipstick was a taser. My entire body seized in pain, but also in a strange sort of euphoria. Every muscle I had contracted, and I was completely powerless.

The sensation stopped abruptly, and I crumpled to the floor, flat on my back. In a daze, I stared at the ceiling.

Lara knelt beside me and pressed a sweet-smelling cloth to my nose.

Not perfume.

Chloroform.

And I was literally too stunned to resist.

MY EYES OPENED TO DARKNESS. So dark that if I hadn't been nauseated with a horrible headache, I would've thought I was still unconscious.

A force flung me into a wall, and a realization hit me like Lara's taser—I was in a moving car.

Oh, God. Is my nightmare coming true? As crazy as the dream had seemed, it was fairly normal for New Orleans.

And for my mom and Nonna.

One positive—I wasn't in a coffin. But I was in a trunk that reeked of tire rubber and new carpet. I didn't know whether Lara had put me in the black BMW or the gray Mercedes. All I knew was that I had to get out.

ASAP.

The emergency trunk release. My hands were behind my back, so I tried to move my arm. But my wrists were bound with a plastic cord, possibly a zip tie, as were my ankles.

And there was a gag in my mouth.

In desperation, I raised my knees to the trunk lid to try pushing it open.

The car swerved, and I smacked back into the wall. We picked up speed and began to weave. I was flung from side to side, which did nothing for my nausea. Or my brain-splitting headache.

Lara drives worse than freaking Phil Redman. You'd think that since she had a kidnapped person in the trunk, she'd follow the traffic laws. But there was just no accounting for the behavior of psychopaths.

As I tried to steady myself, I wondered where Lara was taking me. As the taser attested, she was unpredictable.

The car slowed, and I began to bounce. We were on bumpy ground.

But where?

As if in reply, I got a whiff of another unmistakable odor—rotten eggs. And maybe blackened frog legs.

I knew where Lara had brought me.

The Black Swamp.

20

"Time to wake up, Sleeping Beauty." Lara peered down at me in the trunk and yanked the gag from my mouth.

Since I was at a swamp, Tiana from *The Princess and The Frog* was more appropriate. But this was no fairy tale, and I didn't dare contradict her.

Because two sights had me frozen in fear. One, her blonde hair was brown and cropped. And two, she wore the same surgical gloves as Phil Redman had in my nightmare.

Even more disturbing, the moon was out, and I needed sunlight to have a decent shot at saving myself.

"Don't waste your energy on an escape plan. It's not happening." Lara aimed the taser at my heart.

My body tensed, and I braced for impact.

Instead of giving me another jolt, she pulled wire cutters from her back pocket and snipped the zip tie around my ankles. "Get out."

"It's kind of hard without my hands."

"Find a way." Her harsh tone left no room for discussion.

With difficulty, I maneuvered to my knees and stood. My legs were rubbery—oddly so—presumably from the taser. I jumped to the ground and lurched forward, barely avoiding a faceplant. Once I'd regained my balance, I glanced at the sky, confused about why it was night. I'd gone to Agata's mansion at three thirty in the afternoon. "How long was I knocked out?"

"Four hours, give or take. Every time you started coming to, I gave you another dose of chloroform."

And I'd been worried about the nocino's *effects on my esophagus.* Now I faced the very real prospects of brain damage. "Dosing me that many times was a big risk, don't you think? If I'd died, someone might've linked that chloroform to you."

"Believe me," she snarled, "it was a risk I was more than willing to take."

She didn't have to be surly about it. "So, what are you going to do with me?"

"Make it look like you died trying to find Agata's jewelry."

Nausea rose from my gut to my throat. "No one will believe I came to the swamp alone at night, and especially without telling anyone."

"You told Shona you were going to search for the jewels. Although, you said you'd be looking in the area around the Columns Hotel."

Even though I'd been electrocuted and chloroformed, I would've remembered doing that. "I did not."

"Oh, but you did." She flashed a tight smile. "While you were out, I used your face to get into your phone and your fingers to type her a message." She held up her hands. "Good thing I had these gloves."

My heart dropped.

No help was coming.

"Start walking."

"Where?" I squinted. "I can't see in the dark."

"Straight ahead. I'm not fool enough to use a flashlight." She retrieved a coiled rope from the car, which did nothing for my mood, and raised the taser.

I did as she said.

We trudged in silence through thick muck. It had rained, which made the ground extra soggy and slippery. The air was also suffocating and stunk of sulfur and decay, making it hard to breathe.

My biggest concern was the swamp animals. If I wasn't careful, I could become a meal for any number of critters—and quite possibly the Swamp Sasquatch. But I was also worried about my physical state. The more we walked, the worse I felt.

And I was seeing things.

A rock with eyes.

A scowling tree.

Could a taser cause that?

Or was it proof of the chloroform-induced brain damage?

Either way, I had to focus, think this through. Shona and Moira would eventually look for me. They were pretty good sleuths, and Shona *did* have that mystery tote. They'd know to check the swamp. Unless they were committed to tailing Grace, which was a strong possibility.

And unless it was too late...

My wrists writhed against the zip tie, but it was cutting into my skin. And I couldn't run with a taser pointed at me. The only options left were to try to stall Lara or diffuse her determination to do me in.

The swamp was ahead, so it was time to act. "You know, Lara, Edward was right about Agata selling the jewels. I heard Yvette telling someone that she did it to keep them from the Vieux Carré Commission, which is another reason no one will believe I came out here to find them."

Lara snorted. "Even if that were true, the police will never know you overheard Yvette."

She was right. Not even the Lady in Linen herself knew I'd been eavesdropping on her conversation at the park. Dismayed, I kept walking.

My foot splashed water—and never found ground.

"Oh!" I sank into a pool over my head. An electric jolt worse than the taser shot through my body. Because gators dug holes near swamps, and those holes turned into tiny ponds, which they used to sleep, mate—and attract prey.

Kicking frantically, I surged from the water and hurled myself forward, trying to heave my torso onto solid ground.

Lara laughed as I squirmed and wriggled onto land.

Which was so rude.

"Once we get to where I'm taking you, you'll wish you'd stayed in that gator hole." She pointed the taser. "Now get moving."

Stumbling to my feet, I ignored her taunt. I'd figure out something. I always did. I resumed the death march.

Why? WHY had I called it that?

Our destination loomed large before me.

The big ol' cypress, where the Swamp Sasquatch had found Lara's emerald earring.

And where he'd said that a gator stored its food.

The cypress was spooky, and its mournful history reminded me of the walnut tree from my nightmare. And I had no doubt that if Phil Redman saw it, he'd want to carve it into caskets, like the Swamp Sasquatch had mentioned. But that might've proven too difficult. Because the tree's branches were writhing like octopus arms.

Or the snakes on Medusa's head?

"But this isn't a dream," I whispered. "It's real."

Lara sniffed. "I take it the magic mushrooms are kicking in?"

Fear squeezed my body like the tree tentacles. *She'd given me psilocybin? In the swamp?*

"I got the idea from dear Great Aunt Agata. You know, she poisoned her maid with azalea petals to get her hands on a yellow diamond ring Bette Davis wore in a movie. She'd learned that little trick from her Italian mother, who used herbs and other plants for all sorts of nefarious ends."

Like the janare from Benevento. But I didn't say that aloud. I was too shocked to find out that I'd been drugged and that Agata had indeed murdered her maid, the femme fatale's aunt, for the ring. But I was also distracted—by a toad who'd just stuck its tongue out at me.

We came to the water's edge, and I stopped. The scum floating on the surface glowed green. *And orange?*

I blinked and clenched my teeth. Somehow, I had to manage the effects of the shrooms.

My life depended on it.

The problem was, my heart was pounding, and I was sick to my stomach. And increasingly uncoordinated.

Lara jabbed the taser between my shoulder blades. "Speed it up."

Jerking forward, I waded into the swamp. I heard a splash, and my head snapped to the spot.

"Relaaax," Lara drawled, "it wasn't an alligator, or anything. Just your cell phone. I'm leaving your purse here on the bank, where you would've left it if you'd really come out here to look for the jewels."

Losing my contact with the world outside the swamp was almost as scary as the thought of encountering a gator. And the worst part was, I hadn't even seen where she'd thrown my phone.

"Head to those boscoyos. You *do* know what those are?"

"Cypress knees." My tone was hot, even though I'd only recently learned the term from the Swamp Sasquatch.

"Just checking. You strike me as a city girl."

"And you aren't?" I snapped.

"It's not wise to sass a woman with a taser." Her voice was low and ominous. "My grandfather was a cypress hauler, so I grew up on this swamp. All kinds of animals pass through the root systems of these trees, ones you have no familiarity with."

No, but I'd had experience with their human counterparts, which, believe you me, was not inconsequential.

The water was up to my neck, and so was my anxiety. The swamp was terrifying under normal circumstances. Trying to navigate its perilous waters on a hallucinogen was so much worse.

Something slick brushed against my forearm. I looked down and saw a fish with silvery scales glinting in the moonlight.

And a red pitchfork tail?

Lara shoved me forward. "Swim over to that boscoyo in the middle of the water."

"How?" I shouted. "I can't use my arms."

"You've got feet."

Huffing in rage, I reclined onto my back and kicked my way to the cypress knee, which was no easy feat while tripping.

"Hold still. You don't want to get tasered while you're in the water."

No, I didn't.

Lara uncoiled the rope and began tying it around my waist, pinning my arms even tighter to my sides.

I kicked at her underwater, but with my upper body out of commission, I went face-first into the glowing swamp scum—which had the evil face of a jack-o'-lantern—and came up sputtering.

"I'm almost sorry I can't stay to watch this trainwreck." She gave a throaty laugh. Then her face went as dark as the sky, and she tied the end of the rope to the underwater root, leaving enough length for me to move a couple of feet in any direction.

My brain raced to think of something, anything to change her mind about leaving me to die. "No matter what happens to me, the police will find the rope. It's proof that I didn't come here voluntarily."

She chuckled as she semi-swam back to shore. "If the police do find the rope, they'll think it could've been there for some other reason."

"Not with my DNA on it."

Her face remained impassive. "In that case, they'll assume you tied yourself to the boscoyo so you wouldn't drown while searching for Agata's jewelry."

Highly plausible. "What about the zip tie around my wrists? There's no way to explain that."

Lara reached the bank and turned to stare me down. "No, but I guarantee you this. When the swamp animals start tearing into you, they aren't going to leave any part of the rope—or you. You'll be gator food first, and whatever's left will be food for the turtles and fish."

She turned and disappeared into the night.

And all I could think was, *Whatever was left of me would most likely end up in one of Sylvain Fontane's swamp recipes—and possibly in Maxime the osprey's belly.*

"ALL THINGS CONSIDERED, the swamp is pretty chill." I sat on a horizontal cypress root that extended from the boscoyo Lara had tied me to, kicking my feet back and forth in the water. "Either that, or the mushrooms are working their magic."

A piece of evidence that supported the latter theory was that a pair of evil, neon-blue eyes had been watching me for hours—and I was talking to them. At first, I'd thought they belonged to an albino alligator, like the two at the New Orleans Audubon

Zoo, but whatever they were attached to hadn't eaten me yet. Also suspect, they occasionally turned yellow like the one on the sign at the Ra Shop. "Maybe one is the Eye of Ra protecting me, and the other is the Eye of Horus deflecting the malocchio."

"Pff!" I doubled over laughing. "There are no Egyptian animals in Louisiana. What a hoot!"

An owl hooted, as if responding to my hoot reference. It was perched on a branch above me, and it kept hooting.

Loudly.

"Is that you, Shona?"

The owl shot me a harsh stare, which seemed unfair. After all, a loud librarian from Screamer, Alabama, who originally hailed from Belchertown, Massachusetts, was clearly the Eastern Screech Owl incarnate.

The owl flew away, reminding me yet again that help wasn't coming.

But rather than despair, I was delighted. My heart no longer raced, and my nausea had disappeared. And even though I was still uncoordinated, I didn't care. The swamp wasn't a scary place at all. It was full of life and beautiful colors.

A firefly flitted to my nose, its yellow taillight as bright as the sun.

And I was captivated by it—and the beautiful hints of orange and gold.

He hovered between my eyes, close enough for me to see antennae and something resembling hair—in the style of a mullet.

"What's your name, chère?"

His Cajun accent caught me off guard. Although, based on the way the Swamp Sasquatch sounded, it shouldn't have. "I'm Franki. Are you Raymond from *The Princess and the Frog*?"

"Dey call me Lucien. Last name's Luciole, which is French fo' 'firefly.' An' I hate to break dis to ya, chère, but Ray wasn't real."

He gave me a moment to let that sink in. "And I gotta say, de way dey done Ray in dat movie turned me off o' Disney." His taillight went dark to emphasize his disdain.

And frankly, I agreed with him. Because Ray had met a bad end at the hands of Baron Samedi, and I was in no mood to be reminded of him.

Lucien grinned, revealing pink gums. "Now I prefer de History channel and de Home Shoppin' Network."

"So do I," I shouted, surprised at how much Lucien and I had in common.

Whoops and cries erupted as more fireflies arrived.

"Dem's my *frères*, chère."

"Wow." I surveyed the swarm. "You've got at least twenty brothers!"

"Dat's 'cause I come from a big Catholic family. Pleasure to meet ya!" Lucien flew to his siblings. They formed an oval shape, their lights resembling a floating strand of pearls.

The image of the necklace jogged a distant memory I couldn't pin down, but it didn't have anything to do with Agata and the Marie Antoinette pearls, or the ones worn by Yvette, the Lady in Linen. It was something else.

But what?

"Who cares?" I threw up my arms and beamed at the moon. "I'm having fun!" Then I watched Lucien and his big band of brothers frolic-fly in the night.

"Too bad I don't know any of *The Princess and the Frog* songs, because I have an odd urge to sing one." The only thing I remembered was Tiana singing "Almost there" when she danced around her restaurant with her prince, formerly the frog.

Mimicking one of their moves, I wound myself in the rope until I reached the boscoyo I was tied to. Then I spun until I reached the end. Of course, I was dancing with a cypress knee, but I imagined it was my prince, Bradley.

Not that he was ever a frog. Although...

...finding out on our first date that he was still married to Sheilah was certainly frog-like behavior. Toad-like, really. But we'd worked that out after he'd explained the situation.

And after I'd given him a right hook to the cheek.

Sighing contentedly, I drew the outline of his handsome face in the water. Within less than a year, we'd be man and wife, and our never-ending engagement will have been worth the wait. "I can see Bradley and me now, coming down the church steps in our wedding clothes and climbing into a gleaming black hearse—I mean, a limo."

Why had I thought it was a hearse?

In response, my brain produced a vivid memory of Bradley driving the funeral carriage in my nightmare and calling for me to get inside. And the jokes he'd made about inviting Chandra to holidays and family functions.

Anger bubbled in my belly all over again. "That *man*. I'm definitely going to let him have it the next time I see him."

"*If* you see him."

The comment had come from a gator—with Glenda's face!

"This must be what they call a 'bad trip.'" I shook my head and squeezed my eyes shut. I opened them and recoiled.

In the water on either side of Gator Glenda was Snake Nadezhda and Snapping Turtle Carnie, and on the swamp bank sat Black Bear Rosalie, Common Loon Chandra, and Turkey-Necked Ostrich Ruth—with her cat eye glasses.

"We're here, alright, sugar." Gator Glenda stood upright in the water, and her reptilian paw held a cigarette holder made from a cypress twig. "We've come to give you a warning."

My first thought was to warn her that the lit cigarette would catch the twig on fire, but the Swamp Sasquatch *had* said that cypress was extremely durable. "Warn me about what?"

"Well," Glenda breathed smoke from her gator nostrils, "it wasn't one of the things we swamp animals discussed, but I've got something stuck in my craw that I need to get out. Be sure to live a little before you settle down and play house for good. There are so many fine fish in the swamp. And personally, I don't know why you'd want to settle for just one when you could have them all."

"Go on now, Gator Glenda Gurl," Snapping Turtle Carnie drawled in her high-pitched drag voice. "Serve up that Meryl Streep realness!"

Nadezhda the Snake nodded and grinned, still sporting black nubs from the nocino that had eaten the veneer off her "teet."

Gator Glenda flipped her platinum hair. "Now, as for that warning we swamp animals discussed..." Something caught her eye in the water. She submerged her head and popped up with a mouthful of fish—presumably some that weren't fine enough to date—and downed them in a single gulp. "...you've got to snap out of your purple haze, Miss Franki. You're in danger."

"She's right, Franki." Common Loon Chandra parked a wing on her hip. "And I don't mind saying, your behavior is downright embarrassing."

"Does this surprise you?" Turkey-Necked Ostrich Ruth barked. "I could've told you she was a druggie—and a booze hound to boot."

Black Bear Rosalie scratched her rump on a tree trunk. "Yep, I predicted this when she was a kid. As her mother's best friend, I can tell you that Franki's been making that poor woman suffer since she came out of the womb."

On that note, I flung myself into the water. The fact that my brain had conjured up this scenario was proof that I was at the end of my rope, literally and figuratively.

Ignoring the expectant stares of my swamp animal audience, I searched for a way out of my current predicament. And I found it—a narrow boscoyo projecting upright eight inches. I floated over and pressed my back against it. And I slid up and down, catching it between me and the rope. Then I ducked underwater where the rope met the horizontal portion of the root, and I wriggled free.

Giddy with glee!

Until my hair caught on something.

Claws pierced my crown.

Or something caught my hair?

Panicked, I rocketed to the surface and flung my head forward. A sizeable rodent landed in the water with a splash.

He looked at me, and I looked at him.

Nute! Or rather Nute II.

The scream I let out was primal.

And Nute II screamed as well. Either that or he wanted me to take note of his big orange buck teeth.

Leaning back against a root, I kicked my feet furiously to shoo Nute II.

Satisfied he was gone, I returned to my upright position.

And I saw the gator, who no longer resembled Glenda.

Louis from The Princess and the Frog? I scrutinized its light brown eyes. *Nope, this gator doesn't look joyful—or like a jazz trumpet player.*

My hands were still bound behind me by the zip tie, but I managed to hoist myself backwards onto a cluster of boscoyos and pull my legs from the water.

To my horror, the gator glided toward me with a stealthy silence.

It must be the one the Swamp Sasquatch told me about that

stores its food under the cypress roots. Terrified, I threw myself at the trunk.

But with my bound hands, there was no way for me to climb the tree. Flat against the base, I lay frozen in fear.

The gator lunged, and I hurled my body back toward the boscoyo. I was certain I'd reached the proverbial end of the line. After all, the cypress was a cemetery tree.

But the gator continued on its course and climbed the trunk —with the ease of Glenda scaling a stripper pole at Madame Moiselle's.

"Are you sure you're not my landlady?"

The beast raised its head, its white teeth gleaming in the moonlight, and gave a long growl. At which point I noted two key details:

1. The growl was *not* a direct answer, and
2. Glenda's teeth had cigarette stains, but the gator's didn't.

Time to get the hell out of Honey Island Swamp.

Flipping onto my back, I kicked my way to the shore, stunned the gator wasn't giving chase. As I sat on the bank, I managed to grip the handle of my purse with my fingers. Then I stood and took a final look at the big ol' cypress to be safe.

Two yellow lights flashed from the tree.

Lucien and one of his brothers?

No, just the gator's sequined pasties.

"Lara Blain didn't kill me, but the heat might." I clung to my purse with my hands still behind me and continued my hours-long trek through a wildlife refuge toward the Chef Menteur

Highway. I was dehydrated, weak, and hungry for a fried gator po-boy Peacemaker style. Oh, and I had hundreds of bug bites.

How I hadn't noticed being bitten so many times was beyond me—except that I'd obviously been distracted by my conversations with Lucien the firefly and all the swamp animals.

Thinking back on it, I got incensed all over again by Black Bear Rosalie's crack about me making my mom suffer. I knew she hadn't really said that since the whole swamp-animal scenario had been a product of my magic-mushroom-addled imagination. But she would have.

"And all because I removed her as the head of my bomboniere committee—not that I'd ever appointed her." I cut my rage short because I'd arrived at the highway.

A white FIAT, the Gucci model, was coming up the road.

Another hallucination?

Or, one of the nonne?

Regardless, I jumped up and down to get the driver's attention.

The FIAT slowed to a stop. I leaned into the open passenger window. Behind the wheel sat Marie Antoinette—in a swamp green dress adorned with butterflies and twinkling lights in her pouf hair.

"You all right, hon? You look like you've been through it."

She was right about that. *But am I still going through it, as in tripping?*

"Judging from the look on your face, I should explain." She patted her massive updo. "I'm a member of the Merry Antoinette Mardi Gras krewe. I'm on my way into New Orleans for a charity luncheon we're hosting at Galatoire's."

I flashed back to the Merry Antoinettes that Janine Crawford and I had seen at the restaurant. "Right. I've seen you guys there before."

"By the way, my name's Merry Antoinette too."

A Merry Antoinette named Merry Antoinette? Yeah, I was totally tripping. "Franki Amato. And don't be alarmed by the zip tie around my wrists. I'm a local PI, and I had a bad run-in with a perp."

"Impressive!" Her face showed no sign of alarm. "And a fellow Italian. My last name's Mammarella."

Mammarella? Mamma mia! There was no way I was tripping. A drug didn't exist that could warp my brain into fabricating a name like that.

She reached for a bag with the Merry Antoinettes' slogan, *Let them throw cake!* "I have some scissors in here. Where are you headed?"

I took a step back. The word "headed" reminded me of "beheaded" and that guillotine.

"Are you okay? To be honest, you look like you need to go to the hospital."

"I'm fine. It's just that..." Rather than tell her I'd almost been murdered by a maniac who gave me magic mushrooms, I said the first thing that came to mind. "...I got conked in the conk."

She produced the scissors and got out of the car. "That's terrible." She walked up behind me and cut the zip tie. "Although, what does that mean?"

"I'm not sure." I left it at that because I still didn't know what conk meant and because the unexpected Edith-Cook speak had me once again concerned that I'd sustained brain damage. "Could you take me to the Copper Vine restaurant?" I asked, rubbing my injured wrists. "I need to get to my bridal shower."

Merry Antoinette's mouth Mr. Billed. "Dressed like that?"

Honestly, I was a little taken back by her reaction. I realized I looked rough. But she was starting to sound like Janine, and I didn't need any flack about my appearance. "Yes, and could we please hurry? If I miss this shower, I'll have to do it all over again. And managing the guest list will entail a whole new secret operation that I don't have the time, patience, or stamina to plan."

"Get in." She walked back to the driver side and climbed into the seat. "I have extra clothes in the back you can have. Perfume probably won't help, but we'll try. You smell like a sewer."

Actually, a swamp. I climbed into the car and caught sight of a strand of pearls hanging from the rearview mirror like Puppy the python.

A flash of firefly light went off in my head as the memory that I couldn't pin down hours earlier hit me like a hammer.

"Forget the Copper Vine. Get me to the Columns Hotel as fast as this FIAT will take us."

21

———

"The whole time Edward, Lara, and the woman from the Vieux Carré Commission were looking for Marie Antoinette's pearls," I said to my bridal shower guests—and a couple of gatecrashers, "they were hanging from a branch of the oak tree in front of the Columns Hotel."

The faces around the Copper Vine table reacted to my statement with shock. Or maybe they were still shocked by my appearance. To cover my bug bites, Merry Antoinette had dotted my face with beauty marks and put me in a pink 18th-century gown with long sleeves and wide panniers. And even though I'd refused a pouf wig, she'd teased my hair into a high updo—and topped it with a slice of cake.

Bradley's grandmother, Cordelia, reached for her pearls. "That necklace is practically priceless, and Agata threw it in a tree?"

"Yes, to keep Edward from getting it." I glanced at Veronica and Bradley, who hadn't let go of me since he'd found out what happened. "I suspect she knew he was coming to kill her, and tossing the pearls onto a tree branch was probably her best option to hide them."

Lillian shook her head. "Francesca, how did you figure out where they were?"

"A fake pearl necklace hanging from a rearview mirror reminded me that I'd seen a similar strand hanging from the tree the morning I joined you and Cordelia at the Columns for breakfast." I decided to omit the appearance of the pearls in my nightmare to avoid getting mad at Bradley about that funeral carriage stunt in front of his family. "At the time, I mistakenly assumed they were Mardi Gras beads since there are so many of them in the trees around town."

A waiter tripped over one of my panniers and went flying.

"So sorry." I tried to rein in my dress. "This was the only thing I had to wear."

He eyed me like I'd lost my mind.

But I took no offense. Thirty-plus fake beauty marks *were* excessive.

Shona slung her arm over the back of her chair. "When Franki showed up at the Columns, Moira and I were already on the scene."

Too bad they weren't on the swamp scene looking for me, but I couldn't blame them for being fooled by Lara's text.

"Based on our independent investigation," Shona spoke in a tone that smacked of Barney-Fife swagger, "I'd concluded that the most likely location of the jewels was at the hotel."

It was a good thing the case was solved, because the mystery tote had gone from Shona's shoulder straight to her huge head.

Moira looked at Veronica. "We were searching the grounds when Franki showed up with Merry Antoinette and told us Agata's pearls were in the tree."

"Yeah," Shona sniffed, "and Franki made *me* get them down."

"Uh, remember, I don't have full control of my body after the taser and 'the trip,' and you have prior tree-climbing experience picking walnuts for my mom and nonna."

She looked away, and I kept the other reason I'd had her get the pearls to myself, i.e., the legend of the Marie Antoinette curse. I had enough curses on my plate what with the triple malocchio, and Shona was due one after making me take her case pro bono, getting me added to Lara's restraining order, and staying at Veronica's old apartment after I'd paid the rent.

Veronica reached for her Prosecco glass. "The good news is that all charges against Shona have been dropped."

"Hear, hear." Shona shouted.

Meanwhile, the Copper Vine wait staff dropped to the ground as though bullets had been shot.

"Mm. Franki." Moira swallowed a sip of bloody mary. "Before you came to the Columns today, I found out that they have a playlist for the old-timey radios in the rooms. Old jazz numbers and songs with tobacco themes to go with the history of the house."

Shona pursed at her sleuthing partner. "That explains why the radio in Agata's room played that Herman Hermit's song 'The Man with the Cigar.' But it doesn't explain how it spontaneously turned itself on."

"Maybe the radio *was* on," Moira said, "but the volume had cut out."

Shona tapped her chin. "Either that or the ghost of Simon Hersheim was a fan of the British Invasion."

Based on that deduction, it was time for Shona to trade in her mystery tote for a paranormal cozy model.

My mother raised her glass, as she was fond of doing. "You haven't told us what happened to Lara and Grace, dear."

"I'm not sure Grace was involved, but the police found Lara at home packing along with a one-way ticket to Saint-Tropez. They relayed the news to me when they came to the Columns to pick up the pearls."

Bradley slid a protective arm around my shoulder. "The greed of everyone in that family was their undoing."

The same could be said of Yvette from the VCC since she was also under investigation in the deaths of both Pia and Agata.

My mother smoothed her hairdo, which rivaled mine in size. "Veronica, what do you think will happen to Giada's husband, Wolf? Since he talked to Edward before he killed Agata, is there a chance he'll be charged?"

Veronica took a deep breath. "It's possible, but we'll have to wait until the police complete their investigation."

I nodded, but I had a feeling that Giada would take care of Wolf. I'd called her from the Columns to inform her of Lara's arrest, and she'd sounded none too happy that a group of nonne had descended on her home for a rousing round of Suffering Stories.

Nonna raised her handbag. "If-a that Brunella doesn't go to jail-a too, I'll-a take-a care of-a her with-a this."

My mother's eyes were murderous. "I'll help, Carmela."

Even if Brunella *was* a rogue witch as Madge from Hex Old World Witchery had alleged, she was no match for Vito and Michael Corleone.

"As a deli owner," my mother cast a self-important look at Lillian and Cordelia, "I'm stunned Brunella was running a cottage food business without a license. She could've hurt someone—or worse."

"Yeah. Me," I said, irritated my esophagus ordeal hadn't warranted a mention. Then I yawned, which reminded me of something I needed to address with my family. "While we're on the subject of hurting someone—again, me—why didn't you and Nonna use San Giovanni's herbs to diagnose my malocchio instead of that manhandler majara, Nonna Nunzia?"

"Because, Francesca," my mother's shrill voice was defensive, "there are seven herbs, and they all have to be picked in morning dew. Where could we possibly have done that?"

"Ummm, any local nursery right when it opens?"

She turned the color of the wine she sipped.

"Also," I turned to my nonna, "that Benevento consultant, Nonna Titti, said you could've cured my malocchio with a prayer and the sign of the cross. Why didn't you mention that? Or, even better, *do* it?"

Nonna curled her lower lip in contempt. "People from-a Campania are weak-a!"

After that comment, I decided not to tell her that Bradley's great-grandmother was from Benevento. She was still vaguely suspicious of him after I'd once fibbed that he had a weak digestion, and I didn't want to inflame the issue. "That's a stereotype, Nonna."

"It's-a not! The *campani* take-a the easy way out-a with all-a that witch-a-craft nonsense! We *siciliani* suffer."

Yes, we certainly do. To underscore that point, I reached into my purse beside my chair and pulled out the voodoo doll that looked like a cross between my mom and nonna—the one the protestors had thrown at me at the Ra Shop—and rested it in my lap under the table. Then I jabbed the pin in it.

Twice.

A waiter arrived with a pitcher of water, carefully sidestepping my pannier. He filled Bradley's glass. "Your dessert will be out shortly, sir." He looked at me. "Would you like a coffee?"

"No way." My face grew hot. "I mean, no thank you." My resistance to coffee was only natural given my esophagus damage and the NOLA Noir ordeal—but the waiter's resemblance to Vick Villano wasn't. The similarity was so uncanny that I glanced around the airy white-and-blue room.

And I saw Willie Tea.

Maybe. From his profile, I wasn't positive it was him. But his clothes were worn and dirty, and as he bit into a dinner roll, he appeared to have only one front tooth.

I looked at the waiter. "Do you, by any chance, know the name of the gentleman by the window?"

He stole a glimpse. "Mr. Tea, one of our more eccentric customers."

"What does he do?" Bradley asked.

"I'm not sure." He refilled my water glass. "But he's an avid birdwatcher and owns a multi-million-dollar mansion near Audubon Park."

So Willie was being honest when he'd told me he had plenty of room for guests. I shook my head, regretting the fourteen dollars I'd given him—and the fact that I hadn't known about park narcing when I was in college.

A young brunette placed a plate of black walnut pie in front of Bradley. "Enjoy."

"Thank you." He flashed his dazzling smile, and I melted like the whipped cream on top. "Sure you don't want a bite, babe?"

I cleared my throat, which still didn't feel quite normal. "I've sworn off walnuts."

Bradley took a bite. "Oh, wow. You have to try it."

The very thing Vick said to the femme fatale, Hedy, about the sanguinaccio dolce.

But I was being ridiculous. Bradley wasn't Vick, and I was no Hedy. Plus, the love of my life was offering me *pie*.

"Okay. One bite." I opened my mouth, and he fork-fed me. Besides the walnuts, I tasted molasses and a hint of ginger. And orange? "Mmmm. This is amazing."

"So are you." He kissed my lips and rested his forehead against mine.

"Aww," Veronica cooed.

My mother sighed. "They're pure magic together."

We were. So much so that I'd finally forgiven him for the

funeral carriage stunt he'd pulled in my dream. And yes, it had everything to do with him feeding me pie.

Cordelia smiled. "Lillian and I can't wait for the wedding."

Bradley squeezed my hand. He knew how worried I'd been about his grandmother's "deep concerns" that Delilah Delaire had called me before she was killed.

Lillian nibbled on a breadstick. "We're also looking forward to seeing your dress, Francesca."

Out of nowhere, I got an image of myself in a gown the colors of the Italian flag and shuddered. Given that I was at my bridal shower in a Marie Antoinette outfit, "Italian-American bride" was a look I couldn't rule out.

"Speaking of wedding dresses," my mom clasped her hands, "I went back to Wedding Belles and bought the plantation dress with the hoop skirt and petticoats I told you about—er, just in case you need a backup, dear. Can you believe no one had bought it?"

"Yes. I can." Under normal circumstances, I would've told my mother that she was out of line for picking my wedding dress. But I wasn't upset because I knew exactly what I was going to do with the godawful thing—rub the Demon-Be-Gone smudge stick on the fabric and light it on fire with the Uncrossing candle. It was the perfect cleansing ritual for the case.

Chandra marched up in a white dress with a yellow sequined sun that rivaled Lucien the Firefly's taillight—and the pasties on Glenda Gator. "Sorry I'm late." She dropped a solar-system-themed tote on the table and shot me the stink-eye. "But that's what happens when you're not invited to the party."

"If you weren't invited," I said, struggling to keep my tone civil, "then how did you know to come?"

My mom raised her hand. "That was my doing, dear. When Veronica told us you'd be several hours late to your surprise shower, which is a tad scant on guests, I thought it would be nice if we called your friends."

Underneath the table, I pulled the pin from the voodoo doll and inserted it again. Because thanks to my mother, the bridal shower was starting to look like a repeat of my mushroom trip—except that I was enduring it sober. "Who else is coming?"

"Big Chuck." Moira helped herself to a crawfish beignet. "He said he'd drop by after he takes his niece to see her parole officer."

She must be the daughter of the baby brother who had the jail-release party. "Why not invite Phil from the Saint Cecelia Cemetery?"

Bradley rubbed my thigh. "He's on his way with Ruth."

Shona shot up. "We'd best be going, Moira."

"Why? I'm still eating."

"It's time for me to get back to Screamer and the library."

Shona and I both knew the real reason she needed to go was that Ruth was going to insist she pay the money she owed Private Chicks for my services.

The loud-librarian-turned-loud-sleuth slung her mystery tote over her shoulder. "But don't worry. That goes for you too, Franki. Because this isn't goodbye. The Screamer Scullers and I will be back in a week for our race."

Her middle name wasn't Detailed or even Deafening. It was Daft.

"Excuse us for a moment." Chandra grabbed my wrist, making me wince.

"Ow! Hey, I have a zip-tie injury."

"Such a whiner." She dragged me toward the Ladies Room, and I knew she was going to demand her charm bracelet. Thanks to Lara and the zip tie, I hadn't been able to bury the thing at the swamp where it belonged. Nevertheless, I was more than happy to leave the table. In fact, I was thinking about leaving the restaurant.

And New Orleans.

Inside the bathroom, Common Loon Chandra came at me like a crazed Nute II. "I know Bradley's grandmother is a Toccato."

Reeling in horror, I backed into the door. I was spooked—but for the sake of my future, I had to play it cool. "So? That doesn't mean Cordelia and Lou are related."

"*Lou?* What's he got to do with this?"

"He is your husband."

"Yeah, but he took *my* last name when we got married."

My legs collapsed, as if I'd been tasered, and I slid to the floor. *Bradley could be related to Chandra? As in, shared DNA?* The sensation was similar to being submerged in that gator hole. On some level, I'd feared this, but I didn't really believe it was possible.

"Lou's last name was Carpenter. Can you imagine a plumber named Carpenter? It's just too confusing."

It was confusing, but not as much as the Chandra-Bradley connection. *How could this happen?*

And then the answer came to me—the triple malocchio.

There was only one thing to do. I rose to face her. "How much money do you want to go away and take this to your grave?"

"The charm bracelet will do, but only for the time being." Her eyes narrowed. "I'm sensing a reluctance to have me in the family that has given me a sudden interest in genealogy."

Which, in turn, had given me a sudden ulcer. "There's no need for threats, Chandra. Let's go back to the table and handle this like adults."

"Not a word I would use for you, but okay."

Clenching my teeth, I burst from the bathroom and headed toward the table.

And just my luck, Nadezhda and Glenda entered the restaurant. Nadezhda showed her swamp snake essence with her signature python print, but Glenda was in green-and-yellow scales and a spiny tail?

Nadezhda gave my Marie Antoinette dress the onceover. "Who you tink you is? Caterine ze Great?"

You can take the woman out of Russia, but you can't take the Russia out of the woman. "Never mind me. What's your costume, Glenda?"

"Arousing Alligator, sugar."

How could I not have known that?

Glenda rested a hand on her yellow G-string, which represented her alligator underbelly. "Our Swamp Sasquatch discussion inspired a Halloween show idea that I just pitched to Madame Moiselle's, Miss Franki, and they love it. It's called 'Swamp Strippers,' and all us dancers will dress as a different swamp animal and roll around in filthy kiddie pools."

"Sounds..." It was better to leave that sentence unfinished.

"Before I forget, Miss Carnie's still on tour, and she send her disregards."

"Oh, nice. Be sure to thank her for not coming."

"Will do." Glenda flipped her hair and tail. "Unfortunately, we can't stay for the shower. Madame Moiselle's has contracted Hucci Cucci Hot Couture to do the Swamp Stripper costumes, and I have a lot of work to do."

"In that case, see you later, alligator. And snake."

Nadezhda sneered, and I noticed that her eyetooth hole wasn't as prominent among her black nub teeth.

They left, and I returned to the table, marveling at how life mimicked my magic mushroom trip.

Chandra approached exhibiting a gesture characteristic of her species—an outstretched palm.

Down but not out, I relinquished the charm bracelet.

And then Rosalie barreled into the restaurant and barged up to the table.

"Luckily, I was in Beaumont when you called, Brenda, so that shaved an hour off my drive time." She scowled at me and gave a growl reminiscent of a black bear. "First you remove me as head of the bomboniere committee, and then you don't invite me to your bridal shower. Tell me, Franki, what did I ever do to you?"

Hallucinated incident aside, was she really asking me that question?

"Where are your manners, Francesca?" My mother shook her head. "You're being rude, especially since Rosalie has offered to throw your bachelorette party."

Veronica's eyes popped. "Um—"

"No." I slammed my hand on the table. "Just no."

Rosalie threw up her arms. "There she goes again."

Despite my undercover wedding planning, my bridal shower had turned into a swamp fest. But I would sooner spend another night tied to a boscoyo than have my mother's BFF host my bachelorette. "That's right, Rosalie. Because that honor belongs to the matron of honor, and she and I both are already having to fight to keep Ruth Walker from throwing it."

"I have a brilliant idea." My mother's eyes sparkled from excitement—and a good three glasses of wine. "Veronica, Ruth, and Rosalie can plan it together. Of course, I'll help, as needed."

Nonna gripped her handbag handle. "I will-a too, Brenda. This-a bridal shower is-a the pits-a, and a Restaurant-a Week is-a too. Where's-a the Italian food-a?"

The room spun, and the events of the last twenty-four hours whirled around my brain like a tornado. The run-in with Lara and her taser, the ride in her trunk, the magic mushroom trip with real and imagined swamp animals. Then the plantation gown, Chandra and Bradley's potential DNA connection, and now a bachelorette party hosted by Rosalie, Ruth, Mom, and Nonna.

Veronica's gaze met mine, and her eyes reflected a mix of concern and fear. Despite our efforts, the swamp animals had infested my bridal shower.

Operation Black Swamp was dead in the water.

"Like I told you at the Camellia Grill," I whispered, "they're a powerful force, Veronica, stronger and more connected than you and I can ever understand. Like a modern-day Black Hand."

Bradley pushed back his chair. "Let's get you home, babe. You need to rest."

I did. And I also needed to eat Nutella. Not only would it give me the strength and stamina to fight my looming bachelorette battle, it would also cure my triple malocchio. I was sure of it.

Vick's doppelganger—the pre-waxed version—reappeared at the table. "I see you both enjoyed the pie."

"Best we've had." Bradley took my hand.

Woozy, I attempted a smile at the waiter. "Could I get the recipe?"

He picked up the empty pie plate. "I'm not supposed to tell anyone this, but our pastry chef has been out sick, so we had it brought in. It's made by a local caterer," he paused and looked over his shoulder, "Brunella Pagano."

Black stars danced before my eyes.

Or maybe witch hats?

And then...

Noir.

THANK you for reading *Nocino Noir*! If you enjoyed Franki's coffee shop mystery, you'll definitely want to preorder her wedding investigation. Keep reading to see the blurb for *Sambuca Scarlet*!

SAMBUCA SCARLET!

If you liked *Nocino Noir*, read the first chapter of:

SAMBUCA SCARLET

by
Traci Andrighetti

CHAPTER 1

The slasher-flick scream that erupted from my lungs was proof I wasn't dreaming. And if I needed further evidence of my awake state, my Cairn terrier, Napoleon, provided it with a yowl-yelp before burrowing under the hot pink velvet duvet.

And rightly so.

Like me, he'd awoken to my mom and nonna standing silently beside my French bordello-style canopy bed. Their cheeks were flushed, and their eyes were glassy.

Because they were sick—with wedding fever.

But *I* was the bride.

"Honestly, Francesca." My mother huffed, smoothing her

short, brown, Texas-sized hair. "You nearly scared your nonna and me to death with that outburst."

"*Sì, signorina!*" Nonna clutched a black bed post and the rosary at her bosom.

I flopped backwards onto my pillow and stared at the hot pink canopy. It was just like them to pin the blame on me when all I'd been doing was sleeping. "In my defense, it's more than a little startling to wake up to people hovering over you."

"In *our* defense, we thought you'd *never* wake up."

She acted as though I were a teen sleeping until noon, but I was thirty-two, and it was barely six a.m. I pointed at the old-school alarm clock on my nightstand. "Have you seen the time?"

Nonna nodded and raised a knobby index finger. "And-a it is-a wasting, Franki."

"Only five days until you walk down the aisle," my mother sing-songed, "and become Mrs. Bradley Hartmann."

Still on my elbows, I let my head fall back. I would've rather awoken to zombies from the creepy cemetery across the street than these two. With any luck, Thibodeaux's bar next door to said cemetery would help get me through my wedding week and their meddling antics.

Keeping my head hanging backwards between my shoulders, I said, "Since I've got more help than I need," I paused in the vain hope that message would sink in, "I'm caught up on wedding errands."

My mother dropped onto the bedside, sending my nose into the headboard.

"Ow!" I collapsed and grabbed my face.

"Be careful, Francesca! You don't want a bruise on your wedding day."

"No." My gaze was glacial. "I don't."

"Now, I know you think you're prepared, but problems have a way of popping up."

"I'm all too aware of that." I eyed her pointedly as I rubbed my aching nose. "But I'll deal with any problems if and when they happen—"

Nonna raised her chin. "Your mamma and-a I are glad-a to hear-a that, because-a something has-a come up-a."

"What?"

My mother folded her hands in her lap. "We almost forgot a Sicilian tradition."

Blowing out an exasperated breath, I propped myself on my elbows again. "We've already been over this—and over it, and over it again. The only traditions I'm observing are the normal ones, as in something old, something new, something borrowed, and something blue."

My mom and nonna opened their mouths to speak, but I wasn't having it. "Which rules out any and all Italian traditions like cutting up Bradley's tie and auctioning the pieces at the reception."

My nonna stood. "That's-a not—"

"And auctioning one of my shoes."

My mother rose beside her. "This isn't—"

"And kidnapping me and forcing Bradley to come to my rescue by solving riddles."

"Francesca Lucia Amato," my mother admonished. "Show us the courtesy of hearing us out."

We both knew the "courtesy" bit was a ploy to get me to listen to something I didn't want to hear. But because she'd phrased it that way, I had to acquiesce. "Fine. What's the tradition?"

Nonna patted the duvet. "*A cunzata du li lettu.*"

All I caught was the Sicilian word for "bed," which didn't bode well. "Do I want to know what that means?"

My mother pursed her lips. "It's called '*la cunzata del letto*' in Italian, which means 'the setting up of the marital bed.'"

I bolted forward like a bouquet thrown by a bride. "Stop right there."

Her eyes widened. "You said you'd hear us out."

"And given the subject, I'm setting a time limit on this discussion." I reached for the clock, and something stabbed my side. I pulled the culprit from between the sheets. The plastic baby from my late-night slice of king cake.

"Oh, Francesca!" My mother's shrill voice mimicked a drill running out of power.

"What? It's January sixth, and you of all people should know it's a New Orleans tradition to eat king cake on the Epiphany."

"But you have to fit into your wedding dress." No sooner had she uttered the words than the feverish look consumed her eyes. "Speaking of which," she grasped my forearm, "when are we going to see the one you picked out?"

My jaw set, and I wrested my arm from her grip. "On my wedding day, like everyone else."

"But I'm your *mother*."

"And you lost your dress privileges when you surprise-bought me that plantation-style gown—and parasol—at the Wedding Belles boutique last summer."

Nonna tsked. "It's-a bad-a luck not-a to show-a your wedding-a dress to your mamma and-a nonna."

"Everything is bad luck in Italian families," I snapped. "Now, you have one minute to tell me about this cunzata-del-letto thing, and then I'm going back to sleep."

"Well..." My mother paced in front of the adjoining bathroom.

Not a good start.

"The Thursday before the wedding, the mother of the bride and the mother-in-law supervise the preparation of the marital bed."

"Mom, that's weird."

Her head tilted, and her gaze went sideways. "It isn't, Francesca. According to the tradition, the mother and mother-in-law symbolize maturity and wisdom, so we know what we're doing."

If that were true, then they would know their involvement in the marital bed-making was a real romance killer. "What do you mean by 'preparation,' exactly?"

"The bed is made with sheets of fine white linen or silk."

Nonna nodded. "New and-a unused-a, like-a the bride."

My mom coughed, and I silenced her with a lethal look. Then I got back to business because I knew from hard-learned experience that there was more to the tradition than a set of nice sheets. Like a virgin. Or a fertility symbol. Otherwise, bad luck would inevitably result. "What else?"

"The bed has to be made by two virgins."

Right on target.

Nonna wagged a finger. "An odd-a number *porta male*."

There's the bad luck.

"Once the sheets are on, a little girl jumps on the bed to ensure fertility."

And the fertility symbol.

"After that, all the relatives and friends are invited into the room. They put rice, grain, and coins between the sheets and decorate the bed with rose petals, Jordan almonds, chocolate, even bottles of liquor."

Money, chocolate, and booze? "Keep talking."

"For the final touch, they prepare a surprise for the couple."

My mom and nonna exchanged a look and giggled, suggesting a surprise I wouldn't like.

"And-a in-a the old-a days," Nonna's black eyes twinkled, "they attach-a bells and a cheese-a grater under the mattress."

Even though I was fully awake, this cunzata custom was worse than any nightmare I could remember, and I'd had some real brain busters. Not only was it embarrassing, but it also threatened to compromise my fondness for cheese. "Mark my words, I'll call off the wedding before I agree to that."

"It's important to adhere to tradition, dear. It portends a bright financial future with lots of children."

"What it *portends* is," I slid out of bed, "a weird and awkward start to our marriage."

My mom flailed an arm. "The weird, awkward start is you two spending your first night in this apartment before going on your honeymoon."

"I told you," I pulled a robe from the armoire at the foot of the bed, "the construction on Bradley's place is behind schedule. And because the reception will go late at the Piazza d'Italia, and we have an early flight to Rome, it doesn't make sense to go to a hotel."

She sniffed and surveyed the room. "I've always said Glenda's taste in furniture leaves something to be desired."

For the first time since I'd been so rudely awakened, I mustered something approaching a smile, i.e., a smirk. Desire was precisely the point of my ex-stripper landlady's brothel chic décor.

"You should take Anthony up on his generous offer to stay at Le Richelieu Hotel."

"Your mamma is-a right, Franki. Anthony give-a you a deal-a on the honeymoon-a suite."

Something about spending the night at a hotel my brother managed—which was not only around the corner from my office but also where my entire family was staying for my wedding—didn't say "honeymoon" to me. "Blue moon," yes.

No doubt about it, my apartment was the better option, even with a bed that was rigged and decorated by virgins.

I tightened the sash on my robe and slammed the armoire door. "I'm going to say this for the last time, Bradley and I are planning an Italian-tradition-free wedding, and we have every-thing under control."

My mother swooned, and my nonna gasped. Then she pointed her index and pinky fingers to the ground in a *scongiuri* gesture intended to ward off the bad luck I'd brashly cast over my wedding.

A loud thump and whoosh came from inside the armoire.

"What in the...?" I threw open the door. The wooden clothing rod had broken on one end, and my clothes had slid into a pile. At the bottom lay the satin bag that held my wedding dress—with the clothing rod rammed into it.

"All of this bad luck stuff is nonsense," I said, more for myself than for them. "Just silly superstition."

But my mom and nonna's faces were ashen.

Zombie colored.

I ushered them from the room.

The satin bag was torn, but the dress was intact. Logic told me that the incident was a fluke. Nevertheless, I had the awful sensation that it wouldn't be the last thing to go wrong with the wedding.

Or the worst.

"Oh, no." Veronica's fingers gripped the arms of the chair across from my desk at Private Chicks, and her face was as pale as her peach turtleneck. "No no no no no."

"Relax." I held up a hand. "The dress isn't damaged. Just my nerves."

She catapulted forward in relief, her blonde head dropping between her legs. "When I *think* of what we went through to pick out a dress without your mom and nonna finding out—"

"Don't forget the *nonne*."

Veronica shot up. "How could I forget your nonna's friends when at least one of them tailed us everywhere we went?"

The Café du Monde bag on my desk called to me, and I pulled out my second beignet of the afternoon, and I'd had a few that morning. "Fortunately, they weren't savvy enough spies to realize we'd recognize their FIATs."

"True, but if they hadn't been called to cook after that caterer canceled on Nedda Vitrano's granddaughter's reception, you wouldn't have a dress."

"You're leaving out my fitting during Richard Simmons' memorial mass and Sweatin' to the Oldies' workout." I licked powdered sugar off my fingers and, thanks to the mention of the famous fitness instructor, felt remorse—which I promptly brushed off.

Veronica fell silent. "I meant to ask you, did the nonne go to Richard Simmons' funeral because he converted to Catholicism? Or was it because it was held at St. Louis Cathedral?"

"Neither." I bit into the delightfully doughy beignet. "They're devout fans of his first book—actually, just its title, *Never Say Diet.*"

"Ah."

My phone rang. "Anthony," I said, checking the display. "Probably about our mother. She's not only telling me how to run my wedding, she's also telling him how to run the hotel."

Veronica smirked and shook her head.

"Hey," I answered. "What's up?"

"You gotta help me with Giada, Sis. I know she needs a job because of her divorce and all, but she ain't workin' out as a hotel cook."

The news was a surprise. Our cousin had a gourmet food blog that New Orleans society women loved. "Why not?"

"Giada De Laurentis she ain't. Since Le Richelieu used to be a macaroni factory, I asked her to create a special mac and cheese recipe to serve at our bar. And get this—she used cottage cheese."

Sacre bleu. "Tell Mom and Nonna to give her some pointers in the kitchen. They asked you to hire her, and God knows they need something to do."

"*A-ight*, but I don't think that's gonna help." He hung up.

Veronica glanced at her nails. "Giada's not working out?"

"Apparently not, which isn't good." I took another bite of beignet and brushed powdered sugar from my fingers. "Her soon-to-be ex is living up to his name, Wolf. She's still living in their Garden District mansion, but not for long. He's using his legal power to make sure she doesn't get a dime in the divorce. It doesn't help that they don't have kids."

"As an attorney myself, it really upsets me when I see a colleague capitalizing on the profession to cheat a spouse."

"The worst part is, they're splitting up right when I'm getting married."

Veronica leaned forward. "You can't feel guilty about that, Franki. You know Giada's happy for you. The last time I saw her, she mentioned how romantic it is that you're marrying Bradley on the anniversary of the day you met."

My heart fluttered at the memory of the day I walked into Pontchartrain Bank and met the love of my life. "It *is* romantic, but so improbable given our disastrous first date."

She grinned. "And you punching him in the face."

My mouth flat *refused* to grin back. "He deserved that for failing to mention that he was still married to Sheilah, even if the marriage *was* over."

"Speaking of the Sheilah-devil, is she coming to the wedding?"

"Nope." I polished off the beignet. "She and her second husband will be on a non-refundable trip down the Nile."

Veronica raised a brow. "Sounds fabulous."

"Not as fabulous as my Rome honeymoon."

"True. And as your best friend, I couldn't be happier for you. You kissed a few frogs before Bradley."

"Toadally," I joked. "Todd in college, Vince during my rookie-cop stint, and—"

Our eyes met. Neither of us dared to speak his name.

Some people were best left in the past.

My phone rang again. *St Mary's Church* was on the display. I showed it to Veronica. "I hope there's not a problem with my ceremony." I answered the call on speaker. "Hello?"

"Franki," Nonna rasped, "you have-a to come-a to the church-a *subito.*"

"Now? I'm at work. Can this wait?"

"No, it's-a *importantissimo.*"

Suspicious that she hadn't offered an explanation, I decided to probe further. "Is this about a tradition? If so, the answer is 'no.'"

The call ended.

And I massaged my temples. "Will this wedding-tradition nonsense never end?"

"Not until the wedding does." She tilted her head. "But wow. The cunzata del letto is really something."

"Something I'm not even going to mention to Bradley."

Bradley entered the office, as handsome as ever in a black cashmere sweater and brown chinos. "What are you not going to mention to me?"

My eyes met his. "Yet another Sicilian tradition."

He walked around the desk and gave me a peck on the cheek.

"While we're on the subject of traditions," I said in a playful drawl, "what time is your bachelor party tonight?"

"Six p.m. Why?" A devilish smile danced at the corners of his mouth. "Are you worried?"

"Not at all." I leaned back in my chair and crossed my arms. "I trust you."

He bent over me, and his devilish smile descended on my lips and danced there for a time.

"*Ahem.*" Veronica cleared her throat. "Get a room, lovebirds."

My cheeks grew as hot as the kiss.

Bradley rose and squeezed my hand. "Veronica and I have a meeting right now about an insurance case she's going to handle while we're on our honeymoon."

He lingered on the last word, his blue eyes sparkling like the waters of Rome's Trevi Fountain.

And I dove in.

My phone rang, jolting me from my fountain frolic, and I frowned at the display. "The American Italian Cultural Center. Has to be Marcella."

Veronica looked at Bradley. "She's been fighting with Moira about the catering for your reception."

"I heard." He grimaced. "The stereotypical battle of the Italians and the Irish."

"It is." I reached for the phone. "And if I don't figure out a way to help them get along, Moira will cancel like the caterer for Nedda Vitrano's granddaughter's wedding, which means the nonne will man the cooking."

Veronica's eyes popped, and so did Bradley's. We all knew the chaos and calamity that would ensue if my nonna and her friends took over the reception food.

"We'll leave you to it." Veronica hurried from my office.

And Bradley followed.

Understandably. Marcella was a lot, even when she wasn't in Rocky Marciano mode. Sighing, I tapped *Answer.* "Hello?"

"It's Marcella." She paused, and based on her grim tone, I could see her flipping her black curtain of hair with her maroon-lined lips pursed. "Franki, I hate to do this because I know weddings are supposed to be happy occasions, but we have to talk about Moira."

"What hap—"

"After I gave her a list of the drinks and desserts the American Italian Cultural Center is contributing to your reception, she said our Italian flag cocktail won't work with her menu. I repeat, Won't. Work. With her menu."

Honestly, the drink wouldn't work with my wedding vision, but clearly this wasn't the time to say that.

"So I said, 'Tell me, Moira, what doesn't go with Crème de menthe, white chocolate liqueur, and red Sambuca?' And she said, 'Everything.' So I said, 'I beg your pardon, that drink is a knockout.' And she said, 'Yeah, the taste will knock out the guests' stomachs, and the colors will knock out their eyesight.'"

Entirely possible on both counts.

Marcella gave a hot huff. "Can you imagine anyone saying such a thing?"

"Y—"

"You know what I think, Franki?"

"N—"

"Moira insulted the Italian flag! And we both know it's because she's Irish. I mean, her last name is Mulligan! I'll bet she wants me to change the red Sambuca to something orange like Arancello so the drink will look like Ireland's flag, but the only way that's going to happen is over my dead American-Italian body. Because, let's be honest, the Irish flag looks like an Italian flag that's been in the sun too long. And who wants to sip a sad, faded cocktail at a wedding reception?"

"I—"

"*Mamma. Freakin'. Mia,*" she shrieked.

"Wh—?"

"Moira just sent me a text vetoing the Italian rainbow cookies. And you and I both know the reason."

"N—"

"They're the colors of the Italian flag too. What's that woman going to come for next? The *spumoni*? If she puts one finger on the carton, we'll settle this *my way*, to quote Sinatra. And by the time I'm done with her, Notre Dame is going to have to change the name of their mascot from the Fighting Irish to the Fleeing Irish."

I didn't know how the name change was going to go down, but I'd let Marcella tackle that issue with the football team. She could do it too, because she was the size of a linebacker.

Marcella growled. "The nerve of that wo—"

"I'll come down there right now and straighten this out."

"Oh." The growl had gone. "Why didn't you say so sooner?"

On that note, I hung up.

Then I turned off my phone—one way to keep my wedding under control.

Slinging my hobo bag onto my shoulder, I headed up the hallway to the lobby. Our two college-aged employees, David and Standish, aka The Vassal, were nowhere to be seen. Neither was Ruth, Bradley's assistant.

As I crossed the old brick-walled room, I looked with longing at the two opposing couches. I'd had many a nap there, not to mention the occasional night's sleep.

But I quashed the temptation. After all, I was on a peace-keeping mission. And based on Marcella's unauthorized drink and dessert choices, I was on a menu-keeping mission as well.

Grabbing my coat from the rack beside the door, I left the office and bounded down the three flights of stairs to the street below.

I stepped outside in the French Quarter and, per usual, caught a whiff of something peculiar. Not beignets or gumbo or chicory coffee, or even the sour odor of revelry from the night before.

It's smoky and vaguely fami—

Darkness descended over me.

"Hey," I yelled, struggling against a tomb of fabric.

Strong hands shoved my head down, and another pair slung me forward.

Onto a car seat.

The hands bent my legs at the knees, then someone sat beside me. The door slammed and tires squealed as the car set in motion.

My shock gave way to a sick feeling.

I'd been kidnapped!

culprit—it's the "blooming idiot" who bought the portrait before the auction started.

And don't forget to follow me!

BookBub
https://www.bookbub.com/authors/traci-andrighetti

Goodreads
https://www.goodreads.com/author/show/7383577.
Traci_Andrighetti

Facebook
https://www.facebook.com/traciandrighettiauthor

BOOK BACKSTORY

Thank you for reading *Nocino Noir*! As many of you know, I originally wrote it as an 18,000-word short story for a promotion organized by Tanya Kappes called "Twisty Tales and Cozy Crimes." Since then, I've expanded *Nocino Noir* into this 80,000-word book with even more twisty tales and cozy crimes.

As with the story version, I'm amazed that I ever wrote this book. When I started, the only things I knew for sure were the title and that I wanted it to take place in a coffee shop. Then, I just stared at the Word document for a while. A long while. Where the rest of the words came from, I'll never know. It's a mystery. Or maybe a noir...

That reminds me, the title was suggested to me by Italian writer Matteo Bortolotti, and as soon as I heard the "noir," I knew the story would have to involve the film genre. As for the "nocino," don't be afraid to try it—your throat will be fine.

For the record, however, the throat thing really happened to me. But the culprit was Cynar, an Italian liqueur made from artichokes, not walnuts. I love artichokes, so when I was offered Cynar as a digestivo at a restaurant in Bologna, I happily tried it. I'm not kidding when I say that it was the first time in my life that I was "aware" of my esophagus—the entire freaking length of it. It didn't burn or hurt, it was just lit up as though it was glowing. And it stayed that way for a good stretch, which was odd, not to mention concerning.

There are a lot of other things in *Nocino Noir* that are not entirely figments of my imagination. For instance, Marie Antoinette's pearls and other jewels were auctioned by Sotheby's in 2018. I got the idea to hang them in the tree from an article by Rick Bragg about the Columns Hotel in "Garden & Gun" magazine. My friend Victoria Belue and I spent a night at the Columns in 2023 so that I could research this book, and a spooky radio thing happened to us that I wrote about in one of my newsletters. If you'd like to know what happened, send me an email.

The story of the Benevento witches and the preparation of nocino is also true. Before I wrote this story, I watched YouTube interviews with elderly residents of Benevento who told of their experiences with the janare, which were probably not true? And I was able to find the spell the janare recited after they spread unguent under their armpits and prepared to fly on their brooms:

'Nguento, 'nguento,
    mànname a lu nocio 'e Beneviento,
    sott'a ll'acqua e sotto ô viento,
    sotto â ogne maletiempo.

[Unguent, unguent,
    send me to the walnut tree of Benevento,

under the water and under the wind,
under all bad weather.]

Speaking of witches and their spells, I found all of the Hex Old World Witchery products on their website. And there really are four witch stores near the building on Decatur Street that inspired the Private Chicks office, and there is also a Ra Shop that sells The Gotcha! Belt. But perhaps even more surprising than the witches, witch stores, and novelty urine is that the boob-and-sock-money sign is real—and a terrific example of why my stories are set in New Orleans!

Oh, and the food is always real in my books too, including the Taceaux Loceaux tacos and the Peacemaker-style po-boy, because I want to showcase the history and personality of the NOLA cuisine. As an Italian-American myself (whose heritage is from the Veneto and Le Marche regions, not Sicily!), I take all things food very seriously.

I take my history seriously too. Before I got my PhD in Foreign Language Education, I completed an M.A. in History, specializing in Modern Italy. And based on the historical record, so much of New Orleans' rich history, and especially the contributions of Sicilians, has been lost and even suppressed in the interests of promoting the city to tourists as French. If you'd like to know more about how this revisionist history was able to happen, I highly recommend Creole Italian: Sicilian Immigrants and the Shaping of New Orleans Food Culture by Dr. Joseph A. Nystrom. You will be shocked to learn that Sicilians are not only responsible for the New Orleans oyster scene, among many other notable delicacies, they are also responsible for making pasta a mainstream of American cuisine. And for that, this spaghetti-eater says GRAZIE DI CUORE, SICILIANI DI NEW ORLEANS!

And speaking of Sicilian-Americans, I once met Tony Danza when he was promoting his book I'd Like to Apologize to Every Teacher I Ever Had: My Year as a Rookie Teacher at Northeast High, and he is absolutely NOT a villain. In fact, he is exactly like his television persona—exuberant, warm, and funny. His gracious treatment of fans combined with the fact that in 2009 he took a year off from the entertainment business to teach tenth-grade English makes the answer to my "Who's the Boss?" TV show joke in the story and book versions an easy one. Tony Danza is!

And my absolute favorite real thing in *Nocino Noir*—the New Orleans' voodoo community was and still is protesting the VooDoo Doughnuts franchise. The next time you go to Cafè du Monde, look for protestors across the street from the old Tujague's location. But whatever you do, don't mess with Baron Samedi.

Cin cin (Cheers)!
    Traci

LIQUEUR & COCKTAIL

NOCINO

To make this liqueur, it's important to use an odd number of green walnuts and coffee beans. The traditional recipe calls for thirteen, which is a lucky number in Italy. And if you really want to follow tradition, make the nocino on the eve of June 24, the feast day of San Giovanni, and serve on Halloween night or November first.

Ingredients

    1 quart pure grain alcohol
    13 green walnuts
    13 coffee beans
    3 cloves
    3 cinnamon sticks
    1 whole nutmeg
    3 tablespoons sugar
    water

Cut the walnuts into 4 parts, and add them to the pure grain alcohol together with the coffee beans, clove, cinnamon, and nutmeg. Place the ingredients into a hermetically sealed jar and keep outside in direct sunlight for 40 days.

After 40 days have passed, strain the ingredients. In a small pot, make a syrup by boiling one cup of water and 3 tablespoons sugar. Cool and add to the alcohol.

Return all ingredients to the jar and keep inside for an additional 40 days. Then drink—if you dare!

NOCINO SOUR

This cocktail is ideal for fall and winter. It's warming and sort of holidayish, thanks to the walnuts and spices in the nocino.

Ingredients
> 1 and ½ ounces nocino
> ¾ ounce fresh lemon juice
> ½ ounce demerara syrup
> ¼ ounce sweet vermouth
> 3 dashes Angostura bitters

Shake ingredients with ice, and strain into a coupe glass.

Salute!

DEADLY DESSERTS

SANGUINACCIO DOLCE

This decadent (and deadly!) dessert was traditionally made during Carnevale, the Italian equivalent of Mardi Gras. Neapolitans scooped up the pudding with *chiacchiere* (strips of friend dough covered in powdered sugar, similar to Franki's beloved beignets). In other regions, Italians dipped *savoiardi* biscuits, or ladyfingers, into the pudding. However, given the short shelf life of pork blood, the sale of sanguinaccio dolce was banned in Italy in 1992. All I can say is arrivederci!

Ingredients
- ½ quart pork blood (optional, thank goodness!)
- ½ quart whole milk (or 1 quart to replace pork blood)
- 4 ½ tablespoons potato starch
- ¼ cup unsweetened cocoa powder
- 2 cups sugar
- 13 ounces dark chocolate, chopped
- 1 tablespoon vanilla extract

2 and ½ ounces candied citron, chopped
2 ounces pine nuts
½ teaspoon cinnamon
pinch of salt
rind of 1 lemon (or orange), thinly sliced

In a large pot, dissolve the starch and cocoa powder in a small amount of milk. Next, add the pig's blood, remaining milk, sugar, and lemon rind. Stirring over a low heat, add the dark chocolate and vanilla. Bring to a boil, stirring constantly. Once the mixture comes to a boil, reduce heat to a simmer for 5–7 minutes, stirring to prevent the pudding from sticking as it thickens.

Remove from heat and let cool in the pot. Next, remove the lemon rind and add the cinnamon, candied citron, and pine nuts. Stir well and sprinkle with hazelnuts or chocolate flakes.

Buon appetito?

P.S. Hannibal Lecter makes this dessert in the third season of the TV show *Hannibal* with cow's blood. Although, he claims that he made it previously with the blood of a different sort of animal...

BLACK WALNUT PIE WITH MOLASSES AND ORANGE

This pie has been described as a cross between Britain and America's greatest desserts, the treacle tart and pecan pie—unless it's made by Brunella Pagano!

Ingredients
1 pie crust

4 ½ ounces whole raw, unsalted walnuts (about 1 ½ cups)

1 cup plus 1 tablespoon light corn syrup

Zest of half a navel orange (about 1 teaspoon) and 1/4 cup juice (from the whole orange)

1 tablespoon blackstrap molasses

¼ teaspoon ground ginger

¾ teaspoon kosher salt

3 ounces white bread (crusts removed), torn into small pieces, then pulsed in a food processor until fine (about 2 lightly packed cups)

½ cup heavy cream, plus more for serving

1 large egg plus 1 large egg yolk

Prepare (or purchase) your favorite pie crust.

Heat the oven to 350 degrees and arrange two racks near the center of the oven. Place the pie crust on a sheet pan, and the walnuts on a separate sheet pan. Transfer both to the oven. Bake until the walnuts are evenly golden throughout, 12 to 15 minutes. Continue to bake the pie crust until it turns golden and is fully cooked, another 10 to 15 minutes (for a total of about 25 minutes). Finely chop the walnuts to between the size of a steel-cut oat and a pea. Variety in size is nice.

While the pastry bakes, prepare the filling: Add the corn syrup, orange zest and juice, molasses, ginger and salt to a small saucepan and warm over low heat just until the syrups liquefy and loosen. (Do not boil.) Add the bread crumbs and toasted walnuts to the warmed mixture, stir and let sit until slightly cooled.

In a medium bowl, whisk the heavy cream and eggs together with a fork to combine, then fold it into the cooled walnut mixture. Pour into the pie crust and bake on a sheet pan until the center of the pie just sets, about 25 minutes. Serve at room temperature or just above, with plenty of heavy cream for drizzling.

Enjoy (without fear)!

ALSO BY TRACI ANDRIGHETTI

FRANKI AMATO MYSTERIES

Books
Limoncello Yellow
Prosecco Pink
Amaretto Amber
Campari Crimson
Galliano Gold
Marsala Maroon
Valpolicella Violet
Tuaca Tan
Nocino Noir
Braulio Brown (a Thanksgiving novella)
Sambuca Scarlet

Box Sets
Franki Amato Mysteries Box Set (Books 1–3)
Franki Amato Mysteries Box Set (Books 4–6)
The Franki Amato Mysteries Big Box Set (Books 1–7)

Short Stories
Franki Amato Mini Mysteries
(short mysteries free to newsletter subscribers only)

PASTA AND PIAZZA MYSTERIES

Capri, Cannoli, and Conspiracy (preorder now!)
Rome, Ravioli, and Revenge (forthcoming)

DANGER COVE HAIR SALON MYSTERIES

Books
Deadly Dye and a Soy Chai
A Poison Manicure and Peach Liqueur
Killer Eyeshadow and a Cold Espresso

Franki Amato also investigates with the sleuths of Leslie
Langtry, Arlene McFarlane, and Diana Orgain in the

KILLER FOURSOME MYSTERIES

Books
4 Sleuths & A Bachelorette
4 Sleuths & A Burlesque Dancer
4 Sleuths & A Barnstormer

ABOUT THE AUTHOR

Traci Andrighetti is the *USA Today* bestselling author of the Franki Amato mysteries and the Danger Cove Hair Salon mysteries, and she is a co-author of the Killer Foursome mysteries. In her previous life, she was an award-winning literary translator and a Lecturer of Italian at the University of Texas at Austin, where she earned a PhD in Applied Linguistics. But then she got wise and ditched that academic stuff for a life of crime—writing, that is. Get news of Traci's upcoming books and latest capers at www.traciandrighetti.com.

Speaking of capers, Traci and one of her Killer Foursome co-authors, Diana Orgain, take published and aspiring authors on writing retreats to Italy through LemonLit. If you're up for an Italian adventure, then *andiamo*! But be careful. Traci and Diana are a lot like their sleuths, so you never know what—or who—might go down on the trip...